John Clark Marshman

The Story of Carey, Marshman, and Ward, the Serampore Missionaries

SALZWASSER
VERLAG

John Clark Marshman

The Story of Carey, Marshman, and Ward, the Serampore Missionaries

Reprint of the original, first published in 1864.

1st Edition 2022 | ISBN: 978-3-75259-167-5

Verlag (Publisher): Salzwasser Verlag GmbH, Zeilweg 44, 60439 Frankfurt, Deutschland
Vertretungsberechtigt (Authorized to represent): E. Roepke, Zeilweg 44, 60439 Frankfurt, Deutschland
Druck (Print): Books on Demand GmbH, In de Tarpen 42, 22848 Norderstedt, Deutschland

THE STORY

OF

CAREY, MARSHMAN, & WARD,

THE SERAMPORE MISSIONARIES.

BY

JOHN CLARK MARSHMAN.

LONDON

1864.

PREFACE.

THE interest excited by the publication of the "Life and Times of the Serampore Missionaries," the pioneers of Christian civilisation in Hindostan, has led to an inquiry for a Popular Edition, which should put the narrative of their exertions within the reach of a larger class of readers. The present volume is, therefore, an abridgment of the former edition, with the omission of those historical notices which were intended to illustrate the times and the scenes in which they acted. Having, moreover, placed on record the vindication of their character from the aspersions cast on it during the melancholy controversy in which they found themselves involved, I am enabled, with a feeling of no ordinary satisfaction, to omit all its details, and to present a simple memorial of their exemplary life and arduous labours in the cause of Christian truth.

JOHN C. MARSHMAN.

LONDON, February 25th, 1864.

CONTENTS.

CHAPTER I.

CHAPTER II.

CHAPTER III.

CHAPTER IV.

CHAPTER V.

CHAPTER VI.

CHAPTER VII.

CHAPTER VIII.

CHAPTER IX.

CHAPTER X.

CHAPTER XI.

CAREY, MARSHMAN, AND WARD.

CAREY, MARSHMAN, AND WARD.

CHAPTER I.

William Carey, to whose energy the Protestant missions of the nineteenth century owe their origin, was born on the 17th of August, 1761, in the village of Pury, or Paulerspury, in Northamptonshire, where his father and grandfather occupied in succession the position of parish clerk and schoolmaster. His education was limited to the instruction to be obtained in the village school, which was exceedingly scanty. Of his younger days there are few recollections; but it was remarked that he read with avidity books of a scientific and historical character, and more particularly all the records of voyages and travels he was able to obtain. But the bent of his mind lay towards subjects of natural history, and at an early age his room was stored with the insects he had collected and reared to mark their development. To assist these observations he endeavoured to acquire some knowledge of drawing. His fondness for botanical research became more apparent as he grew up. He was likewise remarkable, at an early period of life, for that spirit of indomitable perseverance which distinguished his subsequent career. He took an active share in the boyish sports of the village, and was a great favourite with children of his own age. His manners were necessarily rustic, but his appearance was prepossessing, and some of his more discerning friends are said to have predicted his future eminence. At the age of twelve, he obtained a copy of a feeling of humiliation. Some time after he was solicited to preach at the village of Earl's Barton, and yielded to the request, more from his unwillingness to give pain by a refusal than from any confidence in his own qualifications. There, as well as in his own village, he preached for three years and a half. It was during these ministerial engagements that his views on the subject of baptism were altered, and he embraced the opinion that baptism by immersion, after a confession of faith, was in accordance with the injunctions of Divine Writ and the practice of the apostolic age. He was accordingly baptized by Dr. John Ryland, his future associate in the cause of missions, who subsequently stated at a public meeting, that, on the 7th of October, 1783, he baptized a poor journeyman shoemaker in the river Nen, a little beyond Dr. Doddridge's chapel, in Northampton. Soon after, he joined the church under the pastoral care of the Rev. John Sutcliffe; but when the question of his receiving a call to the ministry came under discussion, the members expressed a doubt whether he possessed sufficient ability to make a useful minister, and the point was carried chiefly through the personal influence of the pastor. The sermon which he preached on this occasion, he described "as having been as crude and weak as anything could be, which is called, or has been called, a sermon." These engagements necessarily enlarged the circle of his studies, and he laid the libraries of all the friends around him under contribution. Among other methods which he pursued of improving his knowledge of languages, was that of reading the portion of Scripture selected for devotional exercises in Latin, Greek, and Hebrew.

Mr. Old died, and Mr. Carey took over his stock and business, and married his sister before he had attained the age of twenty. This imprudent union proved a severe clog on his exertions for more than twenty-five years. His illiterate wife, who possessed no feeling in unison with his own, was altogether unsuited for his companionship; and the great tenderness which always marked his conduct towards her places the meekness and nobleness of his character in a strong light. On his marriage, he rented a neat cottage at Hackleton, the chief recommendation of which was the little garden attached to it, which he cultivated with great assiduity, and which flourished more vigorously than his business. Trade became dull, and though suffering from fever, which hung on him for eighteen months, he was obliged to travel from place to place to dispose of his stock and procure bread. His church and congregation at Barton were not able to raise enough to pay for the clothes worn out in their service. But he was rescued from actual destitution by the contributions of an affectionate brother, and a small collection made for him in his native village. With this aid he removed to the village of Piddington, where he selected a cottage with a garden; but it was situated in a swamp, and he was again attacked with ague and fever, which rendered him bald for the rest of his life.

In the beginning of 1786, he removed to Moulton, and took the charge of a small Dissenting interest. To this place he was attracted by the prospect of a school which had recently been relinquished. Few men have ever had less natural aptitude for this profession than Mr. Carey. "When I kept school," he facetiously remarked, "it was the boys who kept me." He had no notion of management, and was never able to exercise any control over his pupils, who took personal liberties with him, which subverted all discipline. The unexpected return of the old master reduced his receipts to seven and sixpence a week, and extinguished all hope of a livelihood from this source. The church at Moulton could only raise eleven pounds a year, to which an addition of five pounds was made from some fund in London. For a minister of religion this was simple starvation, and he was obliged to betake himself to his former trade for a subsistence. "Once a fortnight," remarks his associate, Mr. Morris, "Carey might be seen walking eight or ten miles to

Northampton, with his wallet full of shoes on his shoulder, and then returning home with a fresh supply of leather." But he was a very indifferent shoemaker, and always entertained a most humble opinion of his own abilities in the craft. Some thirty years after this period, dining one day with the Governor-General, Lord Hastings, at Barrackpore, a general officer made an impertinent inquiry of one of the aide-de-camps, whether Dr. Carey had not once been a shoemaker. He happened to overhear the conversation, and immediately stepped forward and said, "No, sir; only a cobbler."

Mr. Carey's residence at Moulton, notwithstanding his pecuniary difficulties, was rendered agreeable by opportunities of mental cultivation to which he had hitherto been a stranger. He engaged in a regular course of biblical study, and commenced that systematic distribution and rigid economy of time to which he adhered through life, and which enabled him to accomplish labours which appeared almost incredible. He enjoyed the advantage of the critical remarks on his pulpit exercises of the venerable Mr. Hall, whose name is still fragrant in the churches, partly from the treatise we have alluded to, but chiefly through the incomparable genius of his son, Robert Hall. Mr. Carey also improved his acquaintance with Dr. Ryland; but the most important acquisition of this period was the friendship of the Rev. Andrew Fuller, the Baptist minister at Kettering, and subsequently the great champion of the mission. Mr. Carey was unexpectedly requested to preach at a meeting of ministers. On descending from the pulpit, Mr. Fuller grasped his hand, and expressed the delight he felt in finding so close a coincidence of their views, and his hope that they would become better acquainted with each other. Thus was commenced a cordial friendship between two great and congenial spirits, which was subsequently strengthened by their union in a noble enterprise, and the difficulties connected with it, and which became extinct only with the life of Mr. Fuller, twenty years after.

It was from the perusal of Cook's voyages, while instructing his pupils in geography, that Mr. Carey was first led to contemplate the moral and spiritual degradation of the heathen, and to form the design of communicating the Gospel to them. The idea took complete possession of his mind, and absorbed his thoughts. It was still uppermost, when he was obliged to relinquish his school and fall back upon manual labour. Mr. Fuller has related, that on going into his little workshop, he saw a large map suspended on the wall, consisting of several sheets of paper pasted together, on which he had noted down, in their respective places, all the information he had been able to gather regarding the national characteristics, the population, and the religion of the various countries then known. While engaged in making or mending shoes, his eye was frequently raised to the map, and his mind was employed in traversing the different regions of the globe, and devising plans for communicating the truths of Christianity to them. It was to this circumstance Mr. Wilberforce alluded in the House of Commons twenty years after, when, urging Parliament to grant missionaries free access to India, he said:—"A sublimer thought cannot be conceived than when a poor cobbler formed the resolution to give to the millions of Hindoos the Bible in their own language." But these views met with but little encouragement from his own ministerial brethren. At a meeting of ministers held at this time at Northampton, Mr. Carey proposed, as the topic of discussion, The duty of Christians to attempt the spread of the Gospel among heathen nations; when Mr. Ryland, senior, sprang to his feet and denounced the proposition. "Young man," said he, "sit down: when God pleases to convert the heathen, He will do it without your aid or mine." Mr. Fuller himself was startled by the novelty and the magnitude of the proposal, and described his feelings as resembling those of the infidel courtier in Israel, "If the Lord should make windows in heaven, might such a thing be?"

Nothing daunted by these repulses, Mr. Carey embodied his views on the missionary enterprise in a pamphlet, which he shewed to Mr. Fuller, Dr. Ryland, and Mr. Sutcliffe, and they advised him to revise it, more, however, with the hope of escaping from his importunities, than with any serious desire of encouraging a project which appeared to them perfectly utopian. This pamphlet, which may be considered the germ of those missionary efforts which have now grown to the dimensions of a national undertaking, exhibited the extraordinary knowledge which Mr. Carey had acquired of the history, geography, statistics, and creed of the various countries of the world. It exhibited not less the indomitable energy of his character; for while he was engaged in compiling it, his family was in a state bordering on starvation, and passed many weeks without animal food, and with but a scanty supply of bread.

In 1789, Mr. Carey accepted an invitation from the church at Leicester, and removed to that town in his twenty-eighth year. But the poverty of the church obliged him again to have recourse to secular employment, and he made a second attempt to get up a school, but without success. At Leicester he was introduced to Dr. Arnold, said to have been a "great lover of polite literature," and obtained free access to his library, which was rich in scientific works. Mr. Carey was now in his element, in the full enjoyment of opportunities for cultivating his natural tastes, and prosecuting those researches which he continued with great ardour in India. He also made the acquaintance of the Rev. Thomas Robinson, the pious and exemplary rector of St. Mary's, and the author of "Scripture Characters." With him Mr. Carey maintained an uninterrupted and cordial intercourse while he resided in Leicester, and a friendly correspondence when he removed to India. Mr. Robinson one day asked him whether he approved of Dissenting ministers enlarging their congregations at the expense of the Established Church. Mr. Carey replied, "You are a Churchman, and I am a Dissenter; we must each endeavour to do good according to our light. At the same time, you may be assured that I had rather be the means of converting a scavenger that sweeps the streets than of proselytising the richest and best character in your denomination." Mr. Carey considered the union of Church and State, and the establishment of religion by secular power, without warrant from Scripture; but his views, when in comparative obscurity, were always broad and liberal, and they became still more so when placed in a more conspicuous sphere of action. Of his labours at Leicester, Mr. Fuller has left the following record:—"His zeal and unremitted labour in preaching the Word, not only in Leicester, but in the villages near it, endeared him to the friends of religion, and his thirst for learning rendered him respected by others. He has sometimes regretted to me his want of early education. 'I was so rusticated,' he would say, 'when a lad, that I am as if I could never recover myself.' Yet the natural energies of his mind, accompanied as they were with a generous, manly, and open disposition, together with an ingratiating behaviour towards men of every degree, soon rendered him respected, not only by those who attended his ministry, but by many other persons of learning and opulence."

These pastoral labours, however, did not relax Mr. Carey's ardour in the cause of missions. The more he mused on it, the more the fire burned. For four years he had omitted no opportunity of urging it on his ministerial brethren. The aged and more influential considered the scheme visionary, and endeavoured to divert his mind from it; but this disappointment only led him to ply the younger men, then rising into notice in the denomination, with greater importunity. At a meeting of ministers at Clipstone, in 1791, the discourses appeared to bear a missionary aspect, and he urged that something should be done immediately, that very day, towards the formation of a society to propagate the Gospel among the heathen. It was only under the pressure of his earnestness that even his young associates had been led to contemplate the plan with complacency. But when the proposal of actually pledging themselves to embark in the undertaking was placed distinctly before them, they shrank from the responsibility, and pronounced the plan too vast for their obscure position and limited resources. To gain time, however, without wounding Mr. Carey's feelings, they advised him to publish the tract which he had revised, "The Inquiry on Missions." The next Association was held at Nottingham, in May, 1792. The pulpit was ceded to Mr. Carey, and he preached that sermon which was long remembered as having laid the foundation of the Baptist Missionary Society. He took for his text, "Enlarge the place of thy tent, and let them stretch forth the curtain of thy habitations. Spare not; lengthen thy cords and strengthen thy stakes; for thou shalt break forth on the right hand and on the left; and thy seed shall inherit the Gentiles, and make the desolate cities to be inhabited." From this text he deduced and enforced the two principles which were embodied in the motto of the mission, "Expect great things; attempt great things." Into this discourse he poured the accumulated energy of those feelings which had been gathering strength since he read Cook's voyages, and determined on the establishment of a mission. With such vigour did he denounce that indifference with which the cause of missions was then regarded, that Dr. Ryland, who was present, remarked, that "he should not have been surprised if the audience had lifted up their voice and wept." But when the subject came practically under discussion, the old feelings of hesitation and doubt began to predominate, when Mr. Carey seized Mr. Fuller's hand in an agony of distress, and indignantly asked whether they were again going to separate without doing anything. The expostulation was not without effect, and he had the happiness of seeing a resolution recorded, to the effect that a plan should be prepared against the next ministers' meeting for the establishment of a society for propagating the Gospel among the heathen.

This meeting was held at Kettering, on the 2nd of October, 1792. After the usual services of the day, the ministers, twelve in number, proceeded to discuss the question of establishing a missionary society. But fresh difficulties arose as they examined it in its various bearings. There was no experience of any such undertaking to guide their movements. They were ignorant of the mode of constructing a missionary association, or working its machinery. They knew of no favourable opening in any heathen country to which their efforts might be directed. They were without funds or influence, and their position, in the centre of England, was unfavourable to correspondence or action. But all these objections were overruled by Mr. Carey's energy, and, under the irresistible influence of his mind, a society was constituted "to convey the message of salvation to some portion of the heathen world." A committee of five was appointed, consisting of Andrew Fuller, John Ryland, Reynold Hogge, John Sutcliffe, and William Carey. Mr. Fuller was nominated secretary, and Mr. Hogge treasurer, and a subscription was made of £13 2*s.* 6*d.*,—the harbinger of the millions which have since been laid on the altar of this sacred cause. However ludicrous might be the contrast between the resources thus provided, and the magnitude of the object in view, the subscription paper was no sooner filled up than Mr. Carey offered to embark for any country the society might select. His mind was imbued with that noble enthusiasm which creates great enterprises, and which difficulties serve only to stimulate. The church at Birmingham, under the pastoral care of the amiable Samuel Pearce, sent the first contribution of £70 to the infant society. The example was followed by other churches, and the committee soon found themselves in possession of no inconsiderable purse. The ministers and churches in London, however, refused to join in what they considered a wild enterprise, struck out in the heat of enthusiasm, by a few ardent spirits in an obscure country Association. "When we began in 1792," afterwards remarked Mr. Fuller, "there was little or no respectability among us; not so much as a squire to sit in the chair, or an orator to make speeches to him. Hence good Dr. Stennett advised the London ministers to stand aloof, and not commit themselves." Little did the respectable ministers of London dream that the plan from which they were shrinking back was the embryo of a magnificent enterprise, destined ere long to enlist the energy and zeal of the Christian world on both sides the Atlantic, and to embrace within its sphere every heathen tribe under the sun. The only minister from whom Mr. Carey received any sympathy in the metropolis, was a member of the Established Church, the venerable John Newton, who "advised him with the fidelity and tenderness of a father."

The destination of the mission was undecided, when the receipt of a letter from a Mr. Thomas, who had resided in Bengal for some years, and on his return to England was endeavouring to raise funds for the establishment of a mission, determined the committee to adopt that province as the sphere of its labours. At this stage of the narrative, therefore, it may be interesting to glance at the exertions which had been previously made for the dissemination of Christian truth in India, and at the state of religion and morals in the English community in Bengal.

The first Protestant mission in India was established in 1705, under the auspices of Frederick the Fourth, King of Denmark, at the recommendation of Dr. Francke, of Halle, in Saxony; and the first missionaries, Ziegenbalg and Grundlerus, proceeded to the Danish settlement of Tranquebar, on the Coromandel coast. Ziegenbalg returned to Europe in 1714, with one of his native converts, and was introduced by the Danish sovereign, in the following year, to George the First, who manifested greater interest in the success of missionary efforts than any of his successors. The mission on the coast received, from time to time, great assistance from the incorporated society for promoting Christian knowledge, and was maintained by a succession of able and zealous labourers. Among these was numbered Kiernandier, a Swede, and likewise a pupil of Francke, who, after a residence of fifteen years in the south of India, was induced, in consequence of the war then raging in the Carnatic, to transfer his labours to Bengal, and arrived in Calcutta in 1758, fifteen months after the battle of Plassy. The town was rising like a phœnix from its ashes, and the Europeans, enriched by the treasures of Moorshedabad, were diligently employed in improving the brilliant prospects opened to them by the establishment of British ascendancy. Mr. Kiernandier received a cordial welcome from Colonel and Mrs. Clive, and was encouraged to establish a mission for the benefit of the Portuguese Roman Catholics, many of whom were received into the Protestant communion. He erected a church, which, after being greatly enlarged and improved, was consecrated by the labours of Brown, Thomason, and Dealtry. Kiernandier, who was a man of the most generous heart and liberal views, unhappily stood security for a spendthrift son, and became insolvent. The church was sold, the mission all but extinguished, and he himself was obliged to seek an asylum at Chinsurah, where he died in 1794, in his eighty-third year, a pensioner on the bounty of the Dutch Government.

The battle of Plassy, which had transformed the Company from merchants into sovereigns, proved destructive of the morals of their servants, who were suddenly exposed to all the temptations of absolute power. A boundless field for the gratification of ambition and avarice was opened to them, and every feeling of honour, and even decency, was sacrificed to the accumulation of wealth. Their masters in Leadenhall Street deplored that, "in the complicated scenes of corruption which had been revealed, gentlemen who served in the highest offices had shewn that no sense of honour could control that unbounded thirst for riches which pervaded the whole settlement, and threatened the dissolution of all government." For more than a quarter of a century it might be said with truth, that England had conquered Bengal, but Bengal had subdued the morals of its conquerors.

Mr. Charles Grant, one of the most distinguished public servants of the Company, was the first who ventured to advocate the intellectual and religious improvement of the natives. Amidst the general scepticism of the day, he exhibited a noble example of Christian principle and practice. Amidst universal corruption, he was distinguished by the most exemplary probity. Around him was collected a small band of devoted Christians—Mr. Chambers, Mr. Udny, the Rev. David Brown, and others; and it was into this circle that Mr. John Thomas was introduced on his second arrival in Calcutta. Mr. Thomas had been educated for the medical profession, and having obtained an appointment in the service of the East India Company, proceeded to Calcutta in 1783, as surgeon of the *Oxford* Indiaman. Unable, on his arrival, to discover any one of a congenial Christian spirit, he advertised, as he said, for a Christian who would "assist in promoting a knowledge of Jesus Christ in and around Bengal." Mr. Chambers responded to the notice, and offered to encourage the translation of the New Testament into the Persian and Moorish languages. This movement, however, led to no result, and Mr. Thomas returned to England. He embarked in the same vessel, and in the same capacity a second time, and on his arrival in Calcutta was introduced to Mr. Grant, who was delighted with the ardour of his piety and zeal, and raised a subscription in his own circle to enable him to quit the Company's service, and devote his attention to the heathen. A missionary station was thus formed at Goamalty, in the neighbourhood of Malda, where he applied himself diligently and with the greatest success to the cultivation of the Bengalee language, into which he translated a portion of the New Testament. He was employed for three years in itinerating through the district, and made considerable impression on the minds of several natives. But with all his spirituality of mind and his religious zeal, he was often so mystical and extravagant in conversation as to bring his sincerity into question. He was seldom able to restrain his sectarian bigotry, and was withal so irascible and intemperate in his speech, as to render any intercourse with him hazardous. He, moreover, embarked in speculations which he did not understand, and became involved in debts which so completely neutralised his usefulness, that Mr. Grant, on the eve of embarking for England, was constrained to relinquish all further connexion with him. Mr. Thomas then determined to visit England, and seek assistance for the establishment of a mission in Bengal among the friends in his own denomination.

In 1786, Mr. Grant drew up the plan of a "Mission to Bengal." He proposed to divide the province into eight missionary circles, in each of which a young clergyman of the Church of England was to be employed, on a salary of £350 a year, in setting up schools, superintending catechists, and establishing churches. To the success of any such plan, he considered the support of Government indispensable. The Rev. David Brown was therefore deputed to break the subject to the Governor-General, Lord Cornwallis, and to ask his patronage for the establishment of schools, in order to avoid startling him abruptly with the formidable idea of a mission. But Lord Cornwallis was profoundly indifferent to every scheme for the intellectual culture of the natives, and professed to have no other object than to render our Indian empire subservient to the interests of England, and to provide Leadenhall Street with investments from territorial revenue. He dismissed the subject with the dry remark, that "he had no faith in such schemes, and thought that they must prove ineffectual." Mr. Grant, who stood high in his estimation, then propounded the plan to him in person; but he was immovable.

This failure did not, however, damp the ardour of Mr. Grant. He transmitted copies of his address to the Archbishop of Canterbury and the Bishop of London, but he placed his chief dependence on the active co-operation of Mr. Romaine, Mr. Newton, Mr. Simeon, Mr. Cecil, and the other leaders of the evangelical section of the Church of England. He likewise addressed Mr. Wilberforce on the subject, and for the first time drew the attention of that philanthropist to the question of Indian missions, to which, for the next fifteen years, he devoted his great talents and his noble eloquence. The archbishop, Dr. Moore, entertained the project with cold caution. The Bishop of London replied, that he had entered warmly into Mr. Wilberforce's views for the amelioration of the slaves in the West Indies, and had no time to bestow on the East.

The project languished till Mr. Grant's return to England, when he took up the thread of the movement, and spared no labour to enlist in its favour the support of those who presided over Church and State. The Bishop of London, on whom he called, referred him to the Archbishop of Canterbury, as the East lay within his province. His Grace received Mr. Grant with courtesy, expressed his approbation of the proposal, and promised to mention the subject to the king and to Mr. Pitt. Mr. Wilberforce, to whom Mr. Grant reported the progress of his efforts, assured him that any direct plan of a large mission to India appeared to his political friends too formidable to be entertained at a time when Europe was unsettled, and that a new prospectus must be drawn up in lieu of his "address." With no little reluctance did Mr. Grant yield to the painful necessity of weeding it of any missionary allusions, and of diluting his proposals. The prospectus, thus modified, was submitted to Mr. Elliot, Mr. Pitt's brother-in-law, who had taken a very lively interest in the plan; but he concurred with Mr. Wilberforce in concluding, from his acquaintance with the opinions of men in the highest political circle, that it was still too missionary in its character, inasmuch as education and civilisation were evidently intended to be subsidiary to conversion.

The paper was, therefore, again recast, and deprived of much of its vigour, and then sent to the archbishop, in the hope that some decisive movement would be made before the departure of the spring fleet. Four weeks elapsed without any reply; after which Mr. Grant waited on him, and was told, with many apologies, that, in the present state of affairs, time must be allowed for consideration, and that any immediate action was altogether impracticable. He said he had gone so far as to introduce the subject to the king, who had replied, that "humanity alone would induce attention to it." He would bring the subject again before his majesty, and if his opinion was found to be favourable, would speak to Mr. Pitt about it, and get the business brought forward by the Board of Control and the Court of Directors. It was again submitted to the king after a considerable interval, and he admitted the propriety and importance of the scheme, but hesitated to countenance it, "chiefly in consequence of the alarming progress of the French Revolution, and the proneness of the times to movements subversive of the established order of things." From the king, therefore, Mr. Grant had nothing to hope, but both Mr. Pitt and Mr. Dundas, to whom the archbishop stated the plan of the mission, appeared, on the whole, to be favourably disposed to it.

The period for the renewal of the charter of the East India Company was approaching, and Mr. Grant was anxious that some provision should be made in the new arrangement, for the moral and spiritual improvement of India. The India Bill, however, which was introduced by Mr. Dundas in March, 1793, was found to be altogether silent on the subject. Mr. Wilberforce, therefore, took charge of the question on behalf of the friends of religion; and, after the bill had been discussed, proposed two resolutions, the most important of which was to the effect, that "it is the opinion of this House that it is the peculiar and bounden duty of the legislature to promote, by all just and prudent means, the interest and the happiness of the British dominions in the East, and that for these ends such measures ought to be adopted as may gradually tend to their advancement in useful knowledge, and to their religious and moral improvement." The resolution was adopted and entered on the journals. It was then placed in the hands of the law officers of the Crown, who considered that it must be embodied in specific language to be of any legal efficacy, and they accordingly drew up a clause for insertion in the bill, which stated, that the proposed measures of improvement were to consist in the encouragement of missionaries and schoolmasters. The question was thus brought in a distinct shape before the authorities at the India House; and if a petard had suddenly burst upon it, there could not have been a feeling of greater consternation. The Court of Directors and the Court of Proprietors was at this time crowded with men who had passed their lives in India at a period when Christian principles had undergone a total eclipse; and they had returned to England laden with wealth and anti-religious prejudices. While in India, their minds had become thoroughly brahminized, and the rites and practices of idolatry had not only been regarded with complacency, but considered as acceptable to the Deity as the homage of Christian worship. Any idea of interfering with the "religious prejudices," as they were termed, of the Hindoos, aroused a feeling of strong resentment, and they were resolved not to allow these prejudices to be disturbed by fanatics. In the cant phraseology of the day, they had left their consciences and their religion behind them at the Cape when they went out, and neglected to call for them on their way home.

It was to a body infected with these partialities and prejudices, that the proposal to send out missionaries for the conversion of the Hindoos was presented, and the old Indians in Leadenhall Street seized the first opportunity of giving vent to those feelings of alarm and indignation which agitated their breasts. At a court held on the 22nd of May, to receive a report on a measure altogether foreign to the question of missions, they hastened to unburden their minds. They declared, that they had hoped the age was become too enlightened for attempts to make proselytes; that the sending of missionaries out to India would prove utterly destructive of the Company's interests; that the conversion of fifty or a hundred thousand natives, of any degree of character, would be the most serious disaster that could happen; and they thanked God that it was impracticable. They affirmed, that the higher and more respectable natives were men of the purest morality, and the most sterling virtue; that the project of converting them to Christianity was the most wild, extravagant, expensive, and unjustifiable project that was ever suggested by the most visionary speculator; and that the clause was, in short, so obnoxious in principle, that it ought to be most strenuously resisted. They maintained, that one of the leading causes of the separation of America from England was the establishment of colleges and seminaries in the different provinces, and that it should be our object in India to steer clear of the rock on which we had split in America. A resolution was hastily passed condemning the clause; and the directors who were members of the House were requested to appear in their places and oppose it. Such were the sentiments entertained regarding the moral and intellectual improvement of India by those who, at this period, had been appointed to govern its destinies. The people were to be kept in a state of complete and permanent ignorance, and denied all chance of exchanging the puerile fables of the Poorans for the truths of the Bible, that England might be enabled to hold the country without anxiety, and monopolise its trade and drain its resources. It was with this stern and implacable opposition to all missionary efforts that Mr. Carey and his associates were required to struggle until the next renewal of the charter, when Parliament, under the pressure of public opinion, rejected the protests of the India House, and opened the door of India to the introduction of Christian and secular knowledge.

The clause thus vehemently opposed was not inserted in the Charter Act. In the last stages of the bill, Mr. Wilberforce stood forth as "the bold, zealous, animated, and able champion of Christianity," and again pressed the adoption of it on the House. But Mr. Dundas, who was originally lukewarm on the subject, was now assailed by the India House, and surrendered the missionary clause to its clamours. He complimented Mr. Wilberforce on his humanity and his principles, and assured the House that he was equally anxious to promote so beneficent a purpose, but he doubted whether the means proposed would answer the end. He would not, however, lose sight of the object, and if the House would consent to omit the clause, he was ready, on a future occasion, to give it the consideration its importance required. But that future occasion, that more convenient season, never came, and the design of propagating useful knowledge and true religion in India was left for twenty years at the mercy of the Court of Directors. Thus fell to the ground the "grand scheme" of the mission to Bengal, which originated in the zeal and benevolence of Mr. Grant. It was not under the auspices of the Episcopal bench, or of ministers of State, that the Gospel was to be introduced among the natives of Bengal, but through the humble and energetic agency of an obscure denomination. It was while these vain attempts were in progress to enlist the support of the great in the missionary cause, and to establish it by "might and by power," that the small and unpretending society was formed at Kettering, and Mr. Carey was preparing to embark for Calcutta in the face of every difficulty. This circumstance was gracefully alluded to by Mr. Charles Grant, thirty years after, in a letter to Serampore:—"Many years ago, I had formed the design of a mission to Bengal, and used my humble efforts to promote the design. Providence reserved that honour for the Baptists."

To return to the movements of Mr. Thomas. On his arrival in England, in 1792, he heard of the formation of a missionary society in his own denomination at Kettering, and immediately addressed a letter to Mr. Carey, informing him of the efforts he had made in Bengal, and describing in glowing terms the prospects of success which had attended them. This communication was laid before a meeting of the committee, and it was resolved, if possible, to unite their exertions with those of Mr. Thomas. At the same time, the first address of the Society to the public was adopted, which announced that its object was "to evangelise the poor, dark, idolatrous heathen, by sending missionaries into different parts of the world not blessed with the glorious light of the Gospel." Mr. Fuller went up to London to make inquiries regarding Mr. Thomas, which proved satisfactory; and at a committee meeting, held on the 9th of January, 1793, it was resolved that a door appeared to be opened in India for preaching the Gospel to the heathen, and that Mr. Thomas be invited to unite with the society, who would endeavour to procure an assistant to accompany him. Mr. Carey then rose and renewed the offer of his services, which were at once accepted. While the committee was sitting, Mr. Thomas himself was unexpectedly announced, and Mr. Carey, eager to embrace his future colleague, sprang from his seat, and they fell on each other's neck and wept. Mr. Thomas candidly explained to the committee his disagreement with Mr. Grant, and his own pecuniary embarrassments; but his character appeared to be so ingenuous, and his integrity so obvious, that the resolution of the committee was not shaken, and it was resolved that he and Mr. Carey should proceed to Bengal in the spring.

But new difficulties arose. Mrs. Carey, who had never moved beyond the limits of her own county, refused to undertake a sea voyage of fourteen thousand miles. But Mr. Carey was resolved not to abandon an undertaking dear to him as life itself, and he determined to embark with his eldest son, returning for his wife and family as soon as the mission was established. The Society, moreover, after having determined to send two missionaries to India, found that their zeal had outrun their resources, and that their funds were inadequate even to the expense of the voyage. Mr. Fuller proceeded to London to canvass the opulent members of the denomination from door to door; but from the majority of them he met a cold reception and no encouragement, and he frequently retired from the more public streets to the back lanes that he might not be seen to weep over his disappointment. By dint of begging and borrowing, the sum requisite was at length raised. The valedictory services were held on the 20th of March, when Mr. Fuller delivered an address to the two missionaries, with a degree of animation which impressed it ever afterwards on the minds of those who heard it. It concluded in this strain:—"Go, then, my dear brethren, stimulated by these prospects. We shall meet again. Each, I trust, will be addressed by our Great Redeemer: 'Come, ye blessed of my Father—these were hungry, and ye fed them; athirst, and ye gave them drink; in prison, and ye visited them; enter into the joy of your Lord.'"

The important question now arose, how they were to get to India. No English vessels were allowed to proceed to it except those of the East India Company, and their commanders were strictly prohibited to take any passenger on board without a licence from the India House. Mr. Fuller was desirous that the missionaries should not appear to be smuggled out, and two of the members of the committee proceeded to London to inquire whether it would be prudent to apply for permission to the Court of Directors. The temper of the Court on the subject of missions may be gathered from the preceding narrative; and the two members soon found that nothing could be more indiscreet than to bring the subject under their notice. The Rev. Thomas Scott had removed to London, and occupied the post of chaplain of the Lock Hospital. The modest youth, whom he had last seen at Hackleton in his shoemaker's apron, now called on him to state that he was going out as a missionary to India, and to ask his influence with Mr. Charles Grant to obtain permission for him to proceed there. But Mr. Grant, on being informed that he was associated with Mr. Thomas, peremptorily refused to give any countenance to the undertaking, though he offered every assistance to Mr. Carey if he was disposed to go alone, and expressed a desire to see him. From some accidental circumstance the interview never took place, and these two eminent men, who had been making concurrent efforts in different spheres, unknown to each other, to accomplish the same object, never met.

As the prospect of a licence appeared hopeless, it was resolved that the missionaries should run the risk of embarking without one. The commander of the *Oxford*, Indiaman, with whom Mr. Thomas had made two voyages as surgeon, offered them a passage without reference to the India House, and they proceeded to the Isle of Wight, to await the arrival of the fleet. But Mr. Thomas's creditors continued to pursue him, and he was obliged to resort to various devices to elude their vigilance. Mr. Carey's high and honourable feelings were deeply wounded by the disreputable position of his associate; but the die was cast. At length the fleet hove in sight, and they joined the *Oxford*, but they had not been long on board before the captain received an anonymous letter from London, stating that an information was about to be laid against him at the India House for taking out unlicensed persons. He felt that his commission was at stake, and insisted on their quitting the vessel without the delay of an hour. With a heavy heart they unshipped their baggage, and returned to the shore; and Mr. Carey immediately wrote to Mr. Fuller, under feelings of deep affliction, but not of despondency: "Our plans are frustrated for the present; but however mysterious the dealings of Providence, I have no doubt they are directed by an infinitely wise God." Even the indomitable spirit of Mr. Fuller was staggered by this unexpected blow. "We are all undone," he wrote to Dr. Ryland. "I am grieved; but perhaps it is best. Thomas's debts and embarrassments damped my pleasure before. Perhaps it is best he should not go out. I am afraid leave will never be obtained now for Carey, or any other."

Mr. Thomas, on being expelled from the vessel, hastened to London, in the hope of being able to discover the author of the letter, and inducing him to withhold the information, but he returned without success, just as the fleet was getting under weigh. He found Mr. Carey in an agony of distress at the sight of the departing fleet, and determined one moment to go out overland, at another to proceed boldly to the India House, avow his object, and solicit permission to embark. With a firm conviction that some path would open to them, they left their luggage at Portsmouth, and returned to London to consult their friends. Mr. Thomas went to the various coffee-houses in the city in search of some foreign vessel proceeding to Calcutta, and was so happy as to hear of a Danish East Indiaman which was daily expected in the Downs. But the terms demanded by the agent, £100 for each adult, and £50 for each child, damped his ardour. He proceeded that night to Northamptonshire, partly to raise funds, and partly to make a last effort to persuade Mrs. Carey to accompany her husband. To this she at length reluctantly consented, but only on condition that her sister should accompany the party. This addition to their number served, however, to increase the pecuniary difficulty of the question, because it swelled the passage money to £600. But Mr. Carey was resolved not to allow the opportunity to slip, and within twenty-four hours after his wife had agreed to accompany him, he had disposed of all his little property, and was on his way to London with his whole family. There he was authorized to raise as much money as could be obtained on the guarantee of the Society, and the Rev. A. Booth and Dr. Rippon assisted the cause to the full extent of their credit; but, after every exertion, the sum realised fell short of the exigency. But Mr. Thomas, with that generosity which served in some measure to redeem the inconsistencies of his character, proceeded again to the office of the agent, and, after stating their difficulty, proposed that he and Mrs. Carey's sister should be rated as assistants, and take their meals at the steward's mess. These terms, though inadequate, were accepted, and, on the 13th of June, 1793, the whole party embarked in the *Cron Princessa Maria*, commanded by Captain Christmas, an Englishman, but naturalised in Denmark. On the first day after they had weighed anchor, he handsomely requested Mr. Thomas and Mrs. Carey's sister to take their seats at the cuddy table. The voyage was without incident. Mr. Carey employed his time in studying Bengalee under his colleague, and in assisting him in the translation of the book of Genesis into Bengalee by his own knowledge of the original. As they sailed up the Bay of Bengal, his mind expanded at the contemplation of the great field of missionary labour which was presented to view on all sides. In writing to the Society, he said, "Africa is but a little way from England, Madagascar is a little further on. South America, and all the numerous and large islands in the India and China seas, will not, I hope, be passed over. A vast field opens on every side. Oh, that many labourers may be thrust into the field!"

The party landed in Calcutta, unnoticed, on the 11th of November, and immediately hired a house for both families. Rambosoo, one of Mr. Thomas's most hopeful inquirers, was not long in finding out the missionaries; and, as he had acquired a smattering of English, Mr. Carey immediately engaged him as a moonshee. The funds which they took out for their support had been invested in goods, which was then considered the most advantageous mode of making remittances. The disposal of them was entrusted to Mr. Thomas, who was supposed to understand the Calcutta market; and here, at the threshold of the undertaking, their difficulties commenced. He was not only unthrifty, but inclined to extravagance, and set up a more expensive establishment than their means would justify. The money disappeared as rapidly as it came in; and before Mr. Carey had been a month in the country, he was constrained to seek some cheaper residence. He therefore removed to Bandel, about twenty-five miles up the river, where may yet be seen the neat Roman Catholic church erected more than two centuries and a half ago, the oldest edifice of Christian worship in Bengal. It was while residing at this place that he was introduced to the venerable Kiernandier, then in his eighty-fourth year, and derived no small encouragement from the unabated ardour of his missionary feelings. But Bandel was in the immediate neighbourhood of European society, and Mr. Carey found it unsuited to the plan he had formed of accommodating his habits to the native economy of life, which he then considered the most effectual mode of obtaining access to the people. He proceeded, therefore, with Mr. Thomas to Nuddea, where they resided a few days, and established a friendly intercourse with the pundits at that celebrated seat of learning, and were invited to settle there. "We seemed inclined to do so," wrote Mr. Carey, "as it is the bulwark of Hindooism, which, if once carried, all the country must be laid open to us." But they returned, after a brief sojourn, to Calcutta, where Mr. Thomas found that his London creditors had sent out his bonds for realisation; and he was advised by his friends to resume his profession, and thus adopt some visible means of satisfying their demands. The scanty funds brought from England were by this time nearly exhausted, and Mr. Carey was indebted for an asylum to the generosity of an opulent native, who offered him the use of a small house in the southern suburb of the town. It is pleasing to record that twenty years after, this native gentleman, who had experienced a reverse of fortune, was placed, through the influence of Mr. Carey, in circumstances of ease and comfort.

The distress to which Mr. Carey was reduced at this time was greater than he had ever experienced before. He was in a foreign land, without a friend, and without a farthing, except as he could wring it from Mr. Thomas; and it required all the strength derived from a firm confidence in the Divine promises to keep him from being overwhelmed with despondency. His wife, who had accompanied him to India with great reluctance, was constantly upbraiding him with their wretchedness, and contrasting their indigence with the comparative luxury in which Mr. Thomas was living,—though on funds borrowed from a native at exorbitant interest. His family, consisting of seven persons, was crowded into a small, ill-ventilated house, without any of the conveniences requisite for the European constitution in an eastern climate, and his wife and two of his children were attacked with dysentery, from which they recovered but slowly. Driven to distraction by this accumulation of troubles, he resolved to remove to the Soonderbuns, where he was offered the occupation of a small house, and proposed to take a grant of land and cultivate it for the support of his family. But amidst all these difficulties he never lost sight of the great object which had taken him to India. While residing in Calcuttà he visited the places of public resort, day by day, with Rambosoo as his interpreter, and endeavoured to explain the message of salvation to the heathen, while, at home, he was indefatigably employed in the study of the language. Having at length, after repeated disappointments, obtained a small supply of money from Mr. Thomas, he embarked in a boat with his family for the Soonderbuns. It should be explained that the Soonderbuns consist of a vast tract of land, lying to the south of Calcutta, facing the Bay of Bengal, and stretching from the Pudma on the east, to the Hooghly on the west, over an area of more than 6,500 square miles. It was once filled with hamlets and towns, and a rich cultivation, but was depopulated by the piratical Mugs or Aracanese, and was now inhabited only by wild beasts. Here and there, patches of the forest had been cleared for the manufacture of salt, and villages had gradually arisen at intervals. It was in this region of jungle, and tigers, and malaria, far removed from all Christian and civilised associations, that Mr. Carey now planted the hopes of the mission. After several days of navigation, his stock of provisions was reduced to the requirements of a single day, when he fortunately met a European gentleman employed under Government in the salt department, who received him into his house, and in that spirit of hospitality which has always distinguished Europeans in India, invited him to remain for six months or a longer period, till he could obtain suitable accommodation. Soon after, Mr. Carey proceeded to the opposite bank of the river to a place called Hasnabad, and began to erect what he called his huts, on a tract of land cleared of jungle which he had obtained. "Wild hogs, deer, and fowl," he writes to Mr. Fuller, "are to be procured by the gun, and must supply us with a considerable portion of our food. I find an inconvenience in having so much of my time taken up in procuring provisions and cultivating my little farm. But when my house is built I shall have more leisure than at present, and have daily opportunities of conversing with the natives, and pursuing the work of the mission."

From this position, the most unfavourable that could be conceived for the development of missionary plans, he was rescued by a circumstance altogether unexpected. Mr. Udny, the friend of Mr. Charles Grant, who had once contributed to the support of Mr. Thomas, but had been constrained by his follies to withdraw it, was at this time in charge of the Company's commercial factory at Malda, and had recently been plunged into the deepest affliction by the death of his brother and his sister-in-law, who were drowned by the upsetting of a boat off Calcutta. Mr. Thomas, on hearing of this affliction, wrote an affectionate letter of condolence to Mr. Udny, who was so touched by this token of sympathy, as to overlook their differences, and invite him to Malda, and soon after to offer him the charge of one of the indigo factories he had newly erected. Mr. Thomas immediately dropped his professional prospects in Calcutta, which were by no means bright, and accepted the proposal. Soon after, he brought the solitary and desolate condition of his colleague in the Soonderbuns to the notice of Mr. Udny, who authorized him to offer his friend the superintendence of another of his factories. Mr. Carey was delighted with a proposal which not only rescued him and his family from starvation, but opened the prospect of a more extensive field of usefulness. Immediately on accepting the invitation, he wrote to the committee stating that he was no longer in circumstances to need any personal support, though "it would always be his joy and glory to stand in the same relation to the Society as if he required its assistance; but he requested that the sum which might be considered his salary should be devoted to the printing of the Bengalee translation of the New Testament." Some of the members of the committee—which had been enlarged, without being improved in liberality—addressed a letter of "serious and affectionate caution to him, lest he should allow the spirit of the missionary to be swallowed up in the pursuits of the merchant;" though it does not appear that in the course of three years they remitted a larger sum than £200 to India. To this ungenerous admonition, Mr. Carey replied,—"I can only say that, after my family's obtaining a bare subsistence, my whole income, and some months more, goes for the purpose of the Gospel, in supporting persons to assist in the translation of the Bible, in writing out copies of it, and in teaching school. I am, indeed, poor, and shall always be so until the Bible is published in Bengalee and Hindoostanee, and the people want no further instruction."

Mr. Carey reached Malda on the 15th of June, 1794, and immediately took charge of the factory of Mudnabatty, thirty miles distant from that station. In that secluded spot he passed more than five years of his life, free from pecuniary anxieties, and preparing himself for the more extended and important duties that awaited him. Of his salary, which at the time of the offer Mr. Udny had fixed at 200 rupees a month, or about £240 a year, he regularly devoted a fourth, but more often a third, to the objects of the mission. No sooner had he obtained a settled position, than his active mind was turned to the improvement of agriculture; and in one of his earliest letters to England he requested Mr. Fuller to send him a supply of implements, scythes, sickles, plough-wheels, and an annual provision of flower and garden seeds. "I will regularly," he says, "remit the money to you; it will be a lasting advantage to the country, and I shall have an opportunity of doing this for what I may now call my own country." As soon as he had acquired sufficient fluency in the native language, he daily assembled the servants and the labourers of the factory, about ninety in number, for Christian worship, and constantly itinerated in the villages around him. He also established a school for native children, the first ever set up by a European in Hindoostan, in which he proposed to teach not only the vernacular tongue, but Sanscrit, the sacred and classical language of the Hindoos, and Persian, the court language of the Mahomedans, together with various branches of useful knowledge, and the doctrines and duties of Christianity. He found, however, that the poverty of the parents too often obliged them to remove their children prematurely from the advantages of tuition, and he proposed, therefore, to feed and clothe as well as educate them. But the time had not arrived, neither was the obscure village of Mudnabatty the place, for an institution of such magnitude. Mr. Carey's principal attention was devoted to the translation of the New Testament into Bengalee; but when it was at length completed, and he sought the means of printing it, he found that the proprietors of the three or four presses in Calcutta, who expected to make fortunes as rapidly as other Europeans, would not undertake to give him, 10,000 copies, on country paper, for less than £4400, exclusive of binding. He therefore proposed to the Society to send him out a set of Bengalee punches from Caslon, the eminent typefounder in London, a press, a supply of paper, and a "serious printer," if one could be found willing to engage in the work of the mission. Such a printer, he said, he knew at Derby before he left England. Soon after, a printing press was offered for sale in Calcutta, which Mr. Carey lost no time in purchasing; but Mr. Udny claimed the privilege of presenting it to the mission; and it is still preserved in Serampore College, as the press at which the first sheet of the Bible was printed in the northern division of India. When the press reached Mudnabatty, and was put together, the natives flocked to see it, and, on hearing Mr. Carey's description of its wonderful power, pronounced it to be a European idol.

Towards the close of 1796, Mr. Fountain joined the mission at Mudnabatty. He embarked in one of the Company's ships, rated as a servant, and entered the country without attracting notice. He was a man of small mind, devoid of all energy, and added nothing to the strength of the cause. But in the excitement caused in England by the French Revolution, he had imbibed the violent Jacobin notions then prevalent, and Mr. Fuller, who considered it indispensable, under a despotic government like that of India, that the missionary should entirely sink the politician, threatened to recall him if he had not the prudence to check the expression of his views; and he was thus placed under a salutary restraint. Mr. Carey now became anxious for more associates, but the jealousy with which the Government of India guarded the country against the entrance of interlopers, presented an insuperable obstacle to the gratification of his wishes. In 1783, Parliament had thought fit to decree that if any subjects of his Majesty, not being lawfully licensed, should at any time resort to or be found in the East Indies, they should be declared guilty of a high crime and misdemeanour, and be liable to fine and imprisonment. In 1793, the Court of Directors mitigated the penalty to simple deportation. There were, however, hundreds of Europeans residing in the interior of the country, under what was termed the "tacit permission" of Government, and it was felt that any attempt to expel them would bring a storm of public indignation on the India House, which it would not be prudent to provoke. And it is due to the East India Company to state, that the extraordinary power with which they were armed by the Legislature was exercised with exemplary moderation, and that only two Europeans were sent out of the country during the next ten years, and they were political agitators.

In 1795, Sir John Shore, the Governor-General, passed an order that every unlicensed European in the country should enter into covenants with the Company, and find securities for the performance of them, varying from £500 to £2000. This was considered a very arbitrary act, inasmuch as it placed every European in India at the mercy of the public authorities; but it was hailed by Mr. Carey as a boon, because it gave him, and those who might join him, a recognised, though precarious, position in the country, and protected them from expulsion. He was returned as an indigo planter, residing in the district of Malda, and Mr. Udny and another friend stood his securities. On the strength of this arrangement he hastened to apply to Mr. Fuller for more labourers. "Whether," he said, "the Company will or will not molest us, must be left to His care without whose permission a sparrow does not fall to the ground; but, that no human means for our safety may be wanting, I have entered into covenants with the Company, and am permitted to live in the country, and with boldness engage in any line of business, and pursue any line of conduct I choose. The missionaries who come out may be returned as my own or Mr. Thomas's assistants." In the hope of receiving new associates, he proposed to form a

Moravian settlement in the neighbourhood of Malda, consisting of seven or eight families. The wives were expected to be as hearty in the work as the husbands. The establishment was to be the nursery of the mission, and the education of the children was to be entrusted to one of the number. They were to live together in a number of little straw houses, forming a line or a square, and to have nothing of their own, but all things in common. One or two were to be elected as stewards to preside over the management of affairs, which, with respect to eating, drinking, worship, learning, and preaching excursions, was to be reduced to fixed rules. He estimated the expense of eight families living distinct at a thousand rupees a month, and at four hundred rupees a month, or fifty rupees for each, if they messed together. The primitive simplicity and self-denial of this plan exhibited the zeal and devotion to the cause which always animated him, but it was no proof of the soundness of his judgment. Even if his straw huts and mud floors had not sent half the community to the grave during the first rainy season, the inconceivable distress to which European families must have been subjected in such a colony, in such a climate, would have broken it up within a twelvemonth.

Mr. Fuller was, however, sanguine of the success of the plan, and, in anticipation of this new missionary establishment, advised Mr. Carey to wait on Lord Mornington, subsequently Lord Wellesley, who had been appointed Governor-General in 1798, to acknowledge his missionary vocation, and endeavour to establish the mission on a permanent footing, by obtaining a legal settlement. Mr. Carey replied that the proposal of an interview with the Governor-General, which Mr. Fuller had urged in the simplicity of his heart, had raised a smile. "You must," he said, "drop all your English ideas and acquire Indian ones. There can be no legal settlement here, in the English sense of the word. The law prohibiting the settlement of Europeans was passed by

Parliament, and can be reversed only by the same authority. Every European is obliged to report himself and his occupation once a year to the magistrate, and if I were to return myself as a missionary I certainly should not be allowed to remain in the country. You must not, however, suppose that we are obliged to conceal ourselves or our work. We preach before magistrates and judges, and were I in the company of Lord Mornington I would not hesitate to avow myself a missionary, though I would not officially return myself as such."

Mr. Carey had now been labouring at Mudnabatty for more than five years, traversing the district in every direction, and sowing the seed of the Word with untiring zeal, but without any corresponding success. The time was now approaching for his removal, in the course of Providence, to another sphere of labour, with larger scope for the development of his views, and with associates of a congenial spirit and of enterprising minds. The indigo factories had not flourished, and Mr. Udny was obliged to relinquish them. In stating this fact to the committee, Mr. Carey remarked that he expected shortly to be left without an independent income; and they responded to this letter in a spirit of generosity which tended to obliterate the remembrance of their former littleness. They resolved to pay him the arrears of the salary, which he had declined, with much disinterestedness, several years before, and to leave the mode of future maintenance to his discretion. He immediately purchased of Mr. Udny a small factory, at a place called Kidderpore, for £300, from the returns of which he hoped to provide for the support of the mission, and where he began to erect straw huts for the associates whom Mr. Fuller had engaged. But he had little aptitude for business, and the mission, if it had depended on his success as an indigo planter, would probably have been extinct in a twelvemonth. Mr. Udny had, moreover, been promoted to a higher appointment in Calcutta, and his successor was a brahminised

European. He had expressed his desire to take proceedings against Mr. Carey for a letter which appeared in the Periodical Accounts of the Baptist Missionary Society, and would speedily have hunted out the missionary settlement in the Malda district. From these embarrassments Mr. Carey was relieved by an unexpected turn of events.

CHAPTER II.

Mr. Carey's letter, announcing that, under the new system of covenants, missionaries might be introduced into the country as assistant indigo planters, reached Mr. Fuller in August, 1798; and such was his indomitable energy, that, within nine months, four missionaries were sailing down the Thames on their way to Mudnabatty. Two of these, Mr. Grant and Mr. Brunsden, men of great zeal and much promise, were cut off in the dawn of their career; but the two other members of the party, Mr. Ward and Mr. Marshman, were destined, in the course of Providence, to be associated with Mr. Carey in the establishment of the Serampore Mission, of which the present work is a brief record.

William Ward was born at Derby, on the 20th of October, 1769, the son of a carpenter and builder, who died while he was a child. The charge of his education devolved on his mother, a woman of great energy of character and exemplary piety, to whose instructions he was indebted for those religious impressions which preserved him from the common dangers of youth. Under the tuition of Mr. Congreve and Mr. Breary, of Derby, he became proficient in the ordinary branches of learning; but for those mental accomplishments which adorned his subsequent career, he was indebted to his own exertions. On leaving school he was apprenticed to Mr. Drury, then at the head of a large printing establishment in the town. He soon rose to the grade of corrector of the press, which gave him the opportunity of storing his mind with a large stock of knowledge. He was endowed by nature with a lively imagination and a pregnant wit; and by incessant reading, and the constant habit of composition, acquired great fluency of language. At the close of his apprenticeship he undertook the editorial charge of the *Derby Mercury*, which, under his able management, became one of the most popular and influential journals in the county. In the enthusiasm of youth he had imbibed the democratic notions created by the French Revolution, and was led to join a political society established in Derby, and affiliated with the parent society in London, which Mr. Pitt considered dangerous to the constitution. For this association he drew up an address, which was republished by Mr. Perry in the *Morning Chronicle*, and became the subject of a public prosecution. The trial was conducted by the Attorney-General, Sir John Scott, afterwards Lord Eldon, while the defence was intrusted to Mr. Erskine, who succeeded in obtaining a verdict of acquittal from the jury. Another paper which Mr. Ward drew up, which exhibited the same talent and the same republican views, was subjected to a similar prosecution, with the like result. Both these papers were attributed by Mr. Erskine, who was ignorant of the author, to the elegant pen of Dr. Darwin. Some time after, Mr. Ward removed to Stafford, and commenced another journal in connexion with a member of Mr. Drury's family. He subsequently proceeded to Hull, where he undertook the management of the *Hull Advertiser*. Six years of his life were thus passed in the active and animating duties of an editor, at a period of great excitement, and he thus acquired a large view of men and things, great facility of composition, and those habits of business which subsequently proved invaluable to the Serampore mission. It was during these editorial engagements that

Mr. Clarkson, on his tour through England to organise a national opposition to the atrocities of the slave trade, visited Derby, and called on him to enlist his services in the cause of abolition, of which his journal became one of the most faithful and earnest advocates.

In August, 1796, Mr. Ward was baptized at Hull by Mr. Pendered, and began to devote his attention to the instruction of the poor in the neigbourhood. Mr. Fishwick, who is represented as a gentleman of good fortune and great benevolence, often accompanied him to the hamlets around, and was delighted with the fervour of the addresses which he delivered, on a three-legged stool, to the rustic congregation. Unwilling that these ministerial talents should remain in obscurity, he placed him, at his own expense, under the tuition of the Rev. Dr. Fawcett, of Ewood Hall, the tutor of John Foster, the essayist. From that period Mr. Ward renounced all interest in politics and journalism, and gave up his heart and soul to the noble vocation of communicating divine truth to his fellow-men. His feelings on this occasion were communicated to a friend in these terms:—"I had thought I had been fixed at Hull. I had a pleasant lodging facing the Humber, refreshed by its gales, inviting me to its banks, gratifying me by its passing current and its stately barques. I was occupied in a situation in which I often indulged my pen and my fancy. I was surrounded by friends, on whose smiles I sometimes imprudently fed. My mind was calm, and I had some leisure for my book and for my friends. Sometimes I went into the villages to gladden the hearts of my fellow-men with good tidings of great joy. In the midst of these engagements and pleasures, I received an invitation to go to Ewood Hall, to leave Hull, perhaps, for ever. Conscience commands me to go, to enter on a new line of life; to combat difficulties and prejudices; to be subject to the cavils of the bigot and the frowns of the dissipated; to incur the displeasure of the mermaids of professors, half sinners, half saints; to live, perhaps, on thirty pounds a year; to warn men night and day with tears; to tremble lest I myself should prove a castaway."

A twelvemonth after Mr. Ward had been placed under Dr. Fawcett's tuition, a member of the Baptist Missionary Committee visited the seminary at Ewood Hall in search of missionary recruits to respond to Mr. Carey's call for aid. On the eve of Mr. Carey's departure for India, he had been introduced to Mr. Ward at Derby, and observed that if the undertaking in which he was about to embark proved successful, they should need one of his calling to print the Scriptures. This conversation was now vividly recalled to his mind as the Society's representative described the labours of Mr. Carey, the completion of the Bengalee translation of the New Testament, and the need of more labourers. While he was musing, the fire burned within him, and he determined at once to offer his services to the Society. They were gladly accepted, and he prepared at once to proceed to India.

JOSHUA MARSHMAN was born at Westbury Leigh, in Wiltshire, on the 20th of April, 1768. His family traced its descent from an officer in the Parliamentary army, who, like all his comrades, retired into private life when the troops were disbanded by Charles the Second, at Blackheath, in 1660. His grandson realised a little independency as a blacksmith, which he bequeathed at his death, in 1720, to his son, who speedily squandered it in dissipation. His wife was a woman of energetic character, and, when reduced to destitution by his extravagance, determined to support her family by her own labour, and apprenticed her son, John Marshman, the father of the Serampore missionary, to a weaver. He afterwards went to sea, and was present at the capture of Quebec, but eventually settled at Westbury Leigh, where he became the deacon of the Baptist church established there seven years after the Act of Uniformity. In 1764, he married Mary Couzener, the descendant of one of the Protestant refugees driven from France by the revocation of the edict of Nantes, and they lived together in a state of the highest connubial happiness for more than fifty years.

At the age of seven, Joshua Marshman was sent to the little village school, kept by one Coggeshall; but he left it with nothing beyond a mere knowledge of reading, as the village pedagogue did not profess to teach either writing or arithmetic. This was all the tuition he ever received. But from his early years he manifested an insatiable thirst for reading. The single shelf of his father's cottage contained little beyond the works of some of the old Puritan divines, the heirlooms of the family; but his son laid the whole neighbourhood under contribution, often walking a dozen miles for the loan of a book, and before he had attained the age of twelve had read through more than a hundred volumes. A few days before his death at Serampore, he amused himself with noting down from memory the books he had read before he was fifteen, together with the name of the friend from whom it was borrowed; and a glance at the first twenty-five on the list will shew the singular activity of his mind, and the varied but ill-assorted knowledge with which it was stocked. "Borrowed of a neighbour, Baker Ingram: the Fables of Pilpay; Voltaire's Candidus; The Travels of a Philosopher in Cochin-China; Robin Hood's Garland. Of the Rev. Robert Marshman: Josephus, in twenty quarto numbers; Salmon's Geography; The Chinese Traveller (Du Halde abridged); and a work on Astronomy. Of Mr. P. Phipps, Westbury Leigh: The Wonders of Nature and Art; The Natural History of Serpents; The Various Revolutions in the World; The Survey of England, in six volumes; The Conversations of Eusebius. Of Mr. William Clift: Neal's History of the Puritans; The History of England, in letters. Of John Hill: The Present State of England, in the time of Charles the Second; Hudibras. Of Benjamin Roberts: The New History of Troy's Destruction; Cynthia, a Novel of the Old Saxon Time; Historical Remarks on the City of London; Don Quixote; Robinson

Crusoe; Milton's Paradise Lost; Collier's History of England; and Tooke's Pantheon." Nothing could be more unfavourable to mental improvement than this miscellaneous course of reading, except the total absence of all culture; but it was enforced by the necessity of returning one work before he could obtain the loan of another. The disadvantage was, however, in a great measure mitigated by his astonishing and almost miraculous memory, which enabled him to call up, at will, any series of events which had once been deposited in it, and to dovetail all information subsequently received on the subject.

When Mr. Marshman had reached the age of fifteen, Mr. Cater, a bookseller in Holborn, and a native of Westbury Leigh, visited the village, and having made the acquaintance of the youth who was said to have read everything, proposed to take him to London, and provide for him in his own trade. The prospect of being placed in a bookseller's shop, surrounded by hundreds of volumes, was too tempting to be refused, and he started for London in a waggon, and reached it in three days. Every moment of leisure he could obtain by day was devoted to reading, and he often sat up half the night at his books, and, even on his way to the customers, could not refrain from looking into the volumes he conveyed to them. But the labour of trudging through the streets, day after day, with a heavy parcel of books, became at length disheartening, and having been one day sent to the Duke of Grafton with three folio volumes of Clarendon's History, he began to give way to melancholy, and as he passed Westminster Abbey, laid down the load, and sobbed at the thought that there was no higher prospect before him in life than that of a bookseller's porter; but looking up at the building, and recalling to mind the noble associations connected with it, he brushed away his tears, replaced the load on his shoulders, and walked on with a light heart, determined to bide his time. At the end of five months, however, his father, who thought he was unhappy, recalled him to Westbury, where he resumed his labours at the loom, and plunged again into his old habit of desultory reading, and devoured every work of fiction or poetry, history, geography, or travels he could procure, and before eighteen had read through more than five hundred volumes.

His life for the next ten years was monotonous. His father, and farmer Bachelor, the pillars of the church at Westbury Leigh, had always inculcated on him that it was the duty of a Christian man to await the leadings of Providence, in humble contentment, and that it was sinful to make any effort which might wear the appearance of anticipating them. He continued, therefore, to labour in his vocation, in association with the humble God-fearing members of the church, though with endowments of mind immeasurably beyond them. He had been trained up by his pious parents with the strictest attention to all the duties of morality and religion; he was correct in his conduct, and could reproach himself with nothing more heinous than a partiality for the novels of Smollett and Fielding. But he felt that he was not justified in considering himself a converted person. He has left on record that he was led to suppose that conversion, to be genuine, must be preceded by some fearful exercises of mind, which a man must undergo for a longer or shorter period before he obtained the assurance that he was in a state of safety. But as he studied the Scriptures more deeply, his views became more clear. Gradually, as he described it, the light of divine truth shone into his mind, and he was enabled at length to place his entire dependence for acceptance with God, and his hope of salvation, on the all-meritorious atonement of the Saviour. This change in his religious views induced him to enter upon a new course of reading. He gave several months to the study of Luther on the Galatians, and read with his usual avidity a whole library of divinity, devotional and polemical. But the works in which he took especial delight were those of the great Puritan divines of the seventeenth century, which he studied with so much intensity as to acquire the peculiarities of their style, which he was never able in after-life fully to correct. Still he was unable to come up to the standard of the Westbury Leigh church, consisting of about a hundred members, and imbued for the most part with those austere views which had descended to them from their Puritan founders. They maintained that, as a work of grace once begun in the heart could never become extinct, it was more advisable to postpone the reception even of those who appeared to be sincere, than to admit a single unconverted person into the fold. They regarded human learning with suspicion, though Robert Hall had once charmed them with his eloquence; and when Mr. Marshman sought admission into the church, the deacons remarked that he had too much head-knowledge of Christianity to have much heart-knowledge of its truths. He was therefore kept on probation for seven years, and left Westbury Leigh unbaptized.

In 1791, Mr. Marshman married Hannah Shepherd, the grand-daughter of the Rev. John Clark, for sixty years the pastor of the Baptist church at Crockerton, where he preached his last sermon, at the age of ninety-one, in the year 1803. This union was the source of unalloyed happiness for forty-six years. Mrs. Marshman combined great piety and a sound judgment, with a disinterestedness of character which made her a suitable associate with her husband in the work to which his life in India was devoted; and she was, moreover, gifted with so amiable a disposition, that in the long intercourse of life, nothing was ever known to ruffle her temper. At the beginning of 1794 a new field of labour opened to Mr. Marshman. The situation of master of a school, supported by the Baptist church at Broadmead, Bristol, was offered to him, with permission to eke out the scanty stipend attached to it by private tuition. This was so manifest a "leading of Providence," that even the rigorous deacons of Westbury Leigh could not gainsay it, and he removed to Bristol when a little under twenty-six years of age. He was introduced on his arrival to Dr. Ryland, the President of Bristol Academy, who, on being made acquainted with the state of his religious feelings, and the long period of probation to which he had been subjected, urged him to join the church at Broadmead, into which he was immediately admitted by baptism. He was permitted to join the classes of the academy, and for more than five years devoted his leisure hours, with his usual assiduity and success, to the study of the classics, to which he likewise added that of Hebrew and Syriac. The perusal of the Periodical Accounts, which recorded the labours of Mr. Carey, gradually turned his mind to missionary labour in India; and when it was known that the Society was in quest of labourers for that field, he resolved to give up all his prospects of independence, and offer his services to the committee, which were at once accepted.

The four candidates for the mission were received with great delight as fast as they presented themselves, but when Mr. Fuller sat down to calculate the cost of their support in India, his mind was filled with anxiety. The funds in the hands of the treasurer had accumulated to £3000, but of this sum £2000 were already engaged for the printing of the Bengalee New Testament, and the remainder would be in a great measure absorbed by the outfit and passage of the missionaries. Mr. Fuller was, therefore, obliged to fall back upon Mr. Carey's plan of a Moravian settlement, and he wrote to India that he did not conceive it possible that the missionaries could be supported in any other manner. In the memorandum which he delivered to them, therefore, on the eve of their embarkation, he authorised them to draw on the Society for the sum of £360 a year, to cover the expenses of the whole missionary establishment, with the exception of Mr. Thomas, then engaged in manufacturing sugar; but he added, "The Lord will provide." Incredible as it may appear, it was with these prospects that Mr. Ward and

Mr. Marshman, and their two associates, embarked with their families for India. The sum of £360 a year, which, at the exchange of the day, was equivalent only to 2880 rupees a year, was the sole provision which the committee of the Society was able to make for the support of six men, five women, and eight children. Mr. Carey, on receiving intimation from Mr. Fuller of the engagement of the missionaries, commenced building his straw houses for them in that distant and isolated locality where he had a small factory without a vat, and where the missionary families were expected to live, and labour, and flourish, on forty rupees a month.

A passage was engaged for the party in an American ship, the *Criterion*, commanded by Captain Wickes, a pious Presbyterian, of Providence, in the United States; and they embarked at Portsmouth on the 29th of May, 1799. The voyage, which lasted four months and a half, was relieved of its usual weariness by the instruction of the sailors, to whom the missionaries devoted several hours daily; and it was rendered agreeable by the rare kindness and Christian sympathy of the commander. But as they approached their destination, the treatment they were likely to receive from a hostile Government, unfurnished as they were with licences, tended greatly to depress their spirits. Mr. Charles Grant had advised Mr. Fuller that they should not expose themselves to immediate banishment by landing in Calcutta, but proceed direct to the foreign settlement of Serampore, and await an opportunity of proceeding, unobserved, to Mudnabatty. But, as the vessel dropped anchor on the 5th of October, the pilot came on board and delivered to the captain the blank form he was required to fill up with the name and vocation of each of his passengers. The missionaries were at first inclined to return themselves as assistants to Mr. Carey, in his indigo factory, near Malda; but, after a little consultation, they determined boldly to avow their missionary character, and trust to Divine Providence to protect them from the consequences. The captain, therefore, entered their names as Christian missionaries proceeding to Serampore. They reached the town on the morning of the 13th of October; and Mr. Marshman, on stepping ashore, fell on his knees and blessed God for having conducted them in safety to the shores of India.

The little Danish town of Serampore, which has become memorable in the annals of Christian missions, is situated on the right bank of the river Hooghly, about fifteen miles above Calcutta. On the opposite bank lies the military cantonment of Barrackpore, and the elegant country-seat of the Governor-General. The settlement was formed in 1755, about twelve months before the battle of Plassy, and increased in prosperity to such an extent that, within twenty years, the number of vessels which resorted to it in a twelvemonth measured 10,000 tons. Towards the close of the last century, Chandernagore and Chinsurah, the French and Dutch settlements in the neighbourhood, had been occupied by the English Government; and owing to the rigid monopoly of the East India Company, the European trade of the private merchants was concentrated in Serampore, which had reached the zenith of its prosperity at the time when the missionaries entered it.

On Monday, the 14th of October, they waited on the governor, Colonel Bie, and were received with great cordiality. He offered them all the assistance in his power, but questioned whether they would be allowed to proceed into the interior of the country. They began, however, the same day to engage boats and make preparations for their departure; but a bitter disappointment awaited them. The captain's return of his missionary passengers had been immediately submitted by the police to the consideration of the Supreme Government. It was the first instance in which the arrival of missionaries, without the permission of the Court of Directors, had been officially reported, and it was determined that they should be immediately ordered to quit the country. Captain Wickes, on applying to enter his vessel, was informed that instructions had been issued to refuse it, unless the four missionaries appeared at the police-office, and entered into engagements to return forthwith to England. This intelligence, which the captain conveyed to them the same evening, disarranged all their plans, and filled their minds with dismay. The next morning they waited again on the governor, and explained the new difficulties of their position. Colonel Bie had enjoyed the ministry of Schwartz, at Tranquebar, and had learned from him to appreciate the value of missionary labours. For twenty years, moreover, he had resolutely resisted the demands of successive Governors-General to surrender those to whom he had accorded the protection of his flag, and he was now prepared to offer the missionaries an asylum in the teeth of British opposition; but he strongly advised them to present a memorial to Lord Wellesley, which they did not fail to do. Much interest was likewise made with Government by the Rev. David Brown. The Governor-General perceived, moreover, that the missionaries, against whom no crime was charged, were now beyond his reach; he felt that he had no legal right to detain a foreign ship for having brought out passengers for a foreign settlement; and he yielded to circumstances with a grace that did credit to his good sense, and removed the interdict he had laid on the American vessel.

The cause of immediate anxiety—the dread of expulsion from the country—was thus removed, but the difficulties of their position remained. They were shut up in the town; and, as their presence in the country was regarded with a feeling of jealousy, they could not venture into the British territories without the risk of being intercepted. Mr. Brown, who stood high in the estimation of Lord Wellesley, made great efforts to obtain permission for them to settle in the Company's territories, but without effect. The influential members of the Government fully participated in the morbid feelings of the India House, and were determined, if possible, to prevent the establishment of missions in the country.

The missionaries were, therefore, constrained to remain in Serampore till they could receive a communication from Mr. Carey. They hired a small house in the town at thirty-two rupees a month, where each family had the accommodation of a single chamber, fourteen feet square. One room of larger dimensions was reserved for their common table and for divine service, and there they invited the Christian community to join them in public worship on the ensuing Sunday. The governor and many other gentlemen sent their own chairs and filled the room. But the dampness of the house at the close of the rains soon proved fatal to one of their number. Mr. Grant was attacked with a severe cold, which brought on a fever, and he was a corpse on the 31st of October, before his brethren, new to the climate, were aware of his danger. In the peculiar circumstances in which they were placed, with their path blocked up, and their course precarious, this sudden bereavement served to aggravate their distress.

Mr. Carey's reply afforded them little relief. He appeared still to cling to the idea of making the little village of Kidderpore, in the north of Bengal, the seat of the mission. He was not without hope that the opposition of Government might be overcome. He endeavoured to make interest, through a friend, with Mr. Colebrooke, the great Orientalist, who occupied a high position in the public service, but was assured that any application to settle in the country as missionaries would not only prove unsuccessful, but create irritation, and that any attempt to proceed into the interior without permission, would insure their immediate deportation. But the kindness of the governor of Serampore was redoubled as the hostility of the British Government became more manifest. On the 6th of November he called on the missionaries, and renewed his advice to make Serampore the head-quarters of the mission. He offered them the full protection of the Danish Government, and all the privileges of Danish citizenship, as well as passports under his official seal, if they desired to visit the interior of the country. At Serampore they might establish schools for the support of the mission, which, from the vicinity of the British metropolis, would speedily become remunerative; they might set up a press and print the Scriptures, and books and tracts, without molestation. Suitable premises might also be obtained at a reasonable cost, and, as an additional inducement, he engaged to make over to them the church for which he was then endeavouring to raise subscriptions, which he knew would be acceptable to his own Government, as the service in Nonconformist chapels harmonised with that of the Lutheran church. At the same time Mr. Brown, who was well acquainted with the views and policy of Lord Wellesley, assured them that it was hopeless to expect permission to establish a press in the Company's dominions out of Calcutta. During the recent struggle with Tippoo, the editors of newspapers in Calcutta had indulged in remarks which exasperated the Governor-General beyond measure, and he ordered the Vice-President in council to suppress the journals and send the editors back to England. On his return to the Presidency, he imposed such restrictions on the liberty of the press, as even the political difficulties of the time were not sufficient to justify, and which he himself subsequently disapproved, when restored to constitutional associations in England. It was at this inauspicious period that the missionaries sought leave to establish a press in a district two hundred miles from Calcutta, and it was peremptorily refused.

Mr. Ward and Mr. Marshman gathered from their interviews with Mr. Brown that it was not repugnant to Lord Wellesley's wishes that the missionaries should accept Colonel Bie's offer and plant their mission at Serampore. On the contrary, it would rather be agreeable to him to find that they were established under a foreign flag, and that he was relieved from all official necessity of interfering with their movements. He was a despot, but an enlightened despot.

He had no sympathy with the contracted views of the corporation in Leadenhall Street, where the dread of interlopers was an heir-loom, and to name missionaries and schoolmasters was considered treason. He did not consider either of these classes dangerous to British interests in India, and he had no desire to molest them. To avoid a lengthened correspondence with Mr. Carey, Mr. Ward obtained a Danish passport and proceeded to Malda, where the subject of their future course was anxiously discussed. The day after his arrival, a letter was received from Mr. Marshman, stating that some of the higher officers of Government were incensed to find that the missionaries had obtained an asylum beyond their reach in a foreign settlement, and had expressed their determination to arrest any of them who might be found in the Company's territories. This letter appears to have extinguished Mr. Carey's hesitation, and determined the question of his removal to Serampore. At this conference, he and Mr. Ward agreed to advise the Society to remit the whole of the funds in the hands of the treasurer, which they assumed at £3,000, to India, to be invested in Government securities, which then bore interest at the rate of 12 per cent. Mr. Carey, in his letter to Mr. Fuller on this subject, observed that if the Society could only secure a capital of £4,000, yielding an annual return of £480 a year, "the mission could be established without any more labour of begging." He does not appear to have considered it possible that a time might arrive when the credit of the Indian Government would be so firmly established that, with the public debt increased tenfold, they could obtain any amount of subscriptions to a loan at five per cent. Happily this project fell to the ground. An endowed mission would become lifeless and effete, as a matter of course. A feeling of wholesome responsibility to the Christian public, periodically enforced by the necessity of an appeal to its liberality, appears indispensable to the maintenance of animation and zeal in the missionary system. The money then in the hands of the treasurer, instead of being locked up in the Company's securities, was more usefully employed in enlarging the sphere of missionary operations, and in printing the Scriptures.

Mr. Carey arrived at Serampore with his family, consisting of his wife in a state of hopeless insanity, and four sons, on the 10th of January, 1800; and thus, under the guidance of Divine Providence, the opposition of Government, which at first threatened the extinction of the mission, became the occasion of removing the seat of it from one of the most unsuitable localities in Bengal to the immediate neighbourhood of the British metropolis, yet beyond the control of the British authorities. If the settlement of Serampore had not existed, or if it had not been at the time under the Danish flag, Mr. Ward and Mr. Marshman would probably have been driven back to England; no missionary press could have been established in the interior of the country; Mr. Carey would have been precluded from receiving any accession of labourers, and the mission might have expired in its cradle at his death. The day after Mr. Carey's arrival he was presented to the governor, who repeated the assurance of his cordial support. The week was occupied in framing rules for the large family thus brought together, and laying down the plan of future operations. It was resolved to form a common stock, to dine at a common table, and to grant each family a trifling allowance for personal expenses, denominated by Mr. Fuller pocket-money. All the missionaries were to be considered on a footing of equality, and the superintendence of the general arrangements and expenditure was to be entrusted to each one in monthly rotation. Mr. Carey had charge of the public chest, as treasurer, and also of the medicine chest,—for India was at the time considered so unhealthy that medicine was deemed as necessary as food. One evening in the week was to be devoted to the adjustment of differences, and the renewal of their pledge of mutual love. All private trade was interdicted, and any sum which might be earned by any member of the family was to be credited to the general fund.

On his arrival in Serampore, Mr. Carey rented a small house at some distance from the residence of his brethren, but in neither of the houses was there the smallest accommodation for a school or a press. Serampore was, at the time, the seat of an active commerce, and the river was enlivened by the presence of six or seven merchantmen. There being no insolvent court in Calcutta, the town was the asylum of bankrupts; house rent was therefore extravagantly high; and no premises suitable for an establishment such as the missionaries contemplated could be obtained under 120 rupees a month, or one-half the sum Mr. Fuller had allotted for the entire support of the families. Within a week of the arrival of their colleague from Mudnabatty, a house with extensive grounds was therefore purchased, for 6,000 rupees, which was paid for partly out of the money brought with them from England, and partly by bills on the Society, and a loan which they obtained in Calcutta. It afforded moderate accommodation for their families; a spacious hall which it contained was reserved for public worship; and on the site of it now stands the mission chapel at Serampore. A side building was fitted up as a printing-office, and a large plot of ground in the rear of the house was made over to Dr. Carey for a botanical garden. Thus, in the first month of the establishment of the mission at Serampore, did the missionaries abandon those confined views of missionary economy which the Society in England, no less than Mr. Carey, had associated with the enterprise, and launched out into a liberal expenditure corresponding with the enlarged scale on which they were about to conduct their operations.

Their first attention was given to the printing-office. With the exception of two books of the Old Testament, the translation of the whole Bible in the Bengalee language was completed. Mr. Ward set the first types with his own hands, and presented Mr. Carey with the first sheet of the New Testament on the 18th of March. The feeling of exultation with which it was contemplated, and the great prospects which it opened up, may be more easily imagined than described. While Mr. Ward was thus working the press, Mr. Carey and Mr. Fountain were engaged, morning and evening, in preaching to the heathen in the town and its neighbourhood. These addresses, in all places of public resort, brought a constant succession of inquirers to the mission-house, and no small portion of Mr. Carey's time was occupied in answering their questions and explaining the doctrines of Christianity to them. The 24th of April was selected as a day of thanksgiving for the establishment of the mission in circumstances so favourable. At this meeting the missionaries voted an address to the King of Denmark, expressing their warmest gratitude for the generous protection which his servants had extended to their undertaking, and soliciting his permission to continue in the settlement and prosecute their labours. In the ensuing year, his Majesty, Frederick the Sixth, signified the gratification he felt at the establishment of the mission in his dominions, and informed the missionaries that he had taken their institution under his special protection.

On the 18th of May, 1800, Mr. and Mrs. Marshman opened two boarding-schools for the support of the mission, which, before the close of the year, brought in an income of £360 a year, and secured the mission from pecuniary destitution. Under their able management, the schools rose in public estimation, and soon became the most flourishing and remunerative in the country. The missionaries who had recently arrived were now passing through the first ordeal of the scorching month of May, but without any of those conveniences by which the heat of the climate is now mitigated. "We have felt," writes Mr. Ward, "the greatest heat we have ever experienced, but though we perspire profusely, it neither impedes business nor injures health. Our brethren preached as usual four times on Sunday." On the 1st of June they opened a vernacular school for native youth, which soon numbered forty pupils; but even at that early period the natives manifested a greater desire to acquire a smattering of the English language than to obtain knowledge through their own tongue. "Commerce," writes Mr. Marshman, "has raised new thoughts and awakened new energies, so that hundreds, if we could skilfully teach them gratis, would crowd to learn the English language. We hope this may be in our power some time, and may be a happy means of diffusing the knowledge of the Gospel. At present, our hands are full." About the middle of the year, Rambosoo, who had consorted several years with Mr. Thomas, and was for some time Mr. Carey's moonshee, came on a visit to Serampore, on hearing of the establishment of the mission. He had a clearer perception of the truths of Christianity than any other native of that period, and likewise a philosophical contempt for the popular superstition, but he had not sufficient resolution to renounce his family connexions and avow himself a Christian. "All the ties," writes Mr. Marshman, "that twine about the heart of a father, a husband, a child, and a neighbour, must be torn and broken before a man can give himself up to Christ." These ties were stronger than the convictions of Rambosoo. He was one of the most accomplished Bengalee scholars of the day, and wielded the remarkable power of sarcasm inherent in that language, with marvellous effect. At the request of Mr. Carey, he composed a tract,—the first which had ever appeared in Bengal,—entitled the "Gospel Messenger," and thus introduced the doctrines of the Bible to his fellow-countrymen. In another tract, he exposed the absurdities of Hindooism and the pretensions of its priesthood, to ridicule, in the most poignant language. Large editions of both these pamphlets were printed and circulated, and produced no ordinary sensation among the natives.

The expenses of the press absorbed the slender resources

of the missionaries, and before the end of the year they were crippled for funds. In this emergency, they adopted the bold and somewhat hazardous course of appealing to the Christian community in Calcutta for assistance to print the Bengalee New Testament, although only a few months had elapsed since the hostility of Government to their undertaking had been unequivocally demonstrated. The notification which they published did not fail to catch the eye of Lord Wellesley, and his apprehensions were immediately aroused. He considered it vain for him to have placed the Calcutta press under restrictions, if a press was allowed to exist in its immediate vicinity over which he could exercise no control. But instead of committing his Government, as he was at first prompted to do, by an official communication with Colonel Bie, he wisely consulted Mr. Brown, who assured him that the press at Serampore was devoted exclusively to the spiritual benefit of the natives; that the missionaries conscientiously avoided all political discussions, and had recently refused to print a pamphlet animadverting on the proceedings of his Government. Lord Wellesley said that he was personally favourable to the conversion of the heathen, but he questioned whether it would be altogether safe to circulate the Bible, which taught the doctrine of Christian equality, without the safeguard of a commentary. Mr. Brown replied that he himself would be responsible for all the mischief which the Bible might do in India; and at the same time hinted that the Bengalee New Testament would be of great utility in the college which he was about to establish. "Such," writes Mr. Ward, "are the jealousies which our press excites in the British Government, though we are under a foreign jurisdiction. How long would it have been allowed to exist at Kidderpore?" This was, however, the last instance of any manifestation of alarm by Lord Wellesley at the proceedings of the missionaries; his subsequent conduct was invariably marked by feelings of confidence and kindness. The appeal to the public brought the seasonable relief of about 1500 rupees.

On the 20th of August, Mr. Fountain, who had proceeded on a visit to Dinagepore, died at the house of Mr. Fernandez. His bier was escorted to the grave, as was then usual, by a guard of sepoys, and the judge of the district read the burial service over his remains. On the 1st of October, Mr. Marshman delivered his first address to the natives in Bengalee, and three weeks after Mr. Ward went out to preach alone. Neither of his colleagues ever obtained that mastery of the colloquial language which he acquired, and scarcely has any foreigner ever been able, like Mr. Ward, to rivet the attention of a native audience by the ease, and vigour, and humour of his addresses. Mr. Thomas was at this time engaged in superintending some sugar factories in Beerbhoom. It was the redeeming trait in his character, that amid all his secular engagements he never neglected the instruction of the heathen. In the month of October he visited Serampore, bringing with him Fukeer, a skilful workman on his establishment, who had been led by his discourses to relinquish idolatry. On the 25th of November he came before the church, and gave a simple and satisfactory account of the progress of his convictions, and announced his desire to make an open profession of his faith in Christ. This was the first native, after seven years of labour, who had come up to this stage of decision. He was received as a Christian brother. "We all stood up," wrote Mr. Ward, "and sung with new feelings 'Praise God, from whom all blessings flow.' Each of us shook Fukeer by the hand. The rest your imagination must supply."

On the day of these "new feelings," Mr. Thomas was called to set the dislocated arm of a native in Serampore. After the operation was completed, Mr. Thomas began to discourse with his accustomed fervour on the folly of idolatry, and the great truths of Christianity. The man, Krishnu, by trade a carpenter, was deeply affected by the conversation and began to shed tears. He was invited to visit the missionaries, and a day or two after made his appearance at the mission house, where he became a constant visitor, and received the instructions imparted to him with great avidity and affection. Meanwhile, Fukeer proposed to visit his family before he was irrevoçably separated from them by crossing the Rubicon of Christian baptism, and Mr. Thomas, dreading their influence on his mind, determined to accompany him into the district. But on reaching their destination, he asked permission to call on a friend, but he never made his appearance again, and Mr. Thomas returned to Serampore in a state of deep despondency.

The grief occasioned by the defection of Fukeer was, however, overbalanced by the consistency of Krishnu, who, after being convinced of the truth of Christianity, did not long hesitate to offer himself as a candidate for baptism. In writing on the subject to Mr. Fuller, Mr. Ward observed, "We think it right to make many allowances for ignorance and for a state of mind the fruit of a corrupt superstition. We cannot think, therefore, of demanding from the candidates before baptism more than a profession of dependence on Christ, and submission to Him in all things. Had some of our brethren with their supralapsarian covenants been here, they must have made some little abatement for poor Krishnu." On the 22nd of December, he openly renounced his caste by sitting down at the table of the missionaries, to the utter astonishment of the servants. "Thus," again writes Mr. Ward, "the door of faith is open to the Hindoos, and who shall shut it? The chain of the caste is broken, and who shall mend it?" This season of exultation was not, however, without alloy. Mr. Thomas, who was present, became frantic with joy, and soon after began to exhibit symptoms of insanity, and within three days it became necessary to place him under bodily restraint.

The report that Krishnu had thrown up his caste and become a *feringee*—the nickname of a Christian—created an extraordinary sensation in the town, and a mob of some two thousand persons assembled before his door, and after calling down the most savage imprecations on him, dragged him to the residence of the magistrate. But as they had no criminal charge to bring against him, the magistrate ordered the crowd to disperse, and commended Krishnu for following up the convictions of his own conscience. He also placed a sepoy at his gate for his security, and offered to protect the missionaries, if necessary, from all interruption during the administration of the rite of baptism. But no such precaution was necessary. On Sunday morning, the 28th of December, Mr. Carey walked down to the river from the chapel, with his eldest son, about to be baptized, on one side, and Krishnu on the other. At the ghaut, or landing-stairs, the governor and several Europeans, a large body of Portuguese, and a dense crowd of Hindoos and Mahomedans, were waiting to witness this novel scene. To them Mr. Carey explained that they had no belief in the divine virtue of the river, but regarded it as the simple element of water; that Krishnu, who had once professed their creed, had renounced the worship of idols and become a disciple of Jesus Christ. The most perfect silence was maintained, and a feeling of solemnity appeared to pervade the assembly while the ordinance was administered. In the afternoon, the sacrament of the Lord's Supper was for the first time celebrated in the Bengalee language: and thus ended the first year of the Serampore Mission.

At the beginning of 1801, the missionaries had the pleasure of baptizing the first Hindu female, Joyminee, the sister-in-law of Krishnu, and likewise Mr. Fernandez, a gentleman of Portuguese extraction and of independent means, one of the little band of friends clustered around Mr. Carey at Mudnabatty. For more than thirty years subsequently he was one of the most active and successful coadjutors of the Serampore missionaries, and was instrumental in raising a large native church in the district of Dinagepore, which continued to flourish under his pastoral care to the time of his death. A month after, Krishnu's wife and another female were baptized; and Mr. Thomas, after a month's residence in an asylum in Calcutta, was restored to mental health, and proceeded to Dinagepore to take charge of an indigo factory. On the 7th February, Mr. Carey enjoyed the supreme gratification of receiving the last sheet of the Bengalee New Testament from the press; the fruition of the "sublime thought" which he had conceived fifteen years before. The work had been pressed on with such diligence that the printing of the volume, a large portion of which Mr. Ward set with his own hands, was completed under every possible disadvantage within nine months. As soon as the first copy was bound, it was placed on the communion table in the chapel, and a meeting was held of the whole of the mission family, and of the converts recently baptized, to offer a tribute of gratitude to God for this great blessing. In communicating this intelligence to Mr. Fuller, Mr. Ward, with his characteristic modesty, remarked, "I think there have been too many encomiums on your last missionaries in the 6th number of your Periodical Accounts. I cannot get out of my mind a public show while I read these accounts— Very fine missionaries to be seen here; walk in, brethren and sisters. I cannot think that any encomium of this kind can excite public confidence, or produce the least good."

The large and liberal views of Lord Wellesley had induced him, on the close of the Mysore war, to establish the College of Fort-William, in Calcutta, with the object of completing the education of the junior members of the civil service, which had been prematurely interrupted in England by their early appointment, often at the age of fifteen, and of giving them a grammatical knowledge of the languages of the country. Lord Wellesley was the first Governor-General who appears to have appreciated the importance of a thorough acquaintance of the vernacular tongue of the people by those who were selected to govern them. He considered the College one of the most important departments of the State, and it was unquestionably one of the noblest designs which had been devised for the improvement of our Government since the battle of Plassy. In this institution the study of the Bengalee language, the mother-tongue of twenty-five millions of people, was for the first time enforced on the public servants. There was, however, but one person qualified to give instruction in it, and he was a missionary, and the leaders in the Government circle were hostile to any encouragement of missionary efforts. But Lord Wellesley was superior to such prejudices, and when Mr. Brown and Mr. Buchanan, who had been appointed Provost and Vice-Provost of the College, stated to him that Mr. Carey was the only man fitted for the appointment, but would accept it only on condition of being allowed the fullest freedom of action as a missionary, he waived every objection on this ground, and directed his services to be at once engaged. But a greater difficulty arose from the spirit of sectarianism. The laws of England, which imposed disabilities on Nonconformists, had never been extended to the foreign dependencies of the country, and the Government of India had from the earliest period acted upon the broadest principles, not merely of religious toleration, but of religious equality, and thrown open every office of every description unreservedly to candidates of all denominations. The first departure from this enlightened policy was exhibited in the statutes of Fort-William College, drawn up by Mr. Buchanan, who was born and bred a Presbyterian, but had joined the Church of England and obtained a chaplaincy in Bengal. He thought fit to introduce into them a religious test for all the superior offices, the professorships, and even the lectureships. Mr. Carey, as might have been expected, refused to qualify himself to teach the Bengalee language in the College by subscribing to the Thirty-nine Articles, and his appointment hung for some time in suspense. But to meet the case of Dissenters and Roman Catholics, a lower grade of officers, denominated teachers, was created, with inferior allowances, from whom no religious subscription was exacted. Mr. Carey accordingly became teacher of the Bengalee language on a salary of 500 rupees a month. He entered upon the duties of his office on the 12th of May, 1801, and immediately wrote to Mr. Fuller that the increased resources of the mission, from his collegiate salary and from the returns of Mr. Marshman's school, would be sufficient for their support without any further help from England; and with the exception of the few hundred pounds which the Serampore missionaries received from the Society during the first year of their settlement, they never accepted anything from the public subscriptions for their personal support.

The rupture between England and Denmark, at the close of 1800, was followed by the occupation of the Danish settlements in India. On the 8th of May, 1801, a detachment of sepoys from Barrackpore took possession of the town of Serampore. The missionaries were thus deprived of the friendly protection of the Danish crown, but they could not fail to appreciate the mercy of Providence in so ordering this event that it was postponed till the mission had taken root in India, and was no longer regarded with alarm by the Governor-General. During the fourteen months in which the town remained in the hands of British officers, the missionaries were permitted to prosecute their labours without interruption. Soon after this event they were called to mourn the loss of another of their number. Mr. Brunsdon died in Calcutta on the 3rd of July, at the early age of twenty-four, after giving promise of an active and useful career. No sectarian distinction was at that period recognised in the use of the public cemeteries, which had from the earliest period been regarded as the common patrimony of all denominations. Mr. Brunsdon was, therefore, interred in the Presidency burial-ground, and Mr. Carey performed the funeral service. It was not till after the establishment of the bishopric in India, that they were converted, by the ceremony of consecration, into the exclusive property of one body, and all but members of the Church of England were excluded from the use of them.

In the month of August, Goluk, one of the earliest inquirers, was received into the church by baptism. These accessions, and the prospect of others, brought under consideration the question of giving Christian names to the converts on their baptism. The missionaries were decidedly adverse to the practice. They could not perceive any positive connexion between the rite of baptism and an alteration of name. They found, moreover, that in the apostolic age it was not deemed necessary to repudiate names of heathen origin, such as Sylvanus, Olympias, Hermes, Nereus, and Fortunatus, and they determined, therefore, that the converts should be baptized with their original surnames. It was not till a later period that the anomaly of Matthew Chukerbutty or Timothy Tarachand was introduced into the missionary system, and which only served to impart a foreign and repulsive character to Christianity in the eyes of the natives. On the 4th of November another Hindoo female, the wife of Goluk, was baptized, which led Mr. Marshman to remark, "We have now six baptized Hindoos, whom we esteem more precious than an equal number of gems. We need great prudence in our intercourse with them. We are obliged to strengthen, to encourage, to counteract, to advise, to disapprove, to teach, and yet to do all so as to endear the Saviour to them, and to retain a place in their warmest affections." The increase in Mr. Marshman's school constrained the missionaries at this time to purchase an adjoining house and grounds, for which they paid £1,000. But while they were ready to expend large sums for premises adapted to their extended operations, their household expenditure was regulated by the sternest economy. They all dined together at four long tables—missionaries, wives, children, and scholars. "We live moderately," writes Mr. Ward, "and drink only rum and water. We have always a little cheap fruit, goat's flesh—the same as mutton—broth, fowls, with a little beef sometimes, and curry; but we have good wheaten bread."

After a residence of two years at Serampore, the missionaries began to itinerate into the interior. Mr. Ward, accompanied by Krishnu, the first convert, made a tour of a fortnight by water, and excited great attention by the novelty of their message, and the free distribution of Testaments and tracts. The books were received with great avidity, and five times the number they took with them would scarcely have been sufficient to meet the demand. On his return to Serampore, Mr. Ward received information of the death of Mr. Thomas, of fever and ague, at Dinagepore, on the 13th of October. He was the first Protestant missionary who preached to the people in Hindoostan in their own tongue, and his missionary labours were continued, with occasional interruptions, for fifteen years. Few foreigners have ever produced so powerful an impression on a native audience. He was formed to work alone, but his zeal overshadowed his eccentricities. His name will ever be held in estimation as the first, and by no means the least zealous of missionaries. By his death, the number of labourers was reduced to three, Carey, Marshman, and Ward; but they were all giants, and the mission, which they conducted with singular spirit and success, has become hallowed in the annals of the Christian church.

CHAPTER III.

On the first Sunday in 1802, Petumber Sing, the first convert of the kayust, or writer caste, which ranks immediately after that of the brahmins, was baptized at Serampore. He was nearly sixty years of age, of an active and inquisitive mind, and great simplicity of character. He had diligently studied the religious dogmas of Hindooism, and visited every shrine within his reach to discover a system of belief which he could receive with confidence. The result of his inquiries was a feeling of dissatisfaction with the national creed, and he quietly relinquished the worship of idols. In this state of mind, one of the tracts distributed by Mr. Ward in his recent journey, fell into his hands, and he hastened to Serampore, a distance of thirty miles, to learn more of this new way. He soon became convinced of the truth of Christianity, and threw up his caste, and joined the church by baptism. A month after, two other kayusts, and a Koolin brahmin, of the highest and proudest grade of brahminhood, came to Serampore and voluntarily relinquished their caste. It was in reference to these circumstances that Mr. Carey wrote to Mr. Fuller,—"Both Europeans and natives laughed at what they thought our enthusiastic idea of breaking the bond of the Hindoo caste, by preaching the Gospel. When Krishnu and Goluk rejected their caste, many wondered at it, but said, What great thing is it, that a carpenter and a distiller should reject their caste? Have any of the brahmins or kayusts believed on him? Lately, however, the Lord has deprived them of that small consolation, and has given us one kayust who has joined the church; and last week two more of the same order, and a brahmin, have rejected their caste without our proposing it."

The circulation of the tracts, and the result which followed it, roused the indignation of not a few of the influential natives, and a Hindoo of high consideration in Calcutta took them to one of the judges of the Sudder, or chief court of appeal, and inquired whether the Government had authorised such remarks on the religion of the country, to the disquietude of the people. The judge, who was no friend to missions, consulted some other alarmists, and it was resolved to bring the subject under the notice of the Vice-President, Mr. George Barlow, an old Indian in his views and prejudices. Lord Wellesley was absent on a tour through the north-west provinces, and the consequences of this reference might have been embarrassing. Mr. Buchanan, when he became aware of the circumstance, advised the judge to procure a translation of the tracts before he committed himself by a representation to Government. The tracts were sent to Mr. Carey, who furnished a faithful English version of them, and the matter was allowed to drop, to the great relief of the missionaries, who felt that they were safe only as they remained unnoticed. This morbid dread of the consequence of propagating Christianity was necessarily accompanied by a profound homage to the usages of Hindooism. "Last week," records Mr. Ward, "a deputation from the Government went in procession to Kalee ghaut—the most opulent and popular shrine of the metropolis— and presented 5,000 rupees to the idol in the name of the Company, for the success which had attended the British arms."

On the other hand, the year was rendered memorable by the abolition of the practice of sacrificing children at the annual festival held at Gunga Sagor. Government had hitherto studiously abstained from all interference with even the most sanguinary and revolting rites of Hindooism, whenever the brahmins declared that they were sanctioned by the Shastras. Lord Wellesley was the first Governor-General to break up this system of guilty concession, and vindicate the claims of humanity. Mr. Udny, the early and steady friend of Mr. Carey, had been elevated to the Supreme Council in 1801, and he immediately called the attention of the Governor-General to the atrocious practice of sacrificing children at Sagor, in the performance of religious vows. Mr. Carey's position in the College, surrounded with the ablest pundits from all parts of the empire, was supposed to give him peculiar advantages for investigating a question of this nature, and he was directed by Government to report on it. "You may be sure," he writes to Mr. Fuller, "that I shall make my report as full as possible, and do it with the greatest pleasure, for I consider that the burning of women, the burying them alive with their husbands, the exposure of infants, and the sacrifice of children at Sagor, ought not to be permitted, whatever religious motives are pretended, because they are crimes against the State." In his report he stated that even in the opinion of the pundits, the practice was by no means imperative, and he urged the immediate abolition of it. His labours were crowned with success; a law was immediately passed prohibiting it under severe penalties. A detachment of Hindoo sepoys was sent down to Sagor to prevent any further sacrifices, and they ceased at once without any disturbance, and without even a murmur.

With the appointment of Mr. Carey to the College commenced the publication of works in the Bengalee language. When he delivered his first lecture in May, 1801, not a single prose work was found to exist in it. The pundits, who monopolised all learning, and prided themselves on their knowledge of the classical Sanscrit, considered it beneath them to cultivate the language of the people, and a vernacular literature had yet to be created. Mr. Carey, in the first instance, employed the talents of Rambosoo, who has been already mentioned as having almost been persuaded to become a Christian, and he compiled a history of Raja Pritapadityu, the first edition of which was published at Serampore, in July, 1801, and formed the first prose work, the Regulations of Government and the Serampore tracts excepted, ever printed in the Bengalee language. After a lapse of sixty years, when thousands of volumes are annually poured forth from the native presses in Calcutta, it is interesting to trace the germ of Bengalee literature to the missionary press at Serampore, at the beginning of the century. Mr. Carey compiled a grammar of the language for the use of his students, and a series of colloquies to familiarise them with the ordinary modes of conversation among the different classes of native society. These works were followed by a translation, executed by the chief pundit in the College, of the Hitopadesh, one of the most ancient and renowned of the Sanscrit classics. About this time Mr. Carey was likewise appointed teacher of the Sanscrit language, though without any additional remuneration, and immediately undertook the compilation of a grammar of that language.

On the 10th of May, Mr. Ward was married to the widow of Mr. Fountain, at the mission chapel, by Mr. Carey. Her previous marriage had been solemnised by Mr. Buchanan, according to the ritual of the Church of England. But as the missionaries expected soon to have occasion to introduce Christian marriages among their native converts, they inquired of the Rev. Mr. Brown, the head of the ecclesiastical department in Bengal, whether there was any legal obstacle to the performance of the marriage ceremony by themselves. He informed them that the English Marriage Act did not extend to India, and that a marriage by a Dissenting minister was not deemed invalid. It is curious to remark that thirty years after this period the Bishop of Calcutta, Dr. Daniel Wilson, in an address to Government on this subject, asserted that if such irregularities as marriages by any but episcopally-ordained ministers were permitted, "a flood of vice and disorder, the ruin and misery of the young, the disturbance of family relations, the wanton riot of headstrong passion and misrule, and the contempt of the religious vow of marriage, must break in upon society." But so little sympathy was felt in India with these feelings, that Government soon after passed an Act for the express purpose of legalising all marriages performed by Dissenting ministers, as well as by lay marriage registrars throughout the country.

The plan which the missionaries devised in the present year for the education of their children, afforded additional proof of their devotion to the cause in which they had embarked. They had renounced every idea of returning to England, and resolved to make India their home and the home of their families. They repudiated the custom of sending children to England, lest European associations should alienate their minds from India, and from the cause of missions. Mr. Marshman, therefore, proposed that suitable arrangements should be made to conduct and complete their education at Serampore, and that it should then be left to their option to engage in some department of missionary labour, or in some secular avocation. The plan at first received the cordial concurrence of his colleagues, but it was never acted on. It was felt to be repugnant to the best feelings of the heart to deprive the children of those healthy associations in which their parents had been trained up, and which are found essential to the mental and moral, as well as physical, vigour of Europeans in India. Mr. Marshman, with whom the proposal originated, had rendered the school so popular that it already yielded an annual income of £1,000; but he took no larger sum for the personal expenses of his family than £34 a year. The corresponding allowance of Mr. Ward from the press did not exceed £20 annually, and Mr. Carey, with his large family, received £40 a year; to which was added the sum of £20, to appear in what they termed "decent apparel at the College and Government House."

All these plans of usefulness were now, however, in danger of serious interruption by the hostility of the Court of Directors to the College of Fort-William, which not only supplied Mr. Carey with 500 rupees a month, but afforded him the inestimable advantage of intercourse with the most learned natives of the East, and enabled him to prosecute the translation of the Scriptures with greater confidence. Lord Wellesley was no favourite in Leadenhall Street. He had given great cause of offence by his advocacy of free trade; he had, moreover, organised the College without the permission of the Court of Directors, and to sanction such a departure from the established system would, they supposed, weaken their authority. There were likewise two substantial objections to the institution, which would have justified them in proposing a modification of its plans; but they adopted the extreme course of peremptorily ordering all expenses connected with it to cease at once. Lord Wellesley did not conceal his feelings of mortification; but in reference to the peculiar character and spirit of the Court's demands on this unhappy occasion, and as an act of necessary submission to the controlling authority of the Court, passed an order for the abolition of the College; at the same time, however, in the hope that the Court would diligently weigh all the considerations which he placed before them, and reverse their adverse decree, he passed a second order, which directed that the abolition should be gradual, and that the institution should not be finally closed for eighteen months. This resolution gave a hope, that with the aid of those vigorous representations which Lord Wellesley was making at the same time to Mr. Pitt on the subject, the College might yet be saved.

On the 19th of July the settlement of Serampore was restored to the Danish authorities. Towards the end of the month, Morad, a Mahomedan, was deputed by his friends in Jessore to invite the missionaries to their village. Mr. Marshman undertook the journey with two of the converts, and on reaching his destination found a large body of Hindoos and Mahomedans assembled, who listened to the Gospel with the greatest attention. The day after, he went to Garapata, where about two hundred men had separated themselves equally from Hindooism and Mahomedanism, and who received the truths of the Bible with great simplicity. "Never," he wrote, "except in the family of Krishnu, have I seen any men listen to the Gospel like these men. Their affectionate conduct towards me I never saw exceeded, even by brethren in England." After spending three days among them, he commenced his return to Serampore, but turned out of his way to the village of Chundooreeah, the residence of a native, Seebram-dass, who had rejected idolatry and established a new sect, and collected, according to popular report, twenty thousand followers. For several hours Mr.

Marshman expounded the truths of Christianity to him and his disciples, and then retired to a hut where a clean mat had been spread on the floor for him. The conference was renewed for several hours the next morning, Mr. Marshman occupying an old chair, and the gooroo, or spiritual guide, being seated on a blanket. After an animated discussion of several hours, Mr. Marshman was invited to a repast of fish, rice, and plantains, which, in the absence of a fork or a spoon, he was obliged to dispose of with his fingers. He then started on his way back to Serampore, leaving several hundred tracts with these kind and simple-hearted people. About a month after, the inquirers again visited Serampore, and Mr. Ward, and Mr. Carey's eldest son, at their special request, proceeded to their village, and gave them further instruction. The eagerness for Christian knowledge manifested by the people in this part of Jessore, induced the missionaries to place one of the converts on the borders of the district, and the aged Petumber Sing was stationed at Sooksagur. He experienced the most determined opposition from the brahmins, who were resolved to prevent his settlement among them; but a wealthy and liberal-minded Roman Catholic gentleman, Mr. Joseph Barretto, one of the most eminent merchants in Calcutta, accommodated him with a piece of ground near his own princely residence, and offered him all the assistance in his power.

Towards the close of the year, the missionaries remark, in their letter to the Society, that they had now thirteen communicants and eight inquirers. They had compiled a little volume of hymns, some of which were adapted to English, and others to native metres; and they had printed and circulated twenty-two thousand tracts. Their mode of proclaiming the Gospel is thus described:—"When the sun is going down, one of us, taking some tracts in his hands, goes out into some part of Serampore or its neighbourhood, talks to the people, and distributes the papers; another does the same in another direction; while a third goes one evening to the

Bengalee school-house, and another evening to Krishnu's little meeting-house. After this our Hindoo friends come every evening to our house. In our family worship, the chapter in the Old Testament, after being read in English, is translated off-hand and read in Bengalee. When proceeding to a distance, we travel, eat, and sleep in a boat, and, going from place to place, preach and distribute tracts."

At the beginning of 1803 the missionaries baptized the first brahmin convert, an amiable and intelligent youth of the name of Krishnu-prisad. Before his baptism he trampled on his poita, or sacred thread, to indicate his rejection of Hindooism, and then placed it in the hands of Mr. Ward, who records in his journal, "This is a more precious relic than any the Church of Rome could boast of." Mr. Ward gave him money to purchase another. Mr. Carey and his colleagues did not at this time deem it necessary for a brahmin to divest himself of his thread, which they considered as much a mark of social as of religious distinction. The converts were, therefore, not only baptized, but preached to their fellow-countrymen with the poita across the shoulder. Krishnu-prisad continued to wear it for three years, when he and another convert of the same caste voluntarily relinquished it. But while the missionaries were anxious to avoid all unnecessary interference with the national habits and customs of those who embraced Christianity, they resolved to make no concession to the demands of caste, which they considered the great bane of native society. The missionaries on the coast had unhappily permitted the converts to carry their caste with them into the Christian church, and this odious distinction had been allowed to intrude itself even into the celebration of the holy communion. The brahmin Christian received the elements before the soodra Christian, and the cup of salvation was thus converted into a chalice of abomination. The Serampore missionaries considered it a sacred duty to extinguish every vestige of caste in the Christian community, and more especially in the Christian church;

and at the first celebration of the Lord's Supper after the baptism of Krishnu-prisad it was arranged that the brahmin should receive the cup after it had passed the lips of the soodra Krishnu. About four months after, the first marriage among the converts was celebrated by the union of Krishnu-prisad, the brahmin, with the daughter of Krishnu, the carpenter: which was another step towards the extinction of caste. Mr. Carey took his seat before a little table in Krishnu's residence, and, after a brief explanatory address, read a selection he had made of passages of Scripture suited to the occasion, and then united them by the short and simple service he had drawn up in Bengalee. After plighting their faith to each other, both bride and bridegroom signed the marriage contract, the first to which a Hindoo female had affixed her signature for centuries. In the evening the missionaries joined in the repast prepared by the father of the bride, which was the first time they had ever partaken of a meal at the house of a convert. Mr. Ward considered this marriage a glorious triumph over caste; but as it was celebrated by a Dissenter, it was, in the opinion of the prelate who subsequently presided over the ecclesiastical department in India, not only irregular but invalid. Half a century was allowed to elapse before the full validity of such marriages was established by a legal enactment. We are accustomed to dilate on the strength of Hindoo prejudices, but it would be as well also to remember how much more easy it was found to break through the prejudices of twenty-five centuries in India, and marry a brahmin to a soodra, than to overcome the prejudices of Christian caste, and regard the office of a pious Dissenting missionary as in every respect equal with that of his Episcopalian fellow-labourer. While the impression created by this marriage was still fresh, Mr. Ward records in his journal:—"Be assured that whatever Europeans may say about the impossibility of converting the Hindoos, there wants nothing more, as it respects human means, but a few men of gifts and real powerful godliness. The reason why this work has never been done yet is, because the means have never been suited to the end. It will be vain to expect that the Gospel will ever spread widely in this country till God so blesses the means as that *native men* shall be raised up, who will carry the despised doctrine brought into the country by the Mlechas (outcasts) into the very teeth of the brahmins, and prove from the Scriptures that this is the Christ that should come into the world. We hope we see the dawn of this." It was to this plan of training native itinerants, who, while retaining all the simplicity of native habits, would enjoy ready access to the minds and hearts of their fellow-countrymen, whom they addressed with all the fervour of their mother-tongue, that the attention of the missionaries was directed; and it was to this agency they looked for domesticating Christianity in India.

In the month of May they received information from Jessore that one of the inquirers had been seized by a public officer, and threatened with a fine and expulsion from the village if he did not renounce Christianity. They had always avoided an appeal to the public authorities for the protection of the converts, feeling that the mission, after all, existed only by sufferance, and that it was imprudent to draw attention to its operations. On the present occasion, however, they injudiciously wrote to the judge of the district to solicit him to investigate the case, and were justly rebuked by his silence. Mr. Marshman determined, therefore, to pay a visit to the village, and give encouragement to the inquirers. It was the burning month of May, and on reaching Sooksagur by boat, he found that no bearers could be procured for his palankeen; but, disregarding all the dictates of prudence, he walked the whole day across the country, with the thermometer at 115°. He arrived at Sreenugur at dusk, and occupied a temple of Kalee for the night, stretching himself on the plank on which the image was annually paraded through the streets. He reached the house of the inquirers on Sunday morning, examined the case, and after giving them the most suitable advice, returned again on foot to Serampore. Nothing but his iron frame could have stood such exposure. At the end of April, the Rev. D. Brown purchased a house and grounds at Aldeen, immediately adjoining the town of Serampore; and although he remarked in one of his letters that Mr. Carey "dips his brahmins in the river not far from my house," he maintained a close and affectionate intimacy with the missionaries, in whose labours he always manifested the greatest interest. A congeniality of feelings and tastes between him and Mr. Marshman created so cordial a friendship, that he generally passed two evenings in the week at Aldeen House.

On the 3rd of October the missionaries purchased a piece of ground for a cemetery at Serampore, and had occasion to use it within four days. Goluk, who had been baptized two years before, died rejoicing in the hope of the Gospel, and it became necessary to establish a precedent for Christian burial among the converts. Mr. Ward was absent at Dinagepore, and Mr. Carey in Calcutta; the arrangements for the funeral, therefore, devolved on Mr. Marshman. At the interment of Christians in the town it had been usual to employ the lowest class of Portuguese to convey their remains to the grave. They were too often drunk and disorderly, and the occupation, denominated that of "pobrees," was considered degrading. Mr. Marshman was anxious to persuade the converts that they ought to be prepared to perform this last office of kindness themselves; but there was no little hesitation among them to march through the public streets in the humiliating position of pobrees. Among the Hindoos, a soodra is never allowed to touch the dead body of a brahmin, and a brahmin cannot touch that of a soodra without being defiled. The missionaries had set before them the task of extirpating caste from the convert community in every form in which it was exhibited, and of teaching the native Christians that whatever might have been their previous distinctions, they were now "one in Christ Jesus." Mr. Marshman undertook this duty on the present occasion with his wonted resolution, and, to overrule every objection, determined to assist in carrying the body himself. At five in the afternoon he repaired to the house of Krishnu, where all the converts were assembled, as well as a large body of their heathen neighbours. There, in the presence of a silent and astonished multitude, he and Mr. Felix Carey, Bhyrub, a baptized Koolin brahmin, and Peeroo, a baptized Mahomedan, placed the coffin on their shoulders, and singing the Bengalee hymn, "Salvation through the death of Christ," conveyed it through the street to the new burial ground, which received its first tenant in these interesting circumstances. This event may be regarded as having completed the abolition of caste among the converts. It commenced with the extinction of all priority in partaking of the Lord's Supper; it was confirmed by the marriage of a brahmin with the daughter of a soodra; and consummated by the conveyance of the body of a soodra to the grave by one of the purest brahminical blood.

At the close of the year, Mr. Marshman proceeded on another missionary tour to Jessore, with Krishnu and several of the converts, visiting on the route several villages which had given a favourable reception to the Gospel. One little incident on this journey deserves notice, as characteristic of Mr. Marshman's disposition. Perceiving that Krishnu was fatigued with walking, he insisted, in spite of the remonstrances of the bearers, upon his taking his seat in the palankeen, while he himself walked by the side of it. "I felt," he writes, "a thousand times greater pleasure in trudging through the sun than I should have done in riding, from the thought that these little circumstances did more than some of greater value towards convincing our native friends of our entire union in heart with them." The day after this occurrence, Mr. Marshman reached the civil station of the district, and, mounting his palankeen, in the marketplace, began to preach to the people at the top of his voice. Some of the influential brahmins in the town hastened to the judge, and demanded his interference; and a native officer was sent to require Mr. Marshman's attendance. The judge was surrounded by the enraged brahmins, and the "omlas," or ministerial officers of the court, always the most violent opponents of Christianity, and informed Mr. Marshman in a tone of severity, that such addresses to the heathen were not to be permitted. Mr. Marshman explained the nature of his visit to the district in connexion with the object of the Serampore mission, and offered to withdraw from the town if he had done anything to contravene the Company's laws. After this explanation, the judge softened his tone, and eventually asked him to dinner in the evening, endeavouring at the same time to pacify the angry brahmins, but with little success. They left the court abruptly, and having assured the people assembled without that the missionary was a madman, advised them to throw his palankeen into the river, and chastise his native companions. Emboldened by this counsel, they chased Koober out of the town, fell on Seetaram, and pursued Krishnu with mud and cow-dung. It was with difficulty Mr. Marshman collected the converts, and placed them under the protection of the public authorities. In the evening he sat down to dinner with the judge, who discussed the plans and prospects of the mission, and drank success to its labours.

In the beginning of 1804, Mr. Carey received the gratifying intelligence that the Court of Directors had withdrawn their orders for the abolition of the College of Fort-William, but had directed that the students from the other Presidencies should cease to resort to it. On the 9th of January, Mr. Chamberlain, Mr. Felix Carey, and several native itinerants, were sent on a tour to the great annual festival at Gunga Saugur, where they preached and distributed tracts among a hundred thousand pilgrims. They had the great satisfaction of finding that the festival passed over without the sacrifice of a single victim. A non-commissioned officer and fifty sepoys were stationed along the banks of the river to prevent any such attempt; but even this precaution was soon found to be redundant. When it became known throughout the country that the practice was opposed to the wishes of the "ruler," and had been prohibited by law, it ceased, as a matter of course, without creating even a murmur. Soon after, Mr. Fernandez was ordained to the work of the mission, with the view of establishing a missionary station at Dinagepore, where he laboured till his death in 1833, receiving no support from missionary funds, but always contributing liberally to them. About the same time two of the most able and zealous of the native converts, Krishnu and Petumber, were set apart to the ministry by laying on of hands.

It was at the beginning of this year, three months before the institution of the British and Foreign Bible Society in London, that the Serampore missionaries laid before the committee the plans which they had been gradually maturing for the translation and publication of the Scriptures, or portions of them, into the languages of the East. It appears like one of the wild dreams of enthusiasm that three men, in their circumstances, should devise the plan of giving the Divine Oracles to the natives of India in their own tongue at a time when the Christian world was utterly indifferent to the work. But in the proposals they submitted to Mr. Fuller there was no attempt to dazzle the imagination by any reference to the grandeur of the undertaking; their communication was marked by simplicity and earnestness. They stated that there were at least seven languages current in India,—the Bengalee, the Hindoostanee, the Ooriya, the Teloogoo, the Kurnata, the Mahratta, and the Tamul; and they considered it practicable to make a translation of at least the New Testament into some, if not all, these languages; and on the following considerations:—They had been trained to the work in the prosecution of the translations they had already made; they were in a position, through the College of Fort-William, to obtain the services of learned men from all these provinces; they had collected an excellent biblical library; they possessed a large printing establishment and a very efficient type-foundry; and their situation gave them great facilities for distributing the Scriptures. At the beginning of 1803, they had commenced a translation of the New Testament in Hindoostanee. In October of that year, the province of Orissa was annexed to the British dominions, and they began translating it into that language. Lord Wellesley had introduced the study of Mahratta into the College, and that language was added to their list, and Mr. Carey was compiling a grammar for the use of the students. Hitherto they had been enabled to carry forward the plan from their own resources, but they found it impossible to enlarge it without public support. Mr. Fuller's ardent mind was kindled at the proposal, and, under his influence, the committee determined to co-operate with them, and gave them the assurance that the Christian public in Britain would not permit such an undertaking to be interrupted for want of funds.

Simultaneously with this plan of translations, they submitted to the Society a proposal to plant missionary stations in the interior of the country. They proposed that the missionaries at the out-stations should support themselves by engaging in some trade, crediting the profits to the common mission stock, and receiving the same personal allowance as their brethren at Serampore. The traffic in which they engaged would, it was hoped, furnish employment and protection to their converts. It was a part of this plan that the whole body of missionaries should meet once a year at Serampore, "in order to give union, direction, and vigour to all affairs; while a perpetual communication of intelligence, hopes, fears, conflicts, oppositions, mercies, and prospects, would, like the circulation of the blood, spread life and impulse through every part of the body." The scheme was drawn up by Mr. Marshman, who assured Mr. Fuller that it was *not* Utopian. A commencement was made by stationing Mr. Chamberlain at Cutwa, where he began a trade in the cloths then manufactured in the district; but he had no commercial experience, and the loss sustained by his transactions became too serious to warrant a repetition of the experiment. In explanation of this plan of missionary economy, it is to be remarked that from the first establishment of missions in India, the missionaries had always been expected to depend for their support chiefly on their own exertions. The Christian Knowledge Society, with whom the missionaries on the coast had been connected, did not consider itself responsible for their support, or suppose that they were violating any principle by making exertions for it themselves. Schwartz bequeathed the property he had accumulated according to his own intentions. His colleague, Gerické, left £5000 to the mission. Kiernandier became rich by trade, and made a noble use of his money. The Rev. Tobias Ringletaube, sent out by the Christian Knowledge Society to succeed him, was informed that he must eke out his scanty pittance by his own efforts; and the additional allowance of £50 granted to him was limited to one year. The Serampore missionaries, when they resolved to support themselves and encouraged their brethren to follow their example, were only acting on the principle then universally recognised, and which continued in force till the Missionary Societies, strengthened by larger resources, resolved to take on themselves the entire support of the missionaries they appointed. The only difference between the Serampore missionaries and those who had preceded them, consisted in the novel resolution which they had voluntarily adopted, of consecrating the whole of their income to the cause in which they had embarked.

Mr. Fuller, however, considered that they had carried the principle of self-denial too far, and was desirous of proposing to the committee to advise them to appropriate the income, of at least a twelvemonth, as a provision for their own families. But his friends at Serampore positively refused to adopt this counsel. Mr. Marshman replied, "I cannot but feel your kindness in the most sensible manner. I am glad, however, you did not resolve on what you intended. So far from having any wish of the kind, I myself, and I am sure I can answer for Mrs. Marshman and my brethren, esteem it one of the greatest favours conferred on me, that I am permitted by the labour of my hands to contribute in any small degree to the support of His cause to whom I owe my life, my soul, my all." Mr. Carey's reply has not been preserved; but Mr. Ward wrote in this strain:—"I can in some measure perceive the feeling which gave rise to this proposal, and it is honourable to you; but I cannot say I approve it. With respect to myself, I have no idea, because I have not thought of it, what pecuniary profit is derived to the mission by my labours; but I will speak of my brethren. After they have ventured their lives and their families in the mission, can it be supposed that they now count the *cowries* contributed to it? Is it unreasonable that we should subsist by our own labour, and after that contribute a mite to the cause of God?"

At the annual disputations of the College of Fort-William, in 1804, Mr. Gowan, one of Mr. Carey's Sanscrit students, was required to pronounce a declamation, and Mr. Carey was requested to address the Governor-General in that language. The assembly at these exhibitions was, at the time, the most brilliant which the metropolis presented. The Governor-General took his seat on the dais in the throne room, and all the principal officers of Government, civil and military, the judges of the Supreme Court, the most distinguished members of European society in Calcutta, the learned brahmins from all parts of India, the opulent rajahs and baboos, and the representatives of the native princes, were gathered around and before him. On this occasion, Mr. Carey drew up a short and interesting address to Lord Wellesley, complimenting him on the success of his administration, and the benefits derived from the institution he had founded. But Mr. Buchanan was determined not to lose the opportunity of introducing the subject of missions, and trimmed and elaborated the address, in which Mr. Carey was made to say, "I, now an old man, have lived for a long series of years among the Hindoos. I have been in the habit of preaching to multitudes daily, of discoursing with the brahmins on every subject, and superintending schools for the education of Hindoo youth. Their language is nearly as familiar to me as my own. This close intimacy with the natives for so long a period has afforded me opportunities of information not inferior to those enjoyed by any person." He then proceeded to state, as the result of his observations, that the institution of the College was wanting to complete the happiness of the natives; for "it will break down that barrier (an ignorance of their language) which has ever opposed the influence of our laws and institutions, and despoiled our administration of its energy and effect." The draft of the address was submitted to the Governor-General, and both Mr. Brown and Mr. Buchanan expected that the allusion to missionary labour would be objected to; but he sent it back unaltered, with the following note:—"I am much pleased with Mr. Carey's truly original and excellent speech. I would not wish to have a word altered. I esteem such a testimony from such a man a greater honour than the applause of courts and parliaments." But among the official dignitaries who surrounded Lord Wellesley, there were not a few who listened to the open avowal of Mr. Carey's missionary vocation in that august assembly with a feeling of resentment, and only wanted an opportunity to give practical effect to it.

At the close of 1804, the missionaries drew up a review of the transactions of the previous five years, and, in a spirit of the most devout gratitude, without a shade of elation. "We are still a happy, healthful, and highly-favoured family.

But, though we would feel incessant gratitude for these gourds, yet we would not feel content until Nineveh be brought to repentance. We did not come to this country to be placed in what are called easy circumstances respecting this world, and we trust that nothing but the salvation of souls will satisfy us. True, before we set out, we thought we could die content if we should be permitted to see the half of what we have seen; yet now we seem as far from the mark of our missionary high calling as ever. . . . Our whole expenditure has not been less than £13,000, and we have received from England, in money, goods, &c., not more than £5,740 during the five years we have been at Serampore, and this money is not sunk, but invested in premises belonging to the mission. No private fortune, no annual contribution which you could have been expected to raise, could have borne the weight of expense which God has brought us through."

On the 1st of January, 1805, arrangements were made for the erection of a chapel in Calcutta. The metropolis contained, at the time, two places of Protestant worship. One was denominated the Mission Church, built by Kiernandier for his humble congregation, and, on his bankruptcy, purchased by Mr. Charles Grant and his friends, and fitted up in a style suited to a wealthy European community. The other was the Church of St. John, erected twenty-seven years after the battle of Plassy, the history of which is thus given by Sir John Shore:—"Our church has lately been built. It was begun at first by subscription—a pagan gave the ground—all parties subscribed—lotteries, confiscations, donations received contrary to law, have been employed in completing it. The Company contributed little,—no great proof that they consider the morals of their subjects connected with their religion." In the patrician associations of these churches, there was no place for the humbler class of Christians, who passed their Sundays at the liquor shops. To attract them, the missionaries had engaged a room for

Divine service in the house of Mr. Lindeman, an undertaker; but they found that there was a strong and general repugnance to wade, Sunday after Sunday, through piles of coffins and other emblems of mortality, and they determined to attempt the erection of a chapel. So little was sectarian bigotry then known in the European community of Calcutta, that the proposal received the warmest encouragement from Mr. Brown, the senior chaplain, and the subscriptions collected in the first year, amounting to about £700, came chiefly from members of the Church of England. The object of the missionaries was not to establish a chapel for the propagation of their own denominational views, but to bring the forlorn beings who bore the Christian name, but disgraced it by their ignorance and vices, under the influence of religious instruction. It was, therefore, announced to be for the worship of all denominations.

At the beginning of this year, the mission was strengthened by the arrival of four additional missionaries by way of America, who were landed, in the first instance, at Madras. While they were detained there, two of their number received an invitation to remain and establish a mission at that Presidency. The question was referred to Serampore, but Mr. Carey and his associates refused to entertain the proposal, on the ground that it was their duty to plant the Gospel where it was not known, and not to enter on the field of other men's labours. Lord Wellesley being still Governor-General, the missionaries landed in Calcutta without molestation. The mission now embraced eight families, Mr. Felix Carey having been accepted as a missionary by the Society. The school had increased, and the printing-office required enlargement, and the premises to the east of the chapel were accordingly purchased in the name of the Society. On the 18th of May, the settlement of Serampore was deprived of its excellent governor, Colonel Bie. He died at the advanced age of seventy-five, after having administered the government for forty years to the universal satisfaction of the inhabitants. It was through his kindness that Mr. Marshman and Mr. Ward, when they were denied a footing in the Company's territories, were received under the protection of the Danish crown, and the missionary enterprise obtained an asylum where it was enabled to weather the opposition of the British Government, and eventually to take root in Hindoostan.

The church at Serampore had for five years adhered to the practice of what is denominationally termed strict communion, by which all who had not been baptized by immersion on a confession of faith were excluded from the Lord's table. But after Mr. Brown had taken up his residence in the town, the subject was frequently brought under discussion, and he urged the reconsideration of a rule which debarred many Christian friends from partaking of the communion in the mission chapel. Mr. Ward had always been an open communionist; and Mr. Marshman was at length brought to adopt the same view, in which Mr. Carey likewise acquiesced. The communion-table was therefore opened to all who professed the same Christian faith. Mr. Ward records in his journal this change to "the amiable side of the question" with great delight. "I rejoice," he writes, "that the first Baptist church in Bengal has shaken off that apparent moroseness of temper which has so long made us appear unlovely in the sight of the Christian world. I am glad that this church considers *real religion* alone as the ground of admission to the Lord's table. With regard to a church-state, a stricter union may be required; but to partake of the Lord's Supper worthily, it requires only that a man's heart be right towards God."

On the 30th of July, 1805, Lord Wellesley resigned the government to his successor, Lord Cornwallis, and returned to England. The Serampore missionaries—except on their arrival in 1799, when their object was not understood—were treated by him with invariable kindness, and their undertaking was regarded with a favourable eye at a time when the Court of Directors and their servants in India treated it with unequivocal hostility. The strength of the adverse current from which his influence had protected them may be estimated from the following extract of a letter of Mr. Brown to Mr. Fuller at this period:—"The storms within this past year have safely passed over, the danger of which your brethren did not know at the time. They, good people, were securely asleep in the vessel at Serampore, while their printed papers circulated among the Hindoos were lying before Government, charged with inculcating sedition, republicanism, and religious anathemas against the British subjects in India. On these papers I reported largely. At present all is tranquil." Lord Wellesley not only permitted the ingress of additional missionaries, but allowed them to travel freely through the country, preaching the Gospel and distributing tracts. When, therefore, the inhabitants of Calcutta presented him with a valedictory address, Mr. Carey and his colleagues, actuated by feelings of gratitude as well as patriotism, united with them in offering that tribute of esteem which they felt to be justly due to the merits of his administration and to his liberality. This proceeding did not, however, meet with the approbation of Mr. Fuller. Under the influence of those morbid feelings, not yet extinct in England, which considered every extension of British power in India a crime, without any reference to the circumstances in which it originated, he wrote to Serampore:—"Gratitude required your acknowledgments to Lord Wellesley, but not your signature to a paper which approves and boasts of his wars, which are here generally thought to be nearly as ambitious and unjust as those of Buonaparte." But the Serampore missionaries, who had watched the progress of events, and marked how these wars had been forced upon the Government by the native princes, could conscientiously applaud "the discernment of Lord Wellesley in seeing the exigencies of the country, and of the times in which he was called to act,—the promptness and determination with which he had seized on the opportunities of acting, and his masterly use of our own intrinsic strength, which had eminently contributed to establish the ascendancy of the British name and dominion from one extremity of the empire to the other."

It was at this period that the missionaries printed an English translation of the Umur-koshu, the most popular dictionary of the Sanscrit language. Mr. Carey's Sanscrit grammar, which eventually extended to a thousand pages, and had been for some time in the press, was pushed on with rapidity. He likewise undertook a translation of the Vedas into English, but ceased to prosecute it when he found it interfere materially with the translations of the Scriptures. At the same time, he and Mr. Marshman undertook the publication of some of the most celebrated Sanscrit classics with an English translation, under the auspices of the Asiatic Society and the College of Fort-William, and commenced with the Ramayun. This arduous undertaking was now added to their labours, but the toil was lightened by the consideration that "means would thus be obtained of supporting at least one missionary station."

From the period of their settlement at Serampore, Mr. Carey and his colleagues had been unremitting in their endeavours to draw the attention of Government to the atrocious practice of female immolation, which was then regarded by Europeans with perfect complacency, as one of the domestic institutions of "the Gentoos;" and they considered that the first step towards its abolition was to bring the number of annual victims prominently into view. They accordingly sent ten agents in 1804 to travel from village to village, within a circle of thirty miles round Calcutta, to collect information on the subject, when it was found that more than three hundred had been immolated on the funeral pile within six months. At the same time, Mr. Carey requested the pundits connected with the College to furnish him with a collection of the various texts in the Shasters which bore on the subject; and from their report it appeared to be simply encouraged as a virtue, and not enjoined as a duty. These documents were placed in the hands of Mr. Udny, the philanthropic member of the Supreme Council, and embodied by him in a minute which he submitted to Lord Wellesley and to his colleagues. In this paper he dwelt on the enormity of the practice, described the extent to which it was carried, and entreated the Governor-General to concur with him in putting it down by a positive enactment, as Government had done with perfect impunity and eminent success in the case of human sacrifices at Saugur. This was the first official notice regarding *suttees* ever placed on the records of Government. Lord Wellesley had arranged to quit the government in seven days, and he felt that the prohibition of a rite which had been observed, as the natives asserted, from the golden age of the world, and which, though it had not the direct authority of the Shasters, had the more important force of prescription and usage, and was considered the pride of Hindooism, required more deliberation than he could then bestow on it. With his departure, all hope of its speedy abolition vanished; and during the next quarter of a century, seventy thousand more widows ascended the pile, and became the victims of a bloody superstition.

CHAPTER IV.

LORD CORNWALLIS landed in Calcutta a second time in 1805, at the age of sixty-six, after his mental and bodily energies had been exhausted by thirty years of incessant service in America, India, and Ireland, and with the finger of death on him. He hastened to the north-west provinces immediately on his arrival, but died within two months at Gazeepore. He was succeeded in the government, provisionally, by Mr., afterwards Sir George Barlow, a civilian of twenty-seven years' standing: a mere plodding man of routine, without a particle of that mental power which the administration of the empire required. Under the influence of Lord Wellesley's master-spirit, he had freely supported those liberal views which marked his government; but when relieved from this superior influence, his feeble and irresolute mind came under the control of the anti-liberal and anti-missionary party, and the prejudices of the "old Indian" school regained their ascendancy in the Council Chamber. The difficulties of the missionaries date from his accession to power; and the storm of opposition to which they were exposed raged with more or less violence throughout eight succeeding years, until Parliament took the decision of the missionary question into its own hands.

In their direct missionary labours, they experienced great alternations of disappointment and success. In March, they regret "the low state of things; no inquirers, no new converts." Every inquirer had left them clandestinely. The misconduct of some who had embraced Christianity, and the profligacy of others, brought odium on the cause in the eyes of the heathen, and damped the spirits of the missionaries. In August, Petumber Sing, one of the earliest and most exemplary of the converts, died, exhibiting the triumph of the Christian's hope in his dying moments. A brief narrative of his life was drawn up and published both in English and Bengalee, the first of a series of memoirs which served to give fresh interest to the missionary cause in England, and to strengthen the faith of the converts in India. Towards the close of the year, the prospects of the mission began to brighten. Fifteen inquirers resorted to Serampore from the neighbourhood of Calcutta; and the additions to the church in the year, which opened with little promise, amounted to thirty-four.

The number of missionaries now amounted to eight, and it became advisable to distribute this strength over the country at subordinate stations. Before Dr. Carey and his colleagues proceeded in this work, they deemed it their duty to place on record, as the result of their experience, the leading principles of the missionary system they were desirous of establishing. The document is valuable, not only as illustrating the spirit of lofty devotedness which they brought to the work, but likewise for the sound and practical maxims which it embodies. To gain the attention of the heathen, they considered it necessary that the missionary should not only become familiar with the language, but with the habits, the sympathies, and propensities of the people; with the current of thought which prevailed among them, and the mode in which they were accustomed to reason about God, sin, holiness, the way of salvation, and a future state. He should not forget the debasing influence of their worship, feasts, and songs. It was necessary for him to abstain from whatever would tend to increase the repugnance of the natives to the Gospel, and to keep out of sight those European peculiarities which were offensive to their national feelings. At the same time, he was carefully to avoid the exhibition of any degree of acrimony against the sins of their gods; and on no account to do violence to their images, or interrupt their worship, "the real conquests of the Gospel being those of love." It becomes us, they remark, "to watch all opportunities of doing good; to carry on conversations with the natives almost every hour in the day; to go from village to village, from town to town, and from one assembly to another; and be instant in season and out of season." Regarding the character of their addresses to the heathen, they remark: "The doctrine of Christ's expiatory death, and its all-sufficient merits, has been, and ever must remain, the grand means of salvation." They deemed it important that the converts should repose the most entire confidence in the missionary; and that he should be ready to listen to their complaints, to give them the kindest advice, and to decide on every question brought before him in the most open, upright, and impartial manner. Among the means of diffusing Christian truth in India, they considered the training of native preachers one of the most important. "We must form our native brethren to usefulness, foster every kind of genius, and cherish every gift and grace in them. In this respect we cannot be too lavish in our attentions to their improvement. It is only by means of native preachers we can hope for the universal spread of the Gospel through this immense continent. Europeans are too few, and their subsistence costs too much, for us ever to hope that they can possibly be the instruments of the universal diffusion of the Word among so many millions. The whole administration of the church should assume a native aspect, by which means the inhabitants would more readily identify the cause as belonging to their own nation." The paper then refers to the paramount duty of promoting translations of the Scriptures into the native languages, the distribution of tracts, and the establishment of schools; and concludes in this glowing language: "Finally, let us give ourselves up unreservedly to this glorious cause. Let us never think our time, our gifts, our strength, our families, or even the clothes on our backs, our own. Let us sanctify them all to God and to His cause. Oh, may He sanctify us for this work!"

To turn now to the progress of the translations. The proposal of the missionaries to publish the Bible, or portions of it, in seven of the languages of India, if they were able to obtain aid to the extent of £1000 a year, exactly coincided with Mr. Fuller's large views, and he determined to take on himself the charge of introducing it to public notice. With this view he proceeded on a tour through the northern counties of England, and through Scotland,—travelled thirteen hundred miles, and preached fifty sermons. The catholicity of the plan enabled him to appeal with success to the sympathies of all denominations; and he succeeded in raising £1300, which were remitted to India by way of

America, where an addition of £700 was made to the fund. Mr. Fuller's labours on this occasion—which furnish us with an apt exemplification of his talent and energy—laid the foundation of a permanent interest in Oriental translations, and enabled him, at the subsequent stages of the work, to appeal with confidence to the liberality of the public. Unknown to Mr. Fuller, the British and Foreign Bible Society, then recently established, had directed its attention to the translation and distribution of the Sacred Scriptures in the languages of the East. Before this noble institution had been three months in existence, a communication was opened with Mr. Udny, requesting him to unite with Mr. Brown and Mr. Buchanan and the three Serampore missionaries, in forming a corresponding committee to devise the best means of diffusing Christian truth in the Eastern languages. This period was singularly marked by the entire absence of a sectarian spirit among men of evangelical sentiments in India. The Serampore missionaries constantly attended the ministry of the Church of England when in Calcutta, and the evangelical clergymen and their families worshipped with the missionaries in the chapel at Serampore. Mr. Buchanan was a man of liberal spirit, and anxious to promote the cause of religion; but when the communication from the Bible Society placed before him the idea of being publicly and officially associated with Mr. Carey and his colleagues, though in a great and catholic object, he appeared to shrink from the sacrifice of feeling or dignity which it might involve. The concession of religious equality is the last, and, apparently, the most difficult triumph of Christian principle. Mr. Buchanan kept the Bible Society's letter for several months without communicating it to the missionaries. Mr. Carey, on being apprised of it, immediately called on him, and urged the formation of the committee without delay; but he remarked that nothing could be done at present, and expressed his astonishment at the liberality and condescension of the Bible Society in thus inviting Dissenters to form a committee which would have to correspond with bishops. Mr. Marshman and Mr. Ward introduced the subject to Mr. Brown, and found that he was also lost in admiration of that liberality of spirit which had induced the bishops and other members of the Bible Society to nominate three Dissenters to act with them; and he likewise stated that no steps could be taken towards the organisation of the committee at the present time.

But this did not satisfy the ardour of the missionaries. They had no ambition to correspond with dignitaries of the Church of England; but they could ill brook the suspension of the work of translation till Mr. Brown and Mr. Buchanan had recovered from their amazement at the liberality of the bishops. The formation of the committee, which would have brought aid from the Bible Society, was thus indefinitely postponed. No intelligence of Mr. Fuller's success had reached India, and they determined to make an immediate effort to raise funds in the country. Mr. Marshman sat down to the compilation of an elaborate "Memoir on the Translation of the Scriptures into the Languages of the East." It opened with the remark, "that after Europeans had been enriched with the gold, the gems, and the precious things of the Eastern world, gratitude, reason, and religion, required that a small portion of the wealth thus acquired should be appropriated to the purpose of repaying the debt and imparting the Word of Life to their fellow-subjects in India." It went on to enumerate the languages current in India, and pointed out the ease with which translations of the Sacred Scriptures could be made into them, from their mutual affinity and their derivation from a common parent. A calculation was then given of the cost of publishing the New Testament in seven of the languages, and it was proposed to raise the sum of £6000, the interest of which should be perpetually devoted to this object. To this was subjoined a statement of the progress already made at Serampore in the Hindoostanee, Persian, Mahratta, and Orissa versions; and the memoir concluded with a reference to the various sources of encouragement which were presented, and an earnest appeal to the Christian sympathies of the Calcutta public. Such an appeal would have been appreciated and nobly responded to in England; but would have been lost upon a community in which half the public officers (according to the testimony of one of their own body) were "immured in loathsome zenanas;" and the few lawyers and merchants who were amassing fortunes had no other object than to take their flight with them to England at the earliest moment.

Mr. Brown expressed the warmest approbation of the memoir, but advised the omission of the introductory address and the final appeal, as being too strong for an unbelieving public. The paper was therefore revised and pruned, and then sent to Mr. Buchanan. After detaining it for some weeks, he threw it aside altogether, and worked up the materials into another memoir, better calculated, as he said, for the meridian of India. Mr. Marshman could not avoid some annoyance at his unceremonious rejection of his labours; but his own object, and that of his colleagues, was the prosecution of a great public undertaking; so they stifled their feelings, and adopted the new document. Mr. Buchanan proposed that the plan should be ushered into public notice under the patronage of the College of Fort-William, but Sir George Barlow refused to authorise a measure which might appear to identify the Government with an extensive plan for the diffusion of Christian knowledge, and the memoir simply stated, in general terms, that the missionaries rested their hopes of success chiefly on the support of that institution. The memoir was printed with the signature of all the missionaries at Serampore, and, at the particular request of Mr. Buchanan, was surmounted by a vignette with a figure of Britannia presenting the New Testament to a Hindoo. Copies of it were immediately sent by him to the archbishops, bishops, and deans of the Church in England and Ireland, and to the universities, and under a college frank, to all the public functionaries in India, to some of the native princes, and to the Emperor of Russia. The subscriptions raised in Calcutta amounted to £1000, to which Mr. Buchanan added £500, and Mr. Brown £100; and it was agreed that 300 rupees a month should be sent to Serampore to assist the labours which had been commenced.

Animated by this support, the missionaries pushed forward their operations with increased animation. They were now fairly embarked in the work of translation, and their plans had received that measure of public support which committed them to the energetic prosecution of it. Mr. Ward, however, did not enter into the design with the ardour of his brethren. He could not view this partial diversion of their energies from the work of direct evangelisation without some feeling of mistrust; but finding Mr. Carey and Mr. Marshman so enthusiastically bent on it, he determined to second their efforts, and to work the press with redoubled energy. Mr. Fuller likewise regarded these proceedings with misgiving. "I must repeat to you," he writes, "that I and some others are under strong apprehensions that the friendship of Mr. Buchanan to you and to the mission is purchased too dear, and that you are in danger of being drawn into his worldly-political religion. Beware of the counsels of Mr. Worldly Wiseman! He will draw you from the simplicity of Christ, and, under pretence of liberality, you will be shorn, like Samson, of your locks." But Mr. Fuller was mistaken in his estimate of Mr. Buchanan's character. His private letters, written to his bosom friends, breathe a spirit of Christian piety, humility, and devotion, as fervent as the correspondence of Mr. Fuller's own ministerial brethren. There was, undoubtedly, more of diplomacy than simplicity in his natural temperament; but it was not the absence of vital religion which led him to place an exaggerated value on the support of political authorities and ecclesiastical dignitaries, and to court their assistance with such eagerness as to incur the suspicion of worldliness and servility.

At the beginning of 1806, Mr. Marshman commenced the study of Chinese, with the view of translating the Scriptures into that language. For fifteen years did he devote to this arduous and wearisome employment every moment he could create by the severest economy of time, and too often by encroaching on the hours of sleep, and he has the merit of having carried the first Chinese translation of the Bible through the press. Considering the great disadvantages under which the translation was executed, it was necessarily imperfect; but it is a valuable memorial of Christian zeal and literary ardour. China is now blessed with the labours of a hundred Protestant missionaries, who have enjoyed the benefit of access to the rich stores of Chinese literature, and of intercourse with its literati, and their biblical labours have naturally superseded those of the first pioneer; but they will not be backward in acknowledging the deserts of the man who, in the midst of numerous engagements and anxieties, first devoted his time and energy to the prosecution of this enterprise.

In May of the year under review, the Rev. Henry Martyn, who had been appointed a military chaplain by Mr. Charles Grant, arrived in Calcutta. His deep personal piety, and his zealous exertions in the cause of Christian benevolence, during the five years he resided in India, have embalmed his memory in the affections of Christians on both sides the Atlantic. Immediately on his arrival he found his way to the congenial associations of Serampore, where he took up his residence with Mr. Brown, and maintained a constant intercourse with the missionaries. "As the shadow of bigotry is not known among us here," writes Mr. Carey, "we take sweet counsel together, and go to the house of God as friends." A strong conformity of sentiment drew him more particularly into a close intimacy with Mr. Marshman, and they might often be seen walking arm-in-arm for hours on the bank of the river. At the extremity of Mr. Brown's premises there stood an old and massive temple, from which the image had been removed, owing to the encroachments of the river, to a safer locality. It had ceased to possess any sanctity, and was included in Mr. Brown's purchase. He fitted it up as a Christian sanctuary, and on Sunday, the 26th of January, it was consecrated by a prayer meeting to the service of the living and true God, whose praises now resounded through the arches which had for a century echoed with the songs of the idol. In the present day, when the points of sectarian distinction in India are no longer smoothed down by Christian charity, it is delightful to recur to that remote period when Churchmen and Dissenters met each other with cordiality on the broad ground of Christian sympathies. In that pagoda, which is still a prominent object in sailing up from Calcutta, every denominational feeling was forgotten, and Carey, Marshman, and Ward joined in the same hosannas with Brown, Martyn, and Corrie.

The anxiety of the missionaries to establish stations in the interior of the country became daily more earnest; but there were tokens which could not be mistaken of a change in the tone of Government and its servants, on the subject of missions, since the departure of Lord Wellesley. Mr. Moore, one of the missionaries recently arrived, and Mr. Carey's second son, proceeded on a missionary tour through the eastern districts, and on reaching Dacca, went into the heart of the city and began to preach and distribute tracts. They were stopped by order of the magistrate, and summoned to his court. Finding that they were without passports, he ordered them to desist from the work, and to quit the city, as the tracts had created uneasiness among the people. Two months after, Mr. Ward went to Jessore to obtain land for the establishment of a missionary station. The European officers were unwilling that missionary labourers should be brought into their immediate neighbourhood, lest the public tranquillity, and their own repose, should be disturbed. After Mr. Ward had fixed upon a spot which he considered suitable, he was informed that the agreement would not be valid without registration, and the collector refused to register it without the direct sanction of Government for the settlement of a missionary in the district. These difficulties suggested the propriety of making a direct application to Government for a general licence to itinerate through the country, and form stations, or, if that was denied, for a licence renewable from year to year. Sir George Barlow had proceeded to the north-west provinces, and the administration devolved provisionally upon Mr. Udny. In his hands Mr. Carey placed a statement of their proposal, which was to form stations about a hundred miles apart, under the superintendence of a European missionary, to be assisted by seven or eight native preachers or catechists, planted around him in different localities. "We wish," he said, "for no privileges or exemptions, but merely for leave to settle, to preach the Gospel, and to distribute Bibles and religious tracts without being molested by the magistrate of the district, and for a general licence to itinerate through the British dominions. We desire to be subject to the laws of the country in every respect, and we shall teach the people to pay all respect to the Government under which they live. As Hindoo and Mahomedan teachers, and Roman Catholic priests, are at liberty to settle and propagate their sentiments in every place, we hope the same liberty will not be denied to a society of Protestants."

This plan entirely coincided with Mr. Udny's views, and he transmitted it to Sir George Barlow with his recommendation. Sir George, on his return to the Presidency, stated that he was personally favourable to missionary exertions, but he had no power to authorise the establishment of stations, and he was unwilling to act in opposition to the known opinions of his masters in Leadenhall Street. Mr. Carey stated, in reply to Mr. Udny, that whatever might be their respect for the wishes of Government, they *must* establish stations, even without their leave, if it could not be obtained, and that they were prepared to risk the consequences. Mr. Mardon was, accordingly, sent to Malda, where there was happily no magistrate, and he was not reported. Mr. Biss and Mr. Moore proceeded to Dinagepore without a passport; but the judge no sooner heard of their arrival than he sent to inquire whether they had the permission of Government "to go into the interior of the country, and circulate religious writings in the native languages;" and finding that they were without a passport, ordered them forthwith to return to Serampore, leaving them, however, the option of remaining in the district under the guarantee of Mr. Fernandez, while a reference was made on the subject to the Supreme Council. They were fully aware of the inevitable result of any such reference, and returned to Serampore in the hope that interest might be made with Government on their behalf; but they found that new difficulties had arisen, and that the prospects of the mission had become more gloomy.

It was during the prevalence of this feeling relative to the dissemination of Christian truth, that the Government took the shrine of Jugunnath under its especial protection, and passed the first Act to identify it with the interests of the State. Two years after the annexation of the province of Orissa, the draft of an Act was introduced into Council to vest the superintendence of the establishment of the idol in British officers. But Lord Wellesley, who had not then resigned the government, manifested the strongest repugnance to a project which would have associated a Christian government with a temple of idolatry. It was brought forward in the following year, while Sir George Barlow presided in the Council, and Mr. Udny entered a vigorous protest against it; but his colleagues considered a pagan establishment a legitimate source of gain, and the Act was accordingly passed in April, 1806. The Court of Directors, though hostile to all missionary efforts, resented the determination of their servants in Calcutta to mix up the Company with the management of a temple on the establishment of which several hundred courtezans were permanently entertained, and refused to pollute their exchequer with the proceeds of a pilgrim-tax. In their reply to Calcutta, they said they were prepared to permit the native officers of the temple to collect their fees, according to ancient usage, from the pilgrims, while the management of the temple establishment and its ministrations must be left with the brahmins, who were to be appointed by election. The interference of the officers of Government was to be strictly confined to the preservation of the public peace, the collection of the police-rate, and the protection of the pilgrims from extortion.

In the course of the year, the first sheet of the Sanscrit New Testament was printed with the new fount of Devanagree types, which had been three years in preparation. The liberal subscriptions which had been raised in Calcutta enabled the missionaries to prosecute the translations with increased vigour, and they put to press the Mahratta, the Orissa, the Persian, and the Hindoostanee versions. Their literary undertakings kept pace with their evangelical labours. The Sanscrit grammar, compiled by Mr. Carey, was completed and published, with a dedication to Lord Wellesley. The first volume of the Ramayun was also finished at press. It was a faithful translation of that renowned epic, but it wanted the poetic warmth of the original. A prose version of any great poem must necessarily be tame; but in the present case the translators were also fettered by the juxtaposition of the Sanscrit text. The prosecution of the work was abandoned after the publication of the third volume, in consequence of the pressure of missionary engagements. At the same time Mr. Ward put to press his work on the Habits, Manners, and Religion of the Hindoos, for which he had been prosecuting researches and collecting materials since his arrival in India.

The sum obtained for the erection of the chapel in Calcutta, a little exceeding £700, was expended in the purchase of a plot of ground in the Bow bazar, which was quickly cleared of the brothels and liquor-shops which covered it, and a temporary bungalow, or thatched house, was erected in the centre of it, which Mr. Ward opened with divine service on the 1st of June. It was the first instance in which the Gospel had been preached to the inhabitants of Calcutta in their own tongue since Job Charnock erected the British ensign on the banks of the Hooghly. Crowds poured in at the gate and filled the enclosure to see a European gentleman address natives, and in their own tongue. As Mr. Ward and the native preachers moved through the streets, they were followed by hundreds clapping their hands and pouring a torrent of abuse on them. On the third Sunday the appearance of Rammohun, a converted brahmin, exhorting his fellow-countrymen to renounce their idolatry, and embrace a new and foreign creed, created the greatest astonishment. There was the excitement both of novelty and of indignation, but there was no tumult, and no interruption of the peace. The interest thus created in the native community filled the missionaries with animation, and, to add to their delight, the arrival of Captain Wickes, with two additional missionaries, Mr. Chater and Mr. Robinson, was at the same time announced. The next day is recorded by Mr. Ward in his journal as a memorable day. At ten in the morning he preached to a quiet and attentive audience in the enclosure of the chapel, the excitement in the town having subsided. At one, he proceeded to the Chitpore road, and preached again in a house which some Armenians had opened for Protestant worship, and before the close of the day, to a third congregation in the Bow bazar. He considered it one of the happiest days of his life, and hoped to spend many such in Calcutta. But the opposition of Government to the missionary cause had already commenced, and his labours were brought to an abrupt close.

Captain Wickes, the day after his arrival, proceeded to the police-office to make the usual report of his passengers, but was informed that Government had thought fit to issue orders for Mr. Chater and Mr. Robinson not to leave Calcutta without permission. Mr. Carey called at the office the next day, to inquire the cause of their detention, when Mr. Blacquiere, the magistrate, said he had a message to deliver to him from the Governor-General, and had called twice at his residence without being able to see him. The purport of the message was, that as the Government did not interfere with the religious prejudices of the natives, it was requested that Mr. Carey and his colleagues would likewise refrain from such a course. Mr. Carey asked for an explanation of this enigmatical order, and was informed that the missionaries were not to preach to the natives, or allow their converts to do so; they were not, directly or indirectly, to circulate any religious pamphlets; they were not, in short, to take any steps, by conversation or otherwise, to induce the natives to embrace Christianity. Mr. Carey left the office with the dry remark that it "was not his wish, or that of his colleagues, to do anything disagreeable to Government." This injunction placed the missionaries in a serious dilemma. To act in open defiance of the Government might lead to the most serious consequences, and possibly break up the mission, which had been settled with great cost and labour; to relinquish all missionary exertions was intolerable. But they considered that if they were able to bend to the storm, it might pass over, and not only leave them in the enjoyment of their present privileges, but possibly procure for them the liberty they had long sought, of settling missionary stations in the interior without interruption. This storm of opposition had been gathering since the departure of Lord Wellesley, and the resolution had been formed in the highest quarters to take advantage of the first opportunity to put a stop to the proceedings of the missionaries. That occasion was now furnished by the *Vellore Mutiny*.

On the death of Tippoo Sultan, and the extinction of his power, in 1799, the members of his family were pensioned;

but, by an act of singular indiscretion, were sent to reside at Vellore, only forty miles distant from the frontiers of Mysore, and that place soon became the focus of intrigues against the British Government. More than three thousand of the old soldiers and subjects of Tippoo had settled in the town, and the retainers of the family exceeded eighteen hundred. These men were incessantly employed, under the guidance of Tippoo's sons and connexions, in attempts to corrupt the fidelity of the sepoys, and to excite a revolt. The loyalty of the sepoys had been shaken by these machinations, when an act of imprudence on the part of the British officers supplied the spark to the combustible materials, and caused an explosion which occasioned the loss of five hundred lives. The Commander-in-Chief at Madras had obtained permission of the governor, Lord William Bentinck, to consolidate the military regulations, on the express condition that the new code should embrace only those which were actually in force, and that no addition of any kind should be made to them without the positive consent of Government. But Major Pearce, to whom the task was assigned, without, as it was affirmed, the cognizance even of the Commander-in-Chief, introduced a novel rule, directing that the sepoys should appear on parade with the chin shaved, and the moustache trimmed after a particular fashion; that they should cease to wear any distinguishing marks of caste, and adopt a turban of a new pattern. The three first injunctions were sufficiently obnoxious to the Hindoo sepoys, but it was the order regarding the turban which inflamed them to madness. The new pattern bore a strong resemblance to the English hat, which is an abomination to Orientals, who, even when they assimilate their dress to the European model, invariably eschew the hat. To the sons of Tippoo this order was a godsend, and they spared no pains to turn it to account and fan the flame of discontent in the minds of the sepoys, who were assured by their emissaries that the Government had formed the deliberate design of forcing Christianity on them and on the country, and that the order regarding the turban was the first step towards the accomplishment of it. The sepoys, thus worked up to desperation, broke out into open mutiny. At two in the morning, on the 10th of July, 1806, they rose on the European garrison in the fortress of Vellore, when asleep and unarmed, and massacred the colonel and thirteen officers, and ninety-nine non-commissioned officers and soldiers. The mutiny was quelled by the prompt arrival of Colonel Gillespie, and by the destruction of nearly four hundred of the mutineers.

This tragic event created a panic both in India and in Leadenhall Street. Though it was to be attributed entirely to the indiscretion of Major Pearce, who issued the turban order, and to the perfidy of Tippoo's sons, who took advantage of it to alarm the sepoys for their caste and their creed, the cause of missions was made to bear the brunt of obloquy. It was immediately asserted that any interference of any kind with the religious prejudices of the people was fraught with the greatest political danger to Government. The stream of European prejudice against missionary efforts was swelled by the alarm which the mutiny had occasioned, and bore down the voice of reason and equity; and every attempt to convert the natives was denounced as the precursor of rebellion and massacre. It was under the influence of this feeling that Sir George Barlow sent in all haste for the magistrate, and directed him to call on Mr. Carey, and request him and his colleagues at once to desist from their labours.

The restrictions thus imposed on the missionaries amounted to an entire stoppage of their missionary work beyond the limits of Serampore, and they made the most strenuous efforts to obtain a modification, and, if possible, a reversal of the order. Sir George Barlow was at length in some degree mollified, chiefly through the interposition of Mr. Brown, and sent Mr. Carey his "ultimatum," as the magistrate termed it. The missionaries were at liberty to remain at

Serampore,—which the British Government could not prevent. They might circulate the Scriptures. They might preach in any private house in Calcutta, but not in the shed in the Bow bazar, until they had obtained the permission of the Court of Directors to "exercise" there; and natives of the country might teach and preach wherever they pleased, provided they were not sent forth from Serampore. The magistrate, when he delivered this message, fully admitted that the bench had never received any complaints against the missionaries, nor had any class of natives made any adverse representations to Government regarding them. It was evident, however, that no terms more favourable could at the time be obtained from Government. Their operations were thus brought to a dead lock, since the European missionaries could not move without a licence, and native itinerants could no longer be sent from Serampore. They were driven, therefore, to make an effort to move the public authorities in England, through the medium of Mr. Fuller, for that liberty of action which was denied them by the local powers.

The result of this reference will be presently related. After the two missionaries who had arrived in Calcutta had been detained there four days, Mr. Carey called at the police-office, and sent up to Mr. Blacquiere to inquire whether Government wished them to remain longer in the town, to which he sent the supercilious reply, that if any of Mr. Carey's friends were in confinement, he must apply for their release to another magistrate, on which Mr. Carey conveyed them and their families at once to Serampore. The following day they were introduced to the governor, and received under the protection of the Crown of Denmark. But Mr. Dowdeswell, the superintendent of police, one of the opponents of the missionary cause, directed the magistrates of Calcutta to report officially to Government that two missionaries had arrived in the country without a licence from the Court of Directors. Hundreds of Europeans entered Calcutta unnoticed, or simply left their names at the police-office; but here were two men, formally denounced, not only as unlicensed persons, but also as missionaries, and it was decided to be the duty of the Government to "enforce the standing orders of the Court on the subject of interlopers." On the 11th of September, the two missionaries were summoned to the police-office, and informed by Mr. Martyn, another of the magistrates, that the Government had thought fit to order them to return to England forthwith, as they had no permission from the Court to remain. Mr. Marshman, who accompanied them, stated that as they had come out to reside at Serampore, which was a foreign settlement, it would have been preposterous for them to make any application to the Court of Directors. The magistrate appeared to be startled by this information, and requested that it might be sent to him in writing; but Captain Wickes was nevertheless informed that the usual papers would be withheld until he entered into an engagement to take them back. Mr. Carey and his colleagues addressed the Government on the subject; and the governor of Serampore informed the Governor-General that they were now residing under the special protection of the King of Denmark. Of this communication the Government of Calcutta took no notice for a month, after which the magistrate was directed to make inquiries of the governor at whose suggestion the missionaries had left England, and whether they had come out under any promise of protection; to which he replied in general terms, that the King of Denmark had, on the 5th of September, 1801, issued instructions to his servants at Serampore to foster the missionary establishment, and had granted the missionaries and their future colleagues the fullest protection of his Crown, and that the certificate he had given to Mr. Chater and Mr. Robinson was "in accordance with his high order."

But the Governor-General and his Council were determined to push the matter to extremities, and expel the missionaries. Colonel Krefting's representation was treated with silent contempt, and, on the 1st of November, the missionaries were informed that Government had thought fit to confirm its former orders, and that the commander of the *Criterion* would not be allowed to leave the port unless he took the missionaries back. Mr. Carey and his colleagues were anxious to prevent the detention of the vessel, to the detriment of the commander and the owners, and were therefore disposed to surrender the missionaries, or to engage to send them to the territory of some foreign prince in Asia. But it was resolved to make one more effort to obtain the reversal of the order. Captain Wickes accordingly stated to Government, that the detention of the captain of an American vessel, because he would not engage to take back two individuals who were then residing under a foreign jurisdiction and beyond his control, would be immediately represented by the owners of the vessel, to whom he was about to write, to the Government at Washington, and become the subject of a serious remonstrance with the Cabinet of England. He stated, moreover, that the abstraction of two gentlemen from Serampore, after they had been received under the special protection of the Danish Government, would lead to a very disagreeable discussion between the courts of Copenhagen and London. Sir George Barlow and his colleagues began to perceive that they were incurring a serious responsibility in the course into which their anti-missionary feelings had hurried them, and that a remonstrance from two foreign courts would be more vexatious to their masters in Leadenhall Street than even the addition of two members to the "Society of Missionaries at Serampore," as the Government was wont to designate them. Captain Wickes, therefore, received an unconditional port clearance; but a letter was, at the same time, sent to the two missionaries, informing them that they could not be allowed to remain in the country, and desiring them to state the name of the vessel in which they proposed to embark. But as this communication was intended simply to save the dignity of Government, it remained without a reply. These proceedings indicated so unfavourable a change in the sentiments of Government, that the Serampore missionaries felt they could no longer count on its neutrality, and they were constrained to turn their attention to countries not under the British flag, where they might obtain that protection from pagan governments which was denied them by the Christian rulers of India. Within three months of this period, Mr. Chater was on his way to Rangoon.

The effort which was made to obtain greater liberty by an appeal to England, proved unsuccessful. On the receipt of the letter from Serampore, Mr. Fuller immediately called on Mr. Grant, but found that the hostility to missions at the India House had been greatly inflamed by recent letters from India, and that, far from obtaining greater freedom for itinerating and forming stations, there was much reason to fear that they would be restrained from going on British territory, perhaps expelled the country altogether. To counteract the influence of these sinister communications, which were pouring into Leadenhall Street from India, he advised Mr. Fuller to draw up a fair and temperate statement regarding the mission. Mr. Grant, on perusing it, made several alterations and additions, and suggested that it should be submitted to Lord Teignmouth, formerly Governor-General of India, and now a member of the Board of Control, and a cordial friend of missions. He likewise dissuaded Mr. Fuller from any application to Government at the present conjuncture, though no official complaint had been sent from India regarding the conduct of the missionaries.

A meeting of the Court of Proprietors had been convened for the 17th of June, when a motion was to be made regarding the Vellore mutiny; and as this tragedy was attributed to missionary efforts, both in Calcutta and in London, it was expected that a side blow would be aimed at missions during the debate, and it was deemed important that Mr. Fuller should be fully prepared for every emergency. He proceeded accordingly to Northamptonshire, and called a meeting of the committee, who adopted a Statement he had drawn up, and gave him the fullest power to act on behalf of the Society. On his return to London, he met a deputation of the London Missionary Society, who were desirous of co-operating with him; and found that they had been led to entertain the highest confidence of their strength in the Court of Proprietors. They considered Mr. Grant a timid and irresolute man, and were anxious that the missionary question should be fully discussed on the 17th. Mr. Fuller also imbibed this impression, but resolved to consult Mr. Grant, who, on hearing the expression of this desire, fixed his eye keenly on him, and said, "You think I am timid and irresolute. I will shew you two or three letters, which will exhibit the strength of prejudice and power you have to encounter. You say you wish the debate to come on; but you do not expect any other result than to be out-voted. What will you do then?" "Appeal," replied Mr. Fuller, "to the Board of Control, and, if necessary, to the King." "The King," replied Mr. Grant, "is not likely to interfere in any such matter; and, as to the Board, read these letters, and mark the opposition you have to combat in that quarter." These letters convinced Mr. Fuller that their chief danger lay in the members of the Board, who had been incessantly calling on the Court of Directors to order the missionaries home; while Mr. Grant had been vigorously defending their characters and their cause, and boldly asserting that they were not intemperate incendiaries, nor heady, nor ignorant, and that no danger had ever arisen from their labours. Through the kind interposition of Mr. Parry, the chairman of the Court of Directors, who was the steady friend of the mission, the motion of the 17th passed over without any reflection on the missionaries.

Mr. Fuller's Statement was sent to every man of influence in the Government of India or of England, and he waited personally on sixteen of the Directors, of whom he found four or five hostile, four or five friendly, and the rest undecided. But the person of greatest consequence in the councils of India at this time was Mr. Robert Dundas, the son of Lord Melville, and the President of the Board of Control. Mr. Fuller accordingly waited on him, and found that the alarmists in India had sent home to the Board very unfriendly translations of the tracts, and had filled him with complaints of the conduct of the missionaries. He treated Mr. Fuller with much kindness and candour, and advised that his friends in India should proceed with great caution. But when Mr. Fuller stated their earnest desire to obtain express permission to itinerate and establish stations, Mr. Dundas drew up, and replied, "I suppose you do; but you do not mean to apply for it immediately?" "Not," said Mr. Fuller, "till the present excitement has passed over." "That," observed Mr. Dundas, "will be a wise course, and you may possibly receive it in four or five months." But more than six years passed before it was obtained. Mr. Fuller likewise called on Lord Wellesley, and sat with him half an hour, relating what had befallen the missionaries since his departure. He frankly stated that the principle on which he had acted while Governor-General, was to facilitate the proceedings of the missionaries as far as he could do so without implicating Government, or giving rise to the opinion that the mission was patronized by the State. He spoke with the highest respect of Mr. Carey and his two colleagues, and said that, as to their being accessory to the Vellore mutiny, it was simply impossible. The storm blew over in a few months, but only to burst with greater violence in the following year.

At the beginning of 1807, the college of Fort-William was remodelled. The Court of Directors established another college at Haileybury, for the instruction of the young civilians in all those branches of European knowledge which Lord Wellesley had proposed to teach in Calcutta, and for imparting to them the rudiments of the Eastern languages.

The offices of Provost and Vice-Provost in the college of Fort-William were abolished. The professorships were reduced to three; the statutes were reformed, and the clause requiring them to profess the creed of the Church of England, which the episcopal zeal of Mr. Buchanan had introduced, was abrogated. Mr. Carey was raised to a professorship, and his allowance increased from 500 to 1,000 rupees a month.

In the month of January, the little chapel erected by the Armenians in the Chitpore road, the great thoroughfare in the native quarter of Calcutta, was opened by Mr. Ward. In his journal he mentions the unfeigned satisfaction he felt in being the honoured instrument in commencing Christian worship in this place, as he had already done in the Bow bazar, little dreaming that before the close of the year even this little meeting-house would excite the alarm of Government, and be closed by its orders. A little incident connected with it deserves mention. The Armenian to whom the premises belonged had erected a large wooden cross over the gateway; but Mr. Marshman, aware of the superstitious homage which was paid to this emblem by the Armenians, equally with the Roman Catholics, who assembled there for worship, requested that it might be removed, and, on the appearance of some hesitation, called for a ladder, and took it down with his own hands. It should be observed, however, that it was only in reference to the notion of sanctity ignorantly attached to this ecclesiastical symbol, that he considered its removal important. So little objection did he feel to it in a position in which it could foster no error, that he preached for thirty years in the settlement church at Serampore, the steeple of which was surmounted by a gilt cross. On the 8th of March, Mr. Carey received the diploma of Doctor of Divinity from Brown University, in the United States; and seldom has this literary distinction been bestowed on one who did more honour to its choice. Of his colossal labours on the days he spent in Calcutta, a private letter of this period affords the following notice:—"He rises a little before six, reads a chapter in the Hebrew Bible, and spends the time till seven in private devotion. He then has family prayer with the servants in Bengalee, after which he reads Persian, with a Moonshee who is in attendance. As soon as breakfast is over, he sits down to the translation of the Ramayun, with his pundit, till ten, when he proceeds to the college, and attends its duties till two. Returning home, he examines a proof-sheet of the Bengalee translation, and dines with his friend, Mr. Rolt. After dinner he translates a chapter of the Bible, with the aid of the chief pundit of the college. At six, he sits down with the Teloogoo pundit, to the study of that language, and then preaches a sermon, in English, to a congregation of about fifty. The service ended, he sits down to the translation of Ezekiel into Bengalee, having thrown aside his former version. At eleven, the duties of the day are closed, and, after reading a chapter in the Greek Testament, and commending himself to God, he retires to rest."

The chapel in the Bow bazar had made considerable progress, and the walls were rising to view, when the magistrate, Mr. Blacquiere, threatened to denounce the missionaries to Government for erecting a public edifice without its sanction. To prevent an official and hostile representation at a time when the public authorities were unfriendly, Mr. Marshman drew up a memorial to the Governor-General, soliciting permission to erect a place of Protestant worship in Calcutta, and waited in person on the most influential European gentlemen in the town, out of the service, and obtained more than a hundred signatures to it. The Government, in accordance with its traditional policy of liberality and equality in all denominational questions, immediately granted permission for the work to proceed.

The feeling of cordial fellowship which had so long subsisted between the Rev. David Brown and the Serampore missionaries was at this time unhappily interrupted by the profound and affectionate deference which he paid to Mr. Buchanan, whom he described as "the man to do good on the earth, and worthy of being Metropolitan of the East." The ascendancy of Mr. Buchanan over Mr. Brown was that of a bold spirit over a meek and amiable one. Finding the office of Vice-Provost in the College of Fort-William abolished, and all the prospects of usefulness he had built on that association extinguished, he proposed to establish a college of translations at Serampore, on the model of the Propaganda at Rome. It was to be placed under the patronage of the King of Denmark, and of the Society for the Promotion of Christian Knowledge; all the sums collected or received for translations were to be placed at its disposal; the labours of the missionaries in the department of translations were to be merged in it, and the press at Serampore was henceforth to be called the Press of the British Propaganda. The missionaries were required to give their unfeigned assent and consent to the plan; but the more closely they examined it, the more formidable did the objections to it appear. It brought no accession of strength to the work of translations: while the ostentatious establishment of such an institution, with so ominous a designation, would, they apprehended, increase the alarm of the Government, in its present temper, to such an extent, as to lead to the conviction that the toleration of missionaries was no longer compatible with public security. The erection of expensive buildings, and the salaries of five professors, as proposed in the scheme, appeared likely to absorb all the resources before a single copy of the Scriptures left the press. They felt themselves, therefore, constrained to withstand the proposal; but Mr. Brown considered that "possibilities were more within Mr. Buchanan's ken than in that of other men," and a very unpleasant controversy was carried on for several months. But the cordiality which was thus interrupted was at length restored; the prayer-meetings at the pagoda were resumed, and their mutual friendship was more closely cemented by the renewed and increased opposition of Government to missions. Mr. Marshman's remarks on Mr. Buchanan's policy were just without being ungenerous: "Mr. Buchanan is going to England, perhaps never to return. I must, after all, declare that he is a good man, thorough evangelical; a friend to the cause of God, and by no means an enemy to us; a man with whom friendship is desirable, but not coalition. The services he has rendered to our mission *ought* never to be forgotten. A little too much of worldly prudence—not avarice—and perhaps a touch of ambition, are his only blemishes. We come to greater things; we have fallen into deep waters." These deep waters referred to the opposition of Government, which was renewed with greater violence on the arrival of Lord Minto as Governor-General. But as it is desirable to give an unbroken narrative of the strenuous effort which was made at this time, both in India and in England, to root out the missionary enterprise, the remaining events of 1807 will be disposed of in the first instance.

At the beginning of the year, Mr. Chater and Mr. Mardon proceeded to Rangoon to examine the practicability of a mission in the Burmese dominions. They met with a generous reception from the European traders settled there, as well as from the public functionaries, and returned with a favourable report to Serampore. Mr. Mardon, however, was unwilling to return and break up fresh ground in a foreign country; but Mr. Felix Carey, Dr. Carey's eldest son, was induced by the natural elasticity of his mind to offer his services for this new and difficult undertaking. He and Mr. Chater reached Rangoon at the close of the year. The erection of the chapel in the Bow bazar had been pushed on with great vigour, but the subscriptions were completely exhausted, and a large balance was due to the architect, Mr. Rolt. Mr. Marshman therefore determined to solicit in person the aid of the most opulent of the European gentlemen in Calcutta beyond the official circle. He proceeded from house to house, and represented the religious destitution of the Christian population for whom there was no accommodation in the two Episcopal churches in Calcutta, and the effort recently made to erect a chapel for their benefit, which was now interrupted for want of funds. Few men have ever surpassed Mr. Marshman in persuasive importunity; and in less than ten days he succeeded in raising £1100 from gentlemen altogether unconnected with his own denomination. But this exhibition of zeal, so novel in Calcutta, was not allowed to pass without an attempt at ridicule. At one of the fancy balls of the season, at which the Governor-General was present, some gentleman thought fit to personate Mr. Marshman, and assuming his clerical garb, went about the room with a subscription paper. In the description given of the entertainment in one of the local journals, it was announced that among other amusing characters, there was "a pious missionary soliciting subscriptions, and that it was gratifying to remark how well his paper was filled." In the month of September, Mr. Grant, an indigo planter in the Malda district, and one of Dr. Carey's earliest friends, died at Berhampore, bequeathing £2000 to the Serampore Mission, and £1000 to the Translations. On the 7th of December, Mrs. Carey, who had been in a state of mental derangement for twelve years, was released from a life of suffering. It will serve to give some idea of the strength of Dr. Carey's character, to state that the biblical and literary labours in which he had been engaged since his arrival at Serampore, were prosecuted with an insane wife, frequently wrought up to a state of the most deplorable excitement, confined in an adjoining room.

The state of the mission family at Serampore, which was regulated on a principle of republican equality and Moravian economy, had for several years been a source of great anxiety to the three senior missionaries. In addition to their external difficulties, they had to encounter the uneven tempers and disappointed hopes of the junior brethren, some of whom were exasperated at the influence exercised in the missionary counsels by Dr. Carey, Mr. Marshman, and Mr. Ward, who had been required to steer the vessel of the mission through violent tempests and dangerous quicksands. As usual in such cases, the capacity of those who aspired to take the helm, was in an inverse ratio to their qualifications for that post, and in their hands the mission would have become a wreck in a few months. The committee of the Society had always impugned this concession of equality, and Dr. Ryland wrote out, in his own caustic style, "Who ever advanced the democratic nonsense of every apprentice we send out being equal the moment he sets foot in Bengal?" To remove this discord, it was resolved, at a meeting of all the missionaries, that the brethren at Serampore, and those who might be sent to subordinate stations, should in future choose their own coadjutors; and that each station should be considered independent in all its family connexions and concerns; but that these distinct families should still constitute one mission, with a committee of management at Serampore, consisting of the three senior missionaries.

In his letter to Mr. Fuller on the subject of this arrangement, Mr. Ward alluded to some remarks unfriendly to missions which had appeared in the *Theological Repository*, and which he was advised to refute. "These remarks," he replies, "indicate a cavilling, censorious, splitting temper, incompatible with a state of mind earnestly pursuing great objects. You wish me to give you such an answer as you may publish. My dear brother, these drivelling cavillers will go unanswered to all eternity, unless they can find some one who has less to do, and more faith in the use of such answers, than I have." In noticing some small payments which had been made to his mother in England, he said, "I hope the Society will make no payments to my mother, unasked. I hope and believe she does not want. I wish to die leaving the mission as much in my debt as possible, so that I may die poor, having received nothing of the mission but food and raiment. Hitherto I have spent my private property to do this, and no one shall stop my boasting in all Asia." To understand this allusion, it must be remembered that the "mission" to which he alluded was the establishment at Serampore, supported by his labour and that of his two colleagues. To this fund he gave up all the profits of the press, while Dr. Carey and Mr. Marshman, as he remarked in his journal, "were contributing £2400 a year, receiving from it only their food and a trifle of pocket-money for apparel."

CHAPTER V.

The hostility to the mission, which had lulled for ten months, was revived on the arrival of Lord Minto as Governor-General. He was a man of classical tastes and cultivated mind, and anxious to give every encouragement to literary undertakings. But with regard to the evangelisation of the heathen, his views did not appear to differ from those of his great Whig leader, Mr. Fox, who had declared in Parliament that he considered all schemes of proselytism wrong in themselves, and productive in most cases of abuse and political mischief. Unhappily for the Serampore missionaries, the first intelligence which met him on his arrival at Madras, on his way to Calcutta, was that of the Vellore mutiny. At that presidency he imbibed the prevailing opinion that it was to be attributed to an injudicious tampering with the religious prejudices of the natives. This impression was confirmed on reaching Calcutta, where the anti-missionary party assured him that the most imminent peril must attend any interference with these prejudices by whatever agency and in whatever form it might be attempted.

An indefinite dread of the danger which threatened the empire from this source took complete possession of his mind, at a time when he was necessarily obliged to lean on the opinions of others; and an opportunity was soon presented for the development of these feelings.

A pamphlet, which had recently issued from the Serampore press, had just fallen into the hands of one of the secretaries to Government, and on the 2nd of September Dr. Carey was required to attend the office of the chief secretary, where he met Mr. Edmonstone, the secretary in the Secret and Political Department. Mr. Edmonstone was one of the most distinguished servants of the Company, of sound judgment and great official experience. He had been twenty-four years in the public service, and was thoroughly imbued with those principles of Indian despotism which he believed to be essential to the existence of the British dominion in the East. Though kind and considerate in his disposition, he was at this time under the influence of the reigning panic, and believed that no attempt could be made to convert the natives without political danger. At this meeting Dr. Carey was asked whether he was cognizant of the publication of a pamphlet at the Serampore press, containing strictures on the Prophet and his religion, which had been circulated among the inhabitants of the presidency. He replied that though he could not take on himself to assert that no such pamphlet had been published there, he was scarcely aware of its existence. Mr. Edmonstone then read an extract from a translation which had been made of the tract, and commented on those portions which he considered inflammatory and dangerous. Dr. Carey replied that he and his colleagues entirely disapproved of the use of offensive language in reference to the religion of the Hindoos or Mahomedans, and that this course was altogether foreign to their practice in their communications with the natives. He expressed an earnest hope that it was not the intention of Government to prohibit their labouring for the conversion of the people by the only means they were disposed to use—fair argument and persuasion. Dr. Carey then withdrew, after assuring Mr. Edmonstone that measures would be immediately taken by the missionaries to suppress the pamphlet, and that they were prepared to submit for the approval of Government every publication they proposed in future to issue from the press.

At the same time, Lord Minto sent a communication to the governor of Serampore, Colonel Krefting, with a translation of the pamphlet, and remarked that the duty of Government, as guardians of the public safety, would alone require them to prevent the diffusion of such a publication; but that an additional obligation was imposed on them by the faith repeatedly pledged to the natives to leave them in the full, free, and undisturbed exercise of their religion. The letter stated that the Government had not yet determined on the ulterior measures to be pursued to preserve the public tranquillity and vindicate the national faith; but as a matter of immediate urgency, they required that the farther distribution of the pamphlet should be interdicted, and all the remaining copies surrendered. This communication was sent by the governor to the missionaries, who, in their reply, expressed their extreme regret that any such publication should have issued from their press, and at the same time sent him, to be forwarded to Calcutta, the remaining copies on hand, seventeen hundred in number. They likewise stated in explanation, that a few months before this time they had placed in the hands of a Mahomedan moonshee, a convert to Christianity, to be translated into Persian, a short abstract of the life of Mahomed in the Bengalee language, taken almost verbatim from the preliminary dissertation of Sale's Koran. The confidence they reposed in the moonshee had led them to put the translation to press without revision, and they now discovered that he had introduced opprobrious epithets in reference to the Prophet which did not exist in the Bengalee version. They remarked that, although this circumstance did not in any measure exonerate them from the responsibility of the publication, it would serve to vindicate them from the suspicion of being indifferent to the peace of the country. This communication was submitted to Lord Minto by Colonel Krefting, who expressed a hope that "no further measures would be taken, as he was ready on the first application from the British Government to check any abuse that might arise."

The anti-missionary party, now in the ascendant, was resolved, however, that so favourable an opportunity for overthrowing the mission should not be lost. The Supreme Council assembled, apparently under the impression that some great missionary conspiracy which threatened the existence of the British Empire had been suddenly detected, which it was their bounden duty to frustrate by the most prompt and stringent measures. Mr. Blacquiere, the magistrate, a thoroughly brahminised European, was therefore directed to ascertain and report on the proceedings of the missionaries, "in disseminating pamphlets, and in meetings stated to be held in the town of Calcutta for the purpose of exposing to the natives the error of their religion, and of persuading them to embrace the Christian faith." After a short interval, Mr. Blacquiere reported that he had directed a brahmin in his service to attend the missionaries, under a pretended desire to become a convert, and to ask for copies of their publications, of which he had obtained eleven. This clandestine proceeding towards Christian missionaries, as if they had been political incendiaries, was subsequently reported to the Court of Directors as a laudable instance of the zeal of the Governor-General for the public safety. On the 6th of September Mr. Blacquiere sent another of his spies to attend the service in the little chapel in the Chitpore road, and he reported that an elderly native had addressed the assembly, descanting on the wicked lives which the brahmins and other men of respectability lived, under the influence of their own evil passions, denying that the brahmins could forgive sins, and affirming that the religious festivals of the Hindoos tended rather to produce than to expiate transgression. A European then ascended the pulpit and preached to a congregation of Armenians and Portuguese; but, with the exception of two converted natives, there were neither Hindoos nor Mahomedans in the room, though a crowd of disreputable natives was collected at the door.

Two days after, Mr. Edmonstone presented to the Supreme Council the depositions of the informer, and the translation of the various tracts which the brahmin had obtained, and the Council proceeded to deliberate on the perilous position of the British Empire in India, as disclosed by these informations. They then recorded their conviction that such proceedings were evidently calculated to excite among the native subjects of the Company a spirit of religious jealousy and alarm, which might eventually be productive of the most serious evils, and that Government was bound by every consideration of general safety and national faith and honour, to suppress treatises and public preachings offensive to the religious persuasions of the people. A letter was therefore sent to Dr. Carey by Mr. Edmonstone, directing that the preaching in the little chapel in the Chitpore road should be immediately discontinued, and that no publications should issue from the Serampore press of a nature offensive to the religious prejudices of the natives, or directed to the object of converting them to Christianity. The reason assigned for this extraordinary injunction was that to obtrude upon the general body of the people, by means of printed works, exhortations necessarily involving an interference with those religious tenets which they considered to be sacred and inviolable, was contrary to the system of protection which Government was pledged to afford to the undisturbed exercise of the religions of the country. The Governor-General, moreover, directed that the Serampore press should be immediately removed to Calcutta, where alone the necessary control could be exercised over it; and the missionaries were directed to use every effort in their power to withdraw from circulation the pamphlets and treatises they had been distributing.

Well might Dr. Carey exclaim that, "never had such a letter been written by any government before! Roman Catholics have persecuted other Christians under the name of heretics, but no Christian government that I know of has ever prohibited attempts to spread the Gospel among the heathen." It was well known that the press was essential to the mission, and that the removal of it must involve the extinction of the missionary establishment at Serampore. It was to compass this object that the anti-missionary party took advantage of the panic created by the Vellore mutiny, and of Lord Minto's inexperience and ignorance of the proceedings of the missionaries during the previous seven years, to induce him to adopt this arbitrary measure within five weeks after he had assumed the Government. The press, moreover, was known to be under the special protection of a foreign power; and if he had allowed himself time for reflection, he could not have failed to perceive that a demand which he could not enforce without a violation of international law, only served to compromise the dignity of his own Government. He had a right to require the suppression of publications which he conceived likely to endanger the safety of the British dominions, but the demand regarding the press itself was one which even the morbid terrors of his Council could not extenuate. As to the pledge to respect the religious prejudices of the natives, which was now for the first time brought forward, the fact was that the British Government had of its own free will conceded to the conquered the blessing of religious toleration in the fullest sense; but to assert that "any effort directed to the object of converting the natives to Christianity" was a violation of that pledge, in other words, that Government was pledged to the perpetual exclusion of Christianity from India, was a simple absurdity.

The order regarding the press filled the missionaries with dismay. They felt that the transfer of it to Calcutta must break up their establishment. The expense of living in the metropolis would have been ruinous. The mission would also be deprived of the protection of a friendly power, and placed under the direct control of a police worked by Mr. Blacquiere. As the avowed object of removing the press to Calcutta was to suppress all attempts to convert the natives, every movement of the missionaries would have been watched with jealousy, and subjected to interruption, while the mission premises would have been incessantly beset by the magistrate's spies. On the arrival of Mr. Edmonstone's letter they held a meeting to supplicate the Divine guidance at this crisis. Immediately after, they waited on Colonel Krefting, who expressed his surprise that the Government of India should have proceeded to act before they had received his reply to their communication, and that the missionaries should have been treated as though they were living under British jurisdiction. The missionaries then proceeded to the residence of Mr. Brown, under whose advice they simply acknowledged the receipt of the letter, and resolved to wait the progress of circumstances.

A week after, a communication, signed by Lord Minto and two members of Council, was sent to Colonel Krefting. The measures he had adopted to suppress publications obnoxious to the religious persuasions of the people were acknowledged with thanks; but it was stated at the same time that "it was obviously regular and highly expedient that the press of the missionaries should be placed under the immediate control of the Government of India; and it was hoped that his Excellency would not only concur in the expediency of the measure they had adopted in ordering it to Calcutta, but withhold his consent to the establishment of any other press under the Danish flag." This letter was communicated by the governor to the missionaries, who held another prayer-meeting, at which Dr. Carey wept like a child. They then waited on him, and received the assurance that he could not permit the removal of the press without incurring the serious displeasure of his sovereign, and that if the British Government thought fit to resort to compulsory measures, he would strike his flag, and leave the settlement in their possession; but he would endeavour, in the first instance, to procure a reversal of the order by conciliation. Dr. Carey and Mr. Marshman agreed, therefore, to leave the matter in his hands, but Mr. Ward was not satisfied with this determination. In a letter which he addressed to his brethren, he questioned the propriety of "remaining in sullen silence after the English Government had addressed them through the governor of Serampore and Dr. Carey. Even if the press was not removed, it would be a great calamity to have them as avowed and exasperated enemies. They might deprive the mission of Dr. Carey's salary, and put an end to the translations, and prohibit the progress of the new chapel. They might prevent the circulation of everything emanating from the press, and even confine them to the town of Serampore. It would be more judicious to entreat their clemency, and endeavour to soften them. Tender words, with the consciences of men on our side, go a long way. We may tell them that we are willing to do everything they desire, except to renounce our work and character as ministers of the Saviour of the world."

In compliance with Mr. Ward's judicious advice, it was resolved to present a memorial to the Governor-General. He likewise urged, with renewed importunity, the suggestion he had formerly made, that they should seek a personal interview with Lord Minto, and thus dispose him to receive their representations with more favour. While they were discussing this proposal, they received a visit from Dr. Leyden, the renowned Orientalist, and, before his arrival in India, the friend and literary associate of Walter Scott. Lord Minto, who held him in the highest esteem, had invited him from Madras, and given him an appointment in Calcutta. A conformity of literary tastes had led to a very close intimacy between him and Mr. Marshman, and he warmly appreciated the benevolent exertions to which the missionaries devoted their lives. To him they explained the nature of their embarrassment, and he advised them to adopt Mr. Ward's proposal, and wait in person on Lord Minto the very next day, and ask his acceptance of their translation of the Ramayun. He remarked that, even if there should be no opportunity of introducing the subject of their present difficulties, the interview would prove that they did not wish to conceal themselves from any consciousness of guilt. Lord Minto received them with his usual affability, and soon placed them at their ease. Dr. Carey then presented him with a copy of the Ramayun, and made an offer of any other literary works which had issued from their press. Mr. Marshman then touched on the object of their visit, and asked permission to present a private memorial. He drew back at a request which recalled to his mind the order he had recently signed against their press, but immediately after assured them that he would be happy to receive it. The ice having thus been broken, the conversation became less reserved. They explained the origin and progress of the mission, the degree of success which had attended their labours, and the principles on which they acted. Mr. Marshman then brought the conversation dexterously to the immediate object of the audience—the ruin with which their missionary plans were threatened by the order to remove their press to Calcutta. Lord Minto made friendly inquiries regarding their missionary efforts, and assured them that he felt no hostility to them or to their undertaking, and that the conversion of the natives, in a quiet way, was a desirable object, but feared there was danger of provoking the bigotry of the Mahomedans. He observed that missionaries were expected to have a little enthusiasm in them, and to feel more warmly on the subject of conversion than other men, and, moreover, that they should be able sometimes to bear the frowns of men in power. Twenty minutes were thus passed in friendly conversation, and Dr. Carey and Mr. Marshman left him with the strong hope that their object was already half accomplished. They had removed the impression that they were a body of wild fanatics, who were determined to push the project of conversion, though it might set India in a blaze, and they had his promise to peruse their memorial before it was placed in the hands of his colleagues.

Mr. Marshman, on his return to Serampore, sat down to the preparation of the memorial, on which the existence of the mission was supposed to hang; and it may be regarded as a favourable example of the skill with which he could handle a difficult question. It described the formation of the Baptist Missionary Society in 1792, the arrival of Mr. Carey and Mr. Thomas, the settlement of the mission at Serampore under the protection of the King of Denmark, the kindness they had experienced from Lord Wellesley, and the approbation he had expressed of their labours. It stated that they had baptized a hundred natives, of whom twelve were brahmins, and sixteen of the writer caste. They esteemed, it said, the principle which guaranteed to the natives the full, free, and undisturbed exercise of their different religions, and were not conscious of having violated it in their discussions with them. They regretted that the opening of the little chapel in the Chitpore road had been represented as an attempt to inflame the minds of the people, and to disturb the public tranquillity. They enumerated all the pamphlets which had issued from their press, describing their character and contents; and they explained more particularly the circumstances under which the obnoxious epithets had crept into the Persian tract. They stated that they were under obligations to the public to translate and print the Scriptures in six of the Eastern languages, and that they could not contemplate the removal of the press to Calcutta without dread, as involving the ruin of their undertaking.

The perusal of this memorial at Barrackpore enabled

Lord Minto to form an independent judgment of the case before he went to the Council Chamber, where it was read the next day, together with Colonel Krefting's reply. In that communication he stated that he had prescribed such rules for the missionaries as would effectually prevent the issue of any tracts of an objectionable character; and he expressed a hope that the Government would not press the transfer of the printing establishment to Calcutta, which would not only entail ruin on the missionaries, but prove detrimental to the interests of his Danish Majesty's settlement. On the perusal of these documents, Lord Minto proposed a resolution revoking the order, and simply requiring the missionaries to submit works intended for circulation in the Company's territories to the inspection of its officers. In communicating this decision to the missionaries, the secretary was instructed to inform them that the Governor-General in Council was fully convinced of the rectitude of their intentions. The storm which at one time threatened to sweep away the mission was thus dispersed, and the imposition of some minor restrictions seemed to improve the position of the missionaries, by leaving them unfettered in other respects. This favourable change was due, under God, to their gentle and judicious conduct in bending to the necessity of circumstances, and endeavouring to conciliate a despotism which threatened to become a tyranny. It was the irresistible might of Christian meekness which carried them over the crisis and saved their mission. "The crests of our enemies," writes Dr. Carey, "are fallen; for as soon as the orders of Government became public, there was no small exultation among the enemies of religion at the prospect of having the missionary establishment at Serampore broken up, and the missionaries themselves placed under the eye of jealous and arbitrary rulers."

This opposition on the part of the Government in Calcutta to the cause of missions, likewise proved advantageous to it, in eliciting a favourable opinion from the Board of Control.

In the despatch transmitted to Leadenhall Street on the subject of these proceedings in India, the defence of them was based on the duty of maintaining the "public tranquillity" and the "national faith," two favourite expressions which were repeated in every page. It dwelt on the obligation to suppress, within the limits of the Company's authority in India, treatises and public preachings offensive to the religious persuasions of the people, and more especially at the seat of Government, where it might otherwise be suspected that they had the sanction and approval of the public authorities. The despatch fully admitted the correctness of the motives and objects of the missionaries, but at the same time requested that the Court would prevent the embarkation of any others, "as the meritorious spirit of religious zeal which animates these respectable persons can seldom be restrained by those maxims of prudence and caution which local knowledge and experience alone can inspire, and without which the labours of the missionaries become a source of danger."

Mr. Robert Dundas, the President of the Board of Control, whose interesting conversation with Mr. Fuller has been already alluded to, drafted the reply to this prolix Bengal despatch, which the Directors could not refuse to sign, however opposite to their sentiments. "The Court," said the despatch, "wished it to be understood that they were far from adverse to the introduction of Christianity into India; but nothing could be more likely to frustrate that object than any imprudent attempt to introduce it by means which should create irritation and alarm. Some of the publications were open to objection, and the Court approved of the measures adopted to prevent the circulation of them. At the same time the Court passed a high eulogium on the temperate and respectful conduct of the Serampore missionaries, and directed that if upon any future occasion any precautionary measures should become necessary, and the interference of Government should again be required, it would be desirable to see whether a private communication with the missionaries might not effect the object, without bringing into view the instrumentality of Government. The officious advice to prevent any further resort of missionaries to India was dismissed with the curt remark that "none of the meritorious individuals who had devoted themselves to missionary labours had proceeded to Bengal with the Court's licence." The despatch concluded with a covert rebuke to the Supreme Council:—"The Court approved of their having refrained from resorting to the authority vested in them by law, against the missionaries, and relied on their discretion to abstain from all unnecessary and ostentatious interference with their proceedings in future."

While these efforts were made in India to extinguish the missionary enterprise, the most vigorous exertions were directed to the same object in England. The feelings which characterised the opposition to missions in 1793 were revived with increased violence, and the second battle of missions raged with great animosity for many months, and gave birth to more than twenty pamphlets. The Vellore mutiny had created a deep sensation throughout the country, and the public mind was prepared to receive, without inquiry, any representation which the "old Indians" might make regarding the perils of our Indian empire. It was at this period of general alarm and anxiety that some of those who had passed their lives in that country and retired to opulence and ease at home, thought fit to come forward and assert that our sovereignty in India was placed in extreme peril by the labours of the missionaries, who "were invading the dearest rights, and wounding the tenderest feelings of the natives." The campaign was opened by Mr. Thomas Twining, the son of the wealthy tea-dealer, who had been employed for thirteen years in the Company's civil service in Bengal. In a letter addressed to Mr. Parry, the chairman of the Court of Directors, he stated that he had recently heard with infinite alarm of proceedings which evinced a strong disposition to interfere with the religious prejudices of the natives. His fears, he said, had been excited by hearing that a society existed in England,—the Bible Society,—the president of which was a member of the Board of Control, and the chief object of which was the universal diffusion of the Christian faith, more especially among the natives of the East; and his fears were confirmed by the progress which had been made in the translating and printing of the Scriptures by the missionaries at Serampore, whose labours he considered to "threaten the extermination of our Eastern sovereignty." His pamphlet concluded with the remark that "if ever the fatal day should arrive when religious innovation should set her foot in the country, indignation would spread from one end of Hindostan to the other, and the arms of fifty millions of people would drive us from that portion of the globe with as much ease as the sand of the desert is scattered by the wind."

Mr. Twining's assault was promptly and successfully met by Mr. Owen, the first and greatest secretary of the Bible Society, who shewed, by a reference to its fundamental rules, that its object was not the "universal dissemination of the Christian faith, but the general circulation of the Scriptures throughout the world." Mr. Twining had stated in a note that he did not know who these Serampore missionaries were, and Mr. Owen rebuked his ostentatious ignorance by the remark, "As for Mr. Carey, the chief minister of the Baptist mission, he is known I presume to all who do not consider literature disgraced by an alliance with piety. As teacher of the Bengalee, Sanscrit, and Mahratta languages in the College of Fort-William, and a member of the Asiatic Society, he is not a correspondent whom any institution need be anxious to disclaim." As to the Serampore missionaries, Sir George Barlow would have informed him who they may be, in whose printed speech they are acknowledged with respect as the Society of Protestant missionaries at Serampore.

The next champion was Major Scott Waring, who had gone out to India forty years previously in the Company's military service, and was placed on the personal staff of the Governor-General, Warren Hastings. Returning to England with an ample fortune, he purchased a seat in Parliament, where his injudicious defence of his patron acquired for him the appellation of Hastings's evil genius. It was he who had bullied Burke into that memorable prosecution which the political party with whom he was associated was anxious to avoid, but from which they could not recede after the Major had thrown down the gauntlet. In 1807 he published "Observations on the Present State of the East India Company," in which he stated that the Vellore mutiny was excited by the sons of Tippoo, whose emissaries insinuated that the change in the dress of the sepoys was only a prelude to their being compelled to embrace Christianity. With regard to missionaries, he asserted that "if not publicly patronised by Government they could do no mischief. The true line for the Government to pursue was obvious,—let them make as many converts as they can, but give them no support on the one hand or discouragement on the other." But after the publication of this pamphlet, he happened, as he stated, to hear that some one had written from India to say that long after the mutiny the dread of a revolt among our native troops was so great that the officers constantly slept with pistols under their pillows. Though this information was before him when the pamphlet was originally published, he added a preface to the second edition,—it went through four editions,—stating that he considered it his duty, on the strength of this report, to "come forward and assert that if India was deemed worth preserving, we should endeavour to regain the confidence of the people by the immediate recall of every missionary." He asserted that the mind of man had never conceived a wilder or more dangerous plan than that of instituting schools in India. It had been, he said, the invariable practice of the British Government, generally, to foster and protect the religion of the Hindoos, and also to encourage what the Bible Society termed the bloody and degrading superstition of Mahomed; but now India was overspread with sectarian missionaries, upon whom he heaped every epithet of abuse that malevolence could devise, and whom, with an affectation of ignorance, he described as Baptist missionaries, Arminian missionaries, United Brethren missionaries. Who these Baptist missionaries were he did not exactly know; perhaps they were Calvinistic Methodists. The new order of missionaries were the most ignorant and bigoted of men. Their compositions were, in fact, nothing but puritanical rant of the most vulgar kind, worse than that so much in fashion in the days of Oliver Cromwell. The head of the missionaries was a Mr. William Carey, who enjoyed a salary from the Company of £800 a year, as teacher in the College of Fort-William, where he had apartments for the reception of his brother missionaries. They have not made a single Mahomedan convert, and no Hindoos but men of despicable character, who took up a new religion because they were excluded from the old. Are these missionaries, he asked, to be allowed to spread themselves over India, each with a team of hackeries loaded with Bibles and religious pamphlets? Shall a warehouse be opened in Calcutta, Madras, and Bombay, and the people invited by advertisement to take away as many copies as they choose? In a subsequent pamphlet he again enforced the imminent danger to which the empire was exposed by these missionary efforts, and the absolute necessity of suppressing them at once if we would preserve it. He considered it utterly impracticable to convert the natives by *human* means, and if those means should receive the sanction of the legislature, he believed that one year would complete the destruction of the British power in India. We had thirty thousand British subjects there, and humanity required that we should preserve the lives of our countrymen by the expulsion of the missionaries.

The pamphlets of Mr. Twining and Major Scott Waring were intended to prepare the proprietors for the motion which Mr. Twining had announced his intention of bringing forward in their Court for the extinction of missionary efforts. Mr. Fuller came up to London on the appearance of these publications, and found that there was a powerful feeling against missions at the India House, and that it was necessary to muster all the strength the friends of the cause could command, to prevent an adverse decision in the Court of Proprietors. He was, moreover, assured that, as the secretary of the Baptist Missionary Society, it was incumbent on him to prepare a full and satisfactory reply to these hostile pamphlets. A few days after, he was informed that some of the Directors were seriously contemplating the recall of the missionaries, and he immediately waited on Lord Wellesley to solicit the exercise of his influence at this emergency. Lord Wellesley assured him that he was decidedly opposed to any such measure, which he considered most impolitic and unjust; and he promised to use every effort to dissuade the public authorities from adopting it, if they should ask his opinion on the subject. The Court of Proprietors met on the 23rd of December, when Mr. Twining made a long speech, in which he dwelt on the new dangers with which the British empire in India was threatened, by the attempts which had been made to interfere with the religious prejudices of the natives. He said he was anxious to avoid discussion, and simply required an assurance from the chair that no such interference would be permitted in future. The chairman, Mr. Parry, the steady friend of the missionaries, refused to give any other than a general assurance that the Directors would do whatever appeared to them most proper. Mr. Twining was thus baffled at the outset, and left the Court threatening to call a special meeting of the proprietors to accomplish his purpose; but no other gentleman appeared desirous of continuing the discussion.

A new opponent now appeared in the field, under the

character of a "Bengal Officer," who was, in fact, Colonel Stewart, generally known through India as "Hindoo Stewart." He had abjured Christianity and embraced Hindooism, and was in the habit of going down daily to the Ganges with sacrificial vessels and flowers to perform his ablutions according to the Hindoo ritual, which exposed him not only to the contempt of his fellow-countrymen, but also to the derision of the natives. On the present occasion he published "A Vindication of the Hindoos," which proved of eminent service to the cause of Christian missions, by the ridicule which his extravagance cast on the cause of their opponents. He exhibited the most abject devotion to the religion of the Shasters; he extolled the moral virtues of the Hindoos, and denounced "the sacrilegious attack of the missionaries on the ancient and venerable fabric of Hindooism." Those who preceded him in this crusade had attempted to shew that every effort to convert the Hindoos must be attended with political danger, but he boldly maintained that these efforts were altogether redundant, as the Hindoo system "little needed the meliorating hand of Christianity to render its votaries a sufficiently moral people for all the useful purposes of civilised life." "Wherever," he said, "I look around me in the vast region of Hindoo mythology, I discover piety in the garb of allegory, and I see morality at every turn blended with every tale; and, as far as I can rely on my own judgment, it appears the most complete and ample system of moral allegory the world has ever produced." He admitted that there were some reprehensible customs among the Hindoos, but they were the offspring of superstition, not enjoined in the Veda, and it was the duty of Government to reform them, and to employ the brahmins in that benevolent task. The immolation of widows he represented as an act of deluded heroism, which we could not but admire while we condemned it. By the universal verdict of all classes in India,—Europeans and natives, Christians and Hindoos,—the religious mendicants are the unmitigated pests of society; but the "Bengal Officer" considered that their "pious example might become a source of great edification." He affirmed that he had never met with a people who exhibited more suavity of manners, or more mildness of character, than the Hindoos; or a happier race of beings when left to the undisturbed performance of the rites of their religion. Then apostrophising the Serampore missionaries, he exclaimed, "Cease, then, worthy missionaries, to disturb that repose that forms the happiness of so many millions of the human race. Whenever the Christian religion does as much for the lower orders of society in Europe, as that of Bramha appears to have done for those of India, I shall cheerfully vote for its establishment in that country." His pamphlet concluded with a "solemn appeal to the Honourable Company and to the empire at large, to obviate, by the most prompt and decisive interposition of their authority, the menaced consequences of that current of indignation now raised in the minds of our Indian subjects, by the impolitic, unwise, and improper conduct of these misguided missionaries."

Mr. Fuller's reply to these attacks was embodied in "An Apology for Christian Missions," published successively in three parts, and on no occasion did his controversial acumen appear to greater advantage. He asserted that the question at issue was not whether the natives of India should continue to enjoy perfect toleration, but whether that toleration should be extended to Christian missionaries. To talk of exterminating them if they attempt to convert others, was not toleration, but persecution. He maintained, by an appeal to experience, that the progress of Christianity, in any country or under any circumstances, could not be unfriendly to its political welfare. The assertions of the "Bengal Officer" regarding the moral tendency of the Hindoo system, and the exalted character of the Hindoos, he refuted with great effect by numerous quotations from writers of unquestionable authority, from Tamerlane to Sir James Mackintosh. On these two points public opinion is now so unanimous that it would be superfluous to recapitulate any of Mr. Fuller's observations. With regard to the translation which had been made of the Serampore tracts, he fearlessly asserted that the inflammatory expressions which had been the object of special censure, were not to be found in the originals, but had been foisted in by the translator to excite the fears and the indignation of the public authorities. Mr. Fuller's three apologies produced a very powerful and favourable effect on the public mind, and written as they were in a calm, dignified, and Christian spirit, contributed to stem the current of opposition. The most severe blow, however, which was inflicted on the "Bengal Officer," came from a writer whose name did not transpire, but who had passed many years in India, and was as complete master of the subject as his opponent. He examined one by one the statements of the Vindication, and demolished the assertions and theories of the writer by extracts from the Shasters themselves, and a reference to the practices of Hindooism. This able pamphlet closed with the following remarks:—"Teach the people the knowledge of the true God by an unrestrained circulation of the Holy Scriptures in their own languages, and let holy and sensible men, such as the Serampore missionaries, who exemplify in their life and conversation the truths contained in the Sacred Volume, be allowed to instruct them, . . . then the idolatrous superstition of the Hindoos, and the worldly pride and empty boast of the Mahomedans will yield, not to the force of arms,—for Christianity knows nothing of these,—but to the enlightening and heart-converting influence of that eternal truth, which, when proposed in its simplicity, God will ever accompany with the unction of His Spirit; and the truth, thus becoming mighty, must prevail." One of the most valuable and effective contributions to the cause of missions during this severe struggle, was from the pen of Lord Teignmouth, and was entitled "Considerations on the

Practicability, Policy, and Obligation of communicating to the Natives of India a Knowledge of Christianity." It was distinguished by clear and irrefragable argument, and attracted confidence by its mild and temperate tone, while it derived authority from the large experience acquired by the writer during a residence of thirty years in India, and from the high position he had occupied at the head of the Government. It concluded with these observations :—"I have no wish to limit that toleration which has hitherto been observed with respect to the religion, laws, and customs of the natives. On the contrary, I hold a perseverance in the system of toleration, not only just in itself, but as essentially necessary to facilitate the means used for their conversion. But I should consider a prohibition of the translation and circulation of our Holy Scriptures, and the recall of the missionaries, most fatal prognostics with respect to the permanency of the British dominion in India."

These publications have passed into oblivion with the discussion which gave birth to them. One attack on the Serampore missionaries alone has survived the excitement of the period, and still continues, after the lapse of more than fifty years, to attract public attention in the collected works of Sydney Smith. The letters and journals of the missionaries described the vivid impression made on their minds by the novel scenes into which they were thrown. They were written in the confidence of friendship, and were never intended to meet the public eye, but were injudiciously published in the Periodical Accounts without revision. From these papers Sydney Smith culled whatever was offensive to his taste, or tinctured with evangelical sentiment, and endeavoured to turn the extracts into ridicule by quaint headings, such as "Brother Carey's Piety at Sea; Mr. Ward admires the Captain; Mr. Ward Frightened by a Privateer; Mr. Ward feels a Regard for the Sailors; Mr. Fountain's Gratitude to Hervey." To demonstrate the danger of missionary exertions in India, every instance of opposition which the missionaries had encountered from the natives, and which they had faithfully recorded in their journals, was diligently extracted, and exhibited under the portentous titles of "Alarm of the Natives at the Preaching of the Gospel; Hatred of the Natives to the Gospel; Hatred of the Natives." To these quotations he added the remark that "it would, perhaps, be more prudent to leave the question of sending missions to India to the effect of these extracts, which appear to us to be quite decisive, both as to the danger of insurrection from the prosecution of the scheme, the utter unfitness of the persons employed in it, and the complete hopelessness of the attempt while pursued in such circumstances as now exist." Strange to say, at a time when the hostility to missions was rampant in Leadenhall Street and in the Council Chamber in Calcutta, and the Serampore missionaries were trembling for the very existence of their mission, Sydney Smith asserted that "the evangelical party had got possession of our Indian empire." The article was for the most part a mere repetition of the assertions and arguments of Major Scott Waring, but enlivened by the brilliancy of Sydney Smith's wit. If there had been any validity in his facts, or any soundness in his reasoning, it would have been the duty of England to proscribe every attempt to introduce Christian truth into India, and to rest satisfied with the conclusion that the Hindoos were destined to worship cows and monkeys for ever.

The Rev. John Styles, one of the most vigorous writers of the time in the Congregational denomination, took up the gauntlet, and published strictures on two critiques on Methodism and Missions in the *Edinburgh Review*. His pamphlet exhibited such spirit and talent that Sydney Smith deemed it advisable not to allow it to pass without a rejoinder, which appeared in the same journal, and opened with these characteristic remarks:—"In rooting out a nest of consecrated cobblers, and in bringing to light such a perilous heap of trash as we were obliged to work through in our articles on

Methodists and Missionaries, we are generally considered to have rendered a useful service to the cause of rational religion." Whether Dr. Carey's reputation has suffered any permanent injury by the appellation of "consecrated cobbler," let the present age decide. The article exhibited not only the utmost licence of satire, but an utter indifference to truth. The opinions and the conduct of the Serampore missionaries had always been marked by a singular absence of bigotry; but the reviewer did not hesitate to affirm that "the darling passion in the soul of every missionary is not to teach the great leading truths of the Christian faith, but to enforce the little paltry modification and distinction which he first taught from his own tub." Mr. Fuller and Lord Teignmouth had demanded the same toleration for the propagation of Christian truth which was freely granted to the Hindoos and Mahomedans. Sydney Smith met them by a new exposition of the doctrine of toleration:—"The missionaries complain of intolerance. A weasel might as well complain of intolerance when he is throttled for sucking eggs. Toleration for their own opinions,—toleration for their domestic worship, for their private groans and convulsions, they possess in the fullest extent; but who ever heard of toleration for intolerance? Who ever heard before men cry out that they were persecuted because they might not insult the religion, shock the feelings, irritate the passions of their fellow-creatures, and throw a whole colony into bloodshed and confusion?" But the cause of missions has survived this attack, and the character of the Serampore missionaries has only derived additional brightness from the dirt cast on it by "passion and prejudice." It is to be regretted that the splendid powers of Sydney Smith should have been applied to the object of impeding the progress of Christianity in India. The publication of the two articles on missions was a mistake which he lived to perceive, and he expressed his regret to Lord Macaulay that he had ever written them.

The controversy terminated with an article in the *Quar-*

terly Review, from the pen of Robert Southey, intended to counteract the unfair statements of the *Edinburgh Review*, and to vindicate the character of the Serampore missionaries. It concluded with the following remarks on Dr. Carey and his two associates :—"We who have thus vindicated them, are neither blind to what is erroneous in their doctrines nor ridiculous in their phraseology; but the anti-missionaries cull out from their journals and letters all that is ridiculous, sectarian, and trifling; call them fools, madmen, tinkers, Calvinists, and schismatics; and keep out of sight their love of men and their zeal for God, and their self-devotedness, their indefatigable industry, their unequalled learning. These 'low-born and low-bred mechanics' have translated the whole Bible into Bengalee, and have by this time printed it. They are printing the New Testament in the Sanscrit, Orissa, the Mahratta, the Hindoostanee, the Guzerattee, and translating it into Persic, Telinga, Carnata, Chinese, the language of the Sikhs, and the Burmese. Extraordinary as this is, it will appear still more so, when it is remembered that of these men one was originally a shoemaker, another a printer at Hull, and the third the master of a charity school at Bristol. Only fourteen years have elapsed since Thomas and Carey set foot in India, and in that time these missionaries have acquired this gift of tongues. In fourteen years, these low-born, low-bred mechanics have done more to spread the knowledge of the Scriptures among the heathen than has been accomplished or even attempted by all the world beside."

This review of the missionary controversy may be appropriately closed by an extract from a letter of Sir James Mackintosh to Mr. Charles Grant. "Mr. Twining's pamphlet is the most singular publication I have seen. He seems to think that the preaching of Christianity is generally acknowledged to be a crime so atrocious, 'as to be hated needs but to be seen.' He publishes extracts of the proceedings of a Society which proposed to circulate the Bible in India, as he would private papers proving a conspiracy to commit treason, which requires no comment, and must of themselves excite general indignation. The only measure which he could consistently propose would be the infliction of capital punishment on the crime of preaching, or embracing, Christianity in India, for almost every inferior degree of persecution is already practised by European or native anti-Christians."

CHAPTER VI.

The open hostility to missionary efforts in India was, in a great measure, allayed by the judicious conduct of the missionaries, and Dr. Carey was enabled to write to Mr. Fuller, soon after the interview with Lord Minto, that Government did not appear to entertain any hostile feeling toward them, though there were individuals in high quarters who wished to crush the Gospel. But a morbid dread of danger from "public preachings" still continued to haunt the Council Chamber. The Armenian and Portuguese attendants at the little chapel in the Chitpore road petitioned Government to grant the Serampore missionaries leave to preach to them in Bengalee, the only language in which they could receive instruction; but the request, however innocent, was positively refused. Dr. Carey and his colleagues were required to submit the manuscript of every publication to the public secretary in Calcutta, and as Government was, according to its own allegation, pledged to protect the natives from all molestation in the exercise of their religion, any animadversion on their creed or practice was supposed to come within the scope of the order; but they hoped by patience and perseverance to obtain greater freedom in time.

Happily, the restrictions were never rigidly enforced, and were suffered gradually to die out. In his last communication with the Supreme Council, the governor of Serampore had requested to be informed whether the Bible was included in the interdict, and was told in reply that the "British Government was not aware of any objection to the circulation of the Holy Scriptures in the vernacular tongues, if unaccompanied by any comments on the religions of the country." Of this privilege the missionaries freely availed themselves, and multiplied the circulation of single Gospels.

The rupture between the Courts of London and Copenhagen, in 1807, was followed by the occupation of Serampore, on the 28th of January, 1808. The loss of Danish protection, which it entailed, was naturally calculated to create apprehension in the minds of the missionaries; but Lord Minto had recovered from the panic of the Vellore mutiny, and he had, moreover, become personally acquainted with their characters and their proceedings; and they were allowed to prosecute their labours without interruption. They could not but consider it a most providential circumstance that the settlement should have been continued in the hands of the friendly Government of Denmark long enough to afford them that protection which enabled them to tide over an important and dangerous crisis. The friendly disposition of Lord Minto was still farther manifested towards them in the succeeding month of February, in reference to the cultivation of the Chinese language by Mr. Marshman and his pupils. At the annual disputations of the College of Fort-William, he introduced into his speech a very complimentary notice of the "efforts made by the pious and learned men at Serampore, who had accomplished for the future benefit, we may hope, of that immense and populous region versions in the Chinese character of the Gospels of Matthew, Mark, and Luke: throwing open that precious mine, with all its religious and moral treasures, to the largest associated population in the world."

The missionaries had about this time contemplated the establishment of a station at Chittagong, and another at Pooree, but considered it prudent to sound the disposition of Government before they embarked in the plan. Dr. Carey, therefore, called on his personal and literary friend, Mr. Colebrooke, who had recently been raised to the Council Board, and inquired whether it was likely that permission would be granted to his second son to reside at Chittagong and superintend a coffee plantation. Mr. Colebrooke replied that "there could be no objection to his son's residing in the district any more than to any other person's doing so, provided he had no view to the making of proselytes." The intended mission was therefore relinquished. It appeared still less likely that the Government would sanction the settlement of a mission on the "sacred soil" of Jugunnath, and permit "public preachings offensive to the religious persuasions of the people" at that celebrated shrine, which had now been adopted as one of the public institutions of the State. Mr. Robinson, who had been destined for the Orissa mission, was therefore sent with Mr. W. Carey beyond the British frontier to Bootan; but on entering the country they found it distracted by factions and intestine war, and were obliged to return to Serampore.

In the month of March of the present year, the missionaries were drawn into an unpleasant collision with their friend Mr. Brown. Mr. Buchanan had assumed the absolute control of the "Translation Fund," raised in the name of Dr. Carey and his associates, and intended to promote their biblical labours; and on his return to England delegated this power to Mr. Brown, without whose signature not a rupee could be drawn from the bankers. It is not necessary to remove the veil which time has drawn over this controversy, and it is now alluded to only to explain that the missionaries were reduced to such distress by this suspension of the funds on which they had depended for the prosecution of their extended labours, that Mr. Marshman was induced to canvass

Calcutta for subscriptions, and in the first instance to solicit the patronage of the Governor-General. The lively interest he had taken in the Chinese studies pursued at Serampore rendered it advisable to place the Chinese version in the foreground. The translation of the New Testament had been completed in that language; but a difficulty arose about printing it in the xylographic mode which the Chinese had used from time immemorial. At a little distance from Serampore a factory had been established for printing calicoes, from which Mr. Marshman procured some of the most skilful of the native workmen who had been employed in engraving the wooden blocks, and set them to carve Chinese characters. After repeated failures, they succeeded in producing several pages of Chinese letter-press, sufficiently distinct and legible, and which afforded every prospect of gradual improvement.

With these interesting specimens of the first attempt at Chinese printing in India, Dr. Carey and Mr. Marshman, under the advice of Dr. Leyden, waited on Lord Minto, and at the same time presented him with sheets of the other versions then passing through the press. They explained the nature of their pecuniary difficulties, and asked him to encourage a subscription for the translations. He expressed no little surprise at the extent and success of their labours, but was particularly struck with the first sheet of the Chinese New Testament. Everything connected with the *terra incognita* of China was at this time invested with a romantic interest; and this specimen of the Gospel of St. Matthew, translated into that inaccessible language by one who had never been in the country, and engraved by natives of India, appeared to him a singular instance of spirit and perseverance. But when pressed regarding the proposed subscription list, he desired a few days for consideration; and on their waiting on him a week after, assured them, in the most friendly spirit, that if he could separate his private from his public character he would at once place his name on the list; but it did not appear judicious that the head of the Government should take the lead in an undertaking which might not meet the approval of the Court of Directors. Mr. Marshman passed the evening in discussing the question with Dr. Leyden, who was of opinion that the public functionaries would be deterred by the same consideration from supporting the Translation Fund. But he felt assured that if a proposal for publishing the translation which Mr. Marshman had made of the works of Confucius were laid before the public, it would receive the most liberal encouragement, and Mr. Marshman and his colleagues would be furnished with an early supply of funds. The prospectus of an English version of Confucius was accordingly drawn up without delay, and submitted to Lord Minto, who signified his approbation of it by a liberal subscription for ten copies in a complimentary letter, which served to stimulate the liberality of the public. Mr. Marshman waited in person on every gentleman of eminence in Calcutta, and obtained subscriptions of the value of £2,000, which were intended collaterally to aid the printing of the Scriptures, for which he also received direct contributions to the extent of £300.

The report of the violent proceedings of the Government of Calcutta in August and September, 1807, which have been already related, reached England when the storm raised by the pamphlets of Mr. Twining, Major Scott Waring, and the "Bengal Officer," had scarcely subsided, and the minds of Mr. Fuller and the friends of the mission were filled with the most gloomy forebodings. Mr. Charles Grant was discouraged to find that the tracts were so little able to bear scrutiny, and was mortified at "being obliged, as chairman of the Court of Directors, to lay these communications before its members, with several of whom he had pleaded on behalf of the mission with all his might." "If these translations," he remarked, "are just, the good men have been greatly wanting in prudence. I have a difficult battle to fight, standing on the best ground, but am sadly weakened and hampered when the ground will not support me." Even

Mr. Fuller remarked that if the translations were correct he must give up his friends, as utterly unfit for their stations, and scarcely worthy of toleration. In justice to the missionaries, however, it is necessary to state that the translations were made in a spirit of unscrupulous hostility to them and to their cause; that they were grossly and wantonly incorrect, and that with the solitary exception of the epithet applied to the Prophet, there was not a single expression which was not susceptible of a different and unexceptionable signification. If the Government in Calcutta had not been acting under the influence of panic and prejudice, the unfairness of entering on a crusade against those who had issued the tracts, without giving them an opportunity of offering any explanation of them, and of vindicating their characters, would have been at once apparent. Contrary to established precedent, the fidelity of the translations made for Government was not authenticated by the name of the translator; and the missionaries were condemned unheard.

In the intercourse with Mr. Grant which arose out of these transactions, he stated to Mr. Fuller, that with a prudent, still, and quiet mode of procedure, the missionaries were likely to hold their ground, and to obtain more liberty by degrees. To Mr. Fuller's inquiry whether more missionaries would be allowed to proceed to India, he replied emphatically, None. But what, inquired Mr. Fuller, would be the consequence of sending them out by way of America? Mr. Grant replied they would be sent back immediately, and the good understanding which seemed for the time to exist between the missionaries and the Government would be seriously endangered, "for you have no longer a Danish Serampore to send them to." In his letter to Serampore, narrating this conversation, Mr. Fuller remarked, "It may be that you should go on without a toleration, that the hand of God in preserving the bush on fire from being consumed may be more apparent. . . . Of late, some have said, the Baptists mean well, but they have no security. True, and by our want of strength and security, if we properly feel our dependence on God, we may be more likely to pray and succeed. God has fixed you in a post of eminence and difficulty, but hitherto He has helped you. It may be His will that we should have no legal security granted us in India, that it may appear to be, not by might, nor by power, but by His own Spirit. . . . I rejoice in all your literary undertakings, as they afford not only the means of spreading the word of truth, but a shelter to you. Had you been a company of illiterate men, humanly speaking, you must ere now have been crushed. God gave Daniel and his companions wisdom for a protection."

In the course of this year Dr. Carey took for his second wife Miss Charlotte Rhumohr, who had visited Serampore for the benefit of her health about the time when the mission was established, and had since continued to reside there. She lived on a footing of the most friendly intercourse with the missionaries, in whose labours she took a lively interest. She was a member of the patrician family of Ahlfeldt, in the duchy of Schleswic, and her sister was married to Count Wornstedt, chamberlain of the King of Denmark. She was about the same age with Dr. Carey, diminutive in stature, and somewhat deformed in figure; but whatever was wanting in symmetry of form was compensated by the endowments of the mind. She had received that complete and finished education given to families of distinction on the Continent, and she conversed with equal fluency in French, German, Danish, and English. She was not less distinguished by deep piety, and an ardent desire for the spread of Christian truth in India. She was eminently fitted for the companion of a man like Dr. Carey, and their happy union enabled him to enjoy that bracing relaxation in the conversation of his accomplished wife to which he had hitherto been a stranger.

It has been stated in a previous chapter, that at the time when the missionaries sought an asylum in Serampore, in 1799, Colonel Bie, the governor, offered, as an additional inducement to them to settle in it, to make over to them the church he was about to erect. It was completed immediately before the second capture of the town. It was a neat and simple edifice, without any architectural pretensions, built in the style of Lutheran churches, with the rudiments of an altar, but altogether deficient in the merit of ornamentation. The spire, which was surmounted with a gilt cross, was visible for many miles, and gave an air of Christian civilization to the scenery around, amidst its heathen associations. It was erected by subscription, to which Lord Wellesley, on the part of the Company, subscribed £800, perhaps as much from the love of the picturesque, as from the impulse of religious feeling, as he was reported to have accompanied the contribution with the remark that nothing was wanting to the park he had laid out across the river but the view of a distant spire. On the occupation of the town by the English Government, the church was made over to the missionaries, but not without the solemn injunction that "they were to confine themselves to the performance of divine service in the usual manner, and carefully to abstain from all discourses of a nature to offend the religious prejudices of the natives." In that edifice Dr. Carey and his two associates, and their successors, Mr. Mack, Dr. Leechman, and Mr. Denham, continued to preach the vital doctrines of Christian truth for forty-five years.

During this year the difficulty of devising a plan for the management of the mission, which should secure harmony and promote efficiency, became a source of great depression. It was scarcely reasonable to expect that ten men, with the usual diversities of temper, the greater number of whom were married, should be able to live and act together without dissension, in an undertaking based on a rigid and extraordinary self-denial, though enforced by the example as well as the authority of those who had founded and presided over the establishment. The control necessarily exercised by the three senior missionaries was irksome to their junior associates, and gave rise to contentions which proved a greater obstacle to success than even the opposition of Government. They had fallen into the error of creating a system which demanded Moravian self-denial, without conceding Moravian equality. They did not apparently perceive that the individual enthusiasm which could alone sustain such self-denial was destroyed by the principle of submission to superior authority. To extinguish discord, Dr. Carey and his two colleagues proposed that the management of the mission should be vested in a body elected by the majority of the missionaries. Happily, the committee in England, acting under the guidance of Mr. Fuller, refused to ratify this democratic constitution, which would probably have wrecked the mission in a twelvemonth. The Society resolved to retain in their own hands the power of nominating those who were to be intrusted with the expenditure of their funds; and with this authority they invested Dr. Carey, Mr. Marshman, and Mr. Ward, for the period of their lives. But the severe restrictions which the economy established at Serampore imposed on individual freedom continued to prove a fertile source of discontent, and the junior missionaries revolted against the authority of the seniors, who resolved to adopt the only plan likely to cure these disorders, and to establish distinct missionary stations, if possible, within the British territories.

The number of missionaries embraced in this plan was seven, and it was proposed to fix the allowance at the out-stations for man and wife at 70 rupees a month, with an addition of 10 rupees for the first child, and seven for every successive addition to the family. Seven missionaries on this scale would cost £1,000 a year. Of the sum thus allotted for each missionary family, 10 rupees a month were to be appropriated as a personal allowance, and a detailed account of the expenditure of the remainder was to be sent to Serampore to be transmitted to the Society. Any surplus, however, which might remain out of this very scanty provision, was not to be considered individual property, because "this principle, by encouraging a sordid concern for petty savings, would eat out every missionary feeling." The children were to be educated free of all expense to the parents, at Serampore, where an asylum and a suitable allowance was to be provided for the widow and the orphan. Such was the foundation on which Dr. Carey and his two colleagues proposed to build up the missionary edifice, and they expected to see a hundred stations established on this principle. It was a noble and self-denying project, but it supposed the existence of a magnanimous devotedness to the cause of missions in each individual case which was not to be expected in the ordinary course of human events.

In the autumn of the present year, Mr. Fuller, who had been in the habit of making a triennial visit to Scotland, to foster the spirit of missionary zeal, as well as to collect funds for the mission, made a vigorous effort to raise subscriptions for the translations. To pave his way, a memoir on the subject drawn up by Mr. Marshman was reprinted on its arrival, and widely circulated in Scotland, chiefly through the agency of Dr. Stuart, of Dunearn, one of the most cordial friends of the mission and the missionaries. It produced a very unexpected and extraordinary effect in the country. "Money," said Mr. Fuller, "poured in like rain in a thunder-storm. Those who had been disputing for years about discipline, weekly communion, and kindred matters, seemed half ashamed of their differences. One of them said to me: What little things are we employed about compared with this! Thousands flocked to hear me, and hundreds went away for want of room." Mr. Fuller returned to Kettering, after having travelled twelve hundred miles and preached forty-two sermons, with contributions to the extent of £2,000.

The desire which Dr. Carey and his colleagues had long felt of possessing a place of worship in Calcutta for English and native congregations, was gratified on the 1st of January, 1809, by the opening of the chapel in the Bow bazar. It was a spacious and lofty building, with a light and elegant gallery on three sides and a noble portico at the front entrance, and did much credit to the taste of the architect, Mr. Rolt. It was the third Protestant and the first Dissenting edifice for the services of religion in the metropolis. The entire cost, including the purchase of the ground, amounted to £3,200, of which £1,700 were raised by subscriptions, and the remainder advanced by the Serampore missionaries from their own funds. During this year another attempt was made by Mr. Robinson to penetrate Bootan and establish a mission; but as the country was still in a very disturbed state he took up his residence at a frontier town, where he was hospitably entertained by the Bootan officer in charge of it. But before he had completed the erection of his house he was attacked with jungle fever, and obliged to return to Serampore, after which the project was abandoned. The mission to Burmah, however, presented a more favourable aspect. Mr. Felix Carey, who had been trained up under his father's eye, was master of the Sanscrit language, and familiar with the principles of Oriental philology. He discovered, to his delight, that the Pali, the classical language of the country and the parent of the vernacular tongue, was a variety of the Sanscrit. His progress in the Burmese was thus facilitated, and, with the aid of a pundit, he prepared the outline of a grammar, and made a rough beginning with the translation of the New Testament. The affinity which had been found to exist of the Pali and Sanscrit served to stimulate the ardour of Dr. Carey for the translation of the Bible into the languages of the East. "This circumstance," he writes, "will, I suspect, be of incalculable advantage to the translation of the Scriptures into all the languages spoken to the east of Bengal, except the Chinese, as the Pali is the learned language, if I am not mistaken, of Ava, Aracan, Pegu, Siam, Cambodia, and several other countries where the religion of Boodh prevails. The Sanscrit version will generally be understood by the learned men whom we must employ."

Dr. Carey had enjoyed the benefit of unbroken health for nearly ten years at Serampore, and it was to be attributed, under the blessing of God, to his regular and temperate habits, not less than to the animating character of his occupations, which, as he observed, left him no leisure to be ill. He rose early, and immediately proceeded to his garden, where he generally passed an hour or two among his plants, of which he had made the largest collection in any private establishment in India. The garden was also the place of his devotional meditations, and the day, thus opened amidst the most tranquillising associations, was filled up with unremitted labours in the mission and the translations. In the month of July he completed the publication of the Bengalee Bible, and the next day he was seized with a fever, which brought him rapidly to the brink of the grave. He was delirious, at intervals, for several days, and his friends began to tremble for his life; but the fever was at length subdued, and he gradually recovered his strength. During his illness, his place in the College of Fort-William was supplied by Mr. Marshman, who delivered lectures to the students in Bengalee and Sanscrit. This interruption of his labours appeared, however, only to give additional vigour to his missionary zeal. In the letter to Mr. Fuller which mentioned his recovery, he alluded to the circumstance of his having reached the age of forty-eight, and then took a review of the state of Asia, and urged the necessity of a mission to Siam, to Pegu, to Aracan, to Nepaul, and Assam, to all the countries lying on the borders of the British dominions; but to the Company's territories he made no reference, as they appeared to be hermetically sealed against all missionary efforts by the policy of Leadenhall Street.

It was during the present year that the missionaries began to carry out the design of employing in the missionary field young men, born and educated in the country, of European habits, who were found to possess zeal and activity. From the period of their settlement at Serampore, they had always kept in view the necessity of domesticating Christianity in India, and providing for the propagation of it without depending on aid from Europe. Mr. Ward happily expressed their views on this subject when he remarked that for the army of labourers to be employed in assailing the bulwarks of Hindooism, they ought to look to England only for a few superior officers, and endeavour to raise the non-commissioned officers and rank and file in India itself. This plan was now more particularly enforced on them by the determination of the home authorities to prevent any accession to the number of European missionaries in India. The labourers whom they thus obtained in the country were not liable to expulsion for want of a licence, and they could travel about the country without a passport. They might not in every case possess European energy of character, but this deficiency was in some measure compensated by their thorough knowledge of the vernacular tongue, and of the habits and feelings and sentiments of the natives. Two such men were at this time selected for missionary work from the members of the church in Calcutta, Mr. Carapeit Aratoon, and Mr. John Peter. The former was stationed in Jessore, where a considerable number had embraced Christianity; and the latter on the borders of Orissa, that he might embrace opportunities of sending the Gospel into that province.

At the close of 1809 the missionaries transmitted to the Society a report of progress during the ten years of their settlement at Serampore. The whole Bible had been printed off in Bengalee in five volumes, as well as a third and improved version of the New Testament. They had completed the printing of the New Testament and the Psalms in Oriya. The Sanscrit New Testament had been finished at press, and the Pentateuch begun. The translation of the New Testament in the Teloogoo and Punjabee had also commenced. An edition of the Gospels in Hindoostanee had been executed, and much progress made in the Chinese version. With the skilful native workmen whom they had trained, they had completed four founts of native characters, one of which, the Deva-nagree, consisted of seven hundred punches, and had cost only £100, instead of £700, as demanded by the London founders. In the course of ten years, the difference between the cost of their foundry and that of preparing founts in London fell little short of £2,000. In the review of missionary labours for the previous ten years, they remarked that amidst all the opposition of Government, they had succeeded in establishing four missionary stations in Bengal, to send a missionary to Patna and Rangoon, and to fix one on the confines of Orissa. The number of members in church-fellowship exceeded two hundred, while in Calcutta they had collected a large church and congregation, European and native. So great had been their exertions in India as almost to cast the agency of the Society in England into the shade. But they felt that they could never sufficiently appreciate the value of Mr. Fuller's co-operation. He was the life and soul of the cause at home; his indefatigable zeal served to keep alive the interest of the public; his powerful intellect and undaunted spirit baffled all opposition; and his judicious and affectionate counsels diffused animation through the whole system. Seldom has there been an instance of such mutual confidence as that which existed between him and the missionaries. "God has done great things," says the review, "not only by us, but through you. We can never separate ourselves from you for a moment in thinking what He has done for the Baptist mission in India."

The labours of Dr. Carey and his associates in Calcutta, had brought under their notice the condition of hundreds of Christian children, who were growing up in vice and ignorance. They were the remote descendants of European parents and native mothers, chiefly of Portuguese extraction. They were in the lowest stage of social depression and poverty, having some European appearance to maintain often on three or four shillings a week, with a family of four or five children. They reflected nothing but disgrace on the

Christian name which they bore, and were regarded by the Europeans with disdain, and by the natives with contempt. It was for these destitute children that it was now determined to provide the means of instruction. Mr. Marshman took the lead in this undertaking, and the "Benevolent Institution," as the school was designated, owed its rise and prosperity to his exertions. He preached a sermon on its behalf on Christmas-day, after which a collection was made, which, however, did not exceed £30; but with this inadequate sum a house was engaged in the centre of the Portuguese population, and the school commenced. One of its principal objects was to bring the poor children under the influence of the Gospel. The Scriptures were therefore to be read daily and expounded, but no particular creed was to be enforced on the pupils; and those of Roman Catholic parentage were left at liberty to accompany their friends to their own chapels. Dr. Leyden entered heartily into the plan, and assured Mr. Marshman that it would receive every encouragement from Lord Minto; but, before he could attend to the proposal, he was obliged to proceed to Madras to quell a mutiny of the European officers, created by the mismanagement of the Governor, Sir George Barlow, for which he was deposed from the Government. The issue of the prospectus was therefore postponed, and the institution maintained from the donations privately contributed by the friends of religion. The singular popularity it acquired in the first year of its existence was owing to the tact and energy of the master, Mr. Leonard, an Irish soldier, who had served at the capture of Seringapatam, and combined the firmness of military discipline with the warmth of Christian zeal.

During the year 1810, the missionaries were cheered by indications of a more favourable feeling towards their undertaking on the part of Government. This was to be attributed, in part, to their own conciliatory demeanour, and also to the rebuke of the harsh proceedings of the Council in

1807, conveyed in the Court's letter, to which we have alluded. The London Missionary Society had sent Mr. Lee to labour at Vizagapatam; and, to the surprise of Mr. Brown, Dr. Carey, and even Mr. Udny, the Supreme Government granted him permission to reside there. The missionaries at Serampore were not backward to take advantage of this turn of tide. The publication of the Gospels in the Punjabee language had recently been completed, and they were anxious that it should be distributed among the Sikhs. Mr. Chamberlain's natural spirit of enterprise, and his aptitude for the acquisition of languages, induced him to undertake this mission; and the town of Saharempore, on the confines of the British and Sikh territories, was fixed on for this future station. An official application was made to the Governor-General in Council, in September, for permission to send two missionaries to this town to improve the translation of the Scriptures in the Punjabee and Hindoostanee languages. The request was declined, but only on the ground that it was considered imprudent, under existing political circumstances, to allow any Europeans not connected with the public service to settle on the frontier. Here was no allusion to the missionaries being without a licence, or to the pledge of Government to protect the natives from molestation in the exercise of their religion, or to the preservation of the national faith, or to any other of the stereotyped objections to missions. On the receipt of this reply, Mr. Marshman had a private interview with Lord Minto on the subject, and was informed that there would be no objection to the establishment of a mission at Agra or Delhi, but advised that the application should simply be for leave to proceed to either of these places, without any allusion to the object. The Supreme Council acceded to the request; but instead of an official communication, which must have been placed on record, and which might have attracted notice in Leadenhall Street, a simple note was sent to Mr. Chamberlain, informing him that his passport was ready for delivery on the payment of the usual fees. This relaxation of the hostility of Government afforded abundant cause for thankfulness. But it was impossible for the missionaries, who had devoted heart and soul and life to this sacred cause, not to feel that the treatment they had received from a British and a Christian government was such as ought not to have been inflicted on them; and Mr. Ward records the circumstance with this pungent remark:—"Now we shall be tolerated like toads, and not hunted down like wild beasts."

In one of his letters of the present year to Mr. Fuller, Dr. Carey alludes in these terms to himself and his colleagues: "When I first entered on the translation of the Scriptures into the Bengalee language, I thought that if ever I should live to see it completed, I should say with Simeon, 'Lord, now lettest thou thy servant depart in peace, according to thy word;' but He has preserved me not only to see the version finished, but has given me an opportunity of making many corrections in succeeding editions, in various parts of it, and has also preserved me to see portions of the Bible printed in the Oriya, Sanscrit, Hindoostanee, Mahratta, Carnata, Teloogoo, and Punjabee, the Gospel of Matthew in Chinese, and a beginning in Burmese." And he then adds, with his characteristic humility, "I have often thought that the work must be obstructed by me, and that the God who aboundeth in all wisdom and prudence, in the dispensations of His grace, could not give a blessing to the labours of such a one as I am." He then alludes to his natural backwardness for spiritual conversation, a perpetual vagrancy of mind, and a great prevalence of unsanctified affections. "I have for years been obliged to drag myself on, to subject myself to rules, to impose the day's work on myself, and, after all, to sit down in confusion at my indolence and inertness. I often compare myself with my brethren Marshman and Ward. The first is all eagerness for the work. Often have I seen him when we have been walking together, eye a group of persons, as a hawk looks at his prey, and go up to them with a resolution to try the utmost effort of Gospel reasons on them. In point of zeal, he is Luther; I am Erasmus. Brother Ward has such a facility of addressing spiritual things to the heart, and his thoughts run so naturally in that channel, that he fixes the minds of all who hear him on what he says; while I, after making repeated efforts, can scarcely get out a few dry sentences, and should I meet with a rebuff at the beginning, sit like a silly mute, and scarcely say anything at all."

While Mr. Marshman was thus zealously employed in prosecuting his missionary labours, he was happy to avail himself of the opportunity of literary intercourse with Dr. Leyden and other friends in Calcutta. Though there was no harmony between the religious views of Dr. Leyden and Mr. Marshman, they felt a common interest in the pursuits of literature, more particularly in the department of Eastern philology. About the beginning of 1810 a very agreeable addition was made to their circle, by the arrival of Mr. Thomas Manning in Calcutta. After winning honours at Cambridge he had taken a fancy to the Chinese language, and devoted his attention to the cultivation of it. He was the friend and associate of Charles Lamb, some of the most interesting of whose letters were addressed to his Chinese mandarin. He was anxious to establish himself in China to prosecute his studies, and endeavoured to enter it by way of Macao, but, being baffled in the attempt, came round to Bengal to make an effort to penetrate it through Tibet. To facilitate the object of passing for a Tartar, he assumed the Chinese costume, the wooden shoes, the buttoned cap, and the long tail, and cultivated a black beard, which gave additional dignity to his very expressive countenance. On his arrival in Calcutta he sought the acquaintance of the only man who felt a kindred interest in the pursuits of Chinese literature. In the present year, Mr., afterwards Sir Stamford Raffles, then secretary to the government of Penang, came up to Calcutta, at the request of Lord Minto, to confer with him on the expedition to Java. In the Eastern Archipelago he had made the acquaintance of Dr. Leyden, who introduced him to Mr. Marshman. These friends were in the habit of supping together at Dr. Leyden's, and their sitting was often prolonged to midnight. It was the most intellectual coterie in Calcutta. Leyden was a literary colossus, and, with all his vanity,—which was egregious,—a man of undoubted genius. Manning was the most accomplished scholar in India; while Raffles was without a rival in his knowledge of the people and the literature of the Eastern Archipelago. Whatever might be the differences of religious opinion between them, they fully appreciated Mr. Marshman's zeal and earnestness in the cause of religious benevolence, as well as his inexhaustible stores of knowledge; and, on his part, he derived vigour and animation from these literary discussions, in which he found he could take part without any compromise of Christian principle or intrepidity.

In the prosecution of his Chinese studies at this period, Mr. Marshman obtained no little assistance and encouragement from Father Rodrigues, a Roman Catholic missionary, who had passed ten years at Pekin, and was intimately acquainted with the written and colloquial language of China. He manifested that absence of religious antagonism, and that liberality of feeling, which characterised the Roman Catholic missionaries in the East at this period, and he found a corresponding spirit of liberality at Serampore. He was ignorant of English, but spoke and wrote Latin with great fluency; and Mr. Marshman opened a correspondence with him in that language. In noticing these communications to Dr. Ryland, Mr. Marshman remarked: "It is a matter of considerable value, to any young man who may come eastward on missionary work, to acquire a facility of writing Latin correctly; and indeed of speaking it, if he has an opportunity. The Romish missionaries are scattered in almost all parts of the East, and it may often be of service to correspond with them, for which Latin is the appropriate medium. After seeing Manning and Rodrigues, I seem as though I was just beginning my career in Chinese, so great is the pleasure of present study and future anticipation."

It was at this time that Mr. Marshman published the first volume of his English translation of the works of Confucius, with a preliminary dissertation on the language of China. Considering the disadvantages under which it was accomplished, without any of those facilities for the cultivation of the language which are to be obtained in the country itself, it is a monument of literary enterprise, and well merited the hearty encomium passed on it by Lord Minto in his annual address to the students of the College. "He was anxious," he said, "to render the homage which appears due to this laudable effort of modest genius and labour. What Mr. Marshman has already accomplished would have done honour to institutions fostered by all the aids of munificence and power; to have risen in the shade, *ipsi suis pallens opibus*, renders his successful labours only the more worthy of admiration." After the last sheet had passed through the press, Mr. Marshman was enabled to obtain a copy of the Latin translation of Confucius made by the Jesuit fathers, and printed at Paris in 1686. He considered it just, therefore, to add a postscript to his work before it was circulated, pointing out the salient points of difference in the two versions, which, however, were few in number and of little importance.

Towards the close of the present year, Mr. Ward published the first edition of his work on the "History, Literature, and Mythology of the Hindoos, including a minute description of their Manners and Customs, and Translations from their principal works," for which he had been collecting materials since his arrival in the country. The historical sketch, compiled chiefly from treatises written by natives themselves then living, has been superseded by subsequent and more elaborate researches. The least satisfactory portion of the work was that which referred to the different schools of Hindoo philosophy. Since its publication, more profound Orientalists have dived deeply into the mine of Sanscrit literature, and have been able to supply the public with a more ample and accurate exposition of these philosophical doctrines. The most valuable chapters of it were those which treated of the existing divisions of caste, sacerdotal and secular —of their distinguishing customs, duties, and employments —of the manners and observances of the various classes of society—their domestic occupations and habits—the current of their thoughts exemplified in their conversation and correspondence—and the ceremonies practised on the occasions of births, marriages, and deaths. The value of this rich store of information, which exhibits an unexampled acquaintance with the interior economy of native society, has not been diminished by fifty years of subsequent investigation, and the work continues to maintain its character as the most complete and accurate record yet published on these topics. Objections have been raised to the dark colours in which Mr. Ward has depicted the native character; and his remarks on the perfidy, falsehood, and cruelty resulting from the influence of Hindooism have been said to be exaggerated; but the atrocities exhibited in the mutiny of 1857 have fully corroborated his statements, and vindicated the accuracy of his portraiture.

At the beginning of 1811, an Auxiliary Bible Society was formed in Calcutta. It was a gratifying token of the improvement of religious feeling in and around the metropolis, where, thirteen years before, there had been a larger attendance on Sunday at the race-course than in the Christian sanctuary. The subscriptions amounted to £3,500. The committee included men of different creeds,—Protestant, Roman Catholic, and Armenian. Mr. Harington, the judge of the chief native court, and Mr. Edmonstone, the public secretary, were among its vice-presidents. The acceptance of this office in a society for the diffusion of Christian truth, by men of such high standing in the service of the Company, combined with the recent permission to establish a missionary station at Agra, indicated no little mitigation of the hostility of Government to missions; but, as Mr. Ward observed, "the sky was still lowering, notwithstanding an occasional fine day." The freedom they enjoyed was liable to be interrupted whenever any new panic seized the Council Board, or any officious functionary chose to denounce them to Government as being without a licence. As the period approached, therefore, for the Charter discussions, they redoubled their importunity with Mr. Fuller not to allow the golden opportunity to be lost of securing a legal toleration for missionaries in India.

Lord Minto returned to Calcutta, after having suppressed the mutiny of the European officers at Madras; and Mr. Marshman again brought up the question of the Benevolent Institution with Dr. Leyden, who promised to introduce it to his notice. But differences arose regarding the management of it. Dr. Leyden desired to vest it in men who were not likely to look beyond the intellectual progress of the scholars; while Mr. Marshman was determined to make it the instrument of moral and religious culture, and refused to part with the nomination of the teachers. Dr. Leyden considered this resolution as evincing a desire to keep the institution in their own party. "We care nothing for party in this business," replied Mr. Marshman. "I would not for a moment object to a Pædobaptist teacher, but he must be a good man; no one else will care a jot for the souls of the children." And he assured him that from this point they would never swerve, whether he recommended the plan to Lord Minto or not. Dr. Leyden, in bringing the institution before him, did not fail to notice what he termed the "silly and unreasonable determination" of Mr. Marshman; but Lord Minto at once disposed of it by saying that an honest Baptist would be as efficient a teacher as one of any other denomination. He promised to annex a few lines to the prospectus to indicate his approval of it; but his mind was unhappily diverted from it in the bustle of preparations for the expedition to Java, which he had undertaken in obedience to the commands of the home authorities. Dr. Leyden accompanied him to the island, and he and Mr. Marshman, so intimately associated in the congenial pursuits of literature, while so antagonistic in their religious views, never met again. Three weeks after the troops landed, Dr. Leyden imprudently ventured into a library, rich in Oriental treasures, which had not been ventilated for some time, and was at once struck down with malaria, which, notwithstanding the strength of his constitution, carried him to his grave in three days, at the early age of thirty-six.

But the institution was by this time sinking under the weight of a heavy debt; the monthly subscriptions had dwindled down to 45 rupees, while the expenditure had risen to more than 300; and it became necessary to lose no time in appealing to the public for aid. Mr. Marshman drew up a concise statement of the object of the school, and the progress which had been made in carrying it out. He stated very distinctly that it was not intended as a rival, but as an auxiliary of the Free School, the only kindred institution in Calcutta, inasmuch as it received none but day scholars, while the older establishment boarded as well as educated the children, and could therefore provide accommodation for only a limited number. Suddenly there appeared on the scene a violent opponent in the person of the Rev. Dr. Jas. Ward, the junior Presidency chaplain, who came forward and denounced an educational institution unconnected with the Church of England, and promoted by schismatics. This was the first instance since the foundation of Calcutta of any controversy connected with the differences of Church and Dissent. These sectarian distinctions had never been recognised in India, where the religious animosities of England were happily unknown. Indeed, in a country where a gentleman's cook was generally a Bouddist or a Roman Catholic, and his domestics either Mahomedans or Hindoos, there was little scope for the development of Church principles. Dr. Ward's protest fell on the ears of men unaccustomed to such accents. His personal demeanour had been marked by much ecclesiastical assumption; and he was held in no estimation either by his own clerical brethren or by the laity. His denunciation of the missionaries as Nonconformists was therefore received by the community with contemptuous indifference. Mr. Marshman replied to his attack, and dwelt on the necessity of some such institution, and demonstrated that it was impossible there could be any clashing of interests between it and the Free School, as the object of one was to pick up the ragged children wandering through the streets of Calcutta, for whom the other could not find room, and bring them under Christian instruction and discipline. The reply was revised by Mr. Brown, and received the cordial approbation of Mr. Thomason, the evangelical chaplain of the Old Church in Calcutta. Dr. Ward, finding that his first address had made no impression on the public, enlisted the aid of the church-wardens of St. John's Church, who were *ex-officio* governors of the Free School, and issued a paper under their joint signature, entreating the public not to desert an institution connected with the Church of England—which had an endowed income of £4,000 a year—for one projected by sectaries; but neither did this appeal advance his purpose nor check the tide of subscriptions. Finding he could make no way even with this assistance, he proceeded to address the Government, and officially requested the suppression of the Benevolent Institution; but the secretary was desired to inform him that the Supreme Council declined to interfere in such matters. Nothing could have been more opportune for the institution than this attempt to crush it, for it brought in £500 in the course of a few days, and dispelled all fears regarding its support. The number of scholars was increased to more than two hundred; and the encouragement received for several succeeding years emboldened the missionaries to purchase a piece of ground in the heart of the city, and erect a spacious school-room at an expense of £1,200.

One farther effort was made in this year to establish a mission in Bootan. Accompanied by a young man of the name of Cornish, who had offered himself as a missionary, Mr. Robinson returned to his station, but in a few months he and his family were prostrated by a jungle fever, under which his wife sunk into the grave. In the beginning of January his house was attacked by a gang of dacoits, who murdered two of his servants and inflicted several severe wounds on him and his companion. They returned at once to Serampore. Mr. Raffles, before proceeding with Lord Minto on the Java expedition, had urged Mr. Marshman to send a missionary to the island, if it should fall to the British arms, and Mr. Robinson was anxious to avail himself of this opening. Mr. Cornish quitted the mission, and returned to secular employment, with the full concurrence of the senior missionaries, who perceived that he had little heart in the work, and no aptitude for it. Mr. Marshman, writing on this subject to Mr. Fuller, remarked that he could conceive nothing more fatal to the prospects of missions than to allow the occupation of a missionary to be regarded simply as a profession, and that all those who were not found on trial to possess the most ardent zeal for the work should be advised at once to relinquish it. Mr. Ward also wrote about the same time, "In our work, half the Dissenting ministers in England, who merely preach twice or thrice a week, when people come to hear the Word, would be of little use. A man who shall do good here must be incessantly on his legs, or in his saddle, or in his boat. In the hands of a mere domesticated man, who prays at home but never goes out into the highways and ditches, things die a natural death. Men must go out a fishing; the fish will never leave their natural element and walk into their nets; and they must be patient too, though they toil all night and catch nothing."

During the year 1811, the church at Serampore returned to the practice of strict communion, after having for a period of four years followed the more liberal and generous rule of communion at the Lord's table with those Christian friends and missionary brethren who did not coincide in their views on Christian baptism. This retrograde movement was the result of a long and controversial correspondence with Mr. Fuller. The sentiments of Mr. Ward, however, remained unchanged, but with his habitual sweetness of disposition he offered no opposition to the change, and refused to divide the church on this question, simply stipulating that those who were excluded by this rule—the first of whom was an Independent missionary, after he had occupied the pulpit—should be distinctly informed that he was no party to it. But this irreconcilable difference of opinion was never allowed to create any alienation of feeling, or to interrupt the harmony of their mutual co-operation in the missionary cause. Mr. Fuller and Dr. Ryland held very strong and opposite views on this question, which unhappily they did not see fit to exclude from their correspondence with Serampore, and it was with difficulty that their friends there were able to steer between the Scylla and Charybdis of close and open communion. When they adopted the latter course, Mr. Fuller upbraided them with their disregard of a positive ordinance. When they closed the communion-table against all but Baptists, Dr. Ryland reproached them with setting up a Baptist caste. It is a lamentable token of the weakness of human nature that a question of such comparative insignificance should have been allowed to embitter the intercourse of men engaged in an undertaking which ought to have extinguished every minor consideration.

The system of rigid economy which the three senior missionaries adopted themselves, and enforced on others, gave rise to grievous recriminations; and complaints were constantly poured into the ear of the committee at home, the memory of which it is not necessary to revive. The system, though most conscientiously adopted, was altogether erroneous, and the restraints imposed on the junior missionaries were unnatural and irritating. Their hostility was directed more particularly against Mr. Marshman, and Dr. Carey felt himself bound to transmit to Mr. Fuller an ample vindication of his colleague, which is useful as furnishing a valuable delineation of his character by one who was in daily intercourse with him:—"I believe his natural make may in some measure be the occasion of this hostile feeling. He is a man whose whole heart is in the mission, and who may be considered as the soul and life of it. He is ardent, nay sanguine, exceedingly tenacious of any idea which strikes him as right or important. His labours are excessive; his body scarcely susceptible of fatigue; his religious feelings strong; his jealousy for God great; his regard for the feelings of others very little when the cause of God is in question. His memory is uncommonly retentive; his reading has been and still is extensive and general. In short, his activity reproaches the indolence of some; his acquirements reproach their ignorance; and his unaccommodating mind frequently excites sentiments of resentment and dislike." Mr. Marshman's literary labours had attracted much attention in America, and, in the month of June, 1811, he was honoured with the diploma of Doctor of Divinity from Brown University.

In the month of March, 1812, the missionaries experienced the greatest calamity they had yet sustained, which for a time suspended their operations, and put their zeal and perseverance to the severest test. During the night of the 11th the printing-office was totally consumed by fire, and the labour of twelve years destroyed in a few hours. The office was more fully stocked than it had been at any former period. It contained fourteen founts in the Eastern languages, a large supply of English type, and twelve hundred reams of paper recently received from home. The fire was discovered at six in the evening, and the whole building, a hundred feet in length and forty-five feet wide, was quickly filled with a dense and suffocating smoke. A fire-engine was unknown in India, and an attempt was therefore made to stifle the flames by closing the doors and windows, while the roof was opened over the seat of the fire, in the hope of extinguishing it by a stream of water from above. After the lapse of several hours, during which these efforts gave some prospect of success, an injudicious friend opened one of the windows with the view of saving some of the property, but the current of air which was thus introduced speedily set the building in a blaze. By eleven at night the flames had burst forth from every window, and at midnight the roof fell in with a crash, and a steady column of fire rose to the sky like the flame of a candle. After the conflagration became complete, the members of the mission family seated themselves in front of the office, contemplating this scene of desolation with "a feeling of solemn serenity," as Dr. Marshman records, "which seemed to pervade and strengthen every heart." The value of the property was estimated at £7,000, which was a total loss to the mission, as there was no fire insurance office in India at the time. But the loss of numerous copies of the Scriptures, and of valuable manuscripts, was considered to outweigh even the pecuniary damage.

Early the next morning Dr. Marshman went down to Calcutta to communicate the dismal tidings to Dr. Carey, who was so staggered by the blow as to be unable for a time to utter a word. They then called on Mr. Thomason, who burst into tears at the intelligence. After making inquiries regarding a supply of types, of which, however, there was no stock in Calcutta, they returned to Serampore in the evening, and found to their inexpressible delight that Mr. Ward, while employed in clearing the wreck, had discovered the punches and matrices uninjured. There was but one punch cutter in the country, and he had been employed for more than ten years in preparing these various founts. If the punches or matrices had been so far defaced as to be unserviceable, the operations of the press must have been suspended till they could be renewed; but the discovery of them unhurt at once dispelled every feeling of despondency. A building on the premises, more spacious than that which was consumed, had been leased to a commercial firm in Calcutta, and vacated in the previous month; it was resolved, therefore, to convert it into an office. The workmen were called together and paid up to the day, and dismissed for a month, with the assurance that business would be resumed at the end of that period. The pundits were set anew to the work of translation. The number of type-casters was augmented, and they worked by relays, night and day, with such diligence that at the end of thirty days two of the versions were again in the press. In less than six weeks from the night of the fire three other founts were completed. Within a few months the press was in full operation, and by the end of the year there remained no indication of a fire.

The Christian kindness which the missionaries experienced in India on this occasion shewed the estimation in which their labours were held. Their cordial and generous friend, Mr. Thomason, set on foot a subscription among his friends, and in a day or two raised £800 for their immediate exigencies. Throughout the community the loss was considered a public one; and from men of every class, without distinction of sect or creed, they received the warmest expressions of sympathy, and the most liberal aid. The efforts made in England to repair the loss, and establish the press on its former footing of efficiency, presents a singular example of Christian zeal and philanthropy, which cannot be better described than in Mr. Fuller's own language: "When the news reached Norwich, though they had collected £200 for the mission, they added £500 for the fire. At Cambridge, £165 were collected for the loss. The Bible Society voted 2,000 reams of paper. The London Missionary Society voted £100; and the editors of the *Evangelical Magazine*, £50. On the 4th of November I preached at Northampton, where £170 were collected; and £160 at Kettering. Subscriptions are opened at London, Bristol, Birmingham, Leicester, Nottingham, Hull, Leeds, Bradford, Manchester, Liverpool, Edinburgh, and other places. The London subscription cannot be less than £1,000; Edinburgh is £1,000; Leeds amounted to £300; Bradford to £100; Bristol between £300 and £400; Leicester between £200 and £300." The whole of the loss was subscribed in sixty days. Within two months after hearing of the catastrophe, Mr. Fuller received the sheets of the New Testament, printed from the new types, and he cut them into slips and sent them to the friends and associations who had generously poured in their subscriptions, under the designation of the "feathers of the phœnix." In writing to his friends at Serampore, he remarked: "The rapidity with which you have been able to repair the loss of types and to resume your labours is as remarkable as if the pecuniary loss had been made up in a week. This fire has given your undertaking a celebrity which nothing else, it seems, could—a celebrity which, after all, makes me tremble. I see the eagerness of men, after this celebrity, passing all bounds; and we are men. The public is now giving us their praises; if we inhale this incense, will not the Lord be offended and withdraw His blessing, and then where are we? Ought we not to tremble? Surely we need more grace to go through good report than evil. I have less jealousy of you than of ourselves; but we are all in danger. When you pitched your tents at Serampore, you said, We will not accumulate riches, but devote all to God for the salvation of the heathen. God has given you what you desired, and what you desired not. . . . Only beware of flattery and applause, for now you may expect a tide of this to try you. You have stood your ground through evil report; may you stand it under good report. Many who have endured the first have failed under the last. The icy mountain that can stand the winter's blast may melt before the summer's sun. Expect to be highly applauded, bitterly reproached, greatly moved, and much tried in every way. Oh, that having done all, you may stand!"

The trials were close at hand. The missionaries had scarcely recovered from the calamity of the fire when they found the opposition of Government to missions rekindled with double fierceness. The period in which missionaries were to be "tolerated as toads" had expired, and the time for their being "hunted like beasts" was come round again. The intermediate period of repose was very brief. It was on the 16th of November, 1810, that Lord Minto granted a passport to two missionaries to proceed to Agra and establish a station; and it was on the 17th of June, 1812, that Government opened the campaign against missions, and passed an order for the expulsion of two from the country, which, in the course of a few months, was extended to all the missionaries brought under their notice,—those at Serampore excepted—till the number included in the sentence of banishment was increased to eight. The transactions connected with this last and most violent crusade against missions were spread over a period of nine months, and will require to be narrated without interruption; the less prominent events of the year will therefore be previously disposed of.

The missionary labourers raised up in India, chiefly among the members of the Bow Bazar church, were necessarily engaged without reference to the Society; for which, indeed, there was no time, when a twelvemonth usually elapsed between the despatch of a letter to England and the receipt of a reply. Dr. Carey and his colleagues, therefore, took on themselves the entire responsibility, as well as expense, of these nominations, and never allowed the charge to be inserted in the Society's accounts. At the close of this year they had six such labourers dependent on their funds. These generous exertions were gratefully acknowledged by Mr. Fuller in his address to the public: "The annual expenditure of this mission," he said, "at home and abroad, exclusive of translations, amounts at present to five or six thousand pounds. It has not cost the public, however, on an average, during the twenty years of its continuance, more than two thousand pounds. . . . It is owing to the unexampled contributions of the missionaries at Serampore that things have hitherto been thus conducted. This, however, will not be considered by the friends of the undertaking as rendering their exertions less necessary." The mission to Rangoon had been weakened by the retirement of Mr. Chater. His brethren at Serampore had been urged by the Hon. and Rev. Mr. Twisleton, the senior chaplain in Ceylon, to establish a mission on the island, and Mr. Chater accepted the invitation, and proceeded to Columbo, when he laid the foundation of a very interesting and successful mission. Mr. Felix Carey, thus left without the support of a companion, was soon after exposed to unexpected difficulties, and brought under the influence of circumstances which eventually compromised all his prospects of usefulness. He accepted the office of interpreter to the Burmese government,—then engaged in unpleasant discussions with the Governor-General, and was gradually led deeper into this secular connexion. In October of the present year he came round to Serampore to print his translation of the Gospel of St. Matthew and a small Burmese grammar he had compiled. To prevent the interruption of such visits, it was deemed advisable to establish a press at Rangoon; and Mr. Kerr, an East Indian, was associated with Mr. Carey. The missionaries at Serampore embraced this opportunity of addressing a letter to the king at Ava, recommending to his protection their brethren who had proceeded to his dominions to translate the Bible, —"the book of Heaven,—the same from which all Christian nations derived their knowledge of virtue and religion." They then alluded to the press which accompanied them as the instrument employed in England in making known the laws of Government to all the people. This communication created such interest in the royal palace at Ava, that the king ordered a press, with all necessary materials, and a complement of workmen, to be sent from Serampore to his capital; and his envoy, then proceeding to Calcutta, was directed to take charge of it. It was prepared with the greatest alacrity, in the hope that it might lead to the establishment of a mission at Ava; but the vessel in which it was shipped sunk in the Rangoon river, and circumstances prevented the despatch of another. The mission to Agra had raised great expectations of usefulness, but before it had been eighteen months in existence, the refractory disposition of Mr. Chamberlain, whose mind was a stranger to all prudence or discipline, occasioned his sudden and compulsory removal. He fell into the error of a fierce discussion with the commandant of the fort regarding the right which he claimed of giving religious instruction to the soldiers—a right which was not recognised for many years after this period. The commandant referred the matter to Government, and Mr. Chamberlain referred it to his brethren at Serampore, who lost no time in informing him that they considered it the height of imprudence for him to set himself up in opposition to those who were intrusted with power, and whom Government must necessarily support. They saw no hope of his being permitted to remain at Agra, where his work lay among the natives, and not among the European soldiery, unless he would give an unqualified promise to Colonel Bowie, the commandant, to make no attempt to enter the fort without his permission. But no such concession could be obtained from Mr. Chamberlain, and he was sent back to the Presidency.

On the 14th of June the cause of religion in Bengal was deprived of one of its chief supporters by the death of the Rev. David Brown. When he arrived in India in 1786, only a small number of the leading men in the Government recognised the Sabbath by an official attendance at divine service. At the time of his death a large and highly respectable congregation, which had been collected by his labours, crowded the mission church to attend the ministrations of his successor, Mr. Thomason. Of his cordial and affectionate co-operation with the Serampore missionaries after he had taken up his residence in the town, the preceding pages afford ample evidence. He was confined to his couch—from which he never rose—when the printing-office was consumed, but he dictated several letters to Mr. Marshman and his brethren in a spirit of the kindest sympathy, exhorting them not to be dismayed by the magnitude of the calamity, but to raise their minds to a level with this new emergency. Dr. Marshman preached a sermon on the occasion of his death from the text, "Blessed is that servant whom the Lord when He cometh shall find watching."

Three days after the death of Mr. Brown, the final struggle between the Government of India and the missionary enterprise commenced. The first victims were the late Dr. Judson, the apostle of Burmah, and his companion, Mr. Newell, the earliest missionaries from the United States to the eastern hemisphere. For several months, as Mr. Ward remarked, the sky had been lowering. Mr. Thomason had preached a sermon which bore directly on efforts for the conversion of the heathen, but the Government censor refused him permission to publish it. Mr. Thompson, a missionary from the London Society, had come up from Rangoon to Calcutta on his way to Madras. The circumstance was not discovered till after he had sailed, but a peremptory order was sent by post to expel him from the Presidency as soon as he landed, which so deeply affected his spirits that he was attacked by disease, which carried him to his grave in a few days. The anti-missionary party was now again in the ascendant, and it comprised Mr. Charles Milner Ricketts, the cousin of Lord Liverpool, Mr. John Adam, the son of Chief Commissioner Adam, and Mr. George Dowdeswell, the son of Lord North's Chancellor of the Exchequer: men of eminent ability, but unhappily inimical to the introduction of Christianity into India. Lord Minto was naturally most kind and considerate; but he had not sufficient strength of mind to resist the influence of their counsels. One of the most active agents in these proceedings was Mr. Charles Fuller Martyn, a barrister, and one of the magistrates of Calcutta, long after remembered in Calcutta as the type of judicial corruption.

It was in this position of affairs that Mr. Judson and Mr. Newell appeared at the police-office, and reported themselves as missionaries who had come out from America, with passports from the governor of Massachusetts, and landed in Calcutta preparatory to their proceeding to the eastward of Bengal to establish a mission. Mr. Martyn had now missionaries again within his grasp, whom he could worry with impunity under colour of discharging a public duty. He immediately reported to Government that two missionaries had arrived in the *Caravan*, who pretended to be Americans by birth, though he suspected they were British subjects. "The missionary route," he said, "had of late been *viâ* America, because this class of persons knew they could not obtain leave to proceed hither direct in any of the Company's vessels. Many missionaries might be expected, and they would all plead being Americans. He presumed, therefore, to iterate that the only effectual mode of checking these immigrations was to put the commanders to the expense of taking them back." Mr. Dowdeswell, the secretary to Government, informed the magistrate that the Governor-General did not deem it advisable to permit the missionaries to remain, and that the captain would not be allowed a port-clearance unless he gave satisfactory assurance that he would convey them back. Mr. Judson appealed to Government, stating that he and his associate had no intention to continue in Bengal, and had only touched at Calcutta on their way to the eastward, for which they would embark on the arrival of their friends in the *Harmony*. Mr. Dowdeswell replied, that they would not be allowed to establish themselves in any part of the Company's territories, or even in the island of Java; but if they gave the fullest pledge to proceed without loss of time to the territories of any other states than those of Great Britain and her allies, the order for his return by the *Caravan* would be cancelled. Anxious to escape from the seat of a Government so hostile to missions, he requested permission to proceed to the Mauritius, and Lord Minto acceded to his request.

The *Harmony* arrived on the 15th of August with Mr. Judson's three colleagues, and Mr. Johns and Mr. Lawson for Serampore, and Mr. May for Chinsurah. Mr. Martyn immediately reported the arrival of six more missionaries, three of whom were British subjects. "Four of them," he said, "had their wives and children, a presumptive proof that they intended to take up their abode in the country. Their professed object was to preach, but as to whom they were to preach they waited for information from the *officina missionarum* at Serampore." Immediately on the receipt of this intelligence, the Governor-General determined to "enforce the standing orders"—the cant phrase of the day for the order of deportation. The missionaries were therefore commanded to return by the vessel which brought them, and the usual restrictions were laid on the commander. They likewise asked permission to proceed to the Isle of France, which was granted. Mr. Newell embarked in a small vessel which had only one cabin, and the others were therefore obliged to wait for another opportunity. Early in November, Mr. Martyn reported that only one of the missionaries had left the country; and the Government, without deigning to require any explanation from the missionaries of the cause of this delay, determined to adopt the most severe measures against them. Mr. Martyn was informed by the secretary that they had forfeited all claim to the indulgence of Government,—that it was now resolved to send them to England in the fleet then under despatch,—that Government was not bound to incur any expense on their account,—that no larger sum would be allowed for the passage-money of each missionary than £40; and that they were to mess with the gunner.

No reference was made to their wives and families, who were to be left in Calcutta to starve. The vessel in which they were to embark was then lying abreast of Sangor Island, more than a hundred miles below Calcutta; and Mr. Martyn was directed to hire a sloop to convey them down the river under the charge of a police guard.

Armed with this authority, Mr. Martyn sent an order to the American missionaries not to quit their residence in Calcutta without his permission, and planted a police-officer to watch their movements. They felt that to proceed to England would be death to their missionary enterprise, more especially as a war between Great Britain and the United States was then impending, and they determined to run every risk to avoid this infliction. Mr. Judson engaged a passage in the *Creole*, a vessel going to the Mauritius, and went on board at midnight, with his wife and one of his colleagues. Mr. Martyn was no sooner apprised of this circumstance than he procured an order on the pilot not to proceed to sea while the missionaries were on board. They therefore quitted the vessel, and the embargo was taken off. While on shore, bewildered to discover the path of safety, but still feeling that the most dangerous course was to return to Calcutta to fall into the hands of Mr. Martyn, a letter was put into their hands containing permission to embark on the *Creole*. Their friends had made intercession with Government, and Lord Minto, having already granted Mr. Judson leave to embark for the Mauritius, felt the inconsistency of detaining the vessel which was conveying him thither. Mr. Judson hired a boat, and rowing night and day, reached the vessel as the pilot was weighing anchor for the last time.

The two remaining missionaries, Mr. Nott and Mr. Hall, escaped to Bombay. Mr. Martyn, when called upon by Mr. Dowdeswell to account for his apparent negligence, stated that they had clandestinely withdrawn from their usual abode, that they had been secreted by those who espoused their cause, and with their aid had secured a passage to

Bombay. The fact was, that these outrageous proceedings, unexampled in the history of the Company or of the town, had roused public indignation and created a general desire to baffle the tyranny of the Government. A despatch was immediately sent to Bombay, directing that the missionaries should be sent to England as soon as they landed.

Having thus expelled the five American missionaries from India, Lord Minto's government determined to deal summarily with Mr. Johns and Mr. Lawson, who were residing at Serampore. Five months before this time, Dr. Marshman, perceiving the strong current of anti-missionary feeling in the Council chamber, had adopted the precaution of writing to Mr. Edmonstone, stating that he and his colleagues were expecting two brethren in the *Harmony*, and were anxious to obtain permission for them to remain in the country, while a reference was made on their behalf to the Court of Directors. Mr. Edmonstone was directed to state, in reply, that though the Governor-General had no authority to grant licences for residing in India, the two missionaries were at liberty to remain until the pleasure of the Court of Directors regarding them should be known. They were therefore considered safe for at least a twelvemonth. Mr. Robinson, on relinquishing the Bootan mission, accepted the offer of Mr. Raffles, now governor of Java, to proceed to the island and establish a mission, and to this arrangement Lord Minto had given his sanction in Council. The vessel in which Mr. Robinson embarked encountered a gale in the Bay, and returned to Calcutta disabled. The only vessel subsequently bound to the eastern islands was one of the Company's own ships, and the commander required the permission of Government to receive him on board. Dr. Marshman therefore called on Mr. Ricketts, the public secretary, to solicit the usual pass. Mr. Ricketts said he was happy to see him, as he was on the point of writing to him respecting Messrs. Johns, Lawson, and May, the three remaining missionaries who had arrived in the *Harmony*, and of the reason of their having come out by way of America; but as Dr. Marshman had now disclosed the name of another missionary, it was necessary that his case should likewise be included in the report. Dr. Marshman informed him in a letter that Government had given permission to two of the missionaries to remain in the country pending a reference to Leadenhall Street; and to a third to proceed to Java, and that Mr. May was not connected with their body. Mr. Ricketts stated in reply, that these circumstances were not sufficient to warrant their continuance in the country, but before he proceeded to act, he was desirous of knowing why these gentlemen had come out by way of America, instead of coming direct from England, with the permission of the Court of Directors. Dr. Marshman now began to suspect that it was the object of Mr. Ricketts to obtain a written admission that the missionaries were in India without a licence, that he might be enabled to "enforce the standing orders" against them. It was well known in Calcutta that the Court of Directors had already received intimation of the determination of the Ministry to propose a clause in the new Charter, then about to come under discussion, granting permission to Europeans to reside in India. In the hope that some further intimation of this auspicious change of policy might reach Calcutta at an early date, and induce Government to pause in this course of violence, Dr. Marshman endeavoured to prolong the correspondence. Perhaps it is no violation of Christian charity to suppose that the same expectation may have induced the hostile body of secretaries to precipitate their proceedings against the missionaries. But Mr. Ricketts was not to be thus baffled, and after three or four letters had passed on the subject, demanded a categorical reply to his question, when Dr. Marshman informed him that the missionaries had no licence from the Court of Directors, and that they did not apply for one, because they had little hope of its being granted.

The object of this correspondence, which, on the part of

replied that only twenty-four hours had elapsed since the orders of Government had been communicated to them; that they were entirely ignorant of the accommodation of the vessels, as all the cabins were said to be already engaged, and that they intended, moreover, to memorialise the Governor-General for a mitigation of the order. This intimation only served to exasperate Mr. Martyn, who took up the paper, and having made the engagement more positive and stringent, insisted on Mr. Lawson's signing it. Dr. Marshman refused to allow him to commit himself by affixing his name to such a document, but offered in lieu of it an assurance to conform to the ultimate wishes of Government, whatever they might be. "Then I shall commit him," said the magistrate. "You will do as you like," replied Dr. Marshman, "but that paper he shall not sign." Mr. Martyn then made out the order for his committal, and he was conveyed under charge of a European sergeant and a body of native constables to the *Kuttra*, or lock-up house. Dr. Marshman accompanied him thither, and, having seen him deposited in a room with a native cot in it, proceeded to Mr. Ricketts' residence, and expostulated with him on the indignity which had been inflicted on Mr. Lawson, in conducting him like a felon through the streets of Calcutta. Mr. Ricketts did not fail to perceive the odium which the Government must incur by these proceedings, and at once yielded to Dr. Marshman's requisition, and granted an order for his immediate release.

On reaching Serampore a meeting was held the next morning, to consider the best means of obtaining a reversal of the order. Dr. Marshman determined to adopt the same plan which had been successful in 1807, and seek a personal interview with Lord Minto at Barrackpore. Mr. Johns had been assured by the commissioner under whom he served as medical officer at Serampore, that the strongest interest would be made with the Government to retain his services, and with every prospect of success; and he requested that his name might not be coupled with the application about to be made on behalf of Mr. Lawson. Lord Minto had always taken a lively interest in Dr. Marshman's Chinese labours, and there appeared some faint hope of obtaining the indulgence of Government, by dwelling on the value of Mr. Lawson's assistance in perfecting the Chinese fount. It is humiliating to reflect that the only argument which could be employed, with any hope of success, in averting the expulsion of a missionary from India was, that his mechanical skill would be useful in an object of literary interest. In writing to the military secretary for an audience, therefore, Dr. Marshman dwelt more particularly on this circumstance, and enclosed specimens of his delicate and tasteful workmanship. He stated that it was their anxious desire to obtain permission for both these gentlemen to remain till the arrival of a reply to the reference which had been made to the Court of Directors; but if this was considered too great an indulgence, they would limit their solicitation to the case of Mr. Lawson. Lord Minto, anxious to avoid the arguments and the importunity of Dr. Marshman, declined a personal interview, but promised to bring the application before the Council, where alone a mitigation of the order could be passed. At the meeting of Council, it was resolved to allow Mr. Lawson to remain under the charge of Dr. Marshman, to assist him in his Chinese pursuits; but Mr. Johns, whose medical services could be readily supplied, was peremptorily ordered to quit the country. A passage was, therefore, engaged for him the next day, at a cost of £500, and he embarked for England on the 1st of April, 1813.

These arbitrary and violent measures have left an indelible stigma on the administration of Lord Minto. The proceedings of 1807 were sheltered by this plausible excuse, that they were adopted immediately after the Vellore mutiny, and under the influence of the panic which it created, and were prompted by the issue of tracts which were considered likely to endanger the security of the empire, and of which one was, without question, objectionable. The present proceeding admitted of no such extenuation. It could not be said of any of those whom it was the pleasure of Government to hunt out of the country, that they had said or done anything to create alarm. If they came out without a licence, so had hundreds of their countrymen, whom Government never dreamed of molesting. Their only crime was that of being engaged in a religious mission; and Mr. Lawson, who was ordered out of the country as a missionary, was allowed to remain as a punch-cutter. These measures were, moreover, in direct opposition to the spirit of the injunctions which the Court had laid on Lord Minto, when on a former occasion he allowed himself to be drawn into a crusade against the Serampore missionaries. In that instance the Court had commended the local authorities for having "refrained from resorting to the authority vested in them by law, and from enforcing its provisions in all its strictness against the missionaries;" and had expressed a confidence in their discretion "not to bring into view the direct instrumentality of Government, and to abstain from all unnecessary and ostentatious interference with their proceedings." These measures were still more reprehensible as involving a direct breach of the promise which had been unconditionally given by Lord Minto to Dr. Marshman, that Messrs. Johns and Lawson should be allowed to remain till the pleasure of the Court of Directors could be known. The miserable quibble by which it was endeavoured to cover this violation of faith only renders it the more disreputable. Mr. Adam, the secretary, was directed to state that the permission was revoked in consequence of its having subsequently come to the knowledge of the Governor-General that the missionaries had purposely abstained from applying for leave at the India House, because they were aware that it would not be granted, and that a promise obtained under this concealment of facts could be no longer binding;—as if Mr. Adam and Lord Minto were not aware at the time the promise was given that the only reason why these missionaries, and every other private European in India, had not applied at the India House for the safeguard of a licence, was the certainty of its being refused. It would be superfluous to vindicate Dr. Marshman's memory from the charge of having surreptitiously obtained a promise by a suppression of the truth. The mere circumstance of his having applied on behalf of the missionaries for permission to remain pending a reference to Leadenhall Street, carried with it the fullest admission that they were without a licence, for which it was known that they would have applied if there had been any prospect of success. To condescend to such sophistry to cover a glaring breach of promise, was to trifle with the dignity of Government. It afforded a pregnant example of that economy of truth and that contempt for reason and consistency which is fostered by the exercise of despotic power.

In writing to Mr. Fuller on the subject of this transaction, Dr. Carey said:—"I have endeavoured to acquit the Government of religious persecution, but my mind will not do it. Lord Minto has no dislike to us; he is a man of amiable disposition, and a professed friend of liberty. But it is in the power of a secretary to prepare and present such a statement as the Government cannot refrain from noticing. I never before heard of a man like Mr. Johns, of liberal education and scientific acquirements and inoffensive conduct, being sent back to Europe, unless he had meddled with politics, or in some way or other rendered himself troublesome to Government; and in no instance of a man like Mr. Robinson being ordered out of the country after a residence of six years in it. The fault lies in the clause which gives the Company power to send home interlopers, and it is just as reasonable as to forbid every man to look at the moon, and will, I trust, be modified in the next Charter." The excuse alleged for these proceedings was the "standing orders" of the Court of Directors to expel all unlicensed Europeans, which, it was affirmed, had become more stringent in the preceding five years. This assertion, however, is not in the slightest degree supported by the records of the India House. It is only a just tribute to the moderation of the Court of Directors to record that the jealousy of interlopers which belonged to the period of the factory, was greatly relaxed during the period of the empire; that it was rarely exercised, and never without reluctance. It is but too true that they entertained a morbid dread of the introduction of Christianity into India, lest it should endanger the peace of the country, and that they would have refused a licence to a missionary; but the violent proceedings now recorded were altogether foreign to their wishes. They are to be ascribed to the coterie of secretaries in Calcutta, who were enabled to indulge their own animosities under the plea of enforcing the "standing orders." During the vigorous rule of Lord Wellesley, they would have been constrained to bridle their prejudices; under the feeble rule of Lord Minto, they were permitted to give them the fullest license, and to commit the Government to arbitrary measures without precedent, without necessity, and without justification.

The period had now arrived to which the Serampore missionaries had been looking forward with ardent hope to obtain relief from the interruptions and oppression to which they had been subjected for seven years. The Charter, as it was called, of 1793 was about to expire, and the whole question of Indian policy was to be brought under the revision of Parliament. Twenty years had elapsed since the House of Commons had locked the door of India against the entrance of all knowledge, secular as well as religious, and given the key to the Court of Directors, and most strenuously had they resisted every effort to unlock it. Their servants in India, fully participating in their views, had carried them into effect with unexampled violence. While the Court in London steadily refused a licence to any missionary to resort to India, the Council in Calcutta expelled those who ventured out by way of America, and at the period of the Charter discussions, orders had been issued for the banishment of eight missionaries from the shores of India. Matters had come to such a pass that, without the interposition of Parliament, it was impossible for Christian light and truth to obtain admission into India. The eyes of the friends of missions, and more particularly of Mr. Fuller, were therefore fixed with intense anxiety on the proceedings in Parliament; and under the impression that the India question would be brought forward in 1812, the various missionary bodies held a meeting in London to arrange their plans, when it appeared more expedient that their applications to the Government should be made individually than collectively. Mr. Fuller accordingly printed a statement describing the operations at Serampore in the mission and in the translations, and sent a copy of it to every member of Parliament who was likely to take an interest in the subject. On the 9th of May, 1812, he waited on Mr. Spencer Percival, who received him with official urbanity and reserve, and said that he was unwilling to bring the question of religious rights under discussion in the House, but as it was determined to concede various privileges to traders in the new Charter, he thought the same protection would be extended to all classes, and would not be withheld from missionaries. Five days after, he was shot by Bellingham. Mr. Charles Grant, Mr. Wilberforce, Mr. Babington, and others, waited on his successor, Lord Liverpool, and found him apparently more favourable to the cause than Mr. Percival. He was prepared to grant more than they had ventured to expect—to sanction the establishment of seminaries at the Presidencies for training up native ministers; to grant the missionaries licences from the Board of Control; and to consecrate bishops for India.

The question of the Charter was, however, postponed to the following year, and it soon became apparent that the effort to obtain facilities for the missionaries would meet with the most vigorous opposition. The old Indians, who still formed a compact and powerful body, asserted with a degree of assurance bordering on arrogance, that any attempt whatever to evangelise India would result in the loss of the empire. The majority of the Court of Directors entertained the same sentiments. Among the proprietors of India stock, only a small minority was friendly to the cause of missions. Of the members of the House of Commons nine-tenths, in the opinion of Mr. Wilberforce, or at least a large majority, would oppose any motion which might be brought forward by the friends of religion. "Almost all men of influence," as Mr. Charles Grant remarked, "appeared to think and act on the conviction that duty and success lay in slighting Christianity, while they manifested the most delicate regard to the wildest superstitions of heathenism." The periodical press was, with very few exceptions, strongly opposed to the introduction of the Gospel into India. Under such circumstances, the ministers, who had no personal sympathy with the cause, and were officially averse to the agitation of it, were not likely to make any heroic exertions to promote it. Such was the general state of feeling on the subject in the various circles of influence when the contest commenced.

Early in March, 1813, Mr. Fuller went up with a deputation to Lord Buckinghamshire, the President of the Board of Control. He had formerly been governor of Madras, and in its uncongenial atmosphere had imbibed that repugnance to missionary labours which distinguished that Presidency above the others. Mr. Fuller explained to him the two concessions the Society was anxious to obtain—liberty of access to India, and a legal toleration when there. As to the first request, replied Lord Buckinghamshire, "he would see if they could be accommodated." As to the second, he asked what further toleration they could desire than that which they now enjoyed? Mr. Fuller said that the toleration they had was owing merely to the kindness of some of the public authorities, and was liable at any moment to be reversed. By a singular coincidence of time and circumstances, it was only two days before the President of the Board of

Control inquired what further toleration the missionaries could possibly desire in India, that the Government of Calcutta had exemplified the value of the toleration they possessed by issuing an order for the expulsion of three out of the six missionaries residing at Serampore, and that without any motive, except what might be furnished by the wantonness of despotism. Mr. Fuller retired from the interview with very faint hopes of success. "The President," he wrote, "gave us no encouragement. They want to hold you at their discretion. Our liberty folks are mad for getting the Roman Catholics into *power*, while they are very cool as to obtaining even *toleration* for you. But God is above all."

The various missionary bodies are now on the alert. The Church Missionary Society presented a memorial to the ministry. The Methodists brought their quota of influence to bear on the question. The London Missionary Society waited on Lord Liverpool, who told them it was intended "to do something for Christianity in the East; perhaps in the form of an ecclesiastical establishment." Mr. Fuller likewise had an interview with Lord Liverpool, who promised to do everything in his power to promote his views; but we cannot, he said, allow you to send out missionaries without leave, and when there, they must, in common with other Europeans, be under the control of Government. Mr. Fuller replied that he did not object to their being under the laws, but to their being held in restraint, and liable to deportation on mere suspicion and caprice. He complained of the hostile spirit of the Court of Directors, and Lord Liverpool assured him that the missionaries should not in future be left in their hands, but placed under the guardianship of her Majesty's Government. "In short," wrote Mr. Fuller, "we were almost melted down with the candour, openness, and kindness of Lord Liverpool." But Mr. Wilberforce, who was better acquainted with the diplomacy of Downing Street, recorded: "The Baptists have gained nothing from the

Prime Minister but fair words;" and so it eventually turned out.

Mr. Fuller waited in the next instance on Lord Castlereagh, the ministerial leader in the House of Commons, to whom the management of the India Bill had been intrusted, but found that he was not disposed to grant any but the most limited concessions. "We shall probably give your missionaries," said he, "liberty to proceed to India, where they may profess their own faith." "That is a degree of liberty," replied Mr. Fuller, "we can get any day at Constantinople. From a Christian government we certainly expected more liberality." "But," remarked Lord Castlereagh, "the country, in general, seems to be indifferent on the subject of India missions. Whatever interest is manifested in them is confined to two or three missionary bodies." "If," replied Mr. Fuller, "the decision of the question is to depend on the expression of public opinion, your Lordship will soon have an opportunity of judging to what extent we carry the sympathies of the nation with us." The interview, however unsatisfactory, was valuable, inasmuch as it convinced Mr. Fuller that the ministry would make no concession except under the pressure of external influence, and thus pointed out to him the only course of action which was likely to be crowned with success. A day or two after, Mr. Thompson, the member for Hull, and one of the warmest advocates of the missionary cause, informed him that a serious misunderstanding had arisen between the India House and the Ministry regarding the provisions of the India Bill, and that if those differences were reconciled, the Bill would be hurried through the House before petitions in favour of missions could be presented. Happily the two bodies did not come to an agreement, and the cause of missions triumphed.

On the 22nd of March, Lord Castlereagh introduced the measure proposed by the Ministry for the future trade and government of India. He passed a high encomium on the

Company, who had created an empire unexampled in the history of the world, comprising fifty millions of people, and had governed it on principles eminently conducive to the happiness of the country. He proposed to continue, for a farther period of twenty years, the privileges, authorities, and immunities they now enjoyed, but, to suit the necessities of the times, it was intended to throw open the trade to the mercantile community in England. Europeans would likewise be permitted to resort to India under licences from the Court of Directors and the Board of Control, but the local authorities would be left in full possession of the power they had always enjoyed of expelling those whose conduct might be considered dangerous; on the subject of religion, he said, it was unwise to enter on it generally, but there was one provision which appeared necessary "even for the sake of decency"—the appointment of a bishop and three archdeacons to superintend the chaplains, and to give the members of the Church of England the benefit of those parts of their religion to which episcopal functions were necessary. But no allusion whatever was made to the missionary enterprise. Mr. Wilberforce then rose and expressed his regret that the resolutions of the House of Commons of the 14th of May, 1793, relative to the moral and religious improvement of India, had not been attended to; and he was unwilling to leave the same power for twenty years more in the hands of the Court of Directors, who had set their faces against missions for the last twenty years. Lord Castlereagh observed that the subject of religion was one of equal delicacy and importance, and that if the East India Company did not understand what was best for the country, they were not fit to govern it; if they were fit to govern it, it would be invidious to interfere with them in the way proposed by Mr. Wilberforce. This determination on the part of the minister to leave the missionaries for twenty years at the mercy of the India House, convinced the friends of the cause that nothing was to be obtained from the Government except by such an expression of public opinion as they would not venture to despise. Happily, the Court of Directors were equally dissatisfied with the proposal to overthrow, as they termed it, "the whole system of the Company, by abrogating that commercial monopoly which had been confirmed to them during two hundred years by sixteen Acts of Parliament." They therefore demanded permission to bring forward evidence at the bar of the House, to prove the impolicy and danger of these innovations. Lord Castlereagh was constrained to accede to their request. They stated that their witnesses would not occupy more of the time of the House than six days: they consumed six weeks.

The examination of the witnesses during this protracted period, afforded time for rousing the religious spirit of the country and bringing it to act on the Parliament and the Ministry. Mr. Wilberforce and his little cabinet, Mr. Charles Grant, Mr. Babington, and Mr. Stephen, were indefatigable in their efforts to enlighten and to stimulate public opinion. He considered the object "the greatest which men ever pursued," and threw his whole soul into it with the same enthusiasm which he had exhibited on the question of the slave trade. While the various Dissenting bodies were actively engaged in getting up petitions in their respective circles, he was urging the same course on the members of his own community. "Let it not be said," he writes, "that Dissenters only take an interest in the welfare of mankind, and that the members of the Church are not zealous." During this memorable period, Mr. Fuller was at his post, exciting the zeal and organising the operations of his own denomination. Lord Castlereagh's declaration had operated like an electric shock through the country, and united all parties in the common cause. For more than eight weeks the two Houses were overwhelmed with a flood of petitions of which there had been no previous example. They streamed in, night after night, from all parts of the kingdom, from large public bodies and individual congregations, from influential towns and small hamlets, and from every class and denomination. They amounted to nine hundred: a larger number than, it appears, had been presented on any previous occasion; and Lord Castlereagh was reported to have said one night, as they poured in apparently without end, "This is enough, Mr. Fuller."

The House began to receive evidence on the 30th of March. The venerable Warren Hastings was the first witness, and as he entered, the members rose in a body, and paid spontaneous homage to the greatest of Indian rulers. But it was twenty-seven years since he had left India, and his opinions on the management of the trade, the admission of Europeans, and the introduction of Christianity, were only a rehearsal of the views entertained in Calcutta on these subjects during the thirty years which elapsed between the battle of Plassy and the close of his administration—the dark age of our Indian policy—the age of contracted views and gigantic prejudices. Warren Hastings was in advance of the age in which he lived and acted, and behind the age in which he gave evidence. On the subject of religion he stated that if, during his tenure of office, the missionaries had demeaned themselves properly, he should have taken no notice of them, but if they had given any occasion to a belief that the Government itself tacitly encouraged their designs, then, from an apprehension of the consequences of this belief, he should have recalled them to Calcutta, and, if necessary, compelled them to quit the country. At an early period of the session the Court of Directors had printed the papers connected with the transactions between Government and the Serampore missionaries in 1807, and presented a copy to every member. The object of this publication was to demonstrate the impolicy of admitting Christian teachers into India, by a reference to the misconduct of the missionaries at Serampore. It was an *ex parte* statement. These papers included the unauthenticated translation of their tracts. If any opportunity had been afforded them of defending their conduct, or presenting an accurate version of the pamphlets, they would have been enabled to correct the hostile impression which it was now the object to raise against them; but Dr. Carey and his colleagues, whose alleged offences were now to be pleaded against missions, were thus condemned behind their backs by the statements of those who had oppressed them. One of the advocates of the Company in the House endeavoured to turn this missionary blue-book to account, and asked Mr. Hastings whether he considered it consistent with the safety of the empire, to allow missionaries to preach publicly, with a view to the conversion of the natives, that Mahomed was an impostor, and to apply opprobrious epithets to the brahmins and their religious rites; to which he replied that if such a declaration of war was made between the professors of our own religion and those of the native religions, he knew not what would be the consequences.

Lord Teignmouth was then called in, and the same insidious question was put to him regarding these public preachings; and he replied that the practice of preaching such doctrines, as stated in the question, would certainly be attended with danger; but such addresses were not at all necessary for the conversion of the natives, and as far as his experience went, there was nothing offensive to the people of India in the character of a missionary. He was then asked whether, if the Hindoos were possessed with an idea that we had an intention of changing their religion, and converting them to Christianity, it would be attended with disaster. He replied that the Hindoos and Mahomedans had the experience of many years, that every attention had been paid to their prejudices, civil and religious, and that the freest toleration was allowed them, and he did not think they could be brought to believe that Government ever meant to impose on them the religion of this country. There had now, he said, been missionaries in Bengal seventeen years, who had circulated numerous copies of the

Scriptures, and many religious pamphlets in the dialects of India, without creating any alarm among the natives.

The next witness was Mr. Cowper, who had been in the Indian service for thirty years, ten of which he was member of the Supreme Council. He was asked what would be the political effect of sending out a bishop and three archdeacons, and he replied that, a few days before, he should have said that he could see no objection, or very little, to it. But a meeting had just been held at the London Tavern, with Lord Gambir in the chair, which had passed a resolution that there were more than fifty millions of British subjects in India under the influence of inhuman and degrading superstitions, which formed an effectual bar to their civilisation; and he was therefore of opinion that such an appointment would create a general ferment. Regarding the probable result of any attempts at conversion, he said that if the missionaries went without any authority from Government they would make no converts and do no mischief, but if sent forth under that authority, our expulsion from India would be inevitable. He farther asserted, that the mere proposition of the subject within the walls of Parliament would endanger the empire, and that even an express disavowal in the Act of every intention to use compulsion would not be sufficient to avert the danger. In the opinion, therefore, of Mr. Cowper, the Court of Directors were to be at liberty to resist every effort for the introduction of Christianity by voluntary agency, while Parliament was precluded even from receiving a proposal to remove these restrictions, lest the mooting of such a subject should give alarm to the brahmins. Mr. Graham, the next witness, a civil servant of thirty-nine years' standing, admitted that the interference of Government to check the practice of voluntary immolation under the wheels of Jugunnath's car had produced no insurrection or disturbance, though "this act of self-devotion was held in the highest veneration;" but the greatest danger was to be apprehended from the attempts of private individuals to disseminate Christianity. As he had been in Calcutta in 1807, he was asked whether he knew of any insurrection or popular commotion occasioned by the preaching of the Serampore missionaries in the Chitpore road, and he replied that he had heard of one attempt to preach there which ended in an affray.

No further attempt was made to question the India House witnesses on the subject of missions. The House of Commons agreed that the subject of religion should form no part of the examination, and the Lords soon after concurred in this resolution. The friends of missions equally approved of it, feeling assured that nine-tenths of the witnesses would be found hostile to the cause of missions, and that it would be more effectually promoted by leaving it to rest on the "notorious facts of the case, and the plain and undeniable obligation involved in it." The extent to which a long residence in India amidst heathen associations had served to deaden every Christian sympathy, and to create a feeling of animosity towards those who would disturb the native prejudices, was lamentably exhibited in the course of this inquiry, more particularly in the evidence of Colonel, afterwards Sir Thomas, Munro. Though he was considered a statesman of the first grade, and a man of enlightened views and sound judgment, he volunteered a most extravagant panegyric on the Hindoo character and institutions. "If," he said, "a good system of agriculture, unrivalled manufacturing skill, schools established in every village, the general practice of charity and hospitality among each other, and, above all, a treatment of the female sex full of confidence, respect, and delicacy, were among the signs which denoted a civilised people, then the Hindoos were not inferior to the natives of Europe;" and he assured the House that, "if civilisation were ever to become an article of trade between the two countries, England would greatly benefit by the import cargo."

The evidence terminated on the 27th of May. During

its progress the House had been inundated with petitions, demanding with that earnestness and energy which a Constitutional Government may not resist, that India should be opened to the Gospel by an express provision in the Bill. This unanimous expression of public opinion produced a salutary effect on the House, and it was not lost on the Ministry, who now considered it prudent to swim with the stream. Lord Castlereagh accordingly brought forward on the 31st of May the "Christianising Resolution," as Mr. Wilberforce aptly termed it, and proposed that "it was the duty of this country to promote the introduction of useful knowledge and of religious and moral improvement in India, and that facilities be afforded by law to persons desirous of going to and remaining in India to accomplish these benevolent designs." The discussion was postponed to the 22nd of June, when the House met to discuss the question—far exceeding in the importance and magnitude of its results that of commercial monopoly or free trade, Manchester cottons or India piece goods—whether the light of Divine truth should continue to be excluded from the inhabitants of India. The mode in which Lord Castlereagh introduced the subject shewed his utter indifference to it, and the feeling of compulsion under which he was acting. He stated that his reason for bringing forward the proposal was, that the House had adverted to the interests of religion in India in 1793, and it would seem as if they were less disposed to the cause of Christianity than formerly if a proposition of the nature contained in the resolution was not made. No allusion was of course made to the petitions which covered the tables, and overawed both the House and the Ministry. "He did not consider there was any ground for supposing that any dread would be created in the minds of the Hindoos. The voyage to India was long, and the expense of it great; and he was therefore inclined to believe that the spirit of proselytism was not so exuberant in our times as to tempt any very alarming number of persons to proceed on religious missions to India. What progress Christianity might make, it was impossible for him, who had never been in India, to say." Sir Henry Montgomery, who had been twenty years in the Company's military service at Madras, immediately rose to oppose the resolution, and asserted that he had never known an instance of any convert being made, except one, who was converted by "that very respectable individual, Mr. Schwartz." In his opinion, the Hindoo religion was pure and unexceptionable. The immolation of widows was no more a religious rite than suicide was a part of Christianity. If we wished to convert the Hindoos, we ought first to reform our own people there, who at present only give them an example of lying, swearing, drunkenness, and other vices. Though the mutiny at Vellore was not caused by the missionaries, yet if they were allowed to act without restriction, there would be a repetition of those scenes of massacre in every part of the country; and, for his part, he was more anxious to save the lives of thirty thousand of his fellow-countrymen than to save the souls of all the Hindoos, by making them Christians at such a price.

Mr. Wilberforce then addressed the House in support of the missionary cause, in a speech which recalled to the minds of his hearers the noblest of his efforts on behalf of the oppressed Africans. It is justly considered a masterpiece of eloquence, and it produced a powerful effect in the House. One who was diametrically opposed to his missionary views has remarked, that the "unavoidable prolixity of his details was relieved by flashes of the brightest eloquence. With a just confidence in his powers, he ventured to broach the hackneyed subject of Hindoo conversion. He spoke three hours, but nobody seemed to be fatigued; all indeed were pleased, some with the ingenious artifices of manner, but most with the glowing language of the heart." He opened his speech by an allusion to the resolution he had proposed twenty years before, which might serve to shew that he was not treating of a subject of which he was ignorant. Before he entered on his argument, he said he was anxious to clear away a misconception which had arisen, and to assure the House that he abjured all idea of compulsion, and disclaimed all use of the authority, or even the influence, of Government. He adduced the spread of the religion of Nanuk, of Mahomedanism, and of Christianity, as a complete refutation of the dogma that the Hindoos were so unalterably attached to their religion that their conversion was impracticable. He then proceeded to deal with the assertion that the Hindoos were so good and their morals so pure, that any attempt to communicate our religion and morality would, to say the least, be a superfluous, perhaps a mischievous act; and he brought forward the evidence of a dozen authors of the first reputation to disprove it. Referring to the prejudices manifested by the generality of the Anglo-Indians on the subject of Christian missions, while on other topics they were reasonable enough, he quoted the expression of Burke, that Europeans were usually unbaptized on their passage to India. He then dwelt on the moral degradation and social misery of India, the prevalence of polygamy, of infanticide, and of female immolation, the bloody rites and unutterable abominations of the system; and entreated the House to commence, with prudence but with zeal, endeavours to communicate to those benighted regions the genial life and warmth of our Christian principles and institutions, if it could be attempted without absolute ruin to our political interests. This allusion to political danger led him to notice the collision between the Government of India and the Serampore missionaries in 1807, described in a document which was in the hands of every member. He said that there had been but one instance in which their opponents had been able to find any just cause of complaint against them. One of their converts had translated into Persian, and carried through the press, without their cognizance, a tract on the life of Mahomed, containing some abusive and objectionable epithets. But even the circulation of three hundred copies of the pamphlet had produced no disturbance or discontent, and its existence was discovered only by the circumstance of a copy being brought by the son of a wealthy merchant to one of the Mahomedan teachers in the College, with a request that he would reply to it. "These Anabaptist missionaries," said he, as, among other low epithets bestowed on them, they have been contemptuously termed, "are entitled to our highest respect and admiration. One of them, Dr. Carey, was originally in one of the lowest stations in society; but, under all the disadvantages of such a situation, he had the genius as well as the benevolence to devise the plan of forming a society for communicating the blessings of Christian light to the natives of India. To qualify himself for that truly noble enterprise, he had resolutely applied to the diligent study of the learned languages; and, after making a considerable proficiency in them, applied himself to several of the Oriental tongues, and more especially to the Sanscrit, in which his proficiency is acknowledged to be greater than that of Sir William Jones, or any other European. Of several of these languages he has already published grammars, and of one or two of them a dictionary. All this time, sir, he is indefatigably labouring as a missionary, with a warmth of zeal only equalled by that with which he prosecutes his literary labours. Another of these Anabaptist missionaries, Mr. Marshman, has established a seminary for the cultivation of the Chinese language, which he has studied with success scarcely inferior to that of Dr. Carey in the Sanscrit. It is a merit of a more vulgar sort, but to those who are blind to their moral, or even their literary excellences, it may perhaps afford an estimate of value better suited to their principles and habits of calculation, that these men, and also Mr. Ward, another of the missionaries, acquiring from £1,000 to £1,500 per annum by the various exercises of their talents, threw the whole into the common stock of the mission, which they thus support by their contributions only less effectually than by their researches and labours of a higher order." The resolution was violently opposed by those who had been in India, and more especially by Mr. Prendergast, who affirmed as a fact within his own personal knowledge, that Dr. Carey one day harangued the mob, standing on a tub in the streets of Calcutta, and abused the religion of the people to such a degree that he would have been killed but for the interference of the police. This story, however, produced no effect on the House, which, at three in the morning, adopted the resolution by a majority of 89 to 36.

This large majority on the first division, manifestly the result of the petitions, decided the question. But the opponents of the cause were determined to dispute every inch of ground during its subsequent stages. The Bill was again brought under discussion on the 16th of June. Mr. Fuller had intermediately written to Mr. Prendergast to assure him that the assertion he had made regarding Dr. Carey's having preached on a tub in the streets of Calcutta was utterly without foundation, and had therefore called on him publicly to withdraw it; but Mr. Prendergast was more disposed to meet this demand by a challenge than a retraction. He came up to Mr. Wilberforce in the House, and said in a manner which, in a noted duellist, could not be mistaken, "Pray, do you know a Mr. Andrew Fuller who has written to desire me to withdraw the statement I made regarding Mr. Carey?" Mr. Wilberforce answered, with a smile, that he knew him perfectly well, "but, depend on it, you will make nothing of him in your way. He is a respectable Baptist minister at Kettering." On the renewal of the discussion, Mr. Stephen Lushington, who had been in the Company's service at Madras, reprobated the missionaries in language scarcely less opprobrious than that which had been applied to them by his relative twenty years before at the India House. He denounced the remarks made by Mr. Buchanan and the missionaries on the character of the Hindoos as the most infamous and unfounded libels. He affirmed that, to do justice to the Company's Government, they had always acted on a liberal and enlightened principle —that of excluding Christianity from India—till of late years a different system had crept in. God forbid, he exclaimed, that it should be sanctioned by that House, for it was contrary to the faith we had pledged to the natives, "to permit them to pursue their religion, *without molestation*, under our Government." This ingenious and convenient expression was a great favourite with the opponents of missions, because it was supposed to furnish an infallible argument against all attempts to introduce Christianity into India in all time to come; but the merit of having coined it belongs to Lord Minto's administration. Mr. Lushington entered into an elaborate defence of the Hindoo creed and literature, quoted various passages from the shastrus on truth, mercy, charity, and hospitality; he likewise read a Hindoo prayer to the House, and assured the members that it was impossible to behold a brahmin repeat it without being deeply affected by it.

The Bill was again brought up on the 1st of July, when Lord Castlereagh expressed an earnest wish that the clause which referred to missions should be permitted to pass without discussion. But Mr. Charles Marsh, formerly a barrister at Madras, was impatient to counteract the influence of Mr. Wilberforce's eloquent appeal, and to vindicate the honour of Hindooism, and to pour the vials of his indignation on the Serampore missionaries. His speech was the most elaborate and ferocious, but unquestionably the most brilliant, delivered against missions during the struggle; and even those who recoiled from his statements were charmed with his eloquence. It may be taken as an epitome of the views and feelings of the anti-missionary party at this period, and is therefore entitled to a more extended notice. He affirmed that in all former modes of policy for the Government of India the inviolability of the religious feelings and customs of the natives was considered a sacred and indisputable axiom, and that a departure from that policy would shake the empire to its centre. He denounced as most impolitic the clause by which licences were to be given to missionaries. Hitherto, he said, if a missionary misdemeaned himself, the remedy was at hand: the Government banished him from the country, and "the nuisance was instantly abated;" but now he would be able to set up the licence at home against the revocation of it abroad. A governor who exercised this power would do it at the hazard of drawing on himself the clamours and resentments of a body who are daily acquiring fresh accessions of influence and number, and who are knit together by the strongest sympathies. It demands no great effort of fancy to conceive the spiritual denunciations with which every conventicle would ring at the persecution of Brother Carey and Brother Ringletaube. With regard to the Serampore publications, he would not shock the ears of the House by reading any extracts from them, displaying as they did a fearful and disheartening system of terrors, from which the affrighted reason of man would gladly fly to the most barbarous of superstitions for refuge and consolation. Lord Castlereagh had told them not to be alarmed either at the undue increase of missionaries or the kind or description of those who went out, as the Board of Control would exercise a salutary control over their appointment. He confessed that his apprehensions on this head would be put to rest if Lord Buckinghamshire was always to remain at the head of the Board, or if his successors were influenced by his prudence and good sense, for no man was less affected with the cant and fanaticism of the day. But his successor might be of the new evangelical school, who thought the fulness of time was arrived for Hindoo conversion, and that every inspired cobbler or fanatical tailor who felt an inward call had a kind of apostolic right to assist in the spiritual siege already begun against the idolatries and superstitions of that degraded and barbarous country. He then brought up the stereotyped argument against missions drawn from the

Vellore massacre, and asked if it was possible for the House to go off into such a fit of absurdity and fanaticism, or be visited with so fatal a fatuity as not to keep so awful an event before them in the discussion of matters affecting the religion of India. At the same time, he affirmed that no man could be more unaffectedly solicitous than himself for the diffusion of Christianity, and that he should be undeserving of an audience in a Christian assembly were he cold or indifferent to its blessings. But there were no means of accomplishing the object, and the attempt would be attended with dangers that appalled him, though they were treated with indifference by those who were not startled by the miseries they might produce in the glorious object of making sixty millions of people Baptists or Anabaptists. Never will the scheme of Hindoo conversion be realised until you persuade a whole population to suffer the severest martyrdom which has yet been suffered in the cause of religion. And are the men whom this Bill will let loose on India fit engines for the accomplishment of this great revolution? Will these people, crawling from the holes and caverns of their original destinations, apostates from the loom and the anvil, and renegades from the lowest handicraft employments, be a match for the cool and sedate controversies they will have to encounter, should the brahmins condescend to enter the arena against the maimed and crippled gladiators that presume to grapple with their faith? What can be apprehended but the disgrace and discomfiture of whole hosts of tub-preachers in the conflict? He then upbraided Mr. Charles Grant with objecting to the introduction of merchants into India, while he was ready to open every port to swarms of missionaries and fanatics. He considered it strange that those who thought the prejudices of the natives so immutable that they would not buy our woollens should yet consider them prepared to receive the coarsest texture of theology that could be dealt out from the shops of the Anabaptists, or woven in the loom of their fevered and fanatic fancies.

He affirmed that if we adopted the opinions uttered in that House of the degradation of the natives, we were unfit to govern them. He denied the fact of their moral and mental inferiority, and burst forth in a transcendental rhapsody of their ancient and venerable institutions. "When I turn to her philosophers, lawyers, and moralists, who have left the oracles of political and ethical wisdom to restrain the passions and awe the vices which disturb the commonwealth; when I look at the peaceful and harmonious alliance of families, guarded and secured by the household virtues; when I see among a cheerful and well-ordered society the benignant and softening influences of religion and morality; a system of manners founded on a system of mild and polished obeisance, and preserving the surface of social life smooth and unruffled, I cannot hear without surprise, mingled with horror, of sending out Baptists and Anabaptists to civilise or convert such a people, at the hazard of disturbing or deforming institutions which appear hitherto to have been the means ordained by Providence for making them virtuous and happy." He dwelt at great length on the virtues of the native character, and more particularly on the abstinence from intoxicating liquors which was enjoined by the shastrus, but would be overthrown by Christianity. "In exchange for this virtue, they will have been initiated into the mysteries of election and reprobation. I leave it to those who are versed in moral calculations to decide what will have been gained to ourselves by giving them Calvinism and fermented liquors; and whether predestination and gin would be a compensation to the natives of India for the changes which will overwhelm their habits, morals, and religion."

Mr. Wilberforce rose immediately after Mr. Marsh to vindicate the Serampore missionaries. "With the well-founded claims which on a former occasion I stated them to have to your respect, it will not, I trust, be very injurious to them to have received this night, in this House, the contemptuous appellation of Anabaptists and fanatics. . . .

For my own part, I have lived too long to be much affected by such epithets, whether applied to others or to myself. But I should have conceived that the missionaries would have been shielded against such attacks as these from any assailant of a cultivated mind, by their having conceived and planned, and in the face of much opposition undertaken, and so long persevered in carrying on, at a vast expense of time, and study, and money, such dignified, beneficial, and disinterested labours. Anabaptists and fanatics! These, sir, are not men to be so disposed of. Far different was the impression they produced on the mind of Lord Wellesley; far different the language he had bestowed on them. While in India, he patronised their literary labours, and very lately, in another place, publicly, and on a solemn occasion, after describing with a singular felicity of expression which must have fixed his words in every hearer's memory, their claim to the protection, though not to the direct encouragement, of Government, he did them the honour of stating that, though he had no concern with them as missionaries, they were known to him as men of learning. . . . And while the thoughts of a Christian observer of them, and of their past and present circumstances, would naturally dwell upon that providential ordination by which such uncommon men had been led to engage in that important service, even a philosophical mind, if free from prejudice, could not but recognise in them an extraordinary union of various and, in some sort, contradictory qualities—zeal combined with meekness, love with sobriety, courage and energy with prudence and perseverance. When to these qualifications we superadd that generosity which, if exercised in any other cause, would have received, as well as deserved, the name of splendid munificence; and when we call to mind that it is by motives of unfeigned, though it had been misguided, benevolence that these men were prompted to quit their native shores and devote themselves for life to these beneficent labours, is there not, on the whole, a character justly entitled to at least common respect? To use the language of Bishop Hurd, on a similar occasion, I can only admire that eminence of merit which I despair myself to reach, and bow before such exalted merit." Mr. Prendergast repeated the arguments he had used on a former occasion, and felt himself called on to re-state that he had himself seen Dr. Carey stand on a hogshead, and had heard him tell the people that if they continued in their paganism and idolatry, hell-fire would be their portion, and that his life was preserved only by the interposition of the police. Mr. Prendergast assured the House that the attempt to convert the heathen was the most absurd infatuation that ever besotted the weakest mind. Mr. Keene attacked the Serampore missionaries, and declared that they had actually issued an address from their own press to all the inhabitants of India, announcing their intention to preach a new faith to them, and inviting them to renounce their old superstitions. Mr. Robinson, "in pathetic terms, prayed the House would not sanction that clause of the Bill which gave full toleration to missionaries to convert the Hindoos from a religion to the doctrines of which they were so much attached." Mr., afterwards Sir Charles, Forbes, affirmed that it was the opinion of ninety-nine out of every hundred of those acquainted with India, that Christian missions would be attended with the worst possible effects. But, on the division, the cause of missions was supported by a majority of twenty-two, and the Bill passed the third reading on the 13th July. The progress of this measure through the House of Lords was not marked by any of that opposition which had been manifested in the Commons. There were no old Indians among the peers, anxious to exalt the virtues of Hindooism and to deprecate the influences of Christianity. The sanction of the Legislature was thus given to the introduction of the Gospel into India, after a struggle which will ever be memorable in the annals of the Christian Church; and the missionaries at Serampore, who had fought the battle of missions in India alone and unaided for thirteen years, found their reward in the triumph of the cause.

CHAPTER VII.

RESUMING the narrative of events at Serampore, the first occurrence of interest was the establishment of a mission at Sirdhana. In consequence of a difference with the commandant at Agra, Mr. Chamberlain had been sent back to Serampore, with a guard of sepoys on his boat; but before he left the station, he received an earnest invitation from Colonel Dyce to take up his residence at Sirdhana and superintend the education of his children. That town was the capital of a small principality, eleven miles north-west of Delhi, which had been carved out for himself, during the confusion of the times, by Sumroo, the French adventurer, who ordered the massacre of a hundred and fifty European officers and soldiers, the prisoners of the Nabob, Cossim Ali, at Patna, in 1764. He bequeathed this domain to his widow, a Persian lady, and she had succeeded, by her tact and resolution, in maintaining her independence in the midst of perpetual revolutions. The territory was twenty-five miles in length and twelve in breadth. Twelve years before this period, an East Indian of the name of Dyce, proceeding through the north-west in search of employ, was led to visit Sirdhana, and was immediately taken into the service of the Begum Sumroo, and rapidly rose in her confidence, and received her granddaughter in marriage. Out of deference to her deceased husband's wishes, she had made a profession of the Roman Catholic religion, but Colonel Dyce, who had been entrusted with the management of her affairs and the command of her little army, was anxious that his children should be educated in the Protestant faith, and invited Mr. Chamberlain to undertake their tuition. The Serampore missionaries had always been desirous of extending the mission in the north-west, and advised him to accept the offer, but on condition of being allowed to pursue his missionary vocation without any restriction. He was welcomed by the Begum and the Colonel with much cordiality, and received charge of his pupil, who subsequently became noted in England as the wealthy and eccentric Mr. Dyce Sombre. Three or four hours were daily devoted to his education, but the rest of Mr. Chamberlain's time was left at his own disposal, and was passed in preaching, and superintending schools, and translating the New Testament.

The mission to Burmah had by this time become as great an object of anxiety to the missionaries, as it had once been of hope. The king of Ava, hearing of the practice of vaccination which Mr. Felix Carey had introduced at Rangoon, ordered him to repair to the capital and vaccinate the royal household. This circumstance was hailed with delight by Dr. Carey, as likely to lead to the establishment of a mission station at Ava, but it proved fatal to his son's usefulness. He came round to Bengal for a supply of new lymph, and on his return to Rangoon received orders to bring with him the press which had been established in that town. The vessel in which he embarked was upset by a squall in the river, and his wife and two children were drowned. The press was irrecoverably lost, but the king, notwithstanding this disappointment, received him graciously, and after he had resided some time at the court, decorated him with a barbaric title, and prevailed on him to proceed to Bengal as his representative, and bring some negotiations which were then pending with the British Government to a close. He now appeared in Calcutta in the character of a Burmese noble, assumed a diplomatic costume, and proceeded to Government House with a suite of fifty followers. His father was greatly mortified at this transformation, and lamented to Mr. Fuller that his son had sunk from a missionary to an ambassador. The negotiations, for which he had little skill, proved unsuccessful, and drew on him the resentment of the king. On his return to Rangoon he found it more prudent to fly the country than to proceed to the court at the imminent risk of his life. He was thus lost to the mission and to his own family. After leaving Burmah he led a wandering life among the rude and independent tribes on the eastern frontier of Bengal, and passed through a succession of adventures which would be considered extravagant in a novel. After three years of this wild and romantic life, he accidentally fell in with Mr. Ward at Chittagong, and was persuaded to return to repose and usefulness at Serampore.

The missionary field thus deserted in Burmah was soon after occupied by Mr. Judson and his associates, who established the American mission, the labours of which have been prosecuted in a spirit of unexampled zeal and perseverance. That mission has realised all that has been affirmed of the almost fabulous success of Xavier, while it has exhibited a more rigid enforcement of Christian principles and practice. During their voyage from America, Mr. Judson and his companions had employed their leisure in reviewing the authorities for infant baptism, that they might be prepared to combat the arguments in favour of adult baptism which they expected to encounter at Serampore. But they found on their arrival that this was the only topic which their friends could not be prevailed on to discuss. They were too earnestly engaged in the great work of Christian civilisation, and too happy to welcome new labourers into the field, to waste their time on any minor points of difference. Mr. Judson and Mr. Rice were simply referred to the New Testament; their investigations resulted in a change of views, and they were baptized by immersion, on a confession of faith, a few weeks after they had been at Serampore. Driven from Bengal, as already stated, by the hostility of Lord Minto's Government, Mr. and Mrs. Judson took shelter at the Mauritius, which was under the administration of the Crown, while Mr. Rice proceeded to America in the hope of creating an interest in missions in the denomination with which he was now connected. Mr. Judson determined to commence a mission at Penang, and proceeded to Madras in search of a vessel bound to that port, but happily found none, for he would assuredly have been expelled from it without delay, as it was one of the possessions of the Company. His arrival at Madras was immediately reported to Calcutta, and, under the apprehension that the return post would bring an order for him to be sent to England, he hastened to embark with his wife in an old and crazy bark, at the risk of their lives, for Rangoon, which he reached on the 13th of July, and where he commenced the American mission in Burmah. Mr. Rice's exertions in America were crowned with signal success. Societies were rapidly formed in various towns, and contributions were poured into the treasury with unexpected liberality. Delegates from the various societies met at Philadelphia on the 18th of May, 1814, and the "General Convention of the Baptist Denomination in the United States for Foreign Missions" was formed.

In the course of the next year, Mr. Hough, who was well versed in the art of printing, was engaged by the American Board to labour in Burmah. He visited Serampore on his way to Rangoon, and the missionaries prepared another press and types to replace that which had been lost in the Rangoon river, and presented it to the American mission. "Our attempts," they wrote to the Board, "in the Burmese empire have ended in the transfer of the mission to Brother Judson, and those whom you may send to join him. Something, however, has been done: a mission-house has been built; the language has been opened; a grammar printed; materials for a dictionary formed; a portion of the New Testament published, and copies of it circulated. . . . We would recommend you to send missionaries as soon as possible to Bassein, Ava, Martaban, and also to Siam. By thus confining your efforts to countries the languages of which have a strong affinity, your agents will form a united phalanx, having an immense people of the same manners, prejudices, religion, and government, as their object; and being near each other, and in the same country, the experience and acquirements of each will come into the common stock, and bear an ample interest." The letter then alluded in the most animated language to the slow but certain triumphs of Christian truth and benevolence in the East:—"We are sure to take the fortress, if we can persuade ourselves to sit down long enough before it. And then, very dear brethren, when it shall be said of the scene of our labours: The infamous swinging-post is no longer erected—the widow burns no more on the funeral pile—the obscene songs and dances are heard and seen no more—the gods are thrown to the moles and to the bats, and Jesus is known as the God of the whole land—the poor Hindoo goes no more to the Ganges to be washed from his filthiness, but to the fountain opened for sin and for uncleanness—the temples are forsaken, and the crowd say, 'Let us go up to the house of the Lord, and He shall teach us of His ways, and we will walk in His statutes'—the anxious Hindoos no more consume their property, their strength, and their lives in vain pilgrimages, but come at once to Him who can save to the uttermost—the sick and dying are no more dragged to the Ganges, but look to the Lamb of God, and commit their souls into His faithful hands—the children, no more sacrificed to idols, are become the 'seed of the Lord'—the public morals are improved—the language of Canaan is learned—benevolent societies are formed—civilisation and salvation walk arm-in-arm together—the desert blossoms—the earth yields her increase, and redeemed souls from the different towns and villages and cities of this immense country, constantly add to the number and swell the chorus of the redeemed—'Unto Him that washed us from our sins in His own blood, unto Him be the glory'—when this grand result of the labours of God's servants in India shall be realised, shall we then think that we have laboured in vain, and spent our strength for naught?"

In the report of the Translations of the present year, especial reference was made to the important improvement which had been effected in Chinese typography. The first edition of the Gospels was printed, in accordance with the immemorial usage of China, from wooden blocks. But this process was expensive and dilatory, inasmuch as it would be necessary to incur a fresh expenditure of money and time in engraving new blocks for each revised edition. A successful attempt was now made to introduce the system of European printing with moveable metallic types, and with great success. This substitution of typography for xylography, which originated at Serampore, and was in a great measure matured there before it was taken up by other missionary bodies, forms an era in the history of Chinese printing, and will probably be adopted by the Chinese themselves, when their stationary civilisation, of which the block printing is an apt emblem, yields to the impulse of European improvement.

Lord Minto's administration was now drawing to a close. He had signified to the Court of Directors the period at which he desired to be relieved from the government, and it had always been considered an indispensable mark of courtesy to avoid anticipating it. But the new ministry and the Prince Regent were impatient to obtain the post for Lord Moira, and the majority of the Directors submitted to this influence. Mr. Charles Grant, who considered that no Governor-General should be removed abruptly, or contrary to his own wishes, without adequate reason, expressed his deep regret to Lord Minto that he should thus have been dispossessed of his high station without assigned reason or plea. It was a singular coincidence that at the very time the Government of Lord Minto was engaged in hunting the missionaries out of India in servile deference to what was considered to be the wishes of the Court of Directors, he himself was ungraciously superseded in his office by that same body. At the same time, the appointment of Sir George Barlow as provisional Governor-General was cancelled, and he was dismissed from the Governorship of Madras, in consequence of the mutiny of the officers of the Madras army, which was attributed to his mismanagement. Nothing could exceed the kindness of Lord Minto to the missionaries at Serampore, after he had become personally acquainted with them, and there is every reason to believe that even during the hostile proceedings of his administration, his own sentiments were more liberal than those of his council; but he apparently wanted firmness of character to resist the influence of the clique of secretaries in Calcutta, who had been cradled in despotism, and nursed in prejudices. Before he quitted the government, he paid a generous compliment to the missionaries in his last college address. "I am gratified," he said, "by the opportunity which their literary achievements afford me of expressing my regard for the exemplary worth of their lives, and the beneficent principle which distinguishes and presides in the various useful establishments which they have formed, and which are conducted by them." He embarked for England on the 20th of October, 1813, but died a few days after his return.

The arrival of Lord Moira produced an immediate and auspicious change in the policy of the Government with regard to missions. He left England before the Charter Act had become law, but he had witnessed the noble outburst of enthusiasm in every religious community in England; he had seen the nine hundred petitions stream into the House of Lords, and he was not indifferent to this development of national feeling. He was a man of large and enlightened views and great independence and resolution. He had occupied an important position in the political world in England, and enjoyed the entire confidence of the Prince Regent. He did not participate in that morbid dread of missionary efforts which haunted the official functionaries in Calcutta, and the whole tone of Government was changed as soon as his friendly disposition towards missions became known. One of his earliest acts was to stay the persecution of the American missionaries who had proceeded to Bombay. They found an order from the Supreme Government awaiting their arrival to ship them off to England as soon as they landed; but, happily, Mr. Jonathan Duncan, who was the original of Sir James Mackintosh's picture of the brahminised Englishman, had ceased to be Governor of Bombay. His successor, Sir Evan Nepean, a man of evangelical tendencies, was very reluctant to carry out the harsh and unjustifiable orders he had received from Calcutta, and the execution of them was delayed by various circumstances till the arrival of Lord Moira, when Dr. Carey joined Mr. Thomason and Mr. Udny in a memorial intreating his interposition. In the interview with which he favoured them, he "spoke very decidedly about the missionaries being allowed to remain, and expressed his conviction that they meant to do good, and that no conceivable injury could result from their residence in the country." His liberality was equally manifested with regard to Mr. Robinson, who had gone to Java, but was pursued by an order from Calcutta to quit the island. His application for permission to remain was read in Council by the same secretary who had written the order for his deportation, but Lord Moira now presided at the Board, and Dr. Marshman had already obtained an audience of him, and explained all the circumstances of the case. The order was at once reversed. At the same time, Mr. William Byaam Martin, who had been appointed Resident at Amboyna, one of the Molucca islands, recently captured from the Dutch, sent a requisition to Government for a missionary to give instruction to twenty thousand Christian natives, and to establish schools. Lord Moira sent the application to Dr. Carey, and his third son embraced the offer and proceeded to Amboyna.

The progress of conversion among the natives in the present year afforded much encouragement. In the spring, a small body of kayusts, residing in a town a few miles north of Serampore, embraced Christianity as the result of a diligent study of the Sacred Scriptures. They were connected with the most aristocratic families in Calcutta, and possessed of independent means; they were men of cultivated minds, and familiar both with Persian and English. The great hopes raised by this movement in a large and influential circle, were not, however, destined to be fulfilled. Two of the number relapsed into idolatry, but the most eminent among them laboured with true missionary zeal for many years among his own countrymen. It was a source of deep regret to Dr. Carey and his associates that, owing to the heavy engagements which confined them to Serampore, they were unable to itinerate as in the early days of the mission. They therefore employed Mr. Thomas, a member of the church in Calcutta, in visiting the villages around Serampore, in company with five native preachers, which in some measure supplied their lack of personal service. Krishnu, the first native convert, was also sent to the village of Pundooa, near Sylhet, at the foot of the Cossya hills, many of the inhabitants of which had been driven by the oppression of their own chiefs to take refuge in the British dominions. The judge of the district, a former pupil of Dr. Carey, wrote to him to advise that two or three hundred of them should be made Christians at once by baptism, and receive instruction afterwards. Dr. Carey replied that this was to begin at the wrong end; and Krishnu was sent to impart a knowledge of Christian truth to them. His labours resulted in inducing seven of their number to renounce their barbarous superstitions and embrace Christianity. The entire number of baptisms in the missionary circle amounted to a hundred and sixteen. During the present year, Rambosoo, whose name has frequently appeared in these pages, died in Calcutta. He was the earliest of Mr. Thomas's inquirers, and had consorted with the missionaries for more than twenty years. He was always ready to employ his powerful pen in ridiculing the follies of idolatry; but while, in the excellent tracts he composed, he extolled the religion of the Bible and exhorted his countrymen to embrace it, he had not the courage to set them the example. He died in the odour of Hindoo sanctity, and his funeral rites were performed according to the Hindoo ritual, as if he had been a true believer in the gods.

In the original constitution of the Society, the three objects to which its attention and its funds were to be directed were,—the preaching of the Gospel, the translation of the Scriptures, and the establishment of schools. The Serampore missionaries had twenty schools at their different stations, but their attention had been devoted more earnestly to preaching and to the translation and printing of the Scriptures, than to education. The superintendence of the Benevolent Institution in Calcutta, for the instruction of indigent Christians, had drawn Dr. Marshman's attention to the state of ignorance which existed in Hindoo society. At the close of 1813 he drew up a plan for the extension of schools among the heathen on the basis of Lancaster's system, and it received the fullest approbation of his colleagues and of Mr. Fuller. He calculated that a sum of 1,000 rupees a month would be sufficient for the instruction of 4,000 children, and he did not see any other plan of widely diffusing religious and secular knowledge with equal efficiency and economy. The plan was, therefore, recommended to the liberality of the public in England. In the course of the next two years the experiment was brought to greater maturity, and will be noticed in its place.

During the year 1814, the Society in England was deprived by death of the services of Mr. Sutcliffe, who had, from its commencement, been the invaluable coadjutor of Mr. Fuller. His talents were more useful than splendid, and he was better adapted for the cabinet than for the field. He was the Nestor of the missionary circle in England. His counsel was sought on every occasion of difficulty, and his clear perception of the bearings of a case, and his prompt and sound judgment, seemed at once to dispose of a question. His practical good sense may be illustrated by the reply he once gave to Mr. Fuller, when he proposed to call a meeting of the committee on some particular occasion. "Call a committee meeting! why, the matter is self-evident. If you do call one, appoint some place on the turnpike road, at such a milestone; fix the hour and minute. Let us meet, and set our horses' heads together, pass a vote, and separate in two minutes." At the beginning of this year Mr. Fuller availed himself of the privilege granted by the new charter, and obtained a licence from the India House for Mr. Eustace Carey to proceed to Bengal as a missionary in one of the Company's vessels. But a second application on behalf of Mr. Yates was, strange to say, refused. A reference was then made to the Board of Control, and permission was granted without hesitation; and the friends of missions had thus a practical exemplification of the value of the concession which had been extorted from Parliament by the voice of public opinion. It is, however, due to the Court to state that this was the only instance of any reluctance to permit missionaries to proceed to India under the new charter, and that although the Act of Parliament empowered the Government to cancel the licences of the missionaries after their arrival in India, the power was never exercised. The Court was beginning to feel the liberal influences of the age, and, as the old school of Indians died out, a higher tone of sentiment became visible in the counsels of Leadenhall Street.

During the present year Dr. Marshman published his "Clavis Sinica, or Key to the Chinese Language," the result of eight years of study. At the present day it is interesting as one of the earliest efforts to open that difficult, and, at the time, mysterious language to our countrymen. His exertions in this department of Oriental philology have been overshadowed by the subsequent labours of eminent scholars, who have studied the language with superior advantages in the country itself; but the "Clavis" is still an honourable memorial of literary enterprise. Mr. Edmonstone, who was at the time at the head of the Government in Calcutta, in the absence of Lord Moira, evinced his respect for Dr. Marshman, and his esteem for the missionaries, by a generous donation from the public purse of £1,000 towards the expense of the publication.

In 1814, Mr. Chamberlain was a second time removed from the North-West Provinces. In the month of April the Begum proceeded from Sirdhana to the great fair at Hurdwar, the most renowned "teerth," or holy place, in Hindoostan. A particular conjunction of the heavenly bodies in the present year was supposed to enhance indefinitely the merit of bathing in the sacred stream at that place, and more than a hundred thousand pilgrims were attracted to it. Mr. Chamberlain, who accompanied the Begum, was employed, without intermission, for twelve days, in preaching to the devotees at the ghauts, or landing-stairs, and to the crowds who surrounded his elephant, or pressed into his tent to hear this new and strange doctrine, which was now for the first time announced at this great seat of Hindoo superstition. The most profound tranquillity pervaded the multitude, though in a high state of religious excitement, while they listened to discourses which impugned the efficacy of the holy Ganges. An eye-witness thus described the scene:—"During the greater part of the fair, a Baptist missionary, in the service of her highness, daily read a considerable portion from a Hindoo translation of the Sacred Scriptures, on every part of which he commented; he then recited a short prayer, and concluded by bestowing his blessing on all assembled. His knowledge of the language was that of an accomplished native, his delivery was impressive, and his whole manner partook of much mildness and dignity. No abuse, no language which could in any way injure the sacred service he was employed in, escaped his lips. His congregation eventually amounted to thousands. They sat round and listened with attention which would have reflected credit on a Christian audience. On his retiring, they every evening cheered him home, with 'May the padree live for ever!'" Towards the close of the year, Lord Moira made his first progress through the North-West Provinces, accompanied by the secretary, Mr. Ricketts, who had taken the most prominent part in the expulsion of missionaries eighteen months before. Some gentlemen, unfriendly to the cause of missions, brought the subject of Mr. Chamberlain's labours at Hurdwar to the notice of Mr. Ricketts, who made an alarming report on the subject to Lord Moira. Without any investigation of the subject, or any request for an explanation, a peremptory requisition was immediately made to the Begum to discharge Mr. Chamberlain from her service, and he was at the same time ordered to return to the Presidency. On leaving Sirdhana he proceeded to the Governor-General's encampment, and solicited an audience, in the course of which he appealed to the testimony of Lady Hood and Colonel Mackenzie, who were present at Hurdwar, and had assured him of the pleasure they derived from witnessing the peaceable demeanour of the people, and more particularly the brahmins, and the great interest which had been manifested in his addresses. But Lord Moira had been impressed with the danger of preaching to a large concourse of pilgrims, and refused to revoke the order, remarking that one might fire a pistol into a magazine and it might not explode, but no wise man would hazard the experiment. This was the only instance of any unfriendly feeling towards missionaries during his long administration, and it may be sufficiently accounted for by reference to the prejudices of his public secretary. Mr. Chamberlain soon after made choice of Monghir as his station, and there he passed the eight remaining years of his life, in peace, and in the zealous discharge of his missionary duties.

The see established at Calcutta was conferred on Dr.

Thomas Middleton, one of the most eminent scholars of the age. The only missionaries in Bengal were those connected with the Serampore establishment, and his mind had been prepared to appreciate their labours, by the pamphlet recently published by Dr. Marsh, subsequently bishop of Peterborough, in which he said, "Such are the exertions of these extraordinary men, who, in the course of eleven years have contributed so much to the translation and dispersion of the Sacred Scriptures, that the united efforts of no society can be compared with them. These are the men who, before the Bible Society existed, formed the grand design of translating the Scriptures into the languages of the East; these are the men who have been the grand instruments in the execution of this stupendous work; these are the men who are best qualified to complete the design so nobly begun, and hitherto so successfully executed." Such testimony from a dignitary of his own Church gave the missionaries a friendly introduction to the bishop. Dr. Carey called on him a few days after his arrival and found him very open and cordial. In acknowledging the receipt of the Clavis Sinica from Dr. Marshman, he said, "Your name in this department of learning is known to every scholar in Europe, and your labours have received unqualified applause from the very few who are competent to decide on their merits." The bishop soon found that in a society like that of the Europeans in India, utter strangers to religious dissensions, there was a larger scope for liberality of feeling than in England, where every community is segregated by theological animosities. During his episcopate no dissenter had reason to complain of prelatical antipathies.

The review of the mission, drawn up at the beginning of 1815, possesses a melancholy interest from the circumstance of its having been the last transmitted to Mr. Fuller, though he did not live to receive it. As if in anticipation of his speedy removal, the review was a retrospect of the labours in which they had been conjointly engaged for the previous fifteen years. They dwelt on the gradual expansion of the sphere of action, and the extent to which the opportunities of labour had been multiplied and improved. They stated that the planting of the Gospel in any heathen country required three distinct agencies—the formation of missionary stations, where "the standard of the Cross shall be erected, and the Gospel preached to the people, and from whence ultimately spring churches;" the translation of the Scriptures; and the instruction of youth in the truths of the Bible, and the literature suited to the wants of the country. These three objects they remark were intimately linked together. They observed that there were now six missionary stations in Bengal, with resident missionaries, and four occupied by native labourers; four in the upper provinces, and one at Surat and at Amboyna, in Burmah and in Ceylon. These stations were occupied by six missionaries sent out from England, exclusive of those at Serampore,—by fifteen missionaries, European and East Indian, engaged in the country,—and by twenty-seven native preachers and itinerants. The number baptized since Dr. Carey joined his brethren at Serampore had been seven hundred and sixty-five, of whom two-thirds had been natives. In regard to the translations, they observe that the entire canon of Scripture had been printed in the Bengalee and Oriya languages; the New Testament and the Pentateuch in the Sanscrit, Mahratta, and Hindee; the New Testament in the Sikh, and the Gospels in Chinese. The New Testament was, moreover, in the press in fourteen of the dialects of India. Grammars had also been published in seven of these languages. On the question of schools, they observe that the Benevolent Institution in Calcutta contained two hundred and twenty-nine children of both sexes; and twenty schools at nine stations were attended by seven hundred and eighty-eight children. These various exertions, they observe, were necessarily marked by imperfections. The missionary labourers pressed into the service while Government prohibited the access of missionaries from Europe, were defective in some of the qualifications for the work; the native preachers and itinerants lacked evangelical training, and the translations were unavoidably imperfect. But after every deduction had been made by the modesty of the missionaries, it will be apparent that their mission, planted in a country where everything had to be created, and reared amidst the stern opposition of the ruling authorities in England and India, presented a bright example of Christian devotion and energy, and justified the feeling of satisfaction with which they contemplated its progress in this communication to their colleague in England.

This report, however, did not reach him. He expired on the 7th of May, 1815, at the comparatively premature age of sixty-two, for his athletic frame and robust constitution gave promise of a longer life; but he had exhausted his strength in the cause of Christian benevolence. The powerful influence of his writings on the character of his own denomination, and the interests of Christian truth, it would be difficult to exaggerate. But it was in the great cause of missions that his character received its full development and attained its greatest eminence, and his name is indissolubly associated with the early, and as it may be termed, the heroic age of modern missions. His master-mind was peculiarly adapted to the exigencies of a cause which had to encounter the most formidable obstacles. His clear perception discovered the bearings of a complicated question at a glance, and his resolution carried him safely through a sea of difficulties. No little prejudices were ever allowed to disturb his judgment, or divert his mind from the great object before him. He was an administrator of the first order, and combined large and comprehensive views with attention to the minutest details. The natural ascendancy of a great mind placed him at the head of an undertaking which required the exercise of extraordinary talents. During the twenty years in which the cause of missions was struggling for existence, he devoted his mental and physical powers to the support of it with intense zeal and affection; and his life was prolonged till it had attained a position in which his peculiar qualifications were no longer required, and it might safely depend for its future progress on the ordinary impulse of Christian benevolence.

The connexion between the missionaries at Serampore and Mr. Fuller was characterised by that harmony of feeling and action which belongs to the infant stages of a great enterprise. Seldom has the *idem velle et idem nolle* been so clearly illustrated as in their intercourse. In all their communications, from first to last, there was no shade of reserve. The three men at Serampore were prepared to yield without servility to the judgment of their associate in England, and the feeling was fully reciprocated by him. It was not a time for the nice adjustment of the respective limits of authority, and there never was any suspicion of any encroachment on the province or the independence of each other. Dr. Ryland was now the only link which connected the Serampore missionaries with the Society. He had been associated with them in the undertaking from its commencement, and felt a personal attachment to them. But he had none of the genius and dignity of Mr. Fuller, and was unable to keep his own peculiar views in strict subordination to the interests of the mission. The silver cord of confidence was broken by Mr. Fuller's death, and it was not likely to be restored by Dr. Ryland, whose correspondence with Serampore was too often made repulsive by acrimony. This circumstance necessarily produced feelings of anxiety and mistrust at Serampore, and those differences which eventually resulted in an entire separation from the Society may be dated from the lamented death of Mr. Fuller.

Dr. Carey and his colleagues endeavoured to accommodate their course to the new circumstances in which the mission was placed by this event, in order to avoid a collision with his successors. Their management of the missionary establishment, as the constituted agents of the Society, had not given satisfaction to the missionaries sent out from England. Perhaps it was inseparable, from the situation of the parties, that the seniors, who had borne the heat and burden of the day, should expect more deference than the juniors were inclined to yield. They had frequently requested to be relieved from their invidious charge; but Mr. Fuller had invariably refused to listen to their entreaties. It was with difficulty they were enabled to maintain order and economy in the disbursement of the public funds while supported by his co-operation. Now that they were deprived of that support, and a new king was likely to arise who knew not Joseph, they felt it due to the interests of the mission to lay down the authority which had been forced on them. Immediately on the announcement of Mr. Fuller's decease, therefore, they addressed a letter to the Committee, dated the 28th of October, 1815, in which they stated that the extension of the mission, now no longer confined to one station, rendered it advisable for them to resign into their hands the direction of the European brethren. At the same time they engaged to provide from their own resources for the maintenance of the missionary labourers whom they themselves had engaged in the country.

The society formed by the evangelical section of the Church of England for missions to Africa and the East,—now the Church Missionary Society,—which was instituted in 1799, had not deemed it advisable to send missionaries to India while the Government continued hostile to the undertaking, but determined to take advantage of the favourable change which had now taken place, and two missionaries were designated to India in 1814. The address to them was composed by Mr., now Dr., Buchanan, though he was too ill to deliver it in person. It embodied the experience which he had acquired in India, and was generally characterised by sound judgment; but the gold was not without alloy. In his anxiety to stimulate pious clergymen to resort to India, he represented the missionary as going "to experience new modes of comfort," and as being required "to resist the seductions of affluence." He affirmed that a missionary appointment abroad was in general more lucrative than a curacy at home, and equally creditable and permanent; that Christian learning, combined with industry and probity, must frequently become a source of pecuniary advantage, and the accumulation of money was rapid, in consequence of the high rate of interest among the natives. To apply so low and sordid a stimulus to missionary zeal, and to hold out the prospect of a fortune by lending money to natives at usurious interest, appeared to Dr. Carey and his associates a very questionable proceeding, and as they were the only body of missionaries with whom Dr. Buchanan had been on terms of personal intercourse in Bengal, and his remarks might be considered as referring to them, they considered it their duty to counteract this statement. Dr. Marshman accordingly animadverted on it in an appendix to the Report, which furnishes a valuable record of the extreme frugality and simplicity which he and his brethren maintained in the midst of their affluence. "As the reverend and pious author is known to have lived a long time in the neighbourhood of the missionaries at Serampore, and as he has mentioned one of them by name, it may not be improper to state that the individual in question has never indulged himself with a single servant about his own person, a thing done by nearly every Portuguese clerk in the country, and that every article of food and clothing for himself and his family, like those of his missionary brethren, is covered by little more than sixty rupees a month; that notwithstanding the number of females in the family, and the extreme heat of the climate, no conveyance has been retained at the Mission House. Nor did the brethren there relieve the severe effects of a sedentary life by indulging in horse exercise, till the danger of falling into an untimely grave made them doubt whether by this course they were consulting the real interests of the mission."

Of Dr. Carey's habit of extreme frugality, Dr. Marshman gives an amusing account. "For fifteen years we have made the country rum a substitute for all wine and beer; because it was a rupee a gallon, while beer was twelve rupees a dozen, or six rupees a gallon. By mixing it with water it was reduced to the thirtieth part the price of beer; and our regard for missionary economy, which was rigid almost beyond belief, fixed us to this nauseous beverage. When the tumbler of rum-and-water was brought to Dr. Carey, about nine in the evening, as he sat at his desk with his translations, he would drink it down at one draught simply to get rid of it."

Towards the close of 1815, Serampore was restored to the Danish authorities. The great change in the current of trade, which brought Manchester cottons first to compete with, and then to supersede, Indian fabrics, combined with the opening of the trade of India to all British merchants, prevented the revival of its prosperity. Its value as a missionary asylum had ceased with the India Bill of 1813. The event of the restoration of the town to Denmark was communicated by Mr. Ward to a young friend in a letter, which will serve to exhibit the tone of his familiar correspondence. "While I am writing the guns are firing, the office is empty, and the Danish flag is again up. There go the guns from the Danish ship lying off Serampore. All is hushed, and nothing but smoke is left. How different when Christ takes possession of an immortal mind, and sets up His kingdom there; a reign of blessedness commences, measured only by eternity, and every step of progress is advancement towards endless perfection and happiness. O my dear friend, what are all those shows? they are but the monkey and the dancing-bear on a larger scale. O thou Fountain of splendour and moral glory, Thou who art the infinite expansion of everything great, and fair, and excellent, and glorious, never let my friend be content with anything but Thyself, and a portion in that which will last for ever."

Under the auspices of Lord Moira the tide was now turning in favour of Indian improvement. The Court of Directors had endowed a college at Benares for the encouragement of Hindoo learning and theology, and directed that a lecture should be delivered annually by the pundit in each department, and an English translation of it sent to Leadenhall Street. At the same time, any attempt to plant the seeds of moral and intellectual improvement had been pronounced, by the leading men in the Court of Directors and of Proprietors, "the most absurd and suicidal measure which could be devised." Lord Moira was the first Governor-General who repudiated the policy of resting the stability of our empire on the ignorance of the people, and stood forward as the champion of national education. He had written to Mr. Charles Grant to inquire whether the Court could not be persuaded to give support to schools formed on right principles, rather than to the encouragement of the Hindoo shasters and theology; but Mr. Grant assured him that the present time was not suitable for such a proposition. But he determined, notwithstanding, to pursue his own enlightened course. While at Benares, he offered the important aid of Government to Joynarayun Ghosal, a wealthy and educated native, who was anxious to establish and endow a seminary of useful knowledge. Mr. May, the missionary at Chinsurah, had formed a circle of schools in the neighbourhood, and Lord Moira encouraged the effort by a subscription of six hundred rupees a month. The impulse thus given to the cause of education produced a powerful effect on the native gentry in Calcutta, and early in 1816 a meeting was held at the Town Hall, when £11,000 were subscribed to found an institution—the Hindoo College—for giving a generous and liberal education to native youth.

The missionaries at Serampore, who had proposed their plan of popular education while the Government and the community were alike indifferent to it, determined to avail themselves of this improvement in public feeling, to appeal to the public for the means of enlarging it. Dr. Marshman accordingly drew up "Hints relative to Native Schools, together with an outline of an Institution for their Extension and Management." This little pamphlet was an enlarged and improved edition of the proposal they had made two years before, and embodied their more mature views on the subject of public instruction. It produced a powerful impression in India, and on its appearance in England was introduced into an article in the *Encyclopædia*. Under the modest title of "Hints," it exhibited a well-digested system of education for the masses in the vernacular tongue, which no subsequent efforts have rendered obsolete. The plan was never carried out to its legitimate extent, but there can be little doubt that if the missionaries had been enabled to prosecute it with their accustomed energy, the lower provinces of Bengal would now present a different aspect.

The first section of the "Hints" described the state of ignorance and degradation to which the natives were reduced, not one man in a hundred being able to read a common letter. The second section dwelt on the mode in which it was advisable to communicate knowledge, and boldly maintained the theory, then altogether heterodox, and scarcely orthodox at the present day, that any hope of giving instruction to the body of the people of India, or indeed of any country, through the medium of a language other than their own, would be found fallacious. The plan of instruction matured by Dr. Marshman, and detailed in the subsequent sections, embraced, in the first instance, several elementary works, intended to impart a knowledge of orthography and of the grammatical structure of the Bengalee language; a vocabulary of three or four thousand of the words in general use, and a simple treatise on arithmetic. These were to be followed by an outline of the solar system, couched in short axioms, in accordance with the mode in which instruction had been conveyed by the Hindoo sages from the most ancient period; then, a compendium of geography, and a popular treatise on natural philosophy. This was to be followed by a historical and chronological treatise; and, lastly, by a compendium of the doctrines, ethics, and morality of Christianity. "Should any one say, effect this object at once by introducing the Holy Scriptures into the schools; the measure is objected to simply because it does not appear to be the most efficient method which can be adopted. That the Scriptures contain every degree of information relative to the nature of man, his relation to God, a future state, &c., &c., no one can deny. They are, indeed, to the moral world, what the sun is to the natural world, the source of light and illumination. But from that great mass of Divine truth, interwoven in history, narrative, ecclesiastical polity, prophecy, doctrine, and precept, which forms the delightful study of a whole life in Britain, is it to be expected that a heathen youth, totally unacquainted with the nature of the book, should be able, under a heathen teacher, to select precisely those truths which would meet the deficiency in his own ideas? These truths, with which we are familiarised from our earliest infancy, should be laid down in a way no less clear and definite than those which relate to the solar system, natural philosophy, geography, and history. The compendium might be drawn up in the very language of Scripture, or otherwise, as might be deemed advisable."

The next section treated of the new system of instruction, and the new body of teachers it was proposed to create, on the plan which originated with Lancaster, and was then in the height of its popularity. Tables were to be prepared after his model, which were to exhibit the alphabet and its various combinations, together with words of two, three, and four syllables, as spelling exercises; the paradigms of nouns, pronouns, and verbs, and the rules of arithmetic, with a series of examples. These tables, sixty in number, were to be printed in large type, pasted on boards, and suspended round the room, to be used as the reading exercise of a whole class. Instruction of a higher order was to be given by dictation. Each boy was to write down in his copy-book the sentence deliberately pronounced by the monitor, who was to revise the lesson of the day when completed, and note down at the foot of the page the number of errors. It was then to be read in succession by the boys in the class. Thus one printed book served for a dozen children, who were enabled by this exercise to correct their orthography and improve their penmanship, and at the same time acquire a facility of reading and writing their own language. Instruction was thus combined with pleasure, and a spirit of animation as well as of emulation was diffused through the class. The most important facts, moreover, thus written from dictation, and read over repeatedly, could not fail to remain deeply impressed on the memory. If the treatises were comprised, as Dr. Marshman expected, in about four hundred and fifty pages, the whole series, at the rate of half a page a day, might be completed in about three years. Each class was to be placed under the direction of a monitor, and the duties of the master would thus be reduced to the maintenance of discipline, the regulation of the lessons, the registration of the daily exercises, and the general direction of the machinery. Eight or ten classes might thus be managed by a single master, and the progress of the scholars would be secured by the inherent impulse of the system. Schools conducted on this plan might be superintended with great ease. The chief function of the inspector, at his periodical visits, would consist in comparing the registry of attendance with the daily exhibition of work in the copy-books, and in examining each class and pupil in their various exercises. On the subject of expense, it was stated that the outfit of a school in sand-boards, slates, and tables, was not likely to exceed thirty rupees. It was proposed, when practicable, to rent rather than to erect a house, as the proprietor, who would generally be a man of influence in the village, would find his interest in encouraging the undertaking. The rent was taken at a rupee and a half a month; a corresponding sum, would, it was supposed, be sufficient to cover the expense of writing materials and books. The salary of the master was estimated at seven and a half rupees monthly, and a rupee to the monitors would raise the expense of each school to eleven rupees and a half a month. The entire cost of a circle of fifty schools, containing, on an average, seventy scholars each, was estimated at 825 rupees a month, or about £1,000 a year. Such was the plan developed in the "Hints," and it is chiefly interesting, as the first platform ever devised for a system of popular and vernacular education in Bengal.

The pamphlet then proceeded to describe the progress which had been made in carrying the plan into execution. A new fount of types of a size suitable for the tables had been prepared, with which the alphabet and its combinations and the spelling-lessons had been printed; the arithmetical tables were in the press, and of the treatises, some were in the hands of the printer, and others ready for him. The missionaries had established a normal school at Serampore, and a number of masters had been, to a certain extent, trained to their duties. The first school was established at a village across the river, four miles from Serampore. To conciliate the inhabitants, they had been requested to select a master and send him to the training-school. Village after village had followed the example, and despatched the man of their choice to Serampore. Nineteen schools had thus been established, and all at the request of the inhabitants themselves. In some instances men of influence had offered their own residence, and even the family temple for a school-room. Houses had been erected by men of property in the hope of their being rented. Children were attracted to the schools from the most respectable families, and one school contained ten brahmin youths. Instruction was eagerly welcomed in every direction, and there is every reason to believe that if the missionaries had received continuous and energetic support, instead of being distracted by opposition, the country around the metropolis would have been leavened with knowledge.

CHAPTER VIII.

THIS narrative has now reached the period of those unhappy differences with the Baptist Missionary Society, which, from this time forward, and for twenty years, embittered the lives and cramped the energies of the Serampore missionaries; but the writer is anxious to avoid any reference to them, beyond that which may be indispensable to the completeness of this biography. The death of Mr. Fuller was an irreparable loss to the interests of the mission. It broke the bond of confidence and cordiality which had so long united the two bodies in England and India, and had contributed so greatly to the success of their united labours. The management of the affairs of the Society devolved on men who, with one exception, were strangers to those at Serampore, and new feelings and tendencies were developed, foreign to the associations of the preceding twenty years. The old economy of missions, under which Dr. Carey, Dr. Marshman, and Mr. Ward had embarked for India, depending for the means of subsistence mainly on their own exertions, with supplementary aid from England, had passed away. The Societies, strengthened by ample resources, were now enabled to undertake the entire support of their missionaries, and this brought into exercise a principle of subordination to the home authorities, to which the early missionaries had been strangers. Men who had always acted in the spirit of independence, could ill brook the designation, which now began to be applied to them, of the "senior servants of the Society." It was to this state of transition, always beset as it is with embarrassments, that those differences are to be attributed, which gradually became wider and more acrimonious as new elements of irritation were introduced. Those who now came into power at home were new to the management of the mission, and had little knowledge of its traditions. At the first meeting of the committee after Mr. Fuller's death, unfriendly hints were thrown out regarding the conduct of the Serampore missionaries, and they were led to understand that investigations were about to be instituted in reference to some of their proceedings. It is scarcely a matter of surprise that they should have felt some degree of annoyance when they saw themselves regarded in the light of men who were required to vindicate their integrity, rather than as coadjutors in an enterprise which was indebted chiefly to their labours for its present position. Nor could they fail to contrast the mistrust and suspicions of the committee with the unbounded confidence of the Indian public, which they had earned by long and disinterested services.

It was under the influence of these feelings that the annual meeting of the Society was held in October, 1816, when, among other topics, the question of the premises, which the missionaries had bought in the early days of the mission for £3,000, was brought up. The members of the committee, which had been injudiciously enlarged to forty-two, were totally ignorant of the position in which the premises stood, but they appeared very anxious to secure them to the Society. Dr. Ryland entreated them to pause and to make inquiries before they committed themselves to any resolution, and he assured them that "all would be right." A sub-committee of nine was accordingly appointed, which met for the first time three months after, and by its precipitate course of action brought matters to a crisis. Without waiting for any explanation from Serampore, they consulted a Calcutta lawyer, the son of a Baptist minister, who happened to be on a visit to England, and, on his advice, resolved at once to direct that the property at Serampore should be vested in eight trustees, resident in England, in addition to those in India. It has been already stated that, on the death of Mr. Fuller, Dr. Carey and his associates voluntarily resigned the management of the mission, which had been intrusted to them, into the hands of the committee, engaging, at the same time, to support from their own resources the local missionaries whom they had themselves sent into the field. The sub-committee took up this question likewise, and resolved to accept this offer, "to undertake on behalf of the Society the direction of the missionaries already under their care, as an internal regulation." This was the first communication received at Serampore subsequent to the death of Mr. Fuller, and the resolutions appeared to substantiate the worst fears which had been created by Dr. Ryland's private correspondence. During Mr. Fuller's life their contributions to the mission had been regarded by him and by themselves as the donations of independent men. But these funds were now to be expended "on behalf of the Society," and the administration of them was to be considered merely as an "internal regulation," which was interpreted to imply that they were treated as much under the control of the Society as the subscriptions raised in England. The whole question of the independence of the missionaries appeared to be involved in the resolution, which had been evidently penned with great care and precision. On the question of the premises, they felt that to place them in the hands of a majority of trustees in England, chosen by the committee, would effectively place them beyond their control, endanger their continued residence in them, and expose all their missionary operations to the risk of interruption. Their minds were filled with anxiety, and the danger to which they had been exposed by the hostility of Government appeared light in comparison with the danger which now menaced them from home.

The task of framing a reply to the letter of the sub-committee devolved on Dr. Marshman, but it received the fullest approbation of both his colleagues. It was the least happy of all his compositions, decisive in its tone, but unnecessarily prolix and complicated, the simple point at issue being often lost in a cloud of argumentation. The demand of the Society was unequivocally rejected, and the spirit of domination to which it was traced was rebutted in a tone of asperity that was much to be regretted, though great allowance must be made for the feeling of consternation and excitement under which the letter was written. The missionaries stated that, while they had transmitted to England, year by year, detailed statements of the funds sent to them, they had never given, even to Mr. Fuller, any account of the sums realised by their own exertions. With regard to the premises, they executed an "explanatory declaration," which, however, proved to be of no legal force, but which secured them, as they thought, from intrusion. In reference to their pecuniary position, of which most exaggerated reports had been industriously diffused in England, they state that, at the time, "they had scarcely anything left. To support the cause we have exerted ourselves almost beyond our strength, and in a climate which drinks up the spirits have laid on ourselves labours which few constitutions in England could bear. We have deprived ourselves of all recreation, and the hours which, after the labours of the day, others devote to social intercourse with their families, we have given to extra labours or particular studies. We have lived at one common table, and subjected the regimen of our families to each other's will, that we might devote the expense of separate establishments to that cause to which we have devoted ourselves. Were we taken away by death, our families must be turned out on the charity of the public, and, indeed, almost without a rupee, had we not husbanded the little we possessed before we joined the mission, and which, after eighteen years' accumulation, is not equal to four months' produce of the labour we devote to the cause." And this was written when the sums they had acquired since their settlement at Serampore exceeded £50,000. The question of the premises, to which it is not desirable to return, was finally disposed of in a subsequent letter from Serampore. "After the difficult crisis of 1817 had passed over, and the Society's missionaries had established a mission in Calcutta, and we had purchased other and adjoining premises on which our operations might be carried on without risk of future interruption, we felt no hesitation in offering to reconstruct the deeds so as to secure the right of property to your satisfaction, and to admit a new body of trustees. If you will put these two circumstances together—our having resisted the demand for new trustees, when such a step would have been fatal to our honour, and destructive of our missionary plans, and our subsequent voluntary offer of the same concession when it could have done no harm—you will feel convinced that there never was any intention of alienating them." The premises, therefore, remained the property of the Society, who sold them after the Serampore mission had ceased to exist.

The difficulties of this period were exaggerated by the spirit of estrangement shewn by the Society's missionaries, subsequently known as the "junior brethren." They removed to Calcutta, and formed a new mission on the basis of an entire subordination to the committee in England, which they affirmed that Dr. Carey and his colleagues had repudiated. The establishment of another missionary institution in the sphere of labour so long occupied by the Serampore missionaries, and on the ground of their revolt from the Society, could not fail to widen and inflame the breach. It was scarcely possible, by the most exemplary Christian forbearance, to avoid the irritation produced by this proximity. It is not to be questioned, that, apart from the feelings of personal dislike, the junior brethren were actuated by motives which they considered sacred and evangelical; but this, far from mitigating the evil, seemed rather to aggravate it, by giving this antagonism the strength of conscientious motives. The spirit of unlimited submission which the junior brethren professed to the wishes of the committee, with regard both to their funds and their movements, naturally created a feeling of partiality towards them, and of corresponding alienation from what was considered the rebellious station of Serampore. To crown the difficulties of the time, Dr. Ryland, a man of profound learning, but of weak judgment and strong prejudices, whose correspondence with Dr. Marshman had always savoured more of the tutor than the colleague, allowed himself to be carried along by this adverse current to such an extent as to charge him in one of his letters with "canting tortuosity."

The reply of the Society, however, to the letter from Serampore, adopted at a general meeting, held at Reading on the 31st of August, 1818, breathed the old spirit of cordiality; it was not only frank but affectionate. The junior secretary, Mr. Dyer, said, "that if their brethren at Serampore could have been present at the meeting, when silent tears around the circle attested how cordially all united in their petitions for you and us, the flame of holy love would have burst forth with new vigour in their bosoms, and totally consumed every remnant of mistrust and suspicion, should any such be still remaining there." The most sanguine hopes were now entertained of an amicable settlement of all difficulties, and Dr. Marshman wrote on the occasion, "The letters from the Society are in the highest degree pleasing; they breathe the most cordial love to us." But this bright expectation of a return of harmony and confidence was not to be realised. Within three months of the despatch of this communication, Mr. Dyer, who was now beginning to take the lead in the committee, sent a private communication to Dr. Carey, stating that a suspicion had been raised in the minds of the committee that he had signed the letter of July, 1817, without weighing or approving it, under the influence of Dr. Marshman. Mr. Dyer had employed himself in diligently collecting all the calumnies circulated in England regarding Dr. Marshman's extravagant mode of living, his ambition, his attachment to his children, and his ascendency at Serampore, and now desired Dr. Carey, as he said at the request of the committee, to furnish his private opinion on these charges. Dr. Carey, while he treated this clandestine proceeding with the indignation it deserved, still deemed it due to his colleague to place on the records of the Society the fullest vindication of his conduct. But, unhappily, his defence, though triumphant, was considered by the committee only as a fresh proof of his infatuation. The impression produced by this letter of Mr. Dyer it was impossible to banish from the mind. In his public letter, he represented the committee as dissolved in tears at the mistrust entertained of their conduct, and overflowing with love to their beloved brethren at Serampore. In his private letter, written three months after, as the Society's representative, he endeavoured to sow mistrust among them, and to introduce an odious system of espionage into the bosom of their families. They now perceived that, under the official crust of kindliness, there was a current of jealousy and suspicion fatal to all union, and they began to fear that no reliance could be placed on the most friendly professions of the committee.

This unpleasant subject has carried the narrative beyond the year 1817, to which we return. The missionaries at Serampore had hitherto made no provision for their widows and orphans; with the exception of a small pittance for apparel and contingencies, all their income had been thrown into the general stock. Mr. Fuller had often censured this self-denying ordinance, and as a friend, had recommended them to appropriate the receipts of at least a twelve-month for the benefit of their families. This advice they at length adopted, and in the present year resolved to reserve a tenth of their respective incomes for this object. About the same time Dr. Carey united his efforts with those of the Marchioness of Hastings—Lord Moira had been raised in the previous year to the dignity of a Marquis—and Mr. Butterworth Bayley, one of the most enlightened servants of the Company, in the formation of the Calcutta School Book

Society, to supply the wants of the schools which were springing up on all sides. The liberal views of Lord Hastings, which formed a new era in the history of British India, and consigned to the tomb the traditionary policy of the India House politicians, were clearly expounded in the speech he delivered at the College examinations of the present year, in the course of which he said, "This Government never will be influenced by the erroneous—shall I not rather call it the designing?—position, that to spread information among men is to render them less submissive to authority. . . . It would be treason against British sentiment to imagine that it ever could be the principle of this Government to perpetuate ignorance in order to insure paltry and dishonest advantages over the blindness of the multitude." Yet this treason had been deliberately committed by the authorities at the India House, when they compelled Parliament by their clamours to expunge from the India Bill of 1793 the clause which authorised the introduction of schoolmasters into the country. It was in reference to the sentiments thus expressed, that Mr. Charles Grant wrote to Lord Hastings, that the "moral amelioration of so large a portion of the human species may surely be regarded as one of the greatest designs of Providence in placing such a distant region under the care of an enlightened nation. Your Lordship has been, I think, almost the first person in eminent station who has practically acted upon it."

The plan described in the "Hints," for the extension of schools among the natives, had succeeded beyond the most sanguine expectation. Contributions from the European community poured in with unexampled liberality. Forty-five schools were established within a circle of twenty miles around Serampore, in which two thousand children received the elements of knowledge in their own tongue. Dr. Marshman sent a copy of the first report of the schools to Lord Hastings, then engaged in the Mahratta and Pindaree war, to which he replied, "I ought long ago to have acknowledged your obliging attention in sending me the report of the institution for the encouragement of native schools. The weight of business which I have had on me must be my apology for the tardiness of my thanks. You are probably aware of the custom of native princes to present sums destined for distribution in charity. The sums thus offered are carried to what is called the charity fund in the hands of the public secretary. I do not know any charity which can, in this country, be more urgent than the giving to children the means of acquiring the principles of morality. I have directed Mr. Adam to remit you 500 rupees for the institution."

At the close of the present year, the missionaries drew up a review of the mission for the three years subsequent to that which was sent to Mr. Fuller in 1815. It stated that the number of adults baptized during this period amounted to four hundred and seventy, and that the Sacred Scriptures had been brought into circulation, in some cases in single Gospels, in sixteen of the languages and dialects of India. The number of tracts distributed in three years exceeded three hundred thousand, in the missionary stations on the continent of India, and in the islands, in twenty different languages.

For some time past the missionaries had contemplated the publication of a newspaper in the Bengalee language, in order to stimulate a spirit of inquiry, and to diffuse general information. It appeared, however, a hazardous undertaking while the English periodical press in Calcutta was under a rigid and jealous censorship. Dr. Marshman and Mr. Ward, therefore, by way of a feeler, announced the publication in the English journals of the Presidency. The public censor, however, made no communication on the subject, and on the 31st of May, 1818, the first newspaper ever printed in any Eastern language was issued from the Serampore press. It was called the *Sumachar Durpun; or, Mirror of News.* Dr. Carey, who had passed twenty-five years under a suspicious and despotic Government, regarded the enterprise with no little alarm. Though fully aware of the liberal policy of Lord Hastings, he did not think that the Government was prepared for so great a stride in the career of improvement as the introduction of newspapers into the native community, and he feared it might affect the good understanding which then subsisted between the missionaries and the Government. When the proof-sheet was brought for final revision, at the weekly meeting on Friday evening, he renewed his objections to the undertaking, and deprecated its results. But Dr. Marshman assured him that a copy of the journal should be sent the next morning to the chief secretary, with a schedule of the contents, and that it should be relinquished if any disapprobation of it was manifested. But no objection was raised by any members of the Government, and the native periodical press was at once established. The novelty of a weekly paper in their own language gave the *Durpun* great popularity among the natives, and the subscription list, headed by Dwarkenath Tagore, was speedily filled. The postage of newspapers at this time was, however, so heavy, as to restrict the circulation of the *Durpun*, published at only sixpence a number, to the metropolis and its immediate neighbourhood. Dr. Marshman, therefore, addressed Lord Hastings on the subject, and, on his return to the Presidency, he expressed his opinion, that "the effect of such a paper must be extensively and importantly useful," and directed that it should be transmitted throughout the country at one-fourth the usual rate of postage. In the present year, the missionaries also commenced the publication of a monthly magazine, which Dr. Marshman designated the "*Friend of India*," a name which has been associated with the periodical publications of Serampore for nearly half a century. It was intended to include original essays on questions connected with the progress of improvement in India, and notices of the proceedings of Bible, Missionary, and Educational Societies in all parts of the world.

The state of isolation in which Dr. Carey and his colleagues now found themselves placed by the withdrawal of all sympathy with their operations by their brethren in India, and the Society in England, did not, however, produce any relaxation of their exertions. They had for several years been making preparation for the establishment of an institution with the view of more effectually training native preachers and schoolmasters, and giving a more complete education to native students, more especially to those of Christian parentage. They now determined to make an effort for the formation of a college, which should supply these wants, and consolidate their plans for the spiritual and intellectual improvement of the country. On the 15th of July, 1818, they issued the prospectus of a "College for the Instruction of Asiatic Christian and other youth in Eastern Literature and European Science." It was drawn up by Dr. Marshman in his own peculiar and argumentative style, and announced in unequivocal terms, that the institution was intended to be the handmaid of evangelisation. It stated that those who were to be employed in propagating the Gospel in India should obtain a thorough knowledge of the doctrines then held sacred in the country, and that this could not be gained without a knowledge of the Sanscrit language, in which they were enshrined. Hence the necessity of an institution which should impart instruction to the native preacher, not only in the doctrines which he was to teach, but in those he was to combat, inasmuch as while he remained ignorant of the dogmas and arguments of Hindooism, his position as a public teacher in the interests of a nobler creed could not fail to be disadvantageous. Had the apostle Paul been as ignorant of the philosophy of the Greeks, as both European and native teachers, with few exceptions, were of the Hindoo system of philosophy and religion, he could not have cited their own writings or so efficiently fulfilled his mission. "If ever," it was remarked, "the Gospel stands in India, it must be by native opposed to native, demonstrating its excellence above all other systems."

In pursuance of these views, it was proposed to give the students a thorough knowledge of Sanscrit, the sacred language of Hindooism, and of Arabic, the canonical language of Mahomedanism. The students were, moreover, to be well grounded in European science and knowledge, through the medium of epitomes published in their own language, and explained to them in lectures. After this course of study was completed, a select number were to apply to the study of English, and endeavour to attain such a knowledge of it as would "enable them to dive into the deepest recesses of European science and enrich their own language with its choicest treasures." The college was likewise to include a normal school, to educate teachers in the science of instruction, and qualify them for organising and managing schools. But it was to be considered pre-eminently a divinity school, where Christian youths, of personal piety and aptitude for the work of an evangelist, should pursue a course of instruction in Christian theology. It was to be open to native youths from all parts of India, without distinction of caste or creed. A library was to be formed, a philosophical apparatus provided, and an edifice erected at Serampore suited to the objects of the institution. The government of the college was to be vested in the governor of Serampore for the time being, and the three senior missionaries. The expense was calculated at about £2,000 a year, which was considered sufficient for the support of two professors, an English tutor, a staff of pundits and native teachers, and a hundred and fifty students. To this institution, intended to promote the cause of Christianity and the interests of literature of India, the missionaries were anxious to give that degree of independence, by means of endowments, which was necessary to its permanent utility, without removing the necessity of a salutary reliance on the support and confidence of the public. They offered, therefore, to subscribe £2,500 to it from their own resources.

It may appear singular at the present day, that men who

had passed twenty years in India, and were intimately acquainted with its exigencies, should have given the institution so strong an Oriental cast, and postponed the study of English to that of Sanscrit. But it was their full conviction that the evangelisation of India must be accomplished through the vernacular tongues, and the study of Sanscrit was made prominent, because it was not only the depository of the doctrines Christianity was to subvert, but also the parent of Indian philology, and the standard of literary purity and excellence. They were anxious to throw the weight of Oriental scholarship into the scale of Christianity, and they even contemplated a period when the writings of Locke and Bacon, and of the most eminent English divines, should appear in a Sanscrit dress, and supersede the philosophical Dursuns. The idea that English might become the medium of Christian civilisation in India, though cherished by a few ardent spirits, had as yet no practical exemplification. Hitherto, it had been valued only as it opened the path to lucrative employment in the offices of the British Government, as Persian had done under the Mahomedans, and it was not believed that native youths could be induced to remain long enough at their studies to obtain a knowledge of the English classics. These ideas have been corrected by the progress of circumstances. The liberal policy of Lord William Bentinck has opened up situations of dignity and emolument in the public establishments to the natives of Bengal, for many of which a thorough knowledge of English is indispensable. Hundreds of natives have thus been induced to cultivate our language with great assiduity, and have become as familiar with its best authors as the graduates of Cambridge and Oxford. This education has carried them ahead of their national creed, and the influence of Hindooism has been sapped, not, as the missionaries supposed, by learned argumentation, but by the introduction of higher and nobler sentiments. If they could have foreseen this revolution, they would, doubtless, have accommodated their plans to it.

The prospectus of the College was immediately sent to Lord Hastings, who expressed his approbation of it, but regretted that it should appear to announce such broad and unequivocal professions of an intention to aim at converting the native students as would be thought to give great alarm to any of the Hindoos who might have the document translated to them. "This step," he remarked, "was so different from the wise and sagacious patience with which the gentlemen at Serampore were securing ultimate success in their object, that he was satisfied they would excuse his drawing their attention to what they must have overlooked." To this, Dr. Marshman replied that the College embraced two distinct objects. It was intended primarily to educate the children of native Christians, and hence the arrangements for Christian instruction had been more expressly set forth. It was also intended to give Hindoo and Mahomedan youth the benefit of its classes, without putting any strain on their consciences. Perhaps they had not sufficiently guarded against the misapprehension that the particular course of study laid down for Christians would not be compulsory on students of other creeds; but this would be more clearly explained in the first report.

Mr. Ward's severe and incessant labours for eighteen years had now begun to affect his health. A journey which he took in the spring to Dacca and Chittagong brought only temporary relief, and his medical advisers insisted on a voyage to England. He was reluctant to quit his colleagues at a time when the difficulties of their position was becoming more complicated. But it was hoped that a visit to his native land would not only restore him to the vigour of health, but afford the opportunity of healing the breach with the Society, by personal and friendly communications. He embarked on the 18th of December, 1818. During the early part of the voyage, when his frame was invigorated by the sea breeze and the novelty of leisure, he employed his time in composing "Reflections on the Word of God for every

Day in the Year, to be used in Family Devotions." But as the voyage drew to a close his complaint returned, with the addition of dropsical symptoms, and his mind gave way to morbid reflections. He landed in England in May, 1819, enfeebled rather than strengthened by the voyage, and hastened to Bristol, where his friend, Dr. Ryland, was greatly alarmed at his appearance, and immediately called in medical aid. Mr. Ward found that Dr. Ryland still retained all his warmth of affection for Serampore, but had, unfortunately, imbibed the strongest prejudices against Dr. Marshman.

On the first appearance of convalescence, Mr. Ward travelled through the country and visited the friends of the mission; but as he proceeded on his journey his feelings were deeply wounded by the calumnies which had for some time been disseminated in every quarter, and which affected not only the consistency, but the honour and integrity of the Serampore missionaries. Every member of the committee repudiated the imputation of having given them currency, but they predominated in every circle. In one of his letters to his colleagues he stated, that if matters had been straight between Serampore and the Society he might with ease have raised £6,000 for the College, but so fatal an impression had been created, both in England and in Scotland, that contributors hesitated to continue their donations to the Society. They were charged with having amassed colossal fortunes, amidst all their professions of disinterestedness, and throughout the denomination it had become an article of belief that they were no longer to be entrusted with public money. One gentleman, at Birmingham, who had been in the habit of giving £50 a year to the Society, refused to renew the subscription unless he was assured that the funds of the Society did not go to "the men at Serampore." Dr. Stuart, of Dunearne, one of the most enthusiastic friends of the missionaries, informed him that a friend, on reading Dr. Marshman's "Hints on Native Schools," had entrusted him with £500 for that object, but had subsequently forbidden him to transmit it until more satisfactory information could be obtained of the mode in which the missionaries had appropriated other funds. Dr. Stuart likewise placed in his hands a letter of the bulk of a pamphlet which he had received from Calcutta, filled with invectives against Dr. Marshman. In communicating this fact to his brethren, Mr. Ward remarked, that letters of a similar complexion were coming over in great profusion, sufficient to ruin the fairest reputation, and to loosen the bonds of friendship where it was most firmly cemented. He drew up a reply to the letter, which at once disposed of the calumnies. But for one instance where an opportunity was afforded of correcting these misrepresentations, there were ten in which they remained without an antidote. The characters of the absent are always at the mercy of those who are present. Detraction is generally more welcome to human nature than commendation, and these calumnies soon acquired the force of permanent convictions, and the reputation which it had been the labour of a life to build up was blasted beyond recovery in a few months.

Under the feeling of anguish created by these hostile impressions, he wrote to his colleagues in the most importunate strain. "Did ever men place their affairs in such a state of suspicion, since the world began, without the shadow of a reason, and deliver up their fair characters to be spat upon, and themselves to be spoken of as rogues, by those who seek occasion against them, as we have done? Are we not doing everything for Him who 'loved us, and loved us to the death'? Let us do it then in such a way that our friends may rejoice over us, and we rejoice with them. Let us not drive them to the necessity of apologising for us, and making the best of our affairs, as though we were doing something in the dark to give birth to future infamy." He then recommended, in the strongest terms, that they should draw up a deed of settlement, securing the appropriation of the property they had created to the cause of missions, and providing a succession of faithful disinterested men to carry on their labours upon the principle of an entire consecration of all their earnings to the cause of the missions, and that in case of their neglecting to fill up vacancies, the Society should possess the right to do so, and that the property should pass to the Society if the union was broken up. This communication, so novel in its character, after he had cordially approved of all the proceedings of his brethren, created no little surprise in their minds. Three individuals of congenial feelings had been brought together by an extraordinary concurrence of circumstances, and had acquired independent resources, and agreed to throw them into a common stock for the promotion of a great public object, and they were now required, under the penalty of forfeiting the confidence of the public, and "descending to their graves with infamy," to provide for the perpetuation of such a union on the same principles. They were required to find three men of Christian zeal, capable of creating independent incomes, and, in a country where every man husbanded his gains for the luxuries of England, willing to consecrate nine-tenths of them to the mission in India. Well might Dr. Carey and Dr. Marshman exclaim, on hearing what was expected of them in England, "There is no king, lord, nor ruler that asketh such things at any magician, astrologer, or Chaldean."

They determined, however, to lose no time in meeting the impassioned wishes of their colleague; and after long and anxious deliberation, constructed a deed of settlement to meet these requirements, as far as human ingenuity could do so. It provided for the independence of the institution at Serampore, and its union with the Society on the basis of that independence. But the arrangement was too complicated to be of any practical value, and it exhibited rather an earnest desire to meet objections, however unreasonable, which were injurious to the cause of missions, than any solution of the difficult problem propounded to them. It fully satisfied Mr. Ward's ideas; it was a deed to which he could point with confidence as vindicating the honesty and disinterestedness of the Serampore missionaries. From the day of its arrival, every feeling of hesitation regarding his return to Serampore was removed, and every letter breathed a feeling of the warmest affection for the associations of what he termed "the dear old spot." But he was never more mistaken than when he supposed that such a settlement would silence the tongue of censure. After it had been executed, they stood no fairer with the members of their own denomination who were estranged from them, than they had stood before. These hostile opinions had assumed the character of a virtuous indignation against great public delinquents, and it seemed a dereliction of duty to abandon them. Few men have strength of mind sufficient to admit that they have been misled, and calumnies rarely become extinct except with the death of those who have cherished them.

This deed of settlement was, however, anything but satisfactory to the secretary, Mr. Dyer, and other influential members of the committee. The clear determination which it exhibited to maintain the independence of operations at Serampore, produced as great a feeling of consternation as if it involved some conspiracy against the interests of the Society. On the perusal of this document, Mr. Ward was, for the first time since his arrival, invited to attend a meeting of the committee. There, as he wrote out to his colleagues, "the discussion turned on the question of our independence, and I found our finger on the very spot where the bone was out of joint. I wished the Society to be the conservators of the union, as they were the natural guardians of it. I stated that if this point was conceded, minor matters might be adjusted; but that, in the maintenance of their independence, they would find Carey, Marshman, and Ward one. I further urged that the dispute about independence was a war of words; that the Society was contending for a phantom, for over every such station, the control must be nominal; that, seeing union was desirable for both parties, it was wise to establish it on such a basis as would be attended with perfect confidence; and that, after the acknowledgment of our independence, their advice with regard to ulterior measures would weigh with greater force. . . . Mr. Guttridge, Mr. Shaw, Dr. Gregory, and Mr. Broadley Wilson all pleaded that there was a natural and necessary dependence of all stations on the parent Society; the head and the members, the senders and the sent; the very name of missionary implied this. Here, then, the matter is brought to an issue. There is no chance of union with the Society but by acknowledging their supremacy. Mr. Guttridge said they could not, if they would, acknowledge our independence; their duty to the public forbade it. There is no hope, then, whatever, as far as I can see, of our being one with the Society; they will not concede, and we will not relinquish our independence. As a committee, Serampore is to them an object of jealousy, and they will become more and more alienated as the hope of bringing us into a state of dependence lessens or becomes extinct. No effort is ever made in favour of schools or translations. Serampore is a foreigner, and every letter and every article coming from thence is turned over, as though it had a bad odour. It is not *ours*, is the feeling. There is a strong feeling throughout the country in favour of Serampore, but it is stifled, and cannot expand itself on account of incessant rumours of family interests, and some latent villany hatching there, to come out by-and-by. If we would acknowledge our subjection, I believe we might have everything; but, at the same time, subjection to a body always changing, is a dangerous thing. The nature of the union between them and us does not call for this subjection; if they could obtain it they would be none the better, and we might at a future period be the worse." With this irreconcilable difference between the two bodies, on a question of such vital importance, Mr. Ward felt that it would be vain to entertain any hope of cordial union, and he renounced all hope of restoring it.

Forty-five years have passed since the date of this controversy; and, on a calm and historical review of it, there appears to be more cause for regret than surprise. It is matter of regret that the Serampore missionaries should have been checked in their career, just at the time when their plans were matured. So far as any of the members of the committee were actuated by the love of power and domination, and permitted the indulgence of it to impede the progress of Christian truth in India, it is much to be lamented. But there were good and conscientious men in that body, and great allowance must be made for the error of their views. They dwelt on the "first principles of all missionary societies," entirely forgetting that the Serampore mission was established before those principles existed, and could not be amenable to them. Experience has, moreover, taught that, as the object of missionary societies is to plant the Gospel in heathen lands, in the hope that it will grow and flourish without their aid, they are successful in exact proportion as their agency ceases to be necessary. It is their duty, therefore, to foster every independent effort for the support either of missionaries or of native pastors. This doctrine, which no one questions at the present day, was at that period as little recognised as the doctrine of free trade. If it had been applied to Serampore, which, after having been planted by the Society, shot up with such vigour as to require no further succour, the angry discussions of ten years would have been spared. Instead of pottering over the old records in search of some token of subordination to the committee, in the unreserved correspondence of early days, the committee should have taken the *status quo* as the basis of action, and accepted the offer of independent and hearty co-operation in a frank and manly spirit. Twenty years after, when their Jamaica mission had acquired the same independent resources as Serampore, and made the same proposal which was made by Dr. Carey and his colleagues, it was cheerfully accepted.

Mr. Ward's life in England was one of constant activity, and he was incessantly engaged either in the pulpit or on the platform in rousing the public to the spiritual wants of India. He was the first missionary who had ever returned to England from the East, and in every circle he received the most enthusiastic welcome. His warm and animated addresses were well calculated to fix the attention of popular assemblies, and the novelty of his relations gave them a peculiar interest. "I have," he writes, "all the attention and popularity which a greedy man could wish, but I sigh for home. One half-hour in communion with my God is far more precious than 'hear, hear,' echoed by a thousand voices at a public meeting." He published an enlarged edition of his "History of the Religion, Manners, and Philosophy of the Hindoos." He likewise made the most strenuous efforts to promote the establishment of female schools in India. He issued an earnest appeal to the British public on the atrocities of female immolation, and endeavoured to organise an association for the suppression of it. "We must," he said, "inundate England with these horrid tales, till the practice can be tolerated no longer;" but the time had not arrived for extinguishing these fires, which the genius of Hindooism had fed with living victims for twenty-five centuries. He visited the various counties and towns in England, Scotland, and Wales, addressing crowded audiences, and waiting personally on the wealthy and the benevolent on behalf of Serampore College, and succeeded in raising about £3,000—of which £500 were contributed by that eminent philanthropist, the late Mr. Douglas, of Cavers,—which he placed in the hands of trustees in England, whom, to obviate the objections of the most prejudiced, he selected from among the members of the committee.

In the beginning of 1820, Mrs. Marshman, whose constitution had been undermined by twenty years of unrelieved toil in the management of a large school for the support of the mission, was constrained to resort to England to recruit her strength. She landed in England in a state of great debility, and was constrained to follow the example of Mr. Ward, and resort at once to Cheltenham, then the lazaretto of old Indians. To introduce her to the sympathy of the friends of the mission, he sent a paragraph to various magazines, stating that she had been driven to England in search of health, after having contributed many thousand pounds to the cause of missions by her personal exertions; but in the denominational organ, the "Baptist Magazine," the allusion to her contributions was struck out. A few brief extracts from Dr. Marshman's letters to her, will serve to exhibit the temper and tone of his mind under the storm of obloquy which then assailed him:—"I am this day fifty-two; fifty-two years of unspeakable mercy. The evil I feared has not come, and the good expected has exceeded my highest expectations. I look back to the last thirty years more especially, with feelings of deep emotion; what a scene of mercy and blessing, of labour and enjoyment!" "Had not my dependence been upon God, I should either have been transported with anger under the trials I have had to endure, and have given up the support of the mission, or have sunk under the treatment I have received, even from my friend Dr. Ryland, and have died of a broken heart. In our late examination, which the unkindness of others constrained us to make, we found that the sum contributed by my family would have given us an income of £1,200 a year in England and £2,000 a year in India. I rejoice more, unspeakably more, in having thus devoted it to the cause of God than as though the whole sum lay by me at this moment; and I humbly hope, as our income is now much greater, to devote two lacs—£20,000—more to this glorious cause, should your health and mine be spared for a few years to come." "I have learned by experience that it is less painful to suffer in silence the most rancorous defamation, for years together, than by attempting to avenge ourselves, under the idea of doing ourselves justice, to injure the cause of missions, even for an hour."

In his letters to Mr. Ward, he remarks:—"When I write to any one else at home but you, I am never sure what use may be made of my letters. One solitary expression, written in the utmost simplicity at midnight, between sleeping and waking, may be spread through the country, and be made the subject of animadversions for seven years to come. . . . Had we not at Serampore insisted on our rights as men and as Christians, we must at this time have been turned out of the premises purchased with the labour of our hands, or have had insupportable misery with colleagues forced on us. You may possibly hear reflections on me; if you think it worth while to notice them, you may say, that, through the blessing of God, my family is enabled to devote two or three thousand pounds annually to the cause of missions; this, therefore, is sufficient to prove our sincerity. How little do even our own friends in England know me! Why do I not take the next three or four years of the labour of my family, which I can honourably do, and which would produce £10,000? and the interest of this in India would keep me and my family for ever. . . . You have indeed nothing to fear relative to the cause of missions from my feelings, wounded as they have been by the conduct of Dr. Ryland and Mr. Dyer. I think a man ought as much to sacrifice his feelings to the cause of God, as his pecuniary interests. Are we to desert, or even slacken in the cause of our Redeemer, because some of His servants are imperfect?"

The "late examination of their affairs," to which Dr. Marshman alludes above, referred to a statement which they drew up and put in type, to meet various sinister reports circulated against them in England, which Mr. Ward had reported. It was a brief review of all their proceedings, and a clear exposition of their pecuniary disbursements, and went minutely into every point on which, as far as they could learn, their conduct had been impugned. It was twenty years within a fortnight since they first met together at Serampore, and read Mr. Fuller's farewell communication, informing them that the Society was unable to guarantee more than £360 a year for the support of six families, and were thus obliged at once to strike out some plan for their own support. They had not only succeeded in accomplishing this object, but during the subsequent period had acquired a surplus of between £40,000 and £50,000, which they had devoted to the cause in which they were engaged. They had also been entrusted with the administration of public donations to the extent of £80,000, of the expenditure of which the fullest details had been published in annual reports. It is easy to conceive the feelings with which men who had acted with such zeal and devotion would learn that in their own land, and among their own people, they were considered deficient in common honesty, and unworthy to be any longer trusted by the public. But they suppressed every feeling of indignation, and the vindication of their characters was couched in language so singularly mild as to appear almost unnatural. It closed with the remark, that after having exerted themselves to support the cause of missions for so many years, and laid on themselves labours which few European constitutions could sustain in a climate like that of India, and consumed the best of their days in the work, robbing their own families to enrich the mission, they could not but lament that they were required to interrupt their labours to vindicate their characters from these aspersions. This forcible appeal to the justice and common sense of their fellow-countrymen would doubtless have restored the old feeling of confidence, but it was destined never to see the light. Mr. Dyer obtained a copy of it, and laid it before the committee, who were alarmed lest the interests of the Society should be injured by the appearance of a statement which implied the existence of differences they were anxious to conceal from public view. He therefore insisted on the surrender of every copy brought home by Mrs. Marshman, and locked them up, refusing even to allow Mr. Ward the sight of one.

Having canvassed England and Scotland on behalf of the College, Mr. Ward was advised to visit Holland, and endeavour to excite a missionary spirit among the Menonites. The visit, however, produced no result; but he enjoyed an agreeable conference with the Rotterdam Missionary Society, and was enabled to confirm their intention to establish a mission in the Dutch settlement of Chinsurah in Bengal, and place it under the direction of the late Mr. La Croix, who subsequently joined the London Missionary Society, and became one of the ablest and most indefatigable of missionaries. Mr. Ward had also received a pressing invitation from the leading members of the Baptist community in America, of which he now availed himself. He was welcomed with enthusiasm in every circle, and men of all denominations vied with each other in their expressions of esteem for the man who, in conjunction with his two colleagues, had opened up the path of modern missions in the East. But it is due to the memory of the late Mr. Divie Bethune, of New York, to state, that nowhere did Mr. Ward feel himself so completely at home as in the bosom of his family, and from no individual did he receive more cordial support. Mr. Ward's progress through the country was a continuous ovation. During the three months to which his visit was necessarily limited, he made the most strenuous exertions to strengthen the spirit of devotion to missions, and was happy to perceive that America was already preparing to enter upon a career of sacred rivalry with the mother country in that field of Christian benevolence. He succeeded in raising ten thousand dollars for the College, which was invested in American funds, and placed in the hands of American trustees. After his return to England, he appears to have had little intercourse with the committee, whose diplomatic reserve ill accorded with the genial warmth of his own feelings. He found that the concessions made by his colleagues had softened no asperities, and promoted no desire for mutual conciliation. He wrote to his friends at Serampore that he was convinced of the folly of attempting to legislate for posterity; and that he was now about to return to them, content with his own performance of the duties which lay in his path, to which the remainder of his life would be devoted with renewed ardour.

Mr. Ward had been so happy as to engage the services of Mr. John Mack, then twenty-three years of age, as one of the professors of Serampore College. He had gone through the usual course of education in Scotland, first at the High School, and then at the University of Edinburgh, from seven of the professors of which he received the most flattering testimonials. He was originally destined for the Church of Scotland, but his views on the subject of baptism and church polity had undergone a change, and he threw in his lot with the Baptists. It is difficult to speak of the varied excellences of Mr. Mack's character without an appearance of exaggeration. He was an accomplished classic, and deeply versed in every branch of natural science. His intellect was of the first order, and his judgment so sound that his suffrage on any question was considered a tower of strength. He was a powerful and elegant writer, but pre-eminently distinguished for his eloquence, which has seldom been equalled and never exceeded in India. His piety was deep and solid, and he seemed to exhibit a happy union of the resolution of the old Covenanters with the charm of Christian meekness. In all respects he was a congenial associate for Carey, Marshman, and Ward, with whose great work he completely identified himself, and to whom he became as affectionately attached as they were to each other. After having attended a course of Abernethy's surgical lectures, he embarked for India in May, 1821, in company with Mr. Ward, Mrs. Marshman, and several missionary labourers.

During the voyage, Mr. Ward employed his time in writing farewell letters to his friends in England and America, which he was subsequently prevailed on to publish; the work went through three editions. In these letters he presented a vivid picture of the superstitions of the Hindoos, the impurity and cruelty to which they gave birth, and the moral and religious degradation they entailed. He exhibited the hopes, fears, and aspirations of the heathen mind. He carried the reader into the presence of the idol, and brought before him the crowd of prostrate worshippers, and the shouts of frantic votaries. He then conducted him to the funeral pile, and depicted the sufferings of the living victim, and endeavoured to engage him in a crusade against the horrid rite. The letters breathe throughout that spirit of Christian piety and philanthropy with which Mr. Ward was always animated. In this brief epitome of his life, however, there is room for only a single extract, but it will serve to shew that total absence of sectarianism and bigotry which distinguished his character and that of his colleagues: "As for sects, 'a breath may make them as a breath has made.' There is much trash cleaving to us all; but when I see Him, whose right it is to reign, and whose dominion is over mind, going forth conquering and to conquer, I must and will rejoice. I am more than ever anxious, my dear sir, to know no man after his sect—to know no man as an Independent, an Episcopalian, a Presbyterian, a Methodist, or a Baptist. I would say of every one who wears the image of Christ, and who contributes to the improvement of the spiritual desert which surrounds him, and of no one else, 'the same is my brother, and my sister, and my mother.' What a sad thing that while our Lord Jesus Christ loves His people because they bear His image, the cause of our attachment should be that they belong to us! . . . Let us conscientiously profess our opinions, but let us love the man of our sect but little who possesses but little of the image of Christ, while we love him in whom we see much of Christ, though some of his opinions are the very opposite of our own. . . . If I am enabled thus to love all the family 'whose names are written in heaven,' I have property in all; I have fellowship with all; the gifts of all are mine; the spirituality of all is mine; the success of all at home and abroad is mine. 'My Father wrought it all.'"

CHAPTER IX.

To return to the course of events in India. Amidst all his missionary, biblical, and literary labours, Dr. Carey never lost sight of the material interests of the country. The encouragement afforded by Lord Hastings to every plan for advancing the interests of the country, induced Dr. Carey at this time to propose the establishment of an Agricultural Society in Calcutta, of which he drew up the prospectus in the month of April, 1820. It exhibited that clear and practical view of the question which marked all the productions of his pen, of which it may be taken as a fair sample with regard both to matter and style, which was simple and unadorned. Soon after the circulation of the prospectus, he convened a public meeting at the Town-hall of all those who felt an interest in the subject, but the attendance was limited to three European gentlemen, besides Dr. Marshman and himself. Not discouraged by this appearance of apathy to the object, he said he thought the meeting sufficiently strong to make a beginning; and with the same energy of spirit which he had manifested at the formation of the Baptist Missionary Society, voted one of their number into the chair, and inaugurated the Agricultural Society of India. Such was the feeble origin of an institution which now embraces hundreds of members, European and native, in every province of India; and which, during the last forty years, has been one of the most vigorous and successful agencies of improvement in that country. The benefit thus conferred on the interests of India have been held in grateful remembrance by the Society he founded. His bust adorns its hall; and at the annual banquet which follows the distribution of prizes, the memory of the founder is commemorated immediately after the honours paid to the royal family.

In June, 1820, Dr. Marshman, finding that the discussion of topics bearing on the improvement of the country in the monthly miscellany, swelled its bulk and interfered with the punctuality of its appearance, commenced the publication of a *Quarterly Friend*. It was announced to comprise "essays on subjects connected with India, and a review of works tending to promote its welfare." It was not intended to bear a political character; remarks on the conduct or character of the public functionaries were to be avoided, and the discussion of questions of public policy was to be conducted with great moderation, both of tone and language. But it was impossible, even with the best intentions and the greatest circumspection, to avoid a collision with the views of those who were opposed to all innovation and progress. An article advocating the policy of allowing Europeans to settle in India, which was then considered in the light of treason to the Company's interests, was allowed to pass without notice. Another, on the influence of the native press in arousing the national mind from the sleep of ages, created no opposition, though its existence was regarded with no feeling of complacency in official circles on both sides the water. But the third number contained an article on the delicate question of female immolation, which concluded with these remarks:—"This question is one that cannot be permitted to slumber; it ought to undergo the most rigid scrutiny in all its bearings. It *must* yield in time to the voice of humanity. We cannot persuade ourselves that these unnatural fires will be permitted to blaze for another quarter of a century. We cannot for a moment admit the idea that there are 25,000 innocent and helpless females yet destined to the flames under a Christian and a British Government." Great umbrage was taken at the boldness of these remarks, though at the present time they would rather be censured for their timidity. Mr. Adam, the member of Council, denounced the article as an infringement of the rule which prohibited "discussions having a tendency to create alarm or suspicion among the native population of any intended interference with their religious opinions and observances," and he desired that the editors should be enjoined to abstain from all such discussions in future. But when the question came up for consideration, Lord Hastings said he had read the article with great interest and pleasure, and saw nothing to object to in it.

At the beginning of 1821 the missionaries received a letter from Frederick VI., King of Denmark, acknowledging the communication they had sent him on the formation of the College. He assured them of the great interest he felt in the institution, which he desired to take under his especial patronage, and of the progress of which he desired to be informed from time to time. On a previous occasion he had offered them the Order of Dannebrog, which he had recently conferred on Bonhoff, the chief of the Moravian missions in the colony of St. Croix; but they respectfully solicited permission to decline an honour unsuited to their position. He now bestowed on them a gold medal as a token of his approbation of their labours. At the same time he presented them with a large house and extensive grounds, in a very eligible situation in the town, valued at £1,000, the rent of which was to be perpetually appropriated to the support of the College.

On the 30th of May, Dr. Carey was visited with the loss of his second wife. In a letter to Dr. Ryland on this occasion he thus commemorates her Christian virtues: "She was eminently pious, and lived near to God. The Bible was her daily delight; and, next to God, she lived for me. . . . It was her constant habit to compare every verse of Scripture she read in the German, Italian, French, and English versions, and never to pass by a difficulty till it was cleared up. In this respect she was of eminent service to me in the translation of the Scriptures. She entered most heartily into all the concerns of the mission, and the support of schools, more especially those for female native children. So many merciful circumstances attend this very heavy affliction, as still yield me support beyond anything I ever felt in former trials. I have no domestic strife to reflect on, and add bitterness to affliction. She had long lived on the borders of the heavenly land, and I think had latterly become more and more heavenly in her thoughts and conversation." The period in which Dr. Carey was blessed with her society was the happiest of his life. Her mind was enriched with varied acquirements, and her animated conversation was exactly suited to the character of his mind; and he enjoyed a rich feast, when, at the close of a day of severe toil, he was enabled to give himself up to the intellectual enjoyment of the evening. In her deportment there was a blending of patrician grace and Christian simplicity. She fell in cheerfully with the economy of the mission family at Serampore, and contributed by her urbanity to the maintenance of harmony. A day or two after her decease, the following letter of condolence was sent over by the Governor-General: "Lord and Lady Hastings are solicitous, through the kindness of Dr. Marshman, to make their inquiries after Dr. Carey, and to offer him their sincere condolence on his late heavy affliction. They feel assured no one better knows, or will more practically experience, the only consolation which such a case admits of; but while such principles enhance gratitude for one of the best blessings of Providence, it tends to increase their sympathy for the sorrow of one, who, in justly appreciating domestic happiness, is called upon to mourn the interruption of such ties."

The progress made in organising the College in the years 1820 and 1821, was necessarily slow. For an institution of this kind they had everything to create; but, unhappily, at the time when the co-operation of their fellow-labourers in India and of the Society in England would have been of essential service, they were deprived of the sympathy of both bodies. In the report of 1821 they state that the number of scholars was forty-five; but they could make little progress in the arrangements of the institution till the return of their colleague and the arrival of Mr. Mack. Their chief attention was given to the completion of the buildings, and a noble specimen of Grecian architecture did they raise on the ground appropriated to the College, on the banks of the Hoogly, exactly facing Barrackpore Park. The size of the building, which was attributed by the historian of the Baptist mission to "a tincture of ambition," was necessarily adapted to the scale on which they proposed to establish the institution, and which corresponded with the calibre of all their other enterprises. Mr. Ward, while engaged in collecting funds for the support of the College in England, had written to his brethren that they "must raise the buildings themselves in India," and they determined to make a vigorous effort to erect them from their own resources. Neither the ungenerous suspicions which were at the time circulating in England, nor even the charge of malversation brought against them, were allowed for a moment to slacken their exertions. It was while their reputation was under an eclipse, and the pious and benevolent hesitated to subscribe to the Society without the assurance that their donations would not be mixed up with the funds of the men at Serampore, that those men were engaged in erecting a stately edifice for the promotion of knowledge and religion at their own cost, the expense of which eventually amounted to £15,000. To the charge of seeking to alienate from the Society premises of the value of £3,000, which was, after all, their own gift, they replied by erecting a building of five times that value, and vesting it in seven trustees, besides their own body; and it was thus they sought to vindicate the purity of their motives, and to silence the voice of calumny. They were the first to maintain that a college was a most important auxiliary to a missionary establishment in India, and their example has been followed with great vigour by the Episcopalians, the Independents, and the two sections of the Presbyterian Church.

In the course of the previous and the present year, Dr. Marshman was drawn into a controversy with Rammohun Roy, on the doctrine of the atonement. This great Hindoo reformer, who had boldly opposed the superstitions of his own countrymen, now came forward and assailed the fundamental doctrines of Christianity, in a publication entitled "The Precepts of Jesus, the Guide to Happiness and Peace." He maintained that the monotheistic system of the Vedas was sufficient for all the religious wants of man. He extolled the precepts of Jesus, but denied the necessity of an atonement; he questioned the divinity of our Saviour, and declared that His miracles were less stupendous than those of the Hindoo sage, who drank up the ocean and then discharged it from his body. Rammohun Roy was the foremost man in Hindoo society, and any treatise from his pen could not fail to exert a powerful influence among his own countrymen, more especially when it harmonised with their own prejudices against Christianity. Dr. Marshman considered it important to stand forth in defence of the vital principles of the Gospel, thus impugned in the presence of the Hindoo community, on whom the light of Christian truth was then beginning to dawn. In successive numbers of the *Quarterly Friend* he reviewed the arguments of the reformer, and vindicated the doctrines of Christianity. The subject had been the study of his life, and these papers afford a good specimen of his style, both of composition and argumentation. The novelty of a discussion between a Christian missionary and a learned brahmin, on the essential tenets of the Bible, attracted much attention, and the controversy was beneficial to the interests of Christian truth. The Unitarians in England and America united in commending the exemplary temper with which Dr. Marshman conducted the controversy, and the only instance of unfairness which they were able to allege against him was the use on one occasion of the epithet Socinian, which they repudiate, though in general society Rammohun Roy's school was designated that of the "Socinianised Hindoos who retained their caste."

Mr. Ward reached Serampore on the 20th of October, 1821. In his letters to his friends in England, he describes the ecstasy of his feelings in finding himself again on "the hallowed spot." He dwelt on the pleasure he felt in exchanging the cold atmosphere of Fen Court, which had become the head-quarters of the Society, for the genial associations of the family at Serampore. The progress which had been made, during his absence, in the erection of the College buildings, in the assemblage of students, and the arrangement of the classes, exceeded his most sanguine expectations. He returned to his labours with his wonted ardour, and was happy to bury the remembrance of the contentions into which he had been drawn in the animating occupations of the mission. He resumed charge of the secular department of the mission, and of the printing-office, and worked the nineteen presses with increased diligence in the printing of the Scriptures and tracts; but the object to which he gave his chief attention was the training of the more advanced youths in the College for missionary duties. He revised the manuscript of the "Reflections for every Day in the Year," which he had compiled on the voyage to England, and published it in two volumes of moderate size. He also commenced a treatise on the character of Christian missions as exemplified in the life of St. Paul, in which he was anxious to embody the experience which he and his colleagues had acquired in active labours for a quarter of a century among the heathen; but he did not live to complete it.

In the month of March Dr. Marshman was bereaved of his eldest daughter, Susan, who had been married about three years and a half to Mr. Williams, of the Bengal Civil Service. She left two children—a daughter, who died of consumption; and a son, who entered the military service of the East India Company, and in his first campaign was besieged for four months at Ghizni. After the surrender of the fort, the enemy broke faith with the officers and subjected them to the most atrocious treatment. Young Williams appears to have suffered more than his comrades, and his reason was so seriously affected that he was constrained to retire from the public service. His mother was a woman of deep and unaffected piety, and was endeared to her friends by the peculiar sweetness of her disposition. Possessed of a large independent income, it was her delight to imitate the example of those among whom she had been brought up at Serampore, and devote it to the support of schools and missionary itinerants. Dr. Marshman had always exhibited the greatest magnanimity under the severest pressure of difficulties, but this blow appears to have completely prostrated him, and he became, as Mr. Ward expressed it, the prey of settled sorrow. To his bereaved son-in-law he wrote daily for nearly two years, down to the period of his death; and it is in letters like these, written with unreserved confidence, that we have access to the genuine feelings of the heart. No correspondence could exhibit more of the strength of Christian principle and resignation to the Divine will, or a feeling of greater benevolence towards others. There is only one letter out of five hundred in which any epithet appears which might be considered acrimonious. It occurs in reference to the independence of Serampore, which, he says, he would rather part with life than relinquish, while the attempt of the Society to invade it is characterised as an "act of tyranny." It is impossible to peruse these letters without a feeling of surprise that a man so considerate to all, and more particularly towards his opponents, and so warm-hearted towards his friends, should have become the object of hatred to religious men in England.

The chief object to which his attention was directed at this time was the completion of the Chinese version of the Bible, on which he had been engaged for fourteen years, and the last sheet of which left the press in December. This was the first complete edition of the Sacred Scriptures ever printed in that language, and the first Chinese work in which movable metallic types were substituted for the immemorial block-printing. It was prosecuted amidst a crowd of engagements, and without any of those facilities which have been enjoyed in the country itself by subsequent translators. Their versions will, therefore, naturally be found more idiomatic, perspicuous, and acceptable, but Dr. Marshman's labours will nevertheless be recognised as a rare instance of zeal and perseverance in the cause of Christian truth. A copy of it was presented to the British and Foreign Bible Society, at their annual meeting on the 7th of May, 1823, by Mr. Marshman, when the chairman, Lord Teignmouth, remarked that the presentation of the first complete copy of the Scriptures in the Chinese language was one of the most interesting events in the history of the Society. Mr. Wilberforce, who had so nobly defended the character and conduct of the Serampore missionaries in the House of Commons ten years before, was amongst the foremost to offer congratulations on this occasion.

In the course of the present year Dr. Carey married Mrs. Hughes, a widow of forty-five. His friends and colleagues were gratified to find that, though she possessed none of the mental refinement of his late wife, she was most assiduous in endeavouring to promote his comfort. "Perhaps," remarked Mr. Ward, "he could not in this country have found a more suitable match." She was the best of nurses for a man of sixty-two.

Towards the close of the year the missionaries published another Memoir of Translations, in which it was stated that the New Testament had been published in twenty of the languages of India. The sixth edition of the Scriptures in Bengalee, and a second and revised edition of the Hindee, Sanscrit, and Orissa Scriptures was in the press. Of these languages some were of primary importance; others were current in large principalities, and might be more aptly termed provincial dialects. The memoir was accompanied by a miniature map of India, defining, by a distinct colour, the area in which each language and dialect was then understood to be current. It is valuable, as indicating the knowledge of the philological divisions of India which had been attained at that period by those who had most diligently investigated the subject. Unhappily the expense of these heavy undertakings had pressed severely on the resources of the missionaries, and obliged them to seek accommodation from their bankers at the heavy interest of the day.

To explain the cause of this embarrassment it is necessary to state that, in the Translation Memoir of 1816, it was remarked that the expense of translating and printing a version of the New Testament in any of the languages of India would not exceed £500, and that there appeared to be twenty-six such languages and dialects among the hundred and fifty million inhabitants of the continent of India. Mr. Hey, F.R.S., an eminent surgeon at Leeds, and one of the most distinguished philanthropists of the day, was struck with this statement, and considered that £13,000 could not be more advantageously expended than in giving the New Testament, though in an imperfect form, to every tribe in India. He communicated his wishes to the missionaries, who entered into the plan with all cordiality, while he exerted all his influence to raise the proposed sum. But after he had succeeded in collecting £1,500, it appeared to him that the agency of a permanent body like the Bible Society would be more suitable for carrying out a design which must necessarily stretch over a long period, than that of a private individual. He accordingly made over the sum he had raised to that institution, and a resolution was passed to the effect that any one who produced a first version of the New Testament in any Oriental language should, on the examination and approval of his manuscript, receive the sum of £500 to enable him to print a thousand copies of it. This resolution served to augment the ardour of Dr. Carey. The ruling passion of his life was to give the Scriptures to all the people of India, and, disregarding the prudent advice of his colleagues, he pushed the work beyond the limits of discretion. The Translation Fund, to which were charged the second editions of the New Testament, and the books of the Old Testament, as they issued from the press, was already £4,500 in arrears. Of the twenty-six versions of the New Testament, one-half had already passed through the press, but the outlay on only four had been received. The Bible Society had very judiciously appointed a Committee of Translations at Madras and Calcutta, to whose examination versions embraced in Mr. Hey's proposition should be referred. Apparently nothing could be more fair and reasonable than this arrangement, but practically nothing could be more inauspicious to the Serampore missionaries, whom it affected. None of the members of the Translation Committee were acquainted with the languages in which any of these versions had been made, all of which were already in the press when the resolution of the Society reached India, and no satisfactory report on them could be obtained. Meanwhile, the whole expense involved in printing them fell upon the resources of the missionaries.

Dr. Carey and his colleagues were thus reduced to a state of embarrassment which threatened them with dishonour, and weighed heavily on their spirits. In the course of the preceding three years the erection of the College buildings had taxed their resources to the extent of £15,000, and they had, moreover, ten missionary stations dependent on them. Mr. Ward's mind was filled with the most gloomy forebodings. "He did not see how they could get on while they had an obligation on the translations, little short of £10,000, hanging like a millstone about their necks;" but Dr. Marshman, with his usual elasticity, took a more cheerful view of their prospects. It was vain, however, to attempt to evade the fact that their position was one of extreme difficulty. In the ardour of their spirits they had overtasked their strength. As new prospects of usefulness were unfolded, they hastened to take advantage of them, without any rigorous attention to the dictates of prudence. At the end of twenty-three years they may be said to have reached the culminating point of their operations. From this time forward it was with difficulty they were able to maintain the ground they had occupied. They still continued to pursue their labours with unshaken zeal, but with diminished and waning power. For the relief of their immediate difficulties, as regarded the printing of the Scriptures, they sent an urgent application to the Bible Society in London, the result of which will be subsequently stated.

Mr. Mack, on his arrival at Serampore, entered on his duties in the scientific department of the College, and undertook the general superintendence of the classes, the number of students at the end of 1822 being fifty. Mr. Ward took charge of their theological studies, and they laboured together with the greatest harmony and assiduity. At the same time, the first map which had ever appeared in the Bengalee language, was prepared at Serampore, and engraved by Mr. Walker, the eminent artist, in London. To render the College more efficient, it was determined, at the instance of Mr. Ward, to solicit aid from Government. The Serampore missionaries repudiated all State aid for the maintenance of religion, and especially deprecated its patronage for the propagation of the Gospel in India. They felt that the influence of Government might create hypocrites, but could not make converts. But they considered it the bounden duty of Government to employ the revenues of the country in promoting education, and the duty of missionaries to accept and apply this aid. They were entire strangers to the dogma, newly introduced into this country, which proscribes every such subvention as incompatible with the principles of nonconformity. They therefore solicited the assistance of Government to establish a medical department in the College, and Lord Hastings engaged to take the subject into his favourable consideration on the nomination of a professor with satisfactory testimonials. But as he was about to retire from the Government, and his successor might be a man of less liberal tendencies, the plan of the medical class was kept in reserve.

At the beginning of 1822, the writer of this biography embarked for England, and soon after his arrival was invited to meet the committee, as the representative of Dr. Carey and his colleagues. He found the leading members more favourably disposed towards Serampore than he had expected, though they still clung to the principle that all missionary agencies must labour in the strictest subordination to the parent Society. The Serampore missionaries were equally inflexible in the maintenance of their independence, and a majority of the committee considered it idle to prolong a hopeless contest. The conferences with Mr. Marshman, which were conducted in a spirit of reconciliation, were thus brought to an early and definite issue. An agreement was framed for the purpose of removing every ground of misunderstanding between the two bodies, and their future relationship was clearly defined. The independence of the missionaries was distinctly acknowledged under the signature of the two secretaries, and they were to be considered affiliated with the Society, with whom an active and affectionate correspondence was to be maintained. The Society and its auxiliaries were to collect subscriptions for the Serampore institutions, and the reports from its stations were to be embodied in the Society's annual report, that all the missionary labours of the denomination might be presented to the public in one view. It was a kind of federal union with independent agency. The arrangement regarding the premises was likewise placed on a footing which was considered satisfactory to both parties. This convention was hailed by all the friends of the mission in the denomination as a final and most acceptable settlement of differences. But there was, unhappily, one man to whom it gave little delight, and his undisguised displeasure was ominous of future troubles. The secretary, Mr. Dyer, in a letter to Mr. Ward, far from congratulating him on this pacification, indulged in the ungracious remark, "I fear you will now have proof that the committee have been right in their apprehension of the judgment that would be formed by the Christian public of the measures you have been pursuing."

This letter never reached Mr. Ward. After his return from England, he was enabled to resume his labours in the mission with all the vigour of renewed health; but after a brief period of exertion of only sixteen months' duration, his career was suddenly terminated by an attack of cholera. On Wednesday, the 5th of March, 1823, he preached the evening lecture apparently in excellent health and spirits. The next morning he joined his brethren at their weekly breakfast, though suffering from what he considered a simple attack of diarrhœa. He then proceeded to the office, and began a letter to the Rotterdam Bible Society, but was unable to finish it, and retired to his room, which he never quitted. At three in the afternoon he was seized with cramps, and it became evident that the disease was cholera of the most virulent type. Two medical gentlemen were immediately called in, and under their treatment the dangerous symptoms appeared to subside; but at eleven on the forenoon of Friday his pulse began to sink, and at five in the afternoon he was a corpse. The scene of distress around his couch was heart-rending. The three old men had lived and laboured together for twenty-three years, as if animated by one soul, and it seemed difficult to realise the fact that one of them was now gone. Dr. Marshman had been afflicted for some days with deafness, which the present distress served to aggravate, and he paced the room in silent dismay, watching with anguish the dissolution of his beloved colleague, yet unable to receive any communication. Thus, at the age of fifty-three, died the first of the men of Serampore. Mr. Ward's piety was adorned by a most amiable and affectionate disposition, and he never made an enemy. He was not gifted with the ardour of Dr. Marshman, or the indomitable perseverance of Dr. Carey; but in zeal for the cause he fell no whit behind them. He possessed a singular talent for business, a clear judgment, and untiring industry. His knowledge of the character and habits of the natives surpassed that of either of his colleagues, and few Europeans have ever been more successful in dealing with them. He spoke Bengalee with unrivalled ease and fluency, and thus acquired a powerful influence over the native mind, which he had often been known to control by a single flash of native wit. In his person he was of middling stature; his countenance was finely cast, with its bright hazel eyes, Roman nose, and broad expanse of forehead. He left no son; of his two surviving daughters, the eldest was married to Captain Ward, of the Bengal Native Infantry, who died soon after his gallantry in the Sutlege campaign had won him an independent command. The youngest married Mr. Nicholls.

The death of Mr. Ward was the severest blow which had ever fallen on Dr. Marshman. Ten days before this event, he had written to his son-in-law on the anniversary of his daughter's death. "You are quite right in your ideas about death. The Redeemer intended to take away the gloom, and when I contemplate one friend dead five years, and another seven years, and reflect on what they have enjoyed since, with an eternity before them, I cannot help thinking theirs a happy lot. It is only the survivors who die. The pious dead enter into joy and peace unutterable." He was now called to experience the truth of his own remark, that it is the survivors who die. For many days he appeared to be a living death. On the evening of Mr. Ward's decease he wrote again to Mr. Williams. "This is to us the most awful and tremendous stroke, and I have no way left but that of looking upward for help." Four days later he wrote, "Our dear Mr. Ward;—he preached only last Wednesday night—to him death was unspeakable gain. These afflictions make me think far less of life than before. I have, indeed, lost the desire to live, except for the Redeemer's cause. . . . I feel the loss of Mr. Ward as a counsellor, beyond everything. I never did anything, I never published a page, without consulting him."

Immediately after Mr. Ward's death, Dr. Carey wrote to Mr. Marshman, then in England: "Divine Providence has been pleased to remove our beloved brother Ward, after an illness of only thirty-six hours: we are left in circumstances of peculiar distress. The buildings of the College have completely drained us. . . . And our printing the Scriptures in the languages of India, on the faith of supplies from Britain, has involved us in such a state of debt as we never knew before, and in which we little expected to be left in our old age, after so many years' exertion for the cause of God in India. These circumstances are now heightened by the sudden removal of our beloved brother, as it was only from our united and strenuous labours for years to come, with the expense of so many missionary stations on us, that we hoped to recover from our present embarrassments, and save the cause in which we are engaged from ultimate dishonour. In these circumstances, we are constrained to entreat you to return and unite your efforts with ours, that we may be enabled to surmount our present difficulties, and when called home, to have the satisfaction of lying down in the grave free from debt and all fear of thereby dishonouring the cause which is dearer than life." From this state of embarrassment they were relieved by the liberality of the Bible Society, and their gratitude to that body was alloyed only by the reflection that their colleague was not alive to share it with them. The Bible Society had voted £2,000 in 1822 for the general Translation Fund, but information of this generosity was more tardy than usual in reaching India, and to this grant was added the sum of £3,000, on the receipt of the appeal from Dr. Carey and his colleagues. Another sum of £1,000 had been raised for the translations in England, and was remitted through the Society. The missionaries were thus enabled to clear off the sums they had borrowed from their bankers, and to proceed in their work with cheerfulness. Soon after, the Bible Society evinced the interest they felt in the labours of the missionaries, by remitting to them the sums which had been expended in printing five of the versions of the New Testament.

In the month of July, 1823, the labours of Dr. Carey were still further augmented by accepting the office of Government translator in the Bengalee language, for which no man in the country was better qualified. He likewise acceded to the request to edit a grammar and a dictionary of the Bootan language, which had been compiled by Mr. Schræter, a missionary connected with the Church Society, but were left imperfect at his death. The completion of his own Bengalee dictionary likewise demanded no small portion of his time. These herculean labours he was enabled, even in the climate of Bengal, to accomplish without any strain on his constitution, by that methodical distribution of his time to which he rigidly adhered through life, and that cheerfulness which was the spring of exertion. His relaxation consisted simply in turning from one occupation to another. In the course of the present year, he was elected a fellow of the Linnæan Society, a member of the Geological Society, and a corresponding member of the Horticultural Society of London.

On the 8th of October in the present year, he returned from Calcutta about midnight, and as he was stepping on shore from the boat his foot slipped, and the hip-joint was severely injured. During the next two days the inflammation was reduced; the agony he suffered was intense, but the prospect of recovery was very favourable. On the tenth day, however, a violent fever supervened, accompanied by a severe cough and expectoration, and for several days it was apprehended that every hour would prove his last, and that the same year would deprive the mission of two of its founders. But, under the blessing of God, he was brought back from the gates of death, though for six months he was unable to walk without crutches. While he was confined to his couch, the Damooda, a mountain torrent which is swelled by a vast volume of water during the rains, burst through the embankment raised to confine it, and spread desolation through the whole extent of country down to the Hooghly. Dr. Carey's garden was swamped by this inundation, and plants which he had been employed for many years in collecting from all parts of the world, and had watched with the most tender care, were swept away in the course of a single night. The stream rushed violently down on the town of Serampore, and in twenty-four hours the streets were covered with water five feet deep. The effect on the mission premises was most disastrous. The river bank in front of the houses of Mr. Ward and Dr. Carey gave way under the rush of water, and within less than a week there was a depth of fifty feet of water where the public road had recently stood, and a perpendicular and ragged bank was exposed to the abrasion of the river, which daily encroached upon it. The river was at length rolling within ten feet of Dr. Carey's bedroom, and he was obliged to seek refuge in one of the suite of apartments erected for the professors of the College, where he continued to reside till his death. In a few days his old house was absorbed in the river, and totally disappeared. The Hindoos maintained that this was a just retribution on the part of the river goddess for the attacks the missionaries had made on their religion, and some of the older Hindoos remarked that the first encroachment of the river was at the very spot where the first convert had been baptized. Even among the Christians there were some so superstitious as to associate the calamity with the unholy strife of which the premises had been the subject.

The expense of repairing this damage fell heavily on the funds of the missionaries, which had been seriously affected by the death of Mr. Ward, and which were chargeable with the expense of ten stations, while the number supported by the Society did not at this time exceed seven. The report of the labours conducted at the Serampore stations was incorporated with the annual statements of the Society, and contributed to strengthen their claim on public support. Dr. Carey and Dr. Marshman determined, therefore, to solicit aid of the Society, and instructed Mr. Marshman to ask for some portion of the funds raised for missionary objects. The good understanding which had now been established with the committee insured a cordial response to this application, and the sum of £1,000 was voted in March, 1824. Mr. Gutteridge, who now exercised a preponderating influence in the counsels of Fen Court, assured Mr. Marshman, with the utmost cordiality of feeling, that they would have made the grant annual, had it not been that their powers extended only from year to year, but he felt confident that there would in future be no obstacle to the renewal of it.

On the 8th of July, 1822, the learned Bishop of Calcutta, Dr. Middleton, fell a victim to fever, and was succeeded in the see by Dr. Reginald Heber, who united the zeal and piety of the Christian with the accomplishments of the scholar and the gentleman. It would be difficult to name any individual who has ever succeeded to the same extent in acquiring the general esteem of society in India. Towards men of other denominations he manifested the utmost liberality, and always appeared more anxious to promote the general good of the country than the interests of his own section of the Church. Soon after his arrival, he opened a friendly correspondence with the Serampore missionaries, which was continued without interruption to the period of his death. In June, 1824, Dr. Marshman sent him a copy of the report of Serampore College, which he acknowledged in the following letter:—

"I have seldom felt more painfully than while reading your appeal on the subject of Serampore College, the unhappy divisions of those who are servants of the same Great Master. Would to God, my honoured brethren, the time were arrived when, not only in heart and hope, but visibly, we shall be one fold, as well as under one Shepherd! In the meantime, I have arrived, after some serious considerations, at the conclusion, that I shall serve our great cause most effectually by doing all which I can for the rising institutions of those with whom my sentiments agree in all things, rather than by forwarding the labours of those from whom, in some important points, I am conscientiously constrained to differ. After all, why do we differ? Surely the leading points which keep us asunder are capable of explanation or of softening, and I am expressing myself in much sincerity of heart (though, perhaps, according to the customs of the world, I am taking too great a freedom with men my superiors both in age and in talent), that I should think myself happy to be permitted to explain, to the best of my power, those objections which keep you and your brethren divided from that form of church government which I believe to have been instituted by the apostles, and that admission of infants to the Gospel covenants which seems to me to be founded on the expressions and practice of Christ himself. If I were writing thus to worldly men, I know I should expose myself to the imputation of excessive vanity or impertinent intrusion. But of you and Dr. Carey I am far from judging as of worldly men, and I therefore say, that if we are spared to have any future intercourse, it is my desire, if you permit, to discuss with both of you, in the spirit of meekness and conciliation, the points which now divide us, convinced that if a reunion of our churches could be effected, the harvest of the heathen would ere long be reaped, and the work of the Lord would advance among them with a celerity of which we have now no experience.

"I trust, at all events, you will take this hasty note as it is intended, and believe me, with much sincerity,

"Your Friend and Servant in Christ,

"Reginald Calcutta.

"*June* 3, 1824."

Dr. Marshman returned his own and Dr. Carey's cordial thanks for the candid and amiable spirit of this communication; and as the bishop was on the eve of quitting Calcutta on his periodical tour, proposed that the discussion should be in writing. But he replied that he should be unable to find leisure for such a correspondence during his journeys, and it was happily avoided. The time both of the bishop and of the missionaries was too valuable to be wasted in discussing the differences of church and dissent.

In the course of the year 1824, the Abbé Dubois, a Roman Catholic missionary, who had laboured for twenty years in the south of India, published a volume on Indian missions, in which he not only decried the Protestant missions in India, and affirmed that their reports of success were exaggerated and unworthy of credit, but maintained that any mission to the natives of India, whatever Christian community it might be connected with, was a hopeless undertaking. Such an assertion came strangely from the dignitary of a Church which had canonised Xavier. The Serampore missionaries were not spared. The abbé pronounced their statement of conversions to be fabulous, and their translations to be inaccurate and unintelligible. On the appearance of the work, Mr. Charles Grant sent a copy of it to Dr. Carey, and advised that a reply to it should appear without delay. Dr. Marshman undertook the duty, and published a complete answer to the abbé in the *Quarterly Friend of India.* But the most decisive reply to his assertions has since been furnished by the great success of the Church of England missions in the scene of the abbé's labours, which now embrace a Christian population of 60,000. This communication from Mr. Charles Grant was the last he ever sent to Serampore; he died a few months after, at the age of seventy-seven. His memory will always be held in estimation by those who take an interest in Christian missions, more especially to India, of which he was the earliest advocate among public men, and throughout life the firm and unflinching supporter. On every question connected with the moral, religious, and intellectual improvement of India, he was greatly ahead of his colleagues in the Direction. Amidst all their jeers and opposition, he continued for thirty years to maintain his own more enlightened views, and he was rewarded by seeing them at length triumphant in Leadenhall Street. It was only a few months before his death that the celebrated despatch, drafted by the great historian, James Mill, was signed by the Court of Directors, in which they stated that "their great end in India should be not to teach Hindoo learning, but sound knowledge." His esteem for the Serampore missionaries was marked by a legacy of £200, which was generously doubled by his son and executor, subsequently Lord Glenelg.

The missionaries had at this time three institutions dependent on public support in India, and the inconvenience of three successive appeals to the community during the year, while other societies with new claims on public liberality were springing up around them, rendered it advisable to curtail the number. Eight years before this period, when the "Hints" for native schools were first published, the attention of the public had not been drawn to the subject, and the missionaries stood alone. But education had now taken root in the country. Efficient schools had been established by the different missionary bodies, and a society had been formed in Calcutta by the united efforts of natives and Europeans for the prosecution of this special object. Having led the way in which others had earnestly followed them, the missionaries considered that they might in some measure retire from this sphere of labour, and devote their energies more particularly to the College. The number of schools was therefore reduced, and those which remained were incorporated with that institution, the report of which, after it had enjoyed the benefit of Mr. Mack's services for two years, was highly encouraging. The cultivation of Sanscrit was still continued, but the time devoted to it was judiciously abridged. An edition of the renowned grammar of Vopa Deva had been published, with the rules in Sanscrit, and the explanation in the vernacular tongue. The dictionary, which had from time immemorial been committed to memory by students, was published with the words arranged in alphabetical order, and the explanation in Bengalee. A primer and a reader composed of extracts from the Sanscrit classics, was compiled, and the study of the language assimilated to the course pursued in Europe in the study of the ancient classics. For the geographical class, Hamilton's standard work had been abridged and published in Bengalee. Mr. Mack had delivered a course of lectures on chemistry in the native language, and drawn up a brief and simple treatise on natural philosophy. The number of students was fifty-four, of whom forty were resident native Christians. The institution, which was thus gradually acquiring maturity of character, received support from all parties in India, irrespective of class or creed. This circumstance was gratefully recorded in the conclusion of the report:—"When we recur to the list of subscribers and perceive how few of them are of the same religious denomination with the managers of it, we cannot but feel grateful for that disinterested liberality which ranks our obligations to India as Britons and Christians above all minor distinctions of a religious nature. In a country so destitute of everything which elevates the mind, and so dependent on us both for political protection and moral improvement, it is surely the duty of every individual to forget the little distinctions which divide society in England, and to make common cause for the promotion of its welfare. It will be time enough a hundred years hence, when the country is filled with knowledge and truth has triumphed over error, to think of sects and parties."

The plan of perpetuating their missionary labours, drawn up in 1821 to meet Mr. Ward's wishes, did not hold out any great prospect of success. The missionaries were as far as ever from discovering three men fitted, as independent and disinterested contributors, to form a second mission. But in the College, which was a permanent institution, they might calculate, they thought, with some degree of confidence, on a succession of pious, able, and zealous men to superintend the mission after their removal. In that institution they resolved, therefore, to establish a class of missionary students in European habits, to fill up vacancies in the stations connected with them, as well as to form new stations. They considered that the superintendence of their labours when employed in the field could not be entrusted more appropriately than to those who had been instrumental in training them up. It was also a part of their plan that the professors should assist in the preparation of school-books and religious tracts and treatises, and possibly find time for successive revisions of the Scriptures. They provided, moreover, that the professors should visit the stations annually during the winter vacation. It had always been the earnest desire of Dr. Carey and his colleagues to provide, as far as possible, the means of evangelisation in the country itself, depending on England only for a few men of superior character and attainments to regulate the machinery, and the plan they now devised appeared to them to be exactly adapted to the accomplishment of the object. They had already admitted six missionary students into the institution, and hoped shortly to be able to double the number.

In January, 1825, they gratefully acknowledged the grant of £1,000, which had been made for the stations by the committee. But the expense entailed on them of keeping the Society's premises out of the river, and erecting other buildings in the room of those which had been swept away by the inundation, was found to have absorbed the greater portion of the subsidy, and they asked for a renewal of it. A charge had been brought against them in one of the Calcutta journals, of having embezzled £22,000, which the Society was said to have remitted to them. Their character for common honesty was thus impugned in the presence of those before whom their reputation had hitherto been transparent. They consulted their friends in Calcutta, and were advised to bring the subject under the notice of the committee in London, and at the same time to transmit an exact and minute statement of all the sums which had been received from England, with details of the expenditure, and to request the Society to vindicate their integrity by auditing them. They likewise stated that they had associated Mr. Mack with themselves in the management of the missionary stations. The letter was written in that spirit of friendliness and confidence which corresponded, as they supposed, with the feelings of the committee, of which they entertained so little doubt that Dr. Marshman, in a private letter to Mr. Shaw, the treasurer, said that the "affection manifested towards them by the committee in general, and by its members in particular, had been a cordial to their minds of the most refreshing nature."

The reply to this communication unhappily indicated an unfavourable change in the feelings of the committee, which was evidently owing to the intermediate arrival of Mr. Eustace Carey, the nephew of Dr. Carey, and the senior member of the Society's mission in Calcutta. He was received by the committee with that distinction which his great talents and eloquence, not less than his devotion to their service, merited. But his feelings towards Serampore, and everything connected with it, were marked by unqualified aversion, and his animosity towards Dr. Marshman was implacable. On hearing of the application for the grant to the Serampore stations, he expressed, to his intimate friend Mr. Dyer, his surprise that the committee should think "of strengthening an establishment which they knew and felt to be extremely mismanaged, by pouring into its already enormous treasury the ample provision of £1,000." He described the missionary union at Serampore as a "compact more hostile to our Society than any existing religious institution on the face of the earth." It is natural to conclude that these impassioned representations were not without their effect on the minds of the committee, and that the tone of their letter was to be traced to his influence. It was not only frigid, but imperious to a degree which could not fail to be most galling to the Serampore missionaries. The committee declined to audit the accounts, on the plea that they had not sufficient documents; though their own printed accounts would have enabled them to testify to their accuracy, and exonerate honest men from the suspicion of fraud. The letter went on to say:—"Whatever may have been the motives of those who have lately published animadversions on your conduct in Calcutta, we cannot but feel, as we distinctly warned you seven years ago, that on this point your best friends would find it difficult to defend you from the charge of inconsistency." Such a communication to the father of the mission, from a body which owed its existence to his energy, completely overwhelmed his spirits. "Is this," he exclaimed in his letter to Dr. Marshman, "the reward of thirty-three years of labour, and of an entire sacrifice of all personal advantage for so long a period?" Endeared as Serampore was to him by the associations of twenty-five years, he determined to abandon it for ever. He fixed his choice on a very eligible spot on the banks of the river, five miles nearer Calcutta, with a comfortable lodge and seven or eight acres of land for a garden, and it was with extreme difficulty he was induced to relinquish the negotiations he had entered into for it.

CHAPTER X.

Having thus matured their plans for making the College the nursery of the mission, and placing the stations under its superintendence, Dr. Marshman determined to visit England, and make arrangements for carrying them into effect. He embarked in January, 1826, with a letter from his colleagues introducing the subject to the committee. It stated that they had already six students training for the mission, and hoped to be able to double the number; and as no youth would be received into the class who did not exhibit the best evidence of piety and devotion to the cause, they expected to obtain a succession of men well qualified to continue the missionary labours at the stations for which they were now seeking aid. They were anxious that all the operations of the Baptist mission should come before the public in connexion with the Society, and they asked that £1,000, and eventually £1,500 a year, should be appropriated for the support of their stations from the sums raised in England on the combined reports. Dr. Marshman landed at Brighton on the 17th of June, and posted down to Wiltshire. In his diary he describes the ecstasy of his feelings as he gazed on the old white horse chalked out on the slope of the hill near Westbury, and drove through the scenes of his boyhood, and traversed the streets in which every spot called up some cherished recollection. He reached his native village on Sunday morning, and entered the old meeting-house, where he joined some of his old friends, and the sons and grandsons of others, at the communion-table. He passed three days in visiting the few companions of his youth who still survived, and was delighted to find himself again addressed by the familiar name of Joshua.

At Bristol he was, for the first time, introduced to John Foster, who became from that period the bold and unflinching advocate of Serampore, as well as to the Rev. Thomas Roberts, one of its oldest friends. He then hastened to London, to be present at the annual meeting of the Society, and introduced himself to Mr. Dyer, the secretary, and to Mr. Gutteridge, the presiding genius of the committee, and was presented by them to about forty of the ministers present. On the following morning he preached to a crowded audience in Albion chapel, and for the first time in his life read his sermon, but with so little satisfaction to himself that he never repeated the experiment. The next day he returned to Bristol, chiefly with the object of being introduced to Robert Hall. Forty years had elapsed since he had heard him preach to the rustic congregation at Westbury Leigh, among whom he was the only individual capable of fully appreciating his genius. He now listened to his discourses with increased admiration. But it would be redundant to quote from Dr. Marshman's letters any remarks on the unrivalled merits of a speaker of whom Sir James Mackintosh asserted that no man could comprehend why all Greece flocked to hear Demosthenes, till he had listened to Robert Hall. But he was, if possible, more attractive in his study than in the pulpit, and there was not, perhaps, a greater intellectual feast to be found in England at the time than an hour's unreserved conversation with him. He received Dr. Marshman with the cordiality and affection of a Christian brother, and they continued three hours together, discussing every variety of topic connected with the social, political, and religious condition of India. On Dr. Marshman's rising to retire, Mr. Hall pressed him to prolong his stay, and, filling his pipe, sat down for another hour, and at length walked down to the wicket with him, in his dressing-gown and with his head uncovered, and begged him to renew his visit. While at Bristol, Dr. Marshman paid a visit to Barley Wood, where Mrs. Hannah More continued to receive visitors, though in her eightieth year. During the interview, which lasted two hours, Mrs. More ran through India in all its aspects, and Dr. Marshman drew her out on the literary, social, and religious condition of England.

From Bristol he proceeded to Edinburgh, where he was introduced to the acquaintance of Mr. Christopher Anderson, the warm friend of Mr. Ward, and one of the most affectionate supporters of the Serampore mission. To him Dr. Marshman could unbosom himself without reserve, and the privilege was not neglected. Five days were passed in this delightful communion, and in visiting the friends who had welcomed Mr. Ward. From thence he proceeded to Paisley and Glasgow, and on the 22nd of July, 1826, landed at Liverpool, and formed the personal acquaintance of Mr. Samuel Hope, the banker, who from that period to the day of his death continued to be the generous friend and the judicious counseller of the Serampore mission. Proceeding on to Birmingham, he passed many hours in the society of friends, some of whom had been his fellow-students at Bristol, and replied without reserve to all the questions addressed to him, excepting those which referred to the differences with the Society and their missionaries in Calcutta. Though he was fully aware that the strongest prejudices had been excited against him in every missionary circle, yet from the day of his landing he rigidly adhered to the resolution he had formed to speak evil of no man. He assured all those with whom he came in contact that the object of his visit to England was, not to depreciate the character of any, though they might be his opponents, but to foster a missionary spirit, and to obtain succour for those labours in which he was more particularly interested.

Dr. Marshman returned to London in August to make arrangements with the committee regarding the support of the stations. From the last printed report of the Society he found that its gross income was £12,000, and he resolved to base his proposal on this return. The meeting was held at Fen Court, on the 3rd of August, when he delivered in a statement relative to the expenditure of the missionary stations connected with Serampore, and asked for an appropriation of a tenth of their receipts, under the arrangement which had been completed for connecting the superintendence of the stations with the College. Dr. Marshman proposed that a detailed statement of the expenditure of this sum should be published in the Periodical Accounts of the Serampore Mission. The request happily met with the cordial assent of all the members present, and more particularly of Mr. Gutteridge, and it was agreed that Dr. Marshman should be at liberty to make separate collections for the College, and that the most complete confidence and affection should be hereafter cultivated by both parties. So satisfactory a termination of the negotiations filled Dr. Marshman's mind with exultation, under the influence of which he wrote to Dr. Carey, "All is settled between the Society and us on the most solid and equitable basis. I am convinced that, with reference to the troubles with which Serampore has been exercised these last years, 'the days of her mourning are ended.'" This settlement of all differences appeared to be not less grateful to the members of the committee, who stated, in their record of the meeting, that "the result of the explanations which had been mutually given would tend to unite the brethren at Serampore and in this country more closely in love and affectionate confidence than has been the case for years past."

Dr. Marshman soon after attended a meeting of the Bible Society, when the president, Lord Teignmouth, who had zealously defended the Serampore missionaries at the crisis of 1807, and again in 1813, alluded to Dr. Carey and his associates in terms of great esteem, and requested Dr. Marshman to favour the meeting with some account of the translation and distribution of the Scriptures in the north of India. The next day he met the committee of the Religious

Tract Society, and received a very gratifying welcome from all its members. Nothing could exceed the cordiality of his intercourse with these bodies, not less than with the Baptist Missionary committee. He considered half his mission accomplished, and determined to attend without delay to the interests of the College. Before he left Serampore it was resolved to make an effort to obtain a charter for this institution, and thus give stability and permanence to its operations, and he had been desired to take the earliest opportunity of proceeding to Copenhagen and submitting the wishes of the missionaries to the king. Having now, as he hoped, made a final and satisfactory arrangement with the Society regarding the maintenance of the stations, he embarked for Copenhagen, and on his arrival was introduced to Count Schimmelman, a veteran statesman of seventy, who was known to possess more influence with the king than any of his colleagues. He received Dr. Marshman with great affability, examined the ground plan and elevation of the College buildings, and the report of its establishment and progress, and inquired whether he could do anything to promote its interests. Dr. Marshman replied that he had a memorial to his Majesty soliciting the grant of a charter, which he was desirous of being permitted to present in person, and the count promised to take his Majesty's pleasure on the subject. On the day fixed for the audience he accompanied Dr. Marshman to the royal presence and presented him to the king. Dr. Marshman began his address by expressing the deep gratitude which the Serampore missionaries felt for the generous protection and support they had experienced from his Majesty and his Majesty's servants abroad, during the last twenty-five years, and which had been of inestimable value to them, at a time when the British Government was hostile to their undertaking. He then proceeded to describe the establishment at Serampore, the schools, translations, and missionary stations. The king was pleased to remark, that it was he who ought to feel obliged to them for having planted the institution in his dominions. Dr. Marshman then introduced the subject of the College, exhibited the plan and elevation, and solicited his Majesty to confer on it the lasting benefit of incorporation. The king made various inquiries regarding the objects and the progress of the institution, and said that it would afford him much satisfaction to encourage so laudable an undertaking, and referred the question to the chancellor of the University. After a very careful examination of the question, the chancellor made his report, and submitted four points of some little difficulty, of which the king at once dismissed three which he deemed unimportant, and observed that the fourth might be obviated by providing that the degrees conferred by the College should not give any distinction of rank in Denmark without the express sanction of the Crown. Having thus given his royal sanction to the charter, the king directed that it should be engrossed on vellum, and richly bound, at the expense of the Treasury, and sent to Dr. Marshman free of all cost.

From Copenhagen he now proceeded to Hamburg, and preached to a congregation of three hundred of his countrymen, who had assembled on hearing that he was to pass a day in the town. He visited Amsterdam, and at Haarlem indulged his passion for music by engaging the organist to give him an hour on its celebrated organ. In the library of that town, his attention was attracted to a copy of the first book said to have been published in Europe, which he found was printed from engraved blocks of wood, and on one side of the sheet only, similar to the Chinese xylography of the present day, for which he had substituted the use of moveable metallic types. From Haarlem he proceeded to the Hague, where he was introduced to Gutzlaff, who subsequently acquired a European celebrity by his missionary and literary labours in China. At Paris, Dr. Marshman made the personal acquaintance of Remusat, the professor of Chinese, who had long been his indefatigable correspondent in India. He was introduced by the professor to the various literary institutions, and attended a meeting of the Asiatic Society, and was subsequently presented to the great mathematician, La Place. Ten days were thus spent in Paris in visiting the various objects and institutions of interest, and he returned to London after a tour of seven weeks.

Immediately on his arrival in England, Dr. Marshman started for Edinburgh. Mr. Fuller had been in the habit of visiting Scotland every alternate year, to invigorate the missionary spirit, and recruit the funds of the Society, and the practice had been continued with much success since his death. At the request of the committee, Dr. Marshman had undertaken this deputation during the present year. The wearisome journey to Edinburgh occupied him fifty hours; but his iron constitution seemed insensible to fatigue, and having taken his usual stimulant of half-a-dozen cups of green tea, he mounted the pulpit within two hours of his arrival, and preached to a crowded audience. A day or two after he started for the north to collect for the Society, and passed eighteen days in visiting every place of note in the Highlands. He then returned to Edinburgh and devoted ten days to the labour of collecting in the city and its neighbourhood. On the 11th of December he proceeded to the west, and, day after day, addressed large assemblies from the pulpit and the platform. Everywhere he experienced the most flattering reception, and some of the older friends of the mission seemed to feel, as they said, "that the days of Fuller were revived." On the 1st of January he proceeded on his third tour, and on reaching St. Andrews, spent several days in delightful intercourse with Dr. Chalmers, who appointed a prayer-meeting in the town hall, that Dr. Marshman might give an address on India. He returned to Edinburgh in the middle of January, with unimpaired health, though the exposure of travelling, during the severity of a Scotch winter, might have been expected to tell on a constitution which had been subjected for twenty-six years to the heat of Indian summers. The collection amounted to £1,100, which, as he bore his own travelling expenses, was transmitted entire to the Society.

Dr. Marshman was anxious now to return to England, but was persuaded by his friend, Christopher Anderson, to seek a little relaxation in the literary and religious circle of Edinburgh. During his residence there, he breakfasted with Sir Walter Scott and his daughter, and their conversation naturally turned on the reminiscences of their common friend Leyden, whose memory Sir Walter cherished with warm affection. Dr. Marshman was also a frequent guest at the table of Mr. Mackenzie, the Man of Feeling, "a fine, vigorous old man of eighty," as Dr. Marshman records in his diary, "the last link which connected the age of David Hume with the galaxy of genius which now rendered Edinburgh illustrious." He spent some days with Mr. Douglas, of Cavers, the liberal friend of Serampore College, and enjoyed many hours of interesting conversation with him and Mr. George Sinclair. He did not fail to cultivate the acquaintance of Lady Carnegie, at whose house Mr. Ward had always been a welcome guest, and at her table he met Mr. Wolff, who had just returned from Palestine. He also passed a morning with Mr. Jeffrey, and was charmed with his rich and varied conversation. In the company of the editor of the *Edinburgh Review* it was impossible to avoid some allusion to the attacks which had been made on the Serampore missionaries in that journal twenty years before. Mr. Jeffrey had learned, from his friend Leyden, that they were attributed in India to his pen, and he was anxious to clear himself of the imputation: "I did not write them," he said; "bitter as the spirit of them is, they were written by one of your own cloth." Among the gentlemen whose acquaintance he formed in Edinburgh, he particularly enumerates Sir Harry Moncreiff, Bishop Sandford, and the Rev. Henry Grey. Nor from the list of the friends who welcomed him must be omitted the names of Robert and James

Haldane, in whose society he records that "he felt himself almost again at Serampore." His large stores of information, and his genial enthusiasm on every question of Indian improvement, made his presence acceptable in every circle. The General Assembly was at this time contemplating a mission to India, more particularly with a view to the establishment of an institution in which secular education of a high order should be combined with that religious instruction which was excluded from the Government schools. Resolutions had been passed on the subject, but it remained to fix on the sphere of operations, and Dr. Marshman was invited to meet Dr. Inglis, Dr. Anderson, Dr. Brunton, Dr. Gordon, and Dr. Campbell, when the subject was discussed, and the foundation laid of that renowned seminary, known throughout India as "Padre Duff's School."

It has been stated that, in the month of August, Dr. Marshman, having ascertained from the printed reports of the Society that its income was £12,000 a year, had asked for a tenth of that sum, equivalent, as he supposed, to £1,200 a year, for the Serampore stations, which had been granted with much alacrity. But after the meeting was concluded, and the members were about to separate, Mr. Dyer, the secretary, came up to him and remarked that the tenth would not exceed £845; and from this sum was to be deducted fourteen per cent. for "the proportion of expenses." Dr. Marshman, at a subsequent meeting of the committee, explained the embarrassment which this unexpected reduction of the subsidy would occasion, inasmuch as the expenses of the stations exceeded £1,400 a year, and a monetary crisis in Calcutta, consequent on the London crisis of 1825, had for a time extinguished all commercial confidence, and created universal distress, from which the Serampore missionaries had not been exempt. This second meeting was not so friendly as that of the 3rd of August, but Mr. Broadley Wilson, the treasurer, in a very amicable spirit, requested Dr. Marshman to make as accurate an estimate as he could of the aid which was required at Serampore, that "nothing unpleasant might again occur." During his residence in Scotland, he accordingly drew up a statement, in which he explained the requirements of the stations, and proposed that the committee should either grant a subvention of a tenth of its resources, as estimated by Mr. Dyer, allowing the missionaries to receive any supplemental aid which the affection of their friends might supply, or vote a sixth of the subscriptions, without such aid.

To consider this proposal, a meeting was convened at Fen Court, on the 15th of March, 1827, and attended by about forty members. The secretary, Mr. Dyer, produced the statement, and inquired whether Dr. Marshman desired it to be read; to which he replied that such was his object, and that he wished the committee to consider it as his communication on the subject they were assembled to discuss. The paper was read and then thrown aside, and no further notice was taken of it, while Dr. Marshman was subjected for four hours to a cross-examination on which Mr. Foster remarks:—"He was interrogated and spoken of by part of the assembly in a mode and in terms devoid of all manner of respect, or even ordinary civility, insomuch that his friends wondered how it was possible for him to endure such treatment, hour after hour, with patience." After he had been thus badgered for more than four hours, the secretary brought forward a resolution which had been previously prepared, and which proposed that the Society should take over all the stations formed by the Serampore missionaries, and that they should be placed under the management of a committee, consisting of all the Society's missionaries in India, of which Dr. Carey should be chairman. To this proposal Dr. Marshman stated several very cogent objections. It would exclude from the management of the stations, Mr. Mack and Mr. Marshman, who, in conjunction with Dr. Carey, were at the time devoting their time and energies to the superintendence of them. It would at once take away from the Serampore missionaries the establishment which they considered the most substantial part of the mission, and transfer it to a body of men, the majority of whom had for many years acted upon a principle of avowed, even though it might be conscientious, hostility to them. Their feeling of aversion to everything associated with Serampore was so strong, that there could be little prospect of co-operation. To bring such discordant elements together in a committee for the promotion of an object which required the holiest and strongest sympathies, would be the death-warrant of the whole establishment. To such an arrangement, therefore, Dr. Marshman found it impossible to give his consent.

It was then proposed that the stations should be left under the sole care of Dr. Carey and Dr. Marshman during their lives; but he felt that at their advanced age it would be injurious to the mission to deprive themselves of the assistance of their younger associates, whose ardour in the cause was little inferior to their own, while their power of exertion was greater. He therefore offered, as his ultimatum, to transfer all the stations to the Society without reservation, if they were allowed to continue under the superintendence of all his colleagues, who were then employed in directing their labours; with the understanding, as stated in Dr. Carey's letter, that "the management should remain in their hands no longer than they shewed themselves worthy of the trust." "Then," said Mr. Gutteridge, "we must part." "Let us part, then," replied Dr. Marshman, "as becomes Christian men." Thus ended the connexion between the Baptist Missionary Society and the Serampore missionaries, after it had subsisted, in the case of the youngest, for twenty-eight years, and in that of the eldest for thirty-five. The cause of this melancholy disruption Dr. Carey and his colleagues were never able to discover, except so far as it was to be found in the personal feelings of the leading members of the body, for the arrangement proposed by Dr.

Marshman, which the committee refused to sanction, exactly corresponded with that which they had cordially adopted in the previous month of August.

After the separation from the Society, Dr. Marshman called on the Rev. Josiah Pratt, the secretary of the Church Missionary Society, and discussed the events which had just occurred, and the prospects of the mission which had thus been suddenly bereft of all support. Mr. Pratt endeavoured to support his mind under the difficulties which now beset his course, and as a token of his unshaken confidence in the missionaries, became an annual subscriber to the mission. This was the first contribution Dr. Marshman received, and the value of it was enhanced in no small degree by the high Christian character of the donor. At the same time he received a friendly letter from Mr. Wilberforce, who had pressed him to visit his country residence. "I address you a few lines," he said, "to assure you that I look forward with pleasure to the prospect you allow me to entertain of seeing you after your return from Ireland. . . . I cannot conclude without assuring you that the respect I feel for your character renders the kind language you bestow on me truly gratifying. May it please God to grant you a long continuance of usefulness and comfort, and to take you at last to the enjoyment of an everlasting reward." Dr. Marshman had made an engagement, before his interview with the committee, to meet the friends of religion in Ireland, and he now proceeded to Liverpool, and embarked for Dublin, where he landed early in April, and passed a month in the society of friends of all denominations, who seemed to vie with each other in giving him a cordial reception. The atmosphere of Christian benevolence which he now breathed seemed to sustain and invigorate his spirits after the harassing discussions in Fen Court. He attended the meetings of the various Bible, Tract, Missionary, and Educational Societies, and the warm addresses of one fresh from the field of labour in the East were welcomed in every circle. From

Dublin he returned to Liverpool, and visited Mr. Gladstone, Mr. Rathbone, Mr. Cropper, and other gentlemen of influence, who took an interest in the improvement of India. On his return to London, he was introduced to Mr. Mill, the greatest of Indian historians, and passed an evening with him discussing every variety of Indian topic, and was delighted with his broad and enlightened sentiments. At Exeter he visited Sir John Kennaway, one of the great Indian statesmen of the days of Cornwallis, who, since his return to England, had taken a warm interest in the diffusion of Christian truth, and assisted the Serampore mission by a donation of £100. He then proceeded to the north of England, and was welcomed with affection by Dr. Steadman, Mr. Ackworth, and others who still adhered to the cause of Serampore.

On his return to Bristol, he found the minds of his friends deeply depressed by the representations which had been recently disseminated through the country. He had considered the resolution to act independently, which was signed by both parties, as a termination of all strife. He had scrupulously abstained, both in conversation and in writing, from any allusion to past differences, and he expected the committee and their partizans to pursue the same course. But he was now shewn an article in the denominational magazine purporting to give a report of the meeting in Fen Court, in which charges were brought against him utterly destructive of his moral character. It was drawn up by the printer with no mean ability, and had passed under the eye of the secretary. Mr. Foster assured him that this communication gave but a faint idea of the calumnies which had been circulated throughout the country to injure the Serampore missionaries. So deeply had they affected his mind, that he had imposed on himself the task of classifying them in a tabular form, which covered sixteen folio pages. After reading this dark calendar, Dr. Marshman wrote to Dr. Carey:—"I was grieved at the spirit thus manifested, but I felt confident that if the fire was not fed on the other side it would go out, and the command of Holy Writ, 'rest in the Lord and wait patiently for him,' seems to be the only direction I can follow." But Mr. Foster and other friends pointed out to him the indispensable necessity of publishing a statement to vindicate their character and conduct, to which he at length consented; but "it must be drawn up," he said, "in the spirit of the Gospel, just as if nothing repugnant to that spirit had appeared on the other side, and all contention must be avoided, even in self-defence." Soon after, he received a copy of the Report of the Committee on the negotiations which had terminated in the disruption. Though written with great caution, it contained reflections on the conduct pursued at Serampore, and more especially on the proceedings of Dr. Marshman, which went to the destruction of their character, and the annihilation of all confidence in them. The Society had not been attacked, and the publication of the committee was simply aggressive. Dr. Marshman could no longer shut his eyes to the fact, that it was the object of the committee to defeat his attempts to raise funds for the Serampore mission by filling the public mind with prejudices against its conductors. He was therefore constrained to come forward and set himself and his colleagues right with the public, and he determined to add to the statement of the operations at Serampore he was about to publish, an appendix, with a reply to these hostile assertions; but "it must," he said, "exhibit the simple truth, avoiding all recrimination, and every allusion which should appear unfavourable to the committee." The appendix was a calm and dignified answer to the inuendoes of the Society's report, without the remotest reflection on the committee. "Nothing," he wrote to Dr. Carey, "is wanting to make the Baptist Mission a by-word and a scandal in the eyes of the Christian world, but a reply in the spirit of these documents." It is difficult to conceive how any man could place such a restraint on his feelings in this tempest of calumny, as to employ no stronger expression in his defence than the following:—"In conclusion, Dr. Marshman may be permitted to appeal to every impartial reader, whether the Serampore brethren have not acted in the spirit of their original design; whether it is possible for them to have been seeking any object of mean self-interest; and whether they have not adhered as closely to their original agreement, as those duties which were imperatively incumbent on them, as Christian men, would permit." Of the admirable temper he maintained in this contest, the most decisive testimony is furnished by one of his bitter opponents, who, in a review of his statement, said: "The whole world might be challenged to produce, since the establishment of Protestantism, an equally strong example of imputations and differences of so serious a magnitude, being borne down by a defence so inwrought with meekness and Christian simplicity."

Here, therefore, the controversy ought to have closed. Each party had now appeared before the tribunal of the public with its own statement, and that which had been issued on the part of Serampore was clothed in language studiously inoffensive, and intended to obviate the necessity of any rejoinder. Each party was now in a position to bury all differences without any compromise of reputation, and turn its attention to the fulfilment of its missionary obligations in a spirit of sacred emulation. But while Dr. Marshman's friends considered his reply tame, his opponents regarded his moderation as an indication of timidity, and the passions which had hitherto been kept under some kind of restraint were at once let loose against him and his colleagues. So fickle is the breath of public opinion, even in religious circles, that for three years the "Baptist Republic," as Mr. Foster termed it, was deluged with publications tending to destroy the character and paralyse the benevolent exertions of men who had once been the objects of general admiration. Some few of the higher and nobler spirits in the denomination were doubtless influenced by feelings of resentment towards men who were represented as having acquired their reputation by the arts of deception. With the others the assault was the revel of little minds in the humiliation of greatness. Rarely has the conduct of public men, acting in circumstances of extraordinary difficulty, during a period of thirty years, been subjected to so severe an ordeal. To support the allegations brought against them, all their private and confidential correspondence was ransacked and made public. Extracts were given from their letters to establish their delinquency, while the context which would have neutralised the charge was withheld. The letters of the missionaries, who had been irritated by the stringent economy which had prevailed at Serampore, twenty years before, and to which the senior missionaries had equally subjected themselves, were diligently collected and arranged. Circumstances, in themselves insignificant and innocent, were skilfully worked up to sustain the indictment. Injurious reports, which never had any foundation, were pressed into the service. Even the intemperate communications of the deceased members of the Society to Dr. Carey and his colleagues were published to the world without hesitation, and the infirmities of the dead ungenerously exposed to injure the character of the living. But this scrutiny of their words and actions and motives, conducted in a spirit of unscrupulous hostility, has only served to give additional brightness to their characters, now that the animosities and prejudices of the time have died out. It is now fully admitted, that whatever may have been their infirmities and their errors, they were cast into the shade by the disinterestedness and devotedness which marked their career, and the denomination with which they were connected is justly proud of the men who, in conjunction with Fuller, Foster, and Hall, have contributed to raise it to the distinguished position it now holds in our Christian commonwealth.

It would be ungenerous to dwell further on the subject.

Those who take an interest in defunct controversies will find their taste amply gratified by the study of the pamphlets to which the collision gave birth, and which were equal in bulk to two octavo volumes. But though these attacks eventually proved beneficial to the character of the missionaries, they were at the time deeply injurious to the interests of the mission. No pecuniary support could be obtained for the stations without a harassing struggle with the power of a thoroughly organised religious association. Supplies came in but slowly. Men, in general, require no very powerful inducement to slacken their liberality, and, in the present case, the alleged delinquencies of the applicants furnished a virtuous reason for withholding it altogether. Neither while the storm raged was it easy to establish local organisations for the permanent support of the stations. The warm attachment of a few devoted friends was insufficient to counterbalance the general feeling of mistrust infused by incessant activity into every circle. After the separation, Dr. Marshman spent twenty months in visiting various parts of England and Scotland to make collections for Serampore, but whereever he appeared, the delegates of the committee followed in his track and weakened, if they did not neutralise, the impression he had made.

But amidst all these difficulties, and under this load of unmerited obloquy, not an expression of resentment is to be found in the whole of his correspondence. On the eve of his departure from England, he wrote to Dr. Carey: "Let us forget the things that are behind,—namely, that any one has injured us, or wished to do so, except merely to do them the more good in return, and let us press forward to the things that are before us, the calling by Divine grace of multitudes on multitudes of the heathen." He embarked for India on the 19th of February, 1829, leaving the arrangements for the future support of the mission incomplete, and his friends dispirited by what appeared to them a desertion of duty. But the explanation of his abrupt departure was to be found in the morbid state of his mind after the harassing labours of nearly two years. For a time, he had successfully struggled against the effects of this pressure, but his spirits gave way at last, and notwithstanding the apparent calmness of his letters, he was unable either to think clearly, or to act with decision. The ordeal through which he had passed had produced a degree of timidity foreign to his character. Every explanation only brought fresh attacks; even the concessions which candour might induce him to make were turned into new weapons of offence. He felt that the storm must expend itself before the voice of reason and equity could be heard, and he hastened from this scene of tumult to the tranquillising associations of Serampore, where he landed on the 19th of May, looking, as his friends remarked, fifteen years older.

To resume the thread of events in India during Dr. Marshman's absence. The annexation of the province of Aracan to the British dominions induced the missionaries to remove the station of Chittagong to Akyab, where a village was established, which was speedily occupied by more than fifty Christian families. A mile from Serampore another Christian village was formed, to which the families of the converts in the town were removed. During the year 1826 Mr. Mack made his tour of visitation to the various stations in the mission, in pursuance of the arrangement which has been stated in a previous chapter. The increase of Christian and philanthropic institutions at the Bengal Presidency had seriously affected the contributions to the Benevolent Institution, and Dr. Carey determined to submit the case to the consideration of Government. The debt, which had increased to £1,000, was immediately extinguished by a donation from the Treasury; an additional sum of £300 was granted for repairs, and an annual contribution of £240 made towards its maintenance. The province of Assam, which had been conquered from the Burmese during the war, was incorporated with the British territories, and Dr.

Carey importuned his colleagues to respond to a proposal made by Mr. David Scott, the commissioner, and a missionary was accordingly sent to occupy this new field. To the south of Calcutta, a body of more than thirty natives had thrown up their caste and solicited Christian instruction, and a new station was immediately formed in that locality. Mr. Garrett, the judge of Burrisal, had raised a subscription of £1,300 for schools in and around this station, and offered to place it at the disposal of the missionaries; and one of the most advanced of the students in the College was sent to occupy that post. The energy thus exhibited at Serampore in sustaining and enlarging the mission presented a singular contrast to the imputation of unfitness, which was then reiterated throughout the denomination at home. But the funds collected in England in 1827 and 1828, subsequent to the disruption, did not exceed £658, and after crediting £1,131 from the contributions of the missionaries themselves, there still remained a deficit, including the balance of the previous year, of £1,138.

The year 1829 has been rendered memorable in the annals of British India by that intrepid act of mercy, the abolition of suttees. The Court of Directors were not prepared for immediate and peremptory abolition, but looked to the progress of education, and the diffusion of knowledge, for the gradual extinction of this barbarous rite. But Lord William Bentinck landed in Calcutta as Governor-General in July, 1828, with the stern and unalterable determination that there should be no waiting for the progress of education, or the development of favourable circumstances, but that this atrocious practice should cease absolutely and immediately. After suitable inquiries had been made of the public officers regarding the feelings of the country, a regulation was passed on the 4th of December, 1829, declaring the practice of suttee illegal, and punishable in the criminal courts. To prevent any misapprehensions or antagonism in native society, it was deemed advisable to promulgate the English and Bengalee versions of the Act on the same day; and Mr. Henry Shakespear, the secretary to Government, on leaving the council-chamber, despatched a copy of it to Dr. Carey, with this intimation of the wishes of Government. It was twenty-five years since he had submitted the first representation on the subject to Government, and it is easy to conceive the delight with which he now learned the consummation of his wishes. Every day's delay in promulgating the new law might cost the lives of two victims. The regulation reached him on Sunday morning; he felt that the Sabbath was made for man, and, instead of going into the pulpit, he sent for his pundit, and completed the translation of it before night. The orthodox Hindoos, the great landholders, the wealthy merchants and bankers in Calcutta, and the most influential brahmins, were astounded by the decision and promptitude of this measure, and, with the aid of some Hindooised Europeans, got up a memorial to Government. They affirmed that the act of self-immolation was not only a sacred duty, but an exalted privilege. They denounced the missionaries for having endeavoured to persuade Lord Hastings and Lord Amherst to abolish the rite, and demanded the restoration of it in conformity, as they were taught to say, with the various Acts of Parliament, which had provided that there should be no interference in any form with the religion or the customs of the Hindoos. Lord William Bentinck refused to suspend the operation of the Act, but offered to transmit their representation to the Privy Council, before whom the case was argued, on their behalf, with great legal acumen by Dr. Lushington, though without success. The appeal was dismissed, and this great act of humanity received the sanction of the highest authority in the British empire.

The year 1829 closed on Dr. Carey and his associates in gloom and anxiety. The difficulties of 1807, when the mission was threatened with extinction through the morbid terrors of Government, terminated in three months. The anxieties of 1813, during the last crusade of the Indian Government against missions, were removed before the end of the year by the interposition of Parliament. On both occasions they enjoyed the sympathy and support of the Society in England; in its stead they now encountered from the same body a spirit of open opposition. But the succeeding year brought greater embárrassments. At the beginning of it, the great house of John Palmer, the prince of Calcutta merchants, failed for two millions sterling. The interests of Dr. Marshman's seminary, which had necessarily suffered during his absence, were deeply affected by this event. The support of many of the children was derived from funds deposited with the firm, and the parents of others were impoverished by this calamity. Mr. Ward had placed the funds raised by him in America for the College in the hands of trustees, and they now took upon themselves to detain the dividends until an assurance was given them that they would not be expended in teaching science,—in allusion to Mr. Mack's lectures on natural philosophy,—or for the objects of family aggrandisement. In reply to this communication, Dr. Carey asked the American doctor of divinity who had signed the letter on behalf of the trustees, whether they trained up youths for the ministry in America without any knowledge of science? But the Serampore missionaries considered it a gratuitous insult to demand a solemn declaration of the council of a college that they would not embezzle its funds, and they left the American trustees to deal with the dividends as their consciences might dictate.

But a heavier blow was impending. The extravagant expenditure of the Burmese war had converted the surplus of Indian revenue into a deficit, and Lord William Bentinck was constrained on his arrival to appoint a finance committee to make reductions in the public establishments. Among other plans of economy, they recommended the abolition of the professorships of the College of Fort William, and Dr. Carey's allowance was at once reduced to a pension of 500 rupees a month. In this emergency, the missionaries held a meeting to implore the Divine guidance and support, and Mr. Robinson, one of the Society's missionaries, who had joined the Serampore mission, and was present on this occasion, thus describes the scene:—"The two old men were dissolved in tears while they engaged in prayer, and Dr. Marshman, in particular, could not give expression to his feelings. It was, indeed, affecting to see these good men—the fathers of the mission—entreating with tears that God would not forsake them, now gray hairs were come upon them, but that He would silence the tongue of calumny, and furnish them with the means of carrying on His own work.

Having spread their supplication before the Divine Majesty, they drew up an appeal to their Christian brethren in England. For themselves, they said, they had nothing to ask but the goodwill and the prayers of their fellow-Christians at home, but their supplications must be earnest for support to that sacred cause in which they were engaged. Attempts had been made to hold them up as unworthy and unfit, from personal character and the defective organisation of their missionary system, to be entrusted with the contributions of a Christian public, and the further direction of the mission reared under their care. As long as any such representations of their character or conduct were supported by anything like specious argument or allegation, it was not to be expected that the intrinsic importance of the mission would be duly regarded. They had, therefore, been careful to vindicate themselves from these aspersions, and, as far as delicacy would permit, to establish their claims to that integrity and general sufficiency of character which their important trust required. Having done this, they felt that they were now warranted in calling public attention to the real merits of the case, and the pressing necessities of the mission. In the preceding year they had been led to extend the mission by the addition of three new stations, but they were now distressed, not because of their incompetence to undertake new efforts, but their inability to continue their present expenditure. The number of stations now dependent on them for support was thirteen, the number of European and East Indian labourers seventeen, and of native preachers fifteen, and the expense of the mission exceeded £1,500 a year. Their resources had from various causes been reduced. "If," they remarked, "unceasing industry and self-denial could by any means furnish us with the supplies we beg of you, we would toil and deny ourselves, with cheerful alacrity, and leave you unimportuned. But even our present incomes are uncertain. Again we implore your help, and we hope we shall not implore in vain." Before this appeal reached England, the uncertainty of their incomes was exemplified by the further reduction of Dr. Carey's income in consequence of the abolition of the office of Bengalee translator, which had given him £360 a year.

The vindication alluded to in the appeal, referred to three several pamphlets, written by them individually and transmitted to England at the beginning of 1830. Dr. Marshman applied himself to the task immediately on his return from England. At Serampore he was aided by the recollections and the sympathies of his colleagues, and had access to all the information necessary for the completeness of his defence. The associations of the place seemed to revive that spirit of intrepidity which had always marked his character, but which had suffered an eclipse during the storm which had assailed him in England. He grappled manfully with Mr. Dyer's facts and arguments, and triumphantly established the integrity of the missionaries. Mr. Marshman addressed a series of letters to Mr. Foster, in which the validity of the charges brought by Mr. Eustace Carey were investigated. Dr. Carey sent home his own Thoughts on the Discussion, which, independently of the weight of his character and his long and eminent services, carried conviction to the mind by his clear and matter-of-fact mode of dealing with every question. His pamphlet wound up with a characteristic appeal to the Baptist Missionary Society:—"And now what is our trespass? what is our sin, that ye have so hotly pursued us? Whereas ye have searched all our stuff, what have ye found of all your household stuff? Set it here before our brethren and your brethren, that they may judge between us. These thirty-seven years have I been with you—Dr. Marshman thirty years—the rams of your flock have we not eaten. Thus we were,—in the day the drought consumed us, and the frost by night, and our sleep departed from us. . . . Now, therefore, let us make a covenant, we and you, that we will not pass over this heap to you, and that you shall not pass this heap unto us for harm."

The three pamphlets produced an immediate reaction in England. The anxieties of their friends were dispelled, and they were enabled to appeal with renewed confidence to the liberality of the denomination. Contributions came in so rapidly that Mr. Hope was enabled to make an immediate remittance of a thousand pounds, and of a still larger sum in a few days. The relief from embarrassment which this turn of the tide brought them was most seasonable, and excited the strongest emotions of gratitude to God. The allowances of the missionaries at the stations, which had fallen into arrears, were paid up, and they were encouraged to pursue their labours with renewed vigour. "With respect to myself," writes Dr. Carey, "I consider my race is nearly run. The days of our years are threescore years and ten, and I am now only three months short of that age, and repeated bilious attacks have weakened my constitution. But I do not look forward to death with any painful anticipations. I cast myself on, and plead the efficacy of, that atonement, which will not fail me when I need it. . . . But how shall we sufficiently praise and glorify God, who in the time of our great extremity appeared and stirred up His people thus willingly to offer their substance for His cause! My heart goes especially to those faithful and constant friends who have stood by us and defended us when our integrity was called in question, our veracity doubted, and our characters traduced." Dr. Marshman, in writing to Mr. Hope, remarked: "that God has granted us supplies from His people, and their prayers for us in this work, is all the fruit I desire from the pamphlets you have received. Victory is a mean thing any further than it promotes the cause of truth and peace; and revenge, in its fairest and most specious form, utterly unworthy of a Christian."

The missionary labours of the year were prosecuted with unabated zeal, and at no period since the establishment of the mission was there a spirit of greater animation through the whole system. Their own resources had been lamentably curtailed by the advance of age, and the adversity of circumstances. Their friends in England were few and feeble, and every attempt to obtain support for the mission encountered a formidable opposition; but the vital principle of zeal was as vigorous as ever. However humiliating it might be to see men who had worn out their strength, and expended their substance in endeavouring to promote the best interests of India, placed under the ban of their own denomination, the adversity which darkened their closing labours almost ceases to be an object of regret in the aspect of that Christian fortitude which it called into exercise. At the earnest entreaty of Dr. Carey, though not without considerable reluctance, a mission was commenced among the Cossyas, a hill-tribe on the north-east frontier of Bengal. In Assam, now first occupied as a station, the European gentlemen formed an association for the support of native schools. At the new station of Barripore, to the south of Calcutta, the native converts had experienced great opposition from their heathen landlords, and a grant of forest land in the Soonderbuns was obtained, and four hundred men were immediately employed in felling the trees and clearing the land, with the hope of making it the residence of a Christian population. The schools contained twelve hundred scholars, and, notwithstanding the prejudices of the natives against female education, the attendance in the girls' schools at the different stations fell little short of five hundred. In the College, in addition to the other classes, nine students in European habits were engaged in pursuing their studies in classics and philosophy under Mr. Mack, and in divinity under Dr. Carey, some of whom subsequently became very efficient missionaries. But the operations of the College were cramped for want of funds. The American dividends were still withheld, and the agency of the funds raised by Mr. Ward in England, and vested in trustees, having fallen into the hands of Mr. Dyer, he in like manner immediately stopped the remittance of the dividends.

Towards the close of the year, Mr. (now Dr.) Leechman, a graduate of Glasgow, came out, uninvited, with a feeling of generous devotion, to share the labours and anxieties of the Serampore missionaries. Soon after his arrival he accepted the office of professor in the College, notwithstanding the precarious state of its resources, and a seat in the missionary committee; and seldom, if ever, has there been a more efficient association for the management of a missionary establishment. At the head of it were the two venerable founders of the missionary enterprise in Hindoostan, with their rich stores of experience, and their ardent zeal, which appeared to burn brighter as they approached the term of their career. With them was associated Mr. Robinson, the oldest surviving missionary besides themselves, who had served the cause for twenty-five years in Bengal, Bootan, Sumatra, and Java; and Mr. Mack, who for judgment, energy, and genius, had no superior, and few equals in India. Mr. Leechman and Mr. Marshman filled up the number. The number of stations under their superintendence amounted to sixteen; but nothing could be more disheartening than the pecuniary prospects of the mission. Mr. Hope, the treasurer, writing to them after the receipt of the pamphlets, considered it his duty "to caution them against indulging the hope that these publications, or anything else, would materially allay the animosities of their opponents. They have the ear of the public, and they will keep it. The previous writers and their partisans are neither to be won as friends nor conciliated as foes. Their rancour is unquenchable." Towards the close of 1832 he wrote that the reaction created by their vindication was already beginning to die out; and their own denomination continued almost entirely alienated from them, and other denominations were chilled by the fatal spectacle of animosity in bodies which were once united.

The year 1833 was ushered in by commercial disasters greater than any which had visited the country since the sack of Calcutta in 1756. The five great houses of business in Calcutta, the mainspring of all mercantile and agricultural enterprise throughout the Presidency, and the bankers of the European community, were successively obliged to seek the protection of the Insolvent Court, for obligations exceeding sixteen millions. Every local interest was deeply affected by this calamity, but it fell with peculiar severity on the Serampore mission. The funds entrusted to the missionaries for special objects had been lodged with these firms, which had been in existence for half a century, and were considered as stable as the East India Company itself; all these funds were now swept away. Dr. Carey lost his tenths. Dr. Marshman, writing to Mr. Hope, said, "I had about £2,000, the remains of what I had brought with me to India thirty years ago, which had been left accumulating in the hands of one of the houses, but it is now gone, and nothing is left me but the little house I now live in"—he had removed from the Society's premises—"and two bungalows at Barrackpore. Will the public still believe in our scheme of family aggrandisement, now the truth has been unexpectedly brought to light?" The house of Mackintosh & Co. had been the bankers of the mission, and had always been liberal in accommodating their friends at Serampore when supplies were exhausted or delayed. That resource was now dried up; and there was no other quarter to which they could look for assistance in this general wreck, when Mr. Garrett, a member of the civil service, generously came forward, and lodged his Government securities with the Bank of Bengal, and opened a credit in favour of the missionaries till they could receive remittances from England.

A second appeal was now drawn up, and sent home to their friends, stating the wants of the mission, and the difficulties in which they were involved by the mercantile crisis; "two firms," they said, "had already failed for six millions; and the destruction of all credit, and the distress which pervaded all classes, had exhausted the usual sources of support, and thrown them upon the generosity of a single individual." "Our wants," they state, "for the stations are not great; for they do not exceed £2,000 a year; and when sixteen missionary stations, with forty-seven missionary labourers, European, East Indian, and native, can have their wants supplied for such a sum, we know not how missionary operations can be conducted with greater economy." The appeal was responded to with alacrity, and Mr. Hope was enabled to transmit £1,000 by the first vessel. Mr. Gibbs, their missionary agent, was also happy to assure them that public attention had been excited by the silent, unobtrusive, yet efficient operations of the mission, and that one lady had sent him a donation of £1,000, under an anonymous signature. These expressions of sympathy and confidence seemed to justify the hope of a steady and permanent support for the mission, instead of those spasmodic efforts by which it had lately been maintained, and which became feebler at each repetition.

CHAPTER XI.

We come now to the last days of Serampore. At the beginning of 1834 Dr. Marshman experienced another visitation of mental debility. He had never fully recovered from the severe strain on his nervous system by the collision with the committee. The consciousness of integrity made him indifferent to any injury his personal reputation might sustain; but the effect of this opposition on the interests of the mission pressed heavily on his spirits. He experienced the first attack of melancholy nine months after his return to Serampore, when the prospects of support for the cause appeared almost hopeless. A twelvemonth after, he was again visited with the same feeling of morbid depression, when, as Dr. Carey observed, the merest trifle lay on his mind with insupportable weight. The feeling was so intensely painful that he noted in his journal with deep gratitude the day of his deliverance. But the severe calamities of 1833, and the gradual decay of Dr. Carey's health, brought on a third visitation. He wandered about the premises like a spectre. Everything he saw or heard filled his mind with undefinable terror. The days had come when "the grasshopper was a burden." He was not only obliged to relinquish the exercises of the pulpit, but became totally disabled for the ordinary duties of life. During these days of dismay he frequently turned to the record he had made of his former affliction and relief, and entreated the Almighty that "he might be brought out of prison a month earlier." In the beginning of March he appeared suddenly to recover his spirits, and he described his feelings as similar to those of Christian when he escaped from the castle of Giant Despair. During this mental eclipse, nothing seemed to give him such acute distress as the apprehension that his enemies in England might be induced to represent his affliction, in theological phraseology, as "a judicial visitation from God," and thus turn this calamity to the detriment of the mission. His feelings became so buoyant on his recovery that there was some danger of his passing into the opposite extreme. He resumed his old habit of early rising and immoderate reading. "I remain up," he writes to Mr. Hope, "till nine, and sometimes till ten. I long for it to be three, when I rise and enjoy almost a heaven upon earth in reading the Scriptures till five, when I go out for a drive." It was a merciful dispensation of Providence that his mental and bodily vigour was restored in time to enable him to soothe the dying hours of his beloved colleague.

Dr. Carey had experienced several severe attacks of illness in 1833, from which he partially recovered, but his constitution was evidently exhausted by forty years of incessant labour in the climate of Bengal, without a visit to England, or even a voyage to sea to recruit his strength. After he had completed the last revision of the Bengalee translation, he felt that his course was run, and his work accomplished. He had always entertained a dread of "becoming useless," as he termed it, before his death, and he often expressed a hope that life would terminate with his ability for labour. He refused, therefore, to listen to the advice of his friends, and continued his work when scarcely able to sit at his desk. But increasing debility constrained him at length to relax his favourite occupation of revising the proof-sheets of the Scriptures, and take to his couch, to which he was confined several months before his death. Dr. Marshman visited him daily, and often twice in the day, and the interviews always revived his spirits. With the various missionary friends who called to take their farewell of him during his illness, the conversation always turned upon the progress of Christian truth in India. While confined to his couch, Lady William Bentinck repeatedly crossed over from Barrackpore

Park to visit him, and Bishop Wilson came and besought his blessing. In the prospect of death, he exhibited neither rapture nor apprehension. He reposed entire confidence in the all-meritorious atonement of the Redeemer, and felt perfect resignation to the Divine will. "Respecting the great change before him," writes Mr. Mack, "not a single shade of anxiety has crossed his mind since the beginning of his decay, as far as I am aware. His Christian experience partakes of that guileless integrity which has been the grand characteristic of his whole life. . . . We wonder that he still lives, and should not be surprised if he were taken off in an hour; nor is such an occurrence to be regretted. He is ripe for glory, and already dead to all that belongs to life." His decease thus came gently on his relatives and associates. On Sunday, the 8th of June, Dr. Marshman engaged in prayer by his bedside, but was apprehensive that he was not recognised. Mrs. Carey put the question to him, when he feebly replied, "Yes," and for the last time pressed the hand of his colleague. The next morning, the 9th of June, his spirit passed to the mansions of the blest.

Dr. Carey was in his seventy-third year at the time of his death. He had raised himself by his own energy to a position of great eminence and usefulness. He took the lead in a noble enterprise, which embraced the spiritual and intellectual elevation of a great country, and his name is indissolubly associated with the progress of improvement in India, to which he devoted forty years of his life. His exertions were sustained less by the impulse of enthusiasm than by a predominant sense of duty. The basis of all his excellences was deep and unaffected piety. So great was his love of integrity, that he never gave his confidence where he was not certain of the existence of moral worth. He was conspicuous for constancy, both in the pursuits of life and the associations of friendship. With great simplicity he united the strongest decision of character. He never took credit for anything but plodding, but it was the plodding of genius. He was a stern economist of time, and always acted on the principle of taking care of the moments, and leaving the hours to take care of themselves. He was thus enabled to read through so voluminous a work as the Universal History, during his weekly journeys to Calcutta on his college duties. He was greatly attached to the pursuits of science, but his garden was his earthly paradise. His aptitude for the acquisition of languages has seldom been exceeded, and to supply the Sacred Scriptures to the nations of the East in their own tongue became the ruling passion of his life. To him the Bengalee language—the language of thirty millions of people—has been more indebted for its improvement than to any other individual, European or native. His preaching was without ornament, or any attempt at eloquence. His manners were easy, without being graceful. His stature was not above the middle height; the upper portion of his countenance exhibited all the indications of genius, but his figure was of a plebeian cast. Of his four sons who accompanied him to Serampore in 1800, Mr. Felix Carey was endued with much of his father's scientific and philological tastes, and, with the exception of four years, devoted his talents to the service of the mission; he died in 1822. His second son was employed as a missionary for forty years; the third was engaged for twenty years in the superintendence of schools in Amboyna and Rajpootana; and his youngest son embraced the profession of the law in Calcutta, and is the last survivor of the family. Dr. Carey bequeathed his valuable museum to the College, and directed that his library should be sold for the benefit of his widow, who survived him only a twelvemonth. He enjoined on his executors that the only memorial on his tomb should consist of this inscription,—

WILLIAM CAREY,
BORN AUGUST, 1761; DIED
A WRETCHED, POOR, AND HELPLESS WORM,
ON THY KIND ARMS I FALL.

The death of his colleague inflicted a blow on Dr. Marshman's enfeebled constitution, which seemed to threaten a return of his mental debility. They had lived and laboured together in the same spot for thirty-five years, and rarely has there been an instance of such long continued and affectionate union. Notwithstanding the efforts incessantly made to break up the harmony which subsisted between them, by instilling mistrust and suspicion, on no occasion was there the least diminution of cordial confidence. Every object at Serampore now reminded Dr. Marshman of endeared associations, which were finally broken up, and he wrote to Mr. Hope that "everything was tinged with the black hue of melancholy." It was found necessary for him to seek change of air and scenery, and he took a journey to the sanatorium of Chirra Poongee, to which Mrs. Marshman had been obliged to resort for health at the beginning of the year.

On the 20th of March, 1835, Lord William Bentinck resigned the Governor-Generalship, which he had held for seven years. His administration was distinguished by the introduction of the most liberal principles of government, and it constitutes a great and memorable era in our Indian history. All ranks and classes, with one exception, vied with each other in offering the tribute of their gratitude to the ruler who had done more to render the British sovereignty a blessing to the country than the most illustrious of his predecessors. But the greatest compliment to his administration came from the Dhurmu Subha, or association of Orthodox Hindoos in Calcutta, who passed a resolution to the effect that it was incongruous to offer an address of thanks to the ruler who had abolished the rite of female immolation. In reply to the address of the missionaries, he said:—"I have the more reason to be flattered by your kindness on this occasion, inasmuch as it proceeds from those with whom, in their public capacity, I have carefully abstained from holding any communication. The professed object of your lives and labours, is conversion. The fundamental principle of British rule, the compact to which Government stands pledged, is, strict neutrality." But on his arrival at St. Helena, the first port at which he touched on his return to England, he wrote to Dr. Marshman to say, that while he occupied the post of Governor-General, he considered himself precluded from giving support to missionary institutions; but he was happy to embrace the first opportunity, after he was relieved from the responsibilities of the government, of manifesting his esteem for him and his colleagues by a contribution of £50.

The year 1836 was the third centenary of the Reformation in Denmark, and the King, Frederick the Sixth, determined that it should be celebrated throughout the Danish territories by a national recognition of the blessings it had conferred on the country. Instructions were accordingly sent to the public authorities in Serampore to observe three days as public holidays, when solemn thanks were to be offered to Almighty God for the introduction of the Reformation into Denmark; and the congregations were to be exhorted "to implore the continued aid of the Almighty to preserve Christian doctrine in all its purity to the country, that it might bring forth the fruits of faith, sincerity, and love." Dr. Marshman made a metrical version in English of the Danish hymn selected by the king, who also chose the texts for the occasion, from which two sermons were preached by Mr. Mack and Dr. Marshman.

A few days after the celebration of the jubilee, Dr. Marshman's health began to fail. He had never fully recovered from the strain on his constitution by twenty months of incessant anxiety in England, and the repeated renewal of troubles since his return had weakened his strength. His spirits rose and sunk with the prospects of the mission, and those prospects were again gloomy. Mr. Gibbs, the agent of the Serampore mission in England, wrote that he had not been able to obtain a single farthing for its support from the members of the Baptist denomination when he visited Birmingham, though he had received £13 from gentlemen of the Established Church. Just at this period a very distressing calamity in his family served to increase the depression of his spirits. His youngest daughter, the wife of Lieut. Havelock, of H.M. 13th Foot—the late Sir Henry Havelock—was residing at the hill station of Landour, when, on the night of the 18th of October, the bungalow caught fire, and the inmates were roused from sleep by the blaze which surrounded them. Mrs. Havelock rushed out with her infant in her arms, but fell down in crossing the burning straw, and must have perished in the flames, but for the exertions of a faithful native servant, who lifted her up in a state of insensibility, and, wrapping her in his blanket, conveyed her to a neighbouring hut, but the infant was burnt to death. The servant then rushed back to the bungalow, and, at the imminent risk of his life, rescued the two boys from the flames. Lieut. Havelock hastened from the cantonment at Kurnaul to the scene of desolation, and found his wife hovering between life and death. Her medical adviser gave him no hope of her surviving the day; and he wrote to prepare Dr. Marshman for the melancholy tidings which the next mail was expected to convey of the death of his affectionate daughter. By some irregularity in the post, no letters arrived from Landour for the next three days, and Dr. Marshman was in an agony of suspense. He wandered about the house in a state of gloomy abstraction, looking at intervals out of the Venetian windows for the appearance of the postman, and occasionally talking without object or coherence. On the third day, the joyful tidings came that his daughter was out of danger; but the agitation of his feelings during the three days produced an impression from which he never recovered, and he was seldom seen to smile afterwards.

At the beginning of this year, Mr. Mack proceeded on his annual visit to the various missionary stations in the eastern division of Bengal and Assam. On his return to Serampore, he visited Anundpore, the settlement which had been formed in the Soonderbuns, where a hundred families, with a large sprinkling of Christians, were employed in clearing and cultivating the land. The whole community was gradually coming under the influence of Christian institutions, but this useful project fell to the ground on the extinction of the mission, and the grant was disposed of. On reaching Serampore, Mr. Mack was seized with a violent fever, and for several days his life was despaired of. The rush of blood to the head, which threatened momentary dissolution, was happily arrested by the application of Wenham Lake ice, which had been recently introduced into Calcutta, and he gradually recovered his strength. After his convalescence, his medical attendant pronounced a voyage to England indispensable to the complete restoration of his health, and arrangements were made for his departure.

The efforts to sustain the various institutions connected with Serampore were continued during this year with unabated ardour. The younger associates of the Serampore missionaries clustered around the last survivor of the body, animated by the strongest desire to support the character and the usefulness of the establishment. The College continued to maintain its efficiency. The number of students exceeded a hundred, the majority of whom were children of native Christians. Ten students in European habits were likewise preparing themselves for the missionary field; and the report of the year details their progress in the classics, mathematics, logic, natural philosophy, and divinity. Sanscrit had given way to English, the cultivation of which had become the great object of ambition among the natives of the country, some of whom edited journals, and composed poems in the English language. The progress of native youths in mathematics, metaphysics, and mental philosophy, exceeded all expectation, and the authority of the shasters, and the influence of the priesthood, were shaken by these new and powerful influences. The curriculum of study in the College at Serampore was therefore modified to meet the wants of the time; and the study of English was made a paramount object. The number of conversions at the various stations had rather exceeded than fallen short of the returns of former years, and was found to be fully equal to the success experienced at the stations maintained by the Society. Nothing was wanting but the oil to keep the lamp burning.

But the mission was now sinking under an accumulation of difficulties. It was founded on the motto of Dr. Carey —Expect great things; attempt great things: and this principle of action was predominant in all its vitality to the close of its course. Every gleam of prosperity in England induced the missionaries to enlarge the sphere of their operations. Considering that for the last ten years their resources had been affected by all the fluctuations of opinion at home, it must be acknowledged that they were imprudent in not restraining their efforts within more judicious limits. But with the exigencies of the heathen world ever present to the mind, nothing is more difficult than the practical application of this principle of prudence on the part of missionary bodies who have any spring of religious energy in them, and a favourable balance at their bankers. When the Society broke off from Serampore in 1827, the mission comprised fifteen principal and subordinate stations—they now amounted to thirty-three; the number of labourers at the former period was twenty-eight, they now amounted to forty-nine, of whom twenty-four were Europeans and East Indians. The expenditure in 1827 was estimated at £1,400; it was now doubled; and the collections of the past year had fallen short of the sum requisite by £1,200. To add to the difficulties of the missionaries, the pecuniary obligations which they had contracted were in excess of £2,000. In the early portion of 1837, the last year of the existence of the mission, its affairs appeared to be approaching a final and irretrievable crisis. Two appeals had already been made to England, but the last had been responded to with less liberality than the first, and a third did not appear advisable; it was, therefore, determined to hasten Mr. Mack's departure, that he might make an effort to recruit the funds of the mission by personal representations. Soon after his departure, in a state of great debility, it was deemed judicious to depute Mr. Leechman to England to support his exertions. The resignation of two of the European missionaries was accepted, and one station was discontinued. These and other reductions brought the expenditure within 2,000 rupees a month; but they brought also the painful and unquestionable conclusion that a mission which can be maintained only on the principle of contraction, has already passed the meridian of its strength, and is hastening to decay.

Mr. Mack reached England in April, 1837, with his health renovated, and found that the friends of Serampore had grafted on the local association in Liverpool a general society in aid of Serampore, and adopted the same system of organisation as other religious bodies. To this generous movement he gave the most efficient aid, and, being joined by Mr. Leechman, travelled through the country advocating the claims of the missionary establishment. In connexion with this new society, a meeting was held at Liverpool in September, when the position and prospects of the mission were fully discussed, and the question was mooted, whether, viewing the painful exertions connected with the attempt to maintain two missionary societies in the same denomination, the difficulty of stemming the tide of adverse influence, and the animosities arising out of this state of disunion, an attempt to unite the two bodies would not be desirable. Mr. Mack and Mr. Leechman, the representatives of the Serampore mission, were anxious to maintain the principle of independence on which it was founded, and had always been conducted; but they could not fail to perceive a strong tendency on the part of those without whose assistance they were powerless, to seek an alliance with the Society. They reflected on the withering embarrassments which had been so long felt at Serampore, the pressing wants of the stations, and the declining health of Dr. Marshman. To save the missionary stations from extinction, they resolved, as a matter of necessity rather than of choice, to yield to the current of circumstances, and co-operate in the proposed design. This decision was strengthened by the death of Mr. Samuel Hope, who had been, in a pecuniary point of view, the mainstay of the mission for ten years. He brought substantial relief to its funds by constantly anticipating the collections, and on one occasion made a loan of a thousand pounds to the College. He was ever ready to support the benevolent projects of all denominations, but his affections centred in Serampore, and he rarely allowed a mail to leave Liverpool without writing to Dr. Marshman. The loss of his invaluable counsel and support removed whatever hesitation Mr. Mack and Mr. Leechman might have felt, and decided their course. At the same time, Mr. Mack deemed it important to demonstrate that in thus tendering themselves to the Society, those connected with Serampore did not offer them a lifeless burden, but a living body of active and faithful men, whose energetic labours had been blessed with success, and he drew up a full report of the mission, extending to the latest date. An overture was soon after made to the committee in Fen Court that the two societies should be consolidated, and the stations connected with Serampore be annexed to the Baptist Missionary Society, to which the entire superintendence of their labours should be relinquished. The offer was accepted, and it was proposed that a deputation, consisting of two ministers, two laymen, and the two delegates from Serampore, should meet a similar deputation from Fen Court. But the committee of the Society refused to admit either Mr. Mack or Mr. Leechman to the conference, on the singular ground that missionaries should be excluded on both sides, though they were not missionaries, but professors in the College, and principals in the transaction. But as the Fen Court committee appeared to attach the greatest importance to their exclusion, it was deemed expedient to waive the point, rather than mar the negotiation. They were therefore kept in an adjoining room during the conference, but admitted to the repast on its termination. At this conference, held on the 7th December, it was resolved that "the Serampore friends should meet all claims which existed against the mission, and provide for the support of the whole missionary establishment to the end of the ensuing April, when the whole of the stations should pass over to the Society, with the exception of the establishment at Serampore. Dr. Marshman's age and infirmities, it was said, disqualified him from taking any share in this arrangement. The books and translations at Serampore were to be placed at the disposal of the committee. With the College the Society would have nothing to do. Thus fell the Serampore mission, after a bright and useful career of thirty-eight years.

During these negotiations, Dr. Marshman was sinking into his grave. The successive departure of Mr. Mack and Mr. Leechman had deeply affected his spirits, and increased his weakness. The hot season of 1837 was, moreover, the most severe which had ever been experienced. The thermometer in his chamber at four in the afternoon was above blood heat. The rains brought some mitigation of the heat, but nothing could restore the tone of his constitution, and he was disabled from all public services. Under the impulse of that buoyancy of feeling which he was endeavouring to maintain, he wrote, on the 7th of September, to Mr. Godwin, who was acting as secretary to the mission in England, that, taking all things into consideration, and reflecting on the way in which help had been obtained during the absence of his two colleagues, he might well say, "What hath God wrought for us! For my own part, I am grieved at my ingratitude and insensibility in the midst of all God's goodness." During the month of October the symptoms of decay became more decided. He was visited by his missionary brethren of various denominations, with whom he conversed earnestly on the progress of Divine truth in India, encouraging them to redouble their efforts in the sacred cause. Mr. Yates, the senior member of the Society's mission in Calcutta, came up to see him, and was bathed in tears as he knelt by his couch and engaged in prayer. Dr. Marshman assured him of his unabated affection for him and all his associates, however he might have differed from him on minor points. He said he rejoiced in their success, and was convinced the feeling was mutual. There was room enough in India for two missions—for ten missions; and he encouraged them earnestly to persevere in their labours. At the beginning of November he walked downstairs for the last time. The next he made an excursion on the river, and on his arrival at Calcutta was attended by Dr. Nicholson, the most eminent physician at the Presidency, who placed him on a more regular diet, and the dysentery, with which he had been affected for some time, left him; but it was, unhappily, succeeded by dropsy. After the excitement of his trip on the river had subsided, he experienced a relapse, and desired to be taken home without delay, that he might die on the spot where he had passed so many years of his life. The disease increased throughout November, and he was scarcely expected to survive from day to day. But his mind was supported by the blessed hope of immortality, and the richest consolations of the Divine presence were vouchsafed to him. The resignation of his mind, and the serenity of his feelings, afforded the clearest evidence of the value of the Christian hope in the hour of approaching dissolution. When apparently unconscious, he repeatedly exclaimed, "The precious Saviour! He never leaves nor forsakes." Frequently, after a night of broken rest and bodily suffering, the triumph of joy beamed in his eye in the morning, as he assured his friends that he had experienced the greatest delight in communion with God. A week before his death, he was afflicted with lightness of head, but his mind was still fixed on the work of his life, and he conversed on spiritual subjects, and prayed in the Bengalee language. Soon after, he appeared to regain his strength both of body and mind, and was carried about in his tonjohn or sedan-chair, to take his last look at the various objects on the premises. On Thursday morning he caused the bearers to convey him to the chapel where the weekly prayer-meeting was held, and to place him in front of the communion-table, and, while seated in his tonjohn, he gave out, with a firm voice, the missionary hymn which he and his colleagues had been accustomed to use in every season of trial and difficulty, till it came to be designated the chant of the Serampore missionaries:—

"O Lord our God, arise,
The cause of Truth maintain,
And wide o'er all the peopled world
Extend her blessed reign.

"Thou Prince of Life, arise,
Nor let Thy glory cease;
Far spread the conquests of Thy grace,
And bless the earth with peace.

"Thou Holy Ghost, arise,
Expand Thy quickening wing,
And o'er a dark and ruined world,
Let light and order spring.

"All on the earth, arise,
To God the Saviour sing;
From shore to shore, from earth to heaven,
Let echoing anthems ring."

For several days he dictated to his daughter his recollections of the early days of the mission, with a clearness and precision which shewed that his remarkable powers of memory remained unimpaired to the last. On Sunday evening he sat up in his chair, and spent several hours in feasting on the religious periodical publications which had recently been received. At seven on Tuesday morning, he called his family around him, and told them he was dying. He prayed fervently, and with the utmost composure, commending himself, his family, his friends, and the "precious cause," to the Divine keeping. He inquired whether there was anything further he could do for the mission, and then, turning on his side, composed himself as if to sleep. From that position he never moved, and about four hours after breathed his last without a sigh or a groan. He was interred on the afternoon of the 6th of December, in the cemetery which contained the mortal remains of his colleagues. "They were lovely and pleasant in their lives, and in their death they were not divided." During his illness, Dr. Marshman had manifested great anxiety regarding the result of Mr. Mack's and Mr. Leechman's visit to England. Owing to the incompleteness of the overland route, the mails of two months were detained in Egypt, and Dr. Marshman was thus spared the affliction of hearing that the mission, the object of his warmest affection, was about to be broken up, and he went down to the grave without the least anticipation of such an event. As his friends returned from the burying-ground, the letters from Mr. Mack were delivered, which, for the first time, explained the circumstances which had constrained him to submit to the surrender of the mission. By a singular coincidence of time, it was the day after Dr. Marshman's interment that the two deputations met in London, and the Serampore mission ceased to exist. It was emphatically buried in his tomb.

Dr. Marshman was within a few months of seventy at the time of his death. From the humble sphere of life in which he was born, he rose to great eminence in the Christian world by his own genius and his indomitable energy. He plied the shuttle with the Greek grammar before him, and before he was twenty had laid in such stores of knowledge as few even in the most auspicious circumstances have been able to acquire. Whatever object he set before himself, he pursued with enthusiasm which never flagged. His application to business was indefatigable, and he thought nothing of sitting up half the night to accomplish an object. After he had embarked in the cause of missions, the prosecution of it became the ruling passion of his life, and for thirty-eight years every other consideration was absorbed in his devotion to it, and every sacrifice appeared light which could promote its interests. His sterling piety underlay his whole character; and one of his chief opponents has recorded, that "no journals display a more profound piety, sympathy of the noblest kind with the moral condition of the heathen, and a paramount solicitude for the glory of God." He was distinguished by liberality of feeling towards all other denominations, and by the total absence of all bigotry in his intercourse with his fellow Christians. He possessed great powers of reasoning, and a very extraordinary faculty of memory. But his firmness was apt occasionally to degenerate into obstinacy, and the wary and circuitous course he pursued towards the attainment of an object, with the view of meeting every difficulty, led his enemies to charge him with a tortuous and designing policy. As to the love of power which was imputed to him, it was impossible for him to have continued through life to act with perfect cordiality with two such men as his colleagues, without that deference to their opinion which is incompatible with a spirit of domination. It was his strong character which made him bitter enemies and devoted friends. He died, like his colleagues, in graceful poverty, after having, in conjunction with Mrs. Marshman, devoted a sum little short of £40,000 to the mission, and that not in one ostentatious amount, but during a life of privations. While in England, his constitution was feeble; and Huntingdon, the once celebrated preacher, whom he visited before he embarked, exclaimed, on hearing of his design: "You go out to India! why you look as if you had been kept by the parish!" Fortunately there were no medical examiners connected with societies in that early period of missions, and he was permitted to embark without inquiry. Having made up his mind to live and die in the country, he determined to inure himself to the climate, and his frame became gradually so invigorated, that his "iron constitution" came to be a familiar comparison. A few days before his death, he calculated the value of all the medicine he had taken in India in thirty-five years, and found it not to exceed twenty shillings. His stature was about five feet nine inches, and his countenance, with his expansive forehead, presented a rare expression of high intellect and stern energy. Of twelve children, only six outlived infancy. His eldest son has survived to compile this record of his labours and his virtues; the second embarked in the law as a solicitor in Calcutta, but met with reverses; the youngest went the western circuit till his death, and may still be in the remembrance of some of his bar associates for his humour and his memory. His eldest daughter was married to Mr. Williams, of the Bengal Civil Service; the second to Dr. Voigt, the medical officer at Serampore, and, subsequently, to Dr. Brandis, at present superintendent of forests in India, and has died while these pages are passing through the press. The youngest is Lady Havelock.

The Serampore mission, of which the last of the founders was now laid in his grave, was established by three men of humble lineage,—apostates from the loom and the anvil, as their opponents delighted to designate them,—but of sterling genius and deep piety. Brought together by unforeseen circumstances, their characters were immediately put to the test by the occurrence of difficulties which served to cement their union. When their establishment was threatened in its cradle with extinction by their own Government, they were providentially provided with an asylum under a foreign flag, until the storm had blown over. For thirteen years they had to encounter the prejudices and opposition of the governors of India, and it was mainly to their zeal and fortitude, combined with a singular spirit of moderation, that the diffusion of secular and religious knowledge in India, which they had laboured under every discouragement to promote, was at length recognised as the object for which Providence had entrusted the Indian empire to Great Britain. A unity of object produced a unanimity of sentiments and a constancy of friendship, of which there have been few examples. Every private feeling, and every individual predilection, was merged in the prosecution of their great undertaking, and their confidence in each other was never interrupted for an hour. They were exactly fitted for mutual co-operation. They were all embued with the same large views; the same spirit of zeal and animation, and the same pecuniary disinterestedness. Their united energies were thus consecrated to the cause of religion, for the promotion of which they were enabled, by severe and protracted labours, to contribute a sum which, at the close of the mission, was found to fall little short of £80,000.

The Serampore missionaries never considered themselves in any other light than as the pioneers of Christian improvement in India, and it is as pioneers that their labours are to be estimated. In the infancy of modern missions, it fell to their lot to lay down and exemplify the principles of the missionary system. They were the first to enforce the necessity of giving the Scriptures to all the tribes of India. Their own translations were necessarily and confessedly imperfect; but many imperfections may be overlooked in the labours of men who produced the first editions of the New Testament in so many of the Oriental languages and dialects, and gave that impulse to the work of translation which still sustains it. They were the first to insist on the absolute exclusion of caste from the native Christian community and church. They established the first native schools for heathen children in Hindoostan, and organised the first college for the education of native catechists and ministers. They printed the first books in the language of Bengal, and thus laid the foundation of a vernacular literature; and they were the first to cultivate and improve that language, and render it a suitable vehicle for national instruction. They published the first native newspaper in India, and issued the first religious periodical work. In all the departments of missionary labour and intellectual improvement, they led the way, and it is on the broad foundation which they were enabled to lay, that the edifice of modern Indian missions has been erected.

To close this narrative of the Serampore mission, it is necessary to add a few supplemental notices. By the articles of "reunion," everything belonging to it was transferred to the Society, except its debts. In the absence of Mr. Mack and Mr. Leechman from the conference, it was decided that the arrangement should not come into operation before the beginning of the official year in May. The expense of the stations for a period of nearly five months was thus added to the obligations of its conductors, which were thus swelled to more than £3,000. Of this sum, one moiety was due to the estate of the late treasurer, Mr. Hope, the rest was payable in India. Mr. Mack and Mr. Leechman were therefore under the necessity of traversing the country, on the ungracious task of collecting contributions for an extinct mission; but by dint of the most strenuous exertions the whole of the English debt was at length liquidated. The sums due in India fell on the individual who had made himself responsible for them, and they also were paid off by the middle of 1839, without any appeal to public liberality; and the Serampore mission was brought to a termination without any stain on its honour. The year after its dissolution, Mr. Mack returned to India, and revived Dr. Marshman's seminary for his own support. Those who had been connected with the mission were bound by the articles of the 7th December, 1837, never to make any attempt to raise subscriptions for missionary objects; but any station capable of sustaining its own missionary operations was exempt from the control of the Society. Mr. Mack and his surviving colleague claimed this privilege for Serampore, and provided for its missionary exertions, and for the support of the College, by congregational collections and their own contributions.

Though the mission at Serampore was thus become a matter of history, there were many of its old and faithful adherents in England, from whom tokens of affectionate remembrance were received from time to time; one of the most valuable of which was embodied in a letter from John Foster to Mr. Marshman, and may be considered as a true index of that feeling of devotion to Serampore which still lingered in the minds of its friends:—

"It was with regret that I first heard of the indications, premature as they might perhaps be called, of the decline of your father's strength and life. His extraordinary health through life, and the unfailing vigour in which I have invariably seen him while here, might have seemed to promise a somewhat longer term than that which Providence had actually appointed for him. I easily fancied him maintaining onward some measure of the same unsubdued energy.

"But we were informed, and could easily believe, that the loss of his admirable old beloved associate inflicted on him a depression from which he could not recover, causing him to feel as if half his life and power were gone—withdrawn to another world, to which he must thenceforward be looking with a desire to follow.

"I have often imagined the animated mutual recognition and congratulations of the *three* seniors, in that happy region. What ecstasy to find themselves all associated again, in the triumph of a final escape from all evil, and of all hearing together, as each had separately, their Master's sentence of approbation, 'Well done, good and faithful, enter, as a band still indissoluble, into the joy of your Lord!' How insignificant will appear to them now, in their inviolable serenity, all the untoward incidents, the offensive proceedings, the ill offices, the wrongs which had annoyed and harassed them during their mortal sojourn! They will look back on all this as only a discipline to prepare them the more for the new career of service for which they will have all things auspicious, and for ever.

"My inveterate partiality to Serampore made it very unpleasing to hear of the great change in the economy. In passing over to the Society, it has strangely lost in the minds of us, the old and faithful adherents, the interest which it had under the honoured name and administration of Serampore. But *we*, the older portion of us, are fast falling back into the order of men of the past, and have lost, and are losing by death, one and another of those that formed our party. A new race is coming on to be the supporters of the Indian Mission, who are very little acquainted with the matters of this controversy, and will never take any trouble of inquiring."

Towards the close of 1845, the settlement of Serampore was transferred by the King of Denmark to the British Government; but, in conformity with the express wishes of his predecessor, Frederick the Sixth, he made it an indispensable condition that the charter granted to the College should be fully recognised. An article was, therefore, inserted in the treaty of cession, confirming the charter on every point, and a copy of it was attached to that document previously to its receiving the signatures of the contracting parties.

For more than six years after his return to India, Mr. Mack laboured with great zeal and success in his ministerial and pastoral duties, when his career of usefulness was suddenly cut short by a fatal attack of cholera, on the 26th of April, 1846. For twenty-three years he had devoted his splendid talents to the diffusion of Christian knowledge in India, and his name is indissolubly associated with those of his great colleagues at Serampore. A few days before his death, the late Bishop Dealtry, then Archdeacon of Calcutta, visited Serampore, and remarked that there had been but few men at Serampore, but they had all been giants. Mr. Mack was the last of the giants, and his loss was felt to be irreparable. On his death, the missionary establishment was voluntarily transferred to the Baptist Missionary Society, who appointed the Rev. W. H. Denham to take charge of it.

On the 1st of March, 1847, the widow of Dr. Marshman was removed by death at Serampore, at the advanced age of eighty. She was the last survivor of those who had assisted at the formation of the mission forty-seven years before. She fully participated in all her husband's devotedness to the missionary cause, and by her strong mind, and sound judgment, and invariable equanimity, gave him the most important assistance in all his plans of benevolence, while her contributions to the cause fell little short of those which he was enabled to devote to it.

By the year 1855, nearly all those members of the committee who had united in declaring, sixteen years before, that "the Society would have nothing to do with the College," were in their graves, and their adverse feelings were buried with them. In that year, therefore, the committee yielded to the request made by the council of the College to adopt that institution as a part of the Society's operations. The breach with the Society was thus finally healed. Every feeling of prejudice against Serampore has now been completely extinguished, and throughout the denomination there is but one feeling of veneration for the great men who have shed a lustre on its character, while they contributed, in no ordinary degree, to the introduction of Divine and secular knowledge into India.

THE END.